single mama drama

KAYLA PERRIN

single mama drama

MIRA®

MIRA®

ISBN-13: 978-0-7783-2551-2
ISBN-10:   0-7783-2551-2

SINGLE MAMA DRAMA

www.MIRABooks.com

Printed in U.S.A.

This book is dedicated to every woman who is, or has been, a single mother. They say motherhood is the hardest job in the world, and it's even more so when you're parenting alone. Single mothers do their thing—they work hard, love their children and often don't get a break. So I hope as you read this book you're able to put your feet up, relax for a while and smile. You deserve it!

ACKNOWLEDGMENT

I am eternally grateful for the support provided to me by the Writers' Trust of Canada's Woodcock Fund while I was writing this book. At the time, I was involved in an unexpected, time-consuming and expensive legal situation. Thanks to the support I received from the Woodcock Fund, I was able to concentrate on finishing my book, rather than on trying to find a part-time job to make ends meet during this difficult time. Thanks to everyone involved with the Woodcock Fund. Your support of writers in need is truly remarkable!

chapter one

"Damn you, Eli," I muttered when my fiancé's voice mail picked up for the gazillionth time. "Are you planning to *never* talk to me again?"

Cursing softly under my breath, I flipped my cell phone shut. No point leaving another message. It was obvious—painfully so—that Eli was avoiding me.

Great. It wasn't even nine-thirty in the morning yet, and it was clear that the day was going to be full of drama.

I'd been calling Eli since shortly after he stormed out of our apartment the night before, and so far, I hadn't heard a word from him. Did he expect me to grovel? Perhaps take out a billboard ad announcing to all of South Florida that I had overreacted? We'd had a fight. So what? It certainly didn't warrant him acting like I no longer existed.

Enough was enough. If Eli didn't have the decency to get back to me, why should I spend the day moping over him?

Balancing my Starbucks latte in one hand, I shoved my cell

phone into my purse with the other, then strode purposefully into the office building on NE Fifth Street, where I
worked in downtown Miami. I showed my ID card to
security before heading for the bank of elevators. Only one
other person was waiting there, a tall and striking brunette.
She barely glanced my way, but when she did, I saw that her
eyes were red-rimmed. Clearly, she had been crying. I
wondered if she, like me, had dealt with some early-morning
man drama.

Probably. At least I wasn't the only one arriving late to
the office because of a man.

I got off first, on the eleventh floor. My plan was to head
through the glass doors housing the Believe the Dream,
Change Your Life Agency and go straight to my office. But
as I approached the doors, I found myself reaching into my
purse and wrapping my fingers around my cell phone.

Don't do it, don't do it, don't do it....

I did. I pulled the phone out of my purse and once again
punched in Eli's mobile number. What can I say—as frus-
trated as I was with him, there was no way I would stop
trying to reach him. He was my fiancé—the Mr. Right I'd
finally found at the ripe old age of twenty-eight—and I was
determined to marry him.

"Eli, baby," I said when his voice mail picked up. "It's me
again. I'll bet you're still sleeping, which is why I haven't
heard from you yet. Listen, I know I said this before, but I
am sorry about last night. I was stressed to the max, had
worked an incredibly long day—and you know how I get
when I've worked past eight at night." With my shoulder, I
nudged the glass door open and headed into the agency. I

nodded in greeting at Alaina, the receptionist and a friend, as I walked briskly past her. "The good news is, the campaign is now all set," I said a little loudly, hoping Alaina would hear and think I was on a business call, even though she wasn't my superior. "And I'll be home right after work today," I continued, when she was out of earshot. "No later than six, I promise. And then I'm all yours. Maybe Carla can even babysit Rayna for a couple extra hours and we can go for a nice dinner."

I paused as I attempted the fine art of opening my office door with full hands, succeeded, and stepped inside. I quickly placed my coffee on my desk, along with my purse. "Can you just call me, please? Let me know the wedding's still on," I added with a laugh, the kind that said I was sure it was, but in reality, I wasn't entirely confident of that anymore. Anytime Eli and I had had a disagreement before, he'd never taken this long to get back to me. We were the type who patched things up in a couple hours at the most, and we certainly never went to bed angry with one another.

Eli wasn't *that* mad at me—was he?

After all, I was the one with the right to be mad. I was a single mother, and he'd damn near bitten my daughter's head off when she spilled her milk on his lap. At the time, I'd reacted instinctively, like a mother hen protecting her chick, but now the clarity of the morning after had me realizing that Eli had simply overreacted, then I had overreacted, which had led to a stupid fight.

I tossed my cell onto my desk and collapsed in my leather chair with a long-suffering sigh. No sooner had I sat down than my door swung open. My boss, Debbie Noble, walked in and closed the door behind her.

"I'm sorry, Debbie," I began without preamble. "I got held up a little this morning because my sitter had to run an errand, so I couldn't bring Rayna over there at the usual time." A lie, but what the hell. I didn't need any more grief today.

Debbie waved a hand dismissively. "That's not why I'm here."

"Oh?"

A grin slowly spread on her face as she strolled toward my desk. "Ask me what I was doing last night."

I reached for my Starbucks cup and took a quick sip of my latte. "I already know what you were doing. You were having dinner with a potential client." The agency represented motivational speakers and life coaches, and I worked as the office manager. "Did you sign her?"

"After that," Debbie said. "When I came back to the office."

"You came back to the office?" I'd been here until nearly eight, and only the cleaning staff had been around when I left.

"Just ask me."

"Okay, I'll bite. What were you doing last night when you came back to the office?"

"Maybe the better question is *who* I was doing…."

Now my eyebrows shot up. "Debbie—"

"Jason!" she squealed before I could formally ask the question. "And, *oh my God!* I've been dying for you to get here so I could tell *someone.*"

"Whoa, whoa, whoa, whoa, whoa," I said, waving my hands around as I stared up at her in total shock. "You slept with *Jason? Jason* from the *mail room?*"

Debbie grinned proudly and rested her butt on my desk. "Honey, nothing that we did together even remotely resembled sleep."

"I don't understand. What was Jason doing here so late?"

"Meeting me for a scandalous rendezvous."

"You're totally serious."

"As a heart attack."

"But he's so young!" I blurted, not meaning to sound judgmental, but I couldn't help it. "What is he—twenty?"

"Twenty-two, but who cares?"

Which made him sixteen years Debbie's junior. "Does he even shave yet?"

"He's old enough to be legal, but young enough to be horny and hard—*all the time*. Vanessa, he is like a steel rod. And I tell you, girl, that boy couldn't get enough last night! On the floor, against the wall, bent over my desk giving it to me from behind. *Mmmm!*" Debbie closed her eyes and shivered, as if reliving her orgasmic pleasure.

I cast her a wary look as I reached for my latte and gulped it this time. Her story was making me miss Eli all the more.

"I hope you know what you're doing," I said.

Despite my expressed concern, I knew Debbie wouldn't take offense. Not only was she my boss, she was a good friend. We shared all kinds of personal info and didn't hold back on our opinions.

"Of course I know what I'm doing. And I'm doing it again tonight." She laughed airily. "Though this time I'll make sure *he's* on the floor. I got some serious rug burn on my knees...."

"Okay, I think it's a little too early for that kind of talk." I downed more coffee.

"You should try it some time."

"Jason?"

"No, a twenty-two-year-old. Heck, even eighteen."

"*Eighteen!* You have lost your mind. Besides, I have a man." Debbie rolled her eyes.

"And I'm getting married." I waved my three-carat rock. "You remember that important detail, don't you?" I didn't mention that my fiancé was mad at me right now and that he'd spent the night at his best friend's place. I didn't feel like bringing up our stupid fight, especially when I had no doubt that we'd be making up later in the day. Or that a delivery-man with a dozen roses would show up any minute.

"Seriously, Vanessa—don't knock it till you try it. Nothing against Eli, but only the young ones can give it to you the way you want. Talk about stamina! Before you walk down that aisle, I think it's in your best interest to—"

"Enough." I held up a hand to silence Debbie.

"Fine."

"Tell me more about you and Jason," I said.

She raised a perfectly sculpted eyebrow. "You know he's got a tongue ring, right?"

"Yes, I've seen—" I stopped short when the implication of what Debbie was saying hit me. I'd heard plenty about tongue rings, although I'd never dated a guy with one myself.

"Okay, are you saying…?"

"Mmm-hmm." She smiled slyly.

"Don't get coy now. I want the dirty details. Is it true what they say—"

My office line rang, interrupting me, and I groaned in

disappointment. I reached for the receiver, saying to Debbie, "Hold that thought."

She clamped a hand over her mouth as she giggled, either because of the look on my face or because she was remembering everything about the tongue ring that I now wanted to know.

"Vanessa Cain," I said into the receiver, my eyes still on Debbie. "Will you hold a moment?"

I pressed the hold button before the person on the other end of the line could even speak, but Debbie shook her head. "I'll finish the story later," she told me. "You take that call."

"Oh, no you don't! You can't leave me hanging like this!"

She tapped her watch.

"Fine, tell me about the tongue ring later," I said hurriedly, "but do you like this guy or what?"

"I'm married," she said candidly.

"I know, but…" In the last year, Debbie had grown increasingly less attracted to her husband and was now on her third affair. I didn't agree with her infidelity, not in the least, but when I'd made that fact clear in the past, she firmly told me she was a big girl and could do what she wanted. That she didn't need my approval, just my friendship.

Since she was a friend, I tried not to judge her, even if I didn't agree with what she did behind her husband's back. Still, I tried to talk sense into Debbie whenever I could slip my moral opinion in.

"You've found a new boy toy, Debbie," I said. "Obviously, you're not happy in your marriage. That's been clear for a long time. You owe it to Ben—and to yourself—to leave him if you can't be faithful to him."

"And what about my children?" she countered. When I didn't answer, she went on. "Look, screwing Jason is about the sex. Nothing more. He certainly can't offer me anything more than that."

Once, over drinks, Debbie had suddenly gotten emotional and told me how Ben had hurt her while she'd been pregnant with their first child. He and a female colleague had been working together on research about juvenile diabetes, and apparently Ben had almost cheated on Debbie. He couldn't be reached as she'd gone into labor, and had arrived at the hospital after their son was born. When Debbie grilled him as to his whereabouts, he'd broken down and admitted that his colleague had tried to seduce him in his office at the university, and that they'd kissed for quite some time before he came to his senses and realized he couldn't go through with having sex with the woman. He'd been infatuated with her for months, culminating in a moment of weakness.

To his credit, Ben immediately stopped working with her, then stopped working altogether to be a stay-at-home father. Debbie didn't know if he'd been entirely truthful about what had happened, and didn't press the matter, but it was clear to me in her retelling of the story that she had been deeply wounded by what Ben had done. Her trust in him had been forever shattered. Add to the mix the fact that Debbie's father had abandoned her and her mother for a younger woman when she was only nine years old, and it was clear that Debbie had major trust issues where men were concerned. The way I saw it, her infidelity now was a way of guarding her heart, a way of protecting herself from utter devastation should Ben ever say he was leaving her.

I gave Ben credit for having been honest with her, and personally would have written off his actions as immaturity, or even last-minute fear over becoming a new father. And if I couldn't forgive him, I would have moved on.

"I don't see how you can cheat and not feel guilty," I said.

Debbie shrugged. "I guess I did feel a bit guilty when I got home last night—until Ben came out of the kitchen smelling like meat loaf and wearing this ridiculous apron he thinks is cute. My guilt vanished like *that*." She snapped her fingers for emphasis. "Vanessa, we'll chat later. Take that call. It's not like we both don't need to be working. Because I *did* sign Lori Hansen!"

I watched Debbie head out of my office, thinking that in many ways she was like a man. The fierce, ambitious blonde was the breadwinner in the family. Her husband stayed home with their three kids. And here she was, the one having an affair with a subordinate, the way so many men in positions of power do.

Once again I pressed the hold button, realizing for the first time that maybe it was Eli on the line. I cleared my throat and started speaking in my most professional tone. "Thanks for holding—"

"Oh, Vanessa. *Thank God.*"

My heart picked up speed at the sound of Carla's voice. She was my neighbor and babysitter, and if she was calling me so soon after I'd arrived at work, that meant something was wrong with my daughter.

"Carla—"

"Vanessa, you have to come home. You—you just have to. Right now."

"Oh my God. Something happened to Rayna." Had my two-year-old fallen down the stairwell, or gotten into something poisonous, or burned herself? Panic clawed at my throat. "Carla, tell me what happened!" I pushed my chair back and shot to my feet, already reaching for my purse. "How bad is it?"

"No, it's not Rayna."

My pulse was pounding so loudly in my ears, I wasn't sure I heard her correctly. "Rayna's okay?" I asked.

"Yes, she's fine. She and Amani are beside me, coloring." Carla blew out a frazzled breath. "Vanessa, it's…it's Eli."

"Eli?" Panic turned to confusion. Why would Carla be calling about Eli? Had he returned home already and by chance gone to pick up Rayna? I fully expected him to leave Leroy's place and head straight to the studio, where he and a few former athlete friends were working on their new passion—a hip-hop demo. I had my doubts as to whether or not they'd get a record deal, but I supported Eli nonetheless.

"Maybe you don't have to come home," Carla said suddenly. "You have a TV there, right?"

"Why do I need a TV?"

"Vanessa, listen to me. Turn on the TV to CNN. *Right now.* There's a commercial playing, but the story's coming up next. Oh, Vanessa. I'm so sorry."

Carla had me wondering what the heck was going on. Why would Eli be on the news? Had he been arrested for something stupid like drunk driving? I dropped the phone and raced to the conference room. Thankfully, there wasn't a meeting going on, so the room was empty. I found the remote, turned on the television and fumbled around with the buttons until I got to CNN.

I caught the tail end of a Viagra commercial, and then CNN began again. The female news anchor announced this hour's headlines. I bit my fingernail, waiting for her to say something about Eli.

"Also this hour, the bizarre death of Eli Johnson."

I gasped, stumbled backward. I landed against the conference table and gripped it for support.

Bizarre death? Eli was...*dead?*

I sucked in a deep breath and held it for a few seconds before letting it out slowly. Then my mind began to race, searching for answers.

Surely it wasn't *my* Eli Johnson.

Of course not. How could it be him? Eli had stormed out of our apartment just after nine the night before and said he was going to stay at his best friend's place. I knew Eli, and he wasn't a morning person—and definitely not a Monday morning person. It was highly unlikely that he was out of bed already, much less in time to have died a bizarre death. And if anything *had* happened to him, wouldn't Leroy have called me before the media got hold of this info?

No, it didn't make sense. It had to be another Eli Johnson.

Still, the minutes that passed seemed like hours before the full story of Eli's death began. I was anxious to hear confirmation that *my* Eli was alive and well—and still pissed at me.

"And in what the police are calling a bizarre crime of passion, former Atlanta Braves player Eli Johnson was found murdered early this morning."

I didn't have to hear the news anchor say "former Atlanta

Braves player" to know it as my Eli—because a picture of him flashed on the screen to accompany the broadcast.

And then my world crumbled.

"Shortly after seven this morning, Johnson's body was found in an upscale Miami home, in the exclusive area of Bal Harbour…"

I must have cried out, because someone came running into the conference room. And the next thing I knew, arms were wrapping around me. I didn't move, my eyes glued to the television screen.

"Apparently, he was killed by a bow and arrow," the reporter said, enunciating her words to match her shocked facial expression. *"But if that weren't bizarre enough, Johnson and his female companion, Alyssa Redgrave, were both shot with the same arrow, their bodies bonded together in death as they had been in passion. Conrad Redgrave, the victim's husband, reportedly turned himself in to police after the incident. He confessed to shooting Johnson and his wife after returning from a business trip and finding them in bed together."*

Beside me, I heard a gasp. Or had it come from my own mouth?

"Eli Johnson was thirty-nine years old."

"Oh, Vanessa. I can't…I can't believe it."

The news anchor moved on to the next story, and I finally turned to look at who was holding me, and saw my friend Alaina. Her beautiful Cuban-American face was now full of shock and concern. Shock and concern I didn't know how to deal with. I pulled away from her and numbly walked toward the conference room's floor-to-ceiling window.

"He's really dead?" Alaina asked.

I didn't answer. I couldn't find the energy to speak. Instead, I stared out the window at downtown Miami, but didn't see a thing.

Eli was dead. Good God in heaven.

Someone else entered the room—a few people, I think—but I didn't turn around. I heard whispers and words like, "Murdered!" and "with some other woman" and "holy shit."

The next person to approach was Debbie. She stepped between me and the television and rested a gentle hand on my shoulder. "Sweetie, I am *so* sorry for your loss. And I can't believe Eli turned out to be such a pig. Men." She snorted and shook her head. "Obviously, you'll want to head home. You can take as much time off as you need."

I heard but didn't entirely comprehend what Debbie was saying. My head was in a fog. I continued to hear the anchorwoman's words, like some warped drone in my head.

"But if that weren't bizarre enough, Eli and his female companion, Alyssa Redgrave, were both shot with the same arrow, their bodies bonded together in death as they had been in passion."

"Vanessa, are you hearing me?" Debbie asked.

"I'll get her some water," Alaina offered.

I didn't protest as Debbie sat me down on a chair. I could hardly think, much less feel.

Eli was dead.

The reality of it hit me as I stared out the window at the cloudless sky. Eli wasn't only dead, he'd been with another woman. Killed by her jealous husband while in the throes of passion.

My Mr. Right. The man I was supposed to marry a year and a half from now, next October.

I'd known when the day started that it would be full of drama, but I hadn't expected anything like this.

chapter two

"I'm fine," I insisted as my coworkers continued to fuss over me. The initial shock of the devastating news had penetrated my brain, and now I was trying to deal with it.

"Here." Alaina put the mouth of a bottle of water against my lips. "Drink this."

I forced down a couple sips, then turned my head.

"You need more than that," Alaina insisted.

Not facing her, I waved off her concern.

LaToya, one of the agency's administrative assistants, placed her palm on my forehead. "Oh, hell. She's warm. And look at her eyes…they're glazing over. I think she's gonna pass out. Will, go get a damp cloth!"

I pushed LaToya's hand away and got to my feet. "I'm not dehydrated, I don't have a fever and I sure as hell am not about to *pass out*. I'm perfectly okay." I glanced around the conference room at my colleagues. "Please stop treating me like I'm an invalid."

Alaina shot me a look of grave concern. "Honey, your fiancé is dead. How can you be okay?"

"You heard the newscast. He was found in bed with another woman," I said casually, adding a nonchalant shrug. "I guess he got what he deserved."

"Got what he deserved?" Alaina repeated, aghast. "And yesterday, you were showing me travel brochures, telling me where you want to go on your dream honeymoon." She shook her head. "Girl, don't pretend this news isn't devastating."

"I'm shocked, yes," I said, again trying to feign a calmness I didn't feel. "But I'm trying to put things in perspective. Eli was screwing someone else. That makes him a low-down dirty dawg if ever there was one. And one thing I can't stand is a cheating man. Trust me, I'm thanking my lucky stars that I didn't walk down the—"

I couldn't get my words out before I burst into tears.

"Oh, sweetie." Alaina wrapped me in a hug.

With her hugging me and stroking my hair, I allowed myself a total meltdown. The love of my life was dead, as were all our dreams for the future.

And Rayna…my God, how was I going to explain this to my baby?

"Seriously," I heard Debbie say behind me. "You need to go home. Be with your daughter."

"Home… Oh my God," I croaked.

Everyone in the room must have picked up on the alarm in my voice, because there was a chorus of questions.

Pulling out of Alaina's arms, I glanced around and studied the crowd. I think every single person from the agency was in the conference room at that moment, and as much as I appreciated the concern of my true friends, I didn't want to be the day's gossip for the curious.

"Alaina," I began quietly. "Get these people out of here, please. I need to talk to you and Debbie."

Debbie must have heard me, because before Alaina could approach her, she immediately turned off the television, then began to speak in her I'm-the-boss tone. "All right, everyone. Show's over. We have a business to run here. Back to your desks."

When Debbie spoke, people listened. She was that kind of boss. My coworkers started for the conference room door, some more slowly than others, all glancing back over their shoulders to shoot looks of pity at me.

Will appeared holding a wet cloth, and glanced around in confusion as people moved past him.

"Will, back to work," Debbie told him. Not saying a word, he raised the cloth, and she continued. "Forget the wet rag. Just get back to work!"

Will knew better than to piss Debbie off, so he whirled around and disappeared. With him gone, she shut the conference room door to give us some privacy.

"What is it, honey?" she asked when she reached my side again. Debbie, though she could be a total bitch when necessary, did have a soft side for the people she liked. "You sort of freaked out when I said you should go home."

My stomach tightened with the reality that, because Eli was dead, so much in my life would change. "The condo... we've got a mortgage. With Eli gone, I can't afford the payments—not on my own."

The thought of having to move had me on the verge of

hyperventilating. Only three months earlier, Eli and I had purchased the gorgeous apartment in the heart of Miami Beach. It was a place that both Rayna and I loved, in a location that was ideal.

"If I can't afford the payments, I'm going to have to move," I moaned. "And I don't want to leave South Beach! I can't move to…to *Kendall!*"

"What's wrong with Kendall?" Alaina asked, sounding a tad defensive. "It's quiet, beautiful, a great place to raise a family. Not everyone can live on South Beach."

"Alaina," Debbie began, "don't take everything so personally. We know Kendall is a beautiful place. It's just that if it were any farther west, it'd be in Naples."

Despite my misery, I cracked a smile at Alaina's shocked look. If there was one topic that got Alaina riled, it was the subject of Kendall being too far from the center of Miami.

"I love Kendall," I said, then misery gripped me again. "But my perfect sister and her perfect family live there. I'll lose my mind if I have to move in with them. And I love the penthouse Eli and I bought. But I wouldn't be there if it weren't for Eli. I'll have to move, and Rayna…how many changes does my little girl have to deal with in her short life? Carla's been the best babysitter ever. And Eli…" My voice cracked, forcing me to finally slow my rant. "She loved Eli so much."

"And now we know that Eli was a no-good piece of shit," Debbie said frankly. "However, let's hope he had the good sense to have a will written."

"Yes!" Alaina exclaimed, excited. "He played for the Braves. He's got to have a will. And I'm sure he'll have left you enough money to pay off the mortgage."

My heart lifted with hope. "Lord, I hope so. But he hasn't played in seven years. We never really discussed it, but I don't think he's got millions in the bank anymore." I caught myself talking about him in the present tense, as though he were still alive, and my stomach tightened with the sickest of feelings. I wondered when I'd ever get used to referring to him in the past tense.

"And life insurance," Alaina continued. "He must have had life insurance."

"Forget life insurance," Debbie said. "At the very least, you both must have gotten mortgage insurance from the bank. In the event that one of you dies, the mortgage should be paid off."

I heard what Debbie and Alaina were saying, but my brain—and my heart—were stuck on the reality that I'd have to refer to Eli in the past tense.

Dead. Gone. *Was* my fiancé.

Killed while screwing his lover.

A tear rolled down my cheek, and both Debbie and Alaina stopped talking. "I can't believe he was cheating on me," I said as they stared at me. "I can't believe he's dead. I can hardly fathom this. What do I tell my daughter?"

"I don't know," Debbie admitted, her shoulders drooping. "I really don't."

"You've talked to her about heaven, haven't you?" Alaina asked. "When my kids' hamster died, I told them that he'd gone to hamster heaven, where he was running to his heart's content. That brought them a sense of peace."

I didn't see how the fate of a family pet could even compare to the death of a father, but didn't say so. Instead I said,

"No, I haven't talked to Rayna about heaven. I figured she's a little young to understand the concept."

For several moments, no one spoke. What was there to say? Eli was dead, and nothing either of them said would make that reality any easier to deal with.

"I know I need you here," Debbie said, breaking the silence, "but you go on home. I meant it when I said you could take as much time as you need. Paid leave, of course."

I sighed. The idea of going home frightened me more than staying at the office. Going home meant I'd have to deal with Rayna, and I was not in the least bit ready to throw her little world into upheaval.

"Do you mind if I stay here for a while?" I asked Debbie. "Maybe just to rest in my office—if I can. Going home means… I'm just not ready."

Debbie squeezed my hand. "Of course. You do whatever you need to do."

"I think I'll just sit here for a minute, if you don't mind."

"You need anything?" Alaina asked. "Coffee? Water?"

"No." I shook my head.

"All right, Alaina," Debbie said. "Let's give Vanessa some peace and quiet."

Moments later they were gone, the heavy conference door closed behind them.

And I was alone.

The way I would be from now on. Vanessa Cain, single. No significant other.

Except for my baby, of course. She was and always would be my world.

With that thought in mind, I forced myself to stand. As

Debbie had so eloquently said, Eli was a louse. Even if he hadn't been murdered, I would have suffered heartbreak when I learned he'd been cheating on me. This way, I'd been spared the agony of marrying him and then having to deal with a messy divorce.

I was better off—even if it didn't feel that way at the moment.

I headed to my office, not turning to acknowledge the people who were throwing curious glances my way. I'd lost it once. I didn't plan on having another meltdown. Not over Eli, when he so clearly didn't deserve my tears.

In my office, I closed the door and grabbed the bottle of Advil I kept in my desk for the days when the stress at work became too much.

This definitely counted as one of those times. I downed two capsules with my now cold coffee, then made my way to the small love seat near the window. I had a great view overlooking the Port of Miami and Bayside, a trendy area filled with shops and restaurants along the waterfront. It was a view that normally lifted my spirits, but I didn't even peer outside as I plopped down on my sofa and closed my eyes.

I lay there wishing that I could rewind this morning and start over. Actually, I'd rewind to the night before and erase the dumb fight I'd had with Eli. Then he wouldn't have left, and he wouldn't have ended up in another woman's bed.

And he wouldn't be dead right now.

I closed my eyes, tried to force sleep to take me away from this nightmare. It wouldn't come.

I couldn't stop thinking about Eli, trying to imagine the man I'd last seen very much alive suddenly dead. My mind simply couldn't comprehend this information in a real way.

It seemed inconceivable that I wouldn't see him when I went home later. That I would never see him again.

He was with another woman.

Had Eli been killed in a car crash, or gunned down at an ATM, I think I wouldn't have had such a hard time dealing with the news of his death. But the fact that he'd been cheating on me when it had happened was the ultimate bitter pill to swallow.

Who was this woman? Had Eli been involved in an ongoing affair with her? Or had he picked her up in a bar last night after he'd left our place? Had Eli truly been in love with me? Or had I been so blinded by my feelings for him that I'd missed all the signs that he was going to break my heart?

Replaying our life together in my mind, I couldn't think of any signs I'd missed. Eli had chased me. Eli had been the very definition of a romantic. After a whirlwind courtship, he had proposed to me under the stars while we strolled on the beach.

We were engaged, for God's sake. Why propose to me if he didn't love me? And why be such a great father to Rayna? I could see Eli lying to me, breaking *my* heart—but not my daughter's.

My sister, Nikki, said that what attracted me to Eli was his money, but that wasn't it. It was his smile. I vividly remembered the day I'd met him. The exact moment, actually.

I had been at a diabetes fund-raiser at the Eden Roc Hotel, a wine-tasting event that brought out Miami's movers and shakers. Built in the 1950s, the Eden Roc is one of the landmark resorts on South Beach's famous Collins Avenue. It is right on the beach, a definite plus, and has one of the best spas in South Florida. Once, the exterior had been completely white, but with the recent renovations, it had been painted a pale shell-pink with green accents, giving it more of an art deco look.

Debbie knew someone working for the American Diabetes Association, and the organization had needed volunteers for the event. I gladly offered to help out. Free wine and possibly a few bottles to take home—it was a no-brainer.

Even before Eli approached the table I'd been manning, I noticed him among the crowd of happy, stylishly dressed people. I'd finished pouring two glasses of merlot for an older couple, glanced across the room and saw him instantly. He was with a beefy-looking black man in an expensive mustard-colored suit, a man I recognized immediately as Christian Blake, a former Miami Dolphins running back. Christian had retired two years earlier and now appeared in commercials promoting weight training products for men.

Christian Blake was all flash, and yet the man who caught my attention was the one he'd been with. Eli. Eli looked sharp in a loose-fitting black blazer and crisp white shirt. And unlike Christian, he hadn't been sporting a pair of dark sunglasses, so I could easily see his eyes when his gaze met mine. Met and held.

His eyes lit up like he'd just seen the most beautiful woman in the world. Then his lips had curved into a stunning smile, and for that moment, it felt as if we were the only two people in the place.

I know that sounds corny, but it's really the way it happened. Eli didn't stop looking at me as he approached me from across the room, and I tried to be nonchalant, fiddling with one bottle of wine after the next, acting as if I wasn't as instantly smitten with him as he appeared to be with me.

We both knew it was a game, however. Cat and mouse. Hunter and hunted. He was on the prowl, and I was his prey.

"Can I tell you something?" Eli had asked when he'd reached me. "And I hope you won't think I'm crazy."

I made a show of putting an empty bottle under the table, but said, "Sure."

"You have got to be the most beautiful woman I have ever seen in my life."

Now, I've heard that line before, but from Eli's lips, I wasn't compelled to roll my eyes and laugh. Maybe it was because he looked so polished, so damn delicious. Maybe it was because after my last breakup, I needed a good distraction.

Or maybe it was because I couldn't deny the instant attraction between us.

"Would you like some merlot?" I asked, deliberately not responding to his comment. I began uncorking a new bottle, even though there were two open ones on the table.

"I'll take anything you want to give me."

My hands stilled on the cork, and once again I'd looked into his eyes. The charge between us sent a jolt of heat through my body.

I cleared my throat. "One glass of merlot coming right up."

I fumbled to get the cork out of the bottle, all the while making sure not to look at him. He was over six feet tall, strikingly gorgeous, and had an incredible smile; in other words, I needed to keep my guard up around him. Heck, he was friends with Christian Blake, a man who publicly dated women like it was a new sport he'd taken up after foot-ball. And you know what they say about birds of a feather....

I'd already fallen for a smooth-talking pretty boy named Lewis, the guy I had been trying to get over at the time. I didn't want to go down that road again.

"Here you are," I announced, my hand shaking slightly as I passed him the glass of wine.

"My name's Eli," he said.

"That's nice," I replied.

"Ouch." He winced. "So it's like that?"

I should have said yes, that it *was* like that, making it clear that I didn't want to get to know him. But I couldn't bring myself to reject him, even if my brain told me to send him away. He was too fine, with his smooth, dark skin and that dazzling smile. My heart wanted him to stay exactly where he was.

"I hope you like the wine."

"I couldn't care less about the wine. It's you I like."

My heart fluttered at his bold statement. I glanced across the room at his friend, who now had a woman on each arm. "I see you're here with Christian Blake."

"I might be here with him, but I'm not like him, if that's what you're getting at. I'm a one-woman man."

I couldn't help laughing sardonically, a bitter memory of Lewis and his player ways popping into my head. "I've heard that before."

"Yeah, but not from me."

Damn the man, he sounded completely sincere. And to his credit, he was talking to *me*—not one of the groupies tailing Christian. Was it fair to compare him to Lewis? Probably not. Right from the beginning, I knew Lewis saw me as a plaything, and I didn't care. It was my own fault that after six months of hot sex, I'd fallen in love with him.

Eli sipped his wine, eyeing me as I served merlot to another couple. It was clear he wasn't going to leave my station. When the couple walked off, he said, "You gonna tell me your name?"

"Vanessa," I stated. "And before you say anything else, I'm a single mother, raising my baby on my own."

"That supposed to deter me?"

I shrugged.

"You can tell me all about the fool who let you go, over a drink later tonight."

"I get out of here at eleven." My easy answer surprised me. Then I realized that I'd made up my mind about getting to know Eli a little better. A drink was just a drink. I didn't have to see him again if I didn't want to.

We ended up heading to the Delano Hotel, a very chic and trendy South Beach spot. The lobby is beautiful, with two rows of white pillars down the center and interspersed white drapes that billow as the breeze flows through the hotel's open front and back doors. We took a seat on one of the sofas on the large back terrace, also enclosed with drapes, and had a couple of drinks. We talked easily for an hour and a half.

Eli asked about my baby's father, so I told him. I went on and on about Rayna's deadbeat dad, Byron, and how I didn't understand how a man could walk away from his children. Then I talked about Lewis and how he'd broken my heart because he was a player. When I realized I'd bitched for twenty minutes straight, I thought for sure that Eli would be ready to call it a night. But he wasn't. I let him talk, and that was when I learned he used to play for the Atlanta Braves, which didn't surprise me. Even if he hadn't been with Christian Blake, I would have figured him for an athlete. He'd played nine years as an outfielder before a torn rotator cuff had put an end to his career. He said he'd been married before, and that it had ended badly, but didn't offer more information. I didn't ask.

We moved on to more neutral topics, like movies and music, and our favorite places to eat. It had been a perfectly enjoyable evening, and I really liked Eli, but a little voice in my head had told me I shouldn't see him again. That I should remember my vow to concentrate on my career and put men on the back burner.

Only Eli started sending a dozen roses to my office every day when I didn't return his calls. The attention had been as intoxicating as the roses' sweet scent. Still, I was determined to stand my ground. I didn't want to set myself up to get hurt again, as I'd been with Lewis.

With every flower delivery came a note that included Eli's name and number, and the instruction to call him. I didn't. But with the sixth bouquet of roses, the message had been different. It included his name and number as before, with the added note: "I won't stop sending flowers until you call me back."

So I caved and called him. Wouldn't you?

I loved Eli's sense of humor, the way he'd chased me. Lewis was used to women doing the chasing, and I think if he'd spent two days sending flowers with no response, he would have moved on. With Eli committing a solid week to his chase, I decided he was worthy of giving a chance.

Man, how he'd wooed me. Romantic dinners at Miami's top restaurants, gifts of jewelry and adorable toys for Rayna… I've got to say, there wasn't much to *not* like.

He won me over, and more importantly, won my daughter over. Who wouldn't fall for a man who seemed absolutely perfect?

I'm not sure how long I lay curled up on the plush love seat in my office, but when there was a knock at my door, I didn't move. When I heard it open, I turned my head and saw Trisha, Debbie's assistant, peeking her head through the door.

"Hey, Vanessa," she said.

"Hi," I responded weakly.

She entered the room without waiting for an invitation. "I'm so sorry for your loss," she said. "If there's anything you need, please tell me."

"Sure."

Trisha paused at the door, and I expected her to leave, but she didn't. After a moment she asked, "Do you want me to pick you up some lunch?"

"Lunch?" I asked, surprised. "It's already noon?"

"It's almost one, actually. We gave you some time, like you wanted, but we were starting to get worried about you."

Sitting up, I glanced at my watch. Where had the time gone? I must have drifted off to sleep, after all.

"Whatever you want," Trisha said. "My treat."

"I'm not hungry," I told her.

She stepped fully into my office and closed the door behind her. "I know what you're going through. You remember my father died a couple months ago. You need to keep your strength up."

"I'm really not hungry," I reiterated, now getting to my feet. I wasn't in the mood to hear that I'd have to keep my strength up, that I was about to deal with the hardest thing in my life. I already knew that. "I appreciate your concern, Trisha, but I'll get myself something to eat when I'm ready."

She nodded, then silently left the room.

I was still standing before my window, staring outside but seeing only a blur, when I heard the door open again. I didn't know if Trisha said a word to anyone, or if they simply saw her coming from my office and decided that was their cue to enter. But person after person came in to check on me after that, in a steady stream, offering to get me food or whatever I needed, offering to lend me their shoulder to cry on, sharing stories of how they'd learned their lovers had cheated on them, but how they'd gotten over the heartache.

I swear, they drove me nuts with all their sympathy, to the point where I finally left the office to get food, just so I'd have some peace.

I made the short walk from my office to Bayside, where I wandered back and forth along the scenic walkways and perused the two levels of fashionable shops. I was trying to pretend I was a normal woman out for a normal, carefree stroll. When I passed the Hard Rock Café for the seventh time, I realized I couldn't go on like this forever. I couldn't wander around aimlessly like a tourist, pretending everything was right in my world.

Sooner or later, I had to face reality.

Eli was dead.

It suddenly dawned on me that I hadn't called Carla back after I'd watched CNN. Now, I wanted to assure her that grief hadn't caused me to jump out of my office window.

I dug my cell phone out of my purse, turned it on and punched in Carla's home number. She answered on the first ring, exclaiming, "Vanessa!"

"Hey," I said.

"Where are you? Every time I call your office, the phone goes straight to voice mail! I have been totally worried!"

I didn't even remember setting that up, though I must have. Just as I'd obviously turned off my cell phone. "Sorry I didn't get back to you. I just wanted some time."

A moment passed, then Carla said, "When I saw the news, my heart just froze. You had no clue?"

"That Eli would get himself killed one day because he was having an affair with a married woman? No, I had no clue."

Carla tsked. "Sometimes life seriously sucks. I know how much you loved Eli."

"How's Rayna?" I asked, changing the subject. I didn't want to think about what I'd felt for Eli, because I would likely fall apart, right here in front of countless strangers.

"Great. She's having a blast here."

"Good, that's good." A heavy sigh oozed out of my body. At least that was positive news.

"When are you going to be home?" Carla asked.

"Between five-thirty and six, same as usual," I answered.

"What? Tell me your boss isn't that much of a bitch that she's making you stay."

"No, of course not. I chose to stay."

"Why?"

"It's not that I didn't want to head home—I'm definitely no use at the office today—but…I just couldn't. I guess I needed some time to pull myself together. To deal with the shock of all that's happened. And, my God, Carla, I'm afraid I'm going to break down the moment I see Rayna. She's going to ask where Eli is, and how do I tell her…" My voice cracked.

"Oh, sweetie. I'm really sorry. I don't know what else to say."

A weird feeling suddenly passed over me, the kind you get when you sense you're being watched.

It stopped my tears in my eye ducts, because up until that moment, I was certain I'd been about to start crying.

Spinning around, I surveyed the crowd. I saw happy lovers strolling hand in hand, girlfriends carrying multiple shopping bags, people standing near the railing at the edge of the water.

In other words, I saw nothing out of place.

But still, that odd feeling didn't leave me.

"Carla, I'll see you later," I said hastily, then closed the phone.

One more quick glance around and I assured myself I was being paranoid. Who would be following me in this very public place?

I stuffed my cell phone back in my purse and headed for the street. Once again, it hit me that I wasn't in the middle of a nightmare.

Actually, I was—only this nightmare was real.

I pushed that thought aside and forced myself to think about Rayna, how I had to be strong for her.

She was going to need me, and I wouldn't let her down.

chapter three

Needless to say, I didn't get any work done when I went back to my office, but I stayed there the full day nonetheless. I even lingered several minutes after five, giving most of our office staff a chance to leave so I wouldn't have to face them.

I did peek my head into Debbie's office to tell her goodbye, and she told me to make sure I stayed home the next day. There was no mention of Jason, but the fact that she was applying a fresh coat of lipstick told me he would soon be on his way up.

Shortly before five-thirty, I was heading to the lot where I'd parked my car, when I heard my name.

I turned. Kim, a heavyset, dark-skinned woman from the agency, was rushing toward me.

"Vanessa," she said as she reached my side. Sadness creased her forehead. "I didn't get a chance to talk to you earlier because I was out with a client. I'm so sorry about your ex."

"My fiancé," I clarified.

"Fiancé, right. I read the story on the Internet. Holy shit,

it was gruesome. Killed with a bow and arrow! In bed with
another woman! I can't imagine what you're going through.
And when the news hits the papers tomorrow—"

"Thanks for your concern," I said, cutting her off. But I
wanted to say, "Do you think that repeating the dirty details
is making me feel any better?"

I cut her some slack, because none of what had happened
was her fault. I started walking again, picking up my pace a
little.

She clearly didn't get my not-so-subtle hints that I wanted
her to drop the subject, because she fell into step beside me
and continued talking. "I was dating this guy once. Big shot
in some finance company. He took me out for all these fancy
dinners, wooed me on his yacht. I wish someone had shot
that asshole with a bow and arrow, because when I found
out he was married—"

"You know, Kim," I said, halting, "I'm really not in the
mood for this."

A hurt look passed over her face. "I'm just trying to say
I understand what you're going through."

"Yeah, I know," I told her. "Everybody does. More people
have told me today that they've been cheated on than during
the rest of my life combined."

"I'm only trying—"

"It's okay." I placed a hand on her shoulder and offered
her a small smile. "I know you care. Thank you."

I turned to the right, leaving Kim standing on the sidewalk. Perhaps I was abrupt with her, but didn't I have a right
to be? Let's face it, I'd had a really shitty day.

I don't know why, but as I was walking south, I again got

that feeling that someone was watching me. Turning, I saw no one suspicious, not even Kim staring at me with an evil expression. I saw office workers making their way to wherever they'd parked their cars.

And then it dawned on me that perhaps I was sensing Eli.

"Forget it, Eli," I mumbled, imagining him trying to find a ghost whisperer to reach out to me. "Even an apology from the other side isn't going to get me to forgive you."

Only when I exited the MacArthur Causeway onto South Beach did I realize that I had somehow navigated my way home. I didn't remember one bit of the drive, but given my state of mind, I suppose that was only natural.

Glancing at my car's digital clock, I saw that it was ten minutes after six. Rayna would no doubt be anticipating my arrival at Carla's place, as she always did this time of day. And yet when I got to Washington Avenue, I found myself driving past my condo and down to South Pointe Park.

I drove as far south as I could go, to where the street ended and the rocky shoreline began. With my car radio tuned to 99.1, I listened to Kanye West as I stared out at the water.

South Beach had been my home for only three months, but I loved everything about this place. My building was in the historic art deco district. Tourists loved taking walks along Ocean Drive and Collins Avenue, where they could check out the prewar art deco hotels like the Breakwater and the Colony and the South Beach. Buildings with rounded edges, decorative sculptural panels, sleek symmetrical patterns, and a few with futuristic forms. And even though some of the facades appeared small, most of the hotels offered idyllic private courtyards lined with palm trees and boasted pools with stunning designs. During the Depression, the art deco buildings had been designed with bold colors and shapes with the hope of a better future. As such, they had symbolized decadence.

At night, the Ocean Drive strip lit up in an array of neon colors, and that was part of what gave South Beach its appeal. Now, a new generation of architects had designed towering condominiums, which were popping up anywhere there was space. Like Portofino Tower at the southern tip of South Beach, where I now sat in my parked car. But I wasn't partial to skyscraper condos in a part of Miami that had become world-renowned for its low-rise art deco designs. It's one of the reasons I particularly loved my building. It was only six stories high, and featured both angular and rounded edges. The blue-hued windows provided a nice contrast with the white-and-cream-colored exterior. And the private court-yard was to die for.

I glanced up at the Portofino, then back at the stretch of beach that overlooked the bay. It was the end of the workday, and many people were out with dogs that had been cooped up in apartments while they'd been at the office. I watched small dogs prance, big dogs race, and con-templated how odd it was that the world around me was continuing as usual when my personal world would never be the same.

It was the beginning of a slow song that had me getting out of my Honda Accord and walking across the short ex-panse of grass to the rocky shore. I hugged my torso as I did, a wave of sadness crashing over me as I remembered how Eli and I had liked to take walks here in the evenings with Rayna.

And, Lord, the tears started again.

"Vanessa Cain?"

At the sound of my name, I whipped my head around. And saw a tall, thin black woman who looked vaguely familiar.

I brushed away my tears as she approached me. "Vanessa, I'm Cynthia Martin from the *Miami Herald*. You were Eli Johnson's girlfriend, correct?"

My eyes widened. I stood there stupidly, in complete shock.

"I know this has been a very hard day for you."

Suddenly, I realized what was going on. I asked, "You're a reporter?"

"Miami Herald," the woman repeated, this time handing me her card.

And then it clicked. I knew why she looked familiar. I'd seen her today at Bayside. I'd seen her face in the crowd.

Which meant she'd been stalking me.

"I'm very sorry for your loss," Cynthia said. "But I do have some questions about your boyfriend. If I could have just a few minutes of your time."

"Excuse me?" Slowly but surely, outrage was bubbling inside of me.

"A few questions, that's all."

"I heard you. I—I understood what you meant. Why do you want to ask me about Eli?"

"He *was* your boyfriend, right? Or…" Cynthia's eyes lowered to my left hand, landing on my engagement ring. "Oh."

I whipped my hand behind my back. "How do you know who I am?"

"Your fiancé's death has been big news here," Cynthia replied, not at all answering my question.

"You—you're spying on me?"

"It's my job to find people," she said simply.

"How?" I demanded.

"Your name is on the deed with Eli's," Cynthia answered.

"Of course," I mumbled.

"And I don't expect you to remember, but I met you once before," she added. "At a fund-raiser for Jackson Memorial Hospital. I had to coax Eli into letting my photographer take a picture of the two of you together, but that must have been before you got engaged."

"That's right," I said softly, remembering the event. And remembering Eli's reluctance at having us be photographed together. He had explained that he didn't want the media to start harassing me. I'd appreciated his concern, but didn't think that one picture was a big deal, and he'd ultimately agreed to a photograph.

The one thing I'd liked about Eli was that although he'd been a professional athlete, he didn't crave the spotlight. Certainly not like Christian Blake, who was often pictured in the paper at some club, with a different woman on his arm each time. Eli freely admitted that he hadn't been the most popular player on the Braves, but said that had been fine with him because it was the team's superstars who constantly had their privacy violated and dirt dug up about them. He'd made his money, and was happy that he could live a relatively normal life.

After Eli proposed, I'd placed an announcement in the *Miami Herald,* and when I showed it to him, he couldn't have been less enthused. Again, he'd said how he wanted to protect me from any media scrutiny by being associated with him. Personally, it seemed to me that he was overreacting, since during the time I'd been with him we'd been able to walk the streets, shop, and dine at expensive restaurants without any paparazzi bothering us. Yes, some guys recognized him from time to time, but since Eli hadn't played professionally in seven years, he was hardly a blip on the media's radar in terms of current celebrity gossip.

"I followed you from your office this afternoon, but I left you alone because you looked so distraught." Cynthia's words drew me from my thoughts like any slap in the face would. Feeling utterly violated, I grunted and marched past the woman en route to my car.

"Tell me what it was like learning your boyfriend had been murdered," Cynthia called out. "That he'd been gruesomely shot with a bow and arrow."

The words made me halt, but only for a moment. I quickly kept going and scrambled into my car. Cynthia hurried to my window and rapped on it with her knuckles. Ignoring her, I revved the engine, surged forward, then did a fast U-turn and sped down the street. In my rearview mirror, I saw her hurry to her own car, a gold-colored Saturn that had been parked behind mine.

Not about to give her the chance to follow me, I raced down the street, then turned left onto Fifth in a bold move that could have gotten me into an accident if a car had been coming. I zipped into the right lane, glancing in my rearview mirror as I did. Cynthia was stopped at the light. I kept going straight, hoping she'd think that I was heading back to the causeway. But when I hit Alton Road, I made a hasty right turn and sped north.

When I reached Tenth Street and saw no sign of the gold Saturn, I finally started to calm down. But the calm lasted barely a few seconds before my heart spasmed in my chest.

Cynthia had found my name on the deed, which meant she knew where I lived. She wasn't the only reporter in the city. If she could find me, how many others would?

Cynthia, however, had met me before, and therefore knew where I worked. She'd likely tried to get the jump on other reporters by showing up at my office building. But if other members of the media had found my name on the deed and wanted to reach me for comment…

Urged on by the suddenly desperate feeling that I needed to protect my daughter, I made a series of turns and sped the rest of the way home.

Sure enough, I saw a throng of people milling about outside my condo. I didn't need to see the cameras to know they were reporters. In my numbed haze, I'd driven right by my building and not even noticed them before.

Some surrounded the front door. Some hovered near the entrance to the building's parking lot. Slowing, I drove past my condo, wondering what to do.

As I circled the block, I realized that I didn't have a choice. I *had* to get inside, had to get to my daughter. And my best bet was to drive into the condo's parking lot, as I always did. At the very least, it would provide me the protection of my car should the reporters recognize me, and I doubted any of them would risk getting run over simply to get the perfect photo of the grieving fiancée.

Eli and I had been photographed at the hospital fund-raiser, and that picture had made the pages of the *Miami Herald*. So had the photo that accompanied our engagement announcement. Clearly, the reporters surrounding my building figured they could spot me when I approached.

I wasn't about to let that happen.

Before I rounded the corner that would take me back to my condo, I slipped off my sleek sunglasses and put on the large pair I always kept in my car. Then I placed my cell phone at my ear, and acted like I was in the middle of a fun conversation. A short while later, I drove past the reporters as though they didn't faze me one bit. Cameras swung my way, as did curious glances, but I kept my cool and inched forward, even laughing loudly into my phone as I pressed my key card to the electronic sensor.

And then I was on my way into the indoor parking for the residents of Cosmopolitan Towers.

Inside, I breathed a sigh of relief. Good grief, this was insane! Here I was, having to sneak past reporters to get to my own home. Damn Eli. He hadn't just died in the sleaziest of situations. He'd thrown me into a potful of drama.

Oh, he'd been right to be concerned that my association with him might bring out the paparazzi. But never in my wildest dreams had I thought it would be under these circumstances.

Just before I rounded the corner inside the parking garage, I craned my neck for one last look at the reporters pacing the sidewalk.

And I couldn't help thinking, *My life is about to get seriously complicated.*

chapter four

Carla opened her apartment door and immediately swept me into her arms. "Vanessa!"

"Mommy!" The shriek came immediately afterward. I broke apart from Carla in time to scoop up Rayna, who was racing toward me. There's nothing that brings a brighter smile to your face than coming home to a child who loves you so much she'll drop whatever she's doing to throw herself into your arms.

"Rayna, sweetie." I planted kisses all over my daughter's face, which had her in a fit of giggles. "I missed you, baby."

"I miss Mommy."

"Well, Mommy's home now." I held her tight, emotion welling up inside me. "Mommy's home."

Rayna shimmied out of my arms, then headed back to the center of the living room. She lifted a paper full of colorful swirls. "Look, Mommy."

I walked toward her and examined the artwork she held.

"Oh, wow. You made that?" Rayna beamed. "It's beautiful."

"Rainbow."

"Yes, a rainbow," I agreed, amazed at how much the picture *did* resemble a rainbow. "Look at all the beautiful colors."

"This for Daddy." Rayna lifted another picture that had a big circle colored mostly black. "A cat."

I had to swallow back the tears. "Yes. For Daddy."

Rayna planted herself on the floor beside Carla's daughter, Amani, and they resumed playing with a range of colorful ponies that they were both so fond of. It was a bit of a reprieve, thankfully, because I had no clue what I was going to say to Rayna about Eli.

"It's been all over the news," Carla said, her tone quiet. "You must have seen the media camped outside the building."

I nodded. "I assume they were looking for me, but I drove past them and they didn't notice me."

"This is crazy."

"Tell me about it." I crossed my arms over my chest. "I took a detour to the beach for a moment to clear my head, and a reporter from the *Miami Herald* approached me."

Carla's mouth fell open. "What?"

"Yeah. I'd apparently met her once with Eli at an event, and she remembered me. Plus she found my name on the condo's deed. The woman had the nerve to follow me! I saw her when I was at Bayside earlier today. Of course, I didn't realize who she was at the time. Until she approached me twenty minutes ago and said she wanted to ask me a few questions."

"Wow."

"Wow indeed." I sighed softly. "Hopefully by tomorrow, they'll lose interest in this story. Staking me out like this? It's crazy. I'm not Paris Hilton or Britney Spears. I'm a woman whose fiancé was killed by a jealous husband. Happens every day."

"I hate to tell you this, but CNN hasn't stopped running the story. They're saying that neither you, his 'live-in love—'" Carla made air quotes "—nor his family could be reached for comment."

"What family? They tried to reach his mother in Barbados?" Eli's father had died the year before he retired from baseball, and his mother had moved back to Barbados right after that. When we got engaged, I'd asked Eli if he would call his mother and let me say hello, but he didn't want to. Something about her being a Christian and that she'd hate the idea of us living in sin. "I know he's got some cousins somewhere," I told Carla, "but I've never met them. Eli said I'd meet them all at a family reunion this summer, and that he was looking forward to surprising them with news of our engagement."

"They certainly had enough to broadcast without comments from his family," Carla said. "CNN spent the day replaying the scene outside the house where he was…well, you know. Showing the crime scene tape, and that woman's husband in handcuffs. He wasn't shy about talking to the press, that's for sure. They also showed highlights of Eli's career with the Braves, and even had people phone in to share their memories of Eli."

"Share their memories? He hasn't played pro ball in seven years."

"It's still big news. With how he was killed, and why… It's a sensational story."

I grew quiet. What else was there to say? Carla was right—it was the outlandish nature of Eli's murder that had garnered such media interest. I wondered if the reporters were going to stick around until they got a statement from me.

Carla rubbed my forearm. "How are you holding up?"

"Okay. I think. But I don't know how…" I had to stop, take a calming breath. "I'm afraid to go upstairs, Carla, and be there…knowing that Eli won't be coming home."

"You can stay here if you want."

I shook my head, dismissing the idea without giving it a thought. "The routine has to be the same. For Rayna's sake."

Carla gripped both of my hands. "Don't you worry about Rayna. She's perfectly fine."

As if to emphasize that point, my daughter's high-pitched laughter pierced the room.

"I know," I agreed.

"You need to take care of *you,*" Carla insisted. "If it's too soon for you to go upstairs, you tell Rayna we're having a sleepover. Trust me, she'll think it's fun."

"I hear you. I do. But I can't…" I swallowed, considered my words. "I can't avoid this situation forever. I have to go home and deal with…with the truth. If I don't go now, when will I? I may never be ready."

Carla pulled me into her thick arms and gave me a heartfelt hug. "Oh, Vanessa. I'm so sorry. I can't even begin to imagine how you're feeling right now. But you'll get through this."

I nodded, but I didn't entirely believe what she was saying.

As it was, I felt like I was walking an emotional tightrope. One wrong move and I could fall into a pit of despair. The only thing keeping me walking a straight line at the moment was my daughter. She was the reason I was able to summon the strength to keep moving forward.

"What can I do?" Carla asked.

"Nothing. But I love you for caring." I'd met Carla only three months earlier, when I'd moved into the building with Eli, the first time I went down to use the pool one warm January day. Our children had brought us together, the way so many women make friends with other mothers in play groups or at the park. Rayna and Amani had hit it off playing in the water, which had led to me and Carla talking. I soon learned that she was a military wife, and that her husband, stationed at the Homestead Air Reserve Base, was deployed in Iraq. Her daughter, Amani, was a year older than Rayna, and the second cutest child in the world—after Rayna, of course.

We talked for three hours straight that day, as if we'd been friends for years. Carla confided in me her fears that her husband could die any moment, and that sometimes it was a real struggle to stay strong. She also wasn't happy with her weight, and hoped she could lose the twenty-five pounds she'd gained during pregnancy by the time Paul returned home from his tour of duty. Her problem, I'd soon learned, was that Carla ate sweets when she was down, which negated whatever progress she made in the building's gym.

At five foot five, she carried the extra pounds well, I thought. She was pretty, with flawless skin the color of milk chocolate, and whenever we were out together, she attracted her fair share of masculine attention. The brothas appreciated the extra pounds on her butt, something she told me her husband, who was white, didn't at first. Until he'd seen how men had tripped over themselves to get a good look at her behind.

Carla also shared her annoyance at the fact that many of the building's residents had made a point of asking her how she and Paul could afford to live in this building, considering she was a stay-at-home mom and he was in the military. To others, she said they'd invested well in the stock market. But she'd admitted to me that Paul's father had died, and he and his mother, the only two heirs, had split the million-dollar life insurance policy.

I'd never met Paul, but based on everything Carla said about him, I could tell that they had what I wanted—a happy marriage. Why was that so hard to find?

"Let me at least feed you," Carla said, interrupting my thoughts. "I made a pot of spaghetti."

I waved off the suggestion. "No. I'm gonna take Rayna and go."

"This isn't about pity. You know I enjoy the company."

Shortly before Eli and I had moved into this building, Paul had left for Iraq. He was to be gone for a year, which meant he had eight months left to serve before returning home. And ever since his departure, Carla had been lonely. She never said so, but I could tell.

"Another time," I told her. Tonight, I wanted to be alone with my thoughts. Needed to be. I wasn't interested in talking with anyone about how I felt. I simply wanted to be with my baby and act like our world was still normal.

I approached my daughter. "Rayna, sweetie. Time to go home."

She immediately got up and came to me, still holding a pony in each fist. Before I could try to wrestle them from her—a task I knew would be difficult—Carla said, "It's okay. Amani won't miss them. Bring them back next time."

"Are you sure?" I asked.

"I got her double of each pony in case she ever lost one," Carla explained. "Yeah, I'm sure."

"All right, then. Thanks."

I scooped Rayna into one arm, then went back to the door, where I lifted her diaper bag with the other. Amani wrapped an arm around her mother's leg.

Carla lifted her daughter, kissed the girl's cheek, then gave me a look full of sympathy. "If you change your mind, I'll be here. Like I said, the kids can have a sleepover, and we can watch a movie to take your mind off things."

"I'll let you know," I murmured, but I knew I wouldn't be taking her up on her offer. I couldn't watch a movie and pretend everything was okay. A romantic comedy would make me cry. A murder mystery would make me cry.

Anything would make me cry.

Rayna rested her head against the crook of my neck, and I treasured the warm feeling of her little body. She seemed tired, which was good. If she went down early, she wouldn't have a chance to ask me where Daddy was.

No sooner than I had entered my apartment, than the phone rang. Carrying Rayna on my hip, I raced to answer it.

"Hello?" I said breathlessly.

"Vanessa Cain?"

"Yes," I answered, my tone guarded.

"This is Robert Rooney from *Channel 2 News.* Can I set up an interview—"

I hung up the phone. It rang again.

I picked it up, but replaced the receiver without answering.

That happened five more times. So when it rang yet again, I snatched up the receiver and put it to my ear. "No, I won't give you an interview. Please leave me alone."

"Baby, you know the last thing I want from you is an interview."

My eyes narrowed—and then it clicked that Lewis Carter was on the other end of my line. Thankful that it wasn't another reporter, I felt my body relax—then immediately tense. I hadn't heard from Lewis in about six weeks, and the last time he'd called, he had been hoping to get me to cheat on Eli.

"Lewis?" I asked.

"Who else, baby?"

Rayna started to squirm, so I let her down. "What do you want?"

"Is that any way to greet me? After everything we once meant to each other?"

I rolled my eyes. If we meant so much to each other, why hadn't he proposed? "You know exactly what we meant to each other," I said frankly. Lewis had been, for lack of a better word, a booty call. "More importantly, I know it."

"Baby, don't be like that."

"What do you want, Lewis?"

"I'm phoning to see how you're doing. Is that against the law?"

I didn't say anything. I wondered if the timing of his call

was coincidental, or if he, like most of America, had learned about Eli's death on CNN.

"I heard about your fiancé on the radio," he stated, answering my question.

"Of course."

"So how are you?"

I lowered myself onto a chair in my kitchen. "I'm hanging in."

"You sure? Because if I was as shocked as I was to learn that Eli was killed while in the arms of some other honey, I can only imagine how you took the news. Especially after how much you raved about him being the perfect guy."

"If you're calling to gloat, then I'm going to hang up now."

"No, no, I'm not," he said hurriedly. "Look, I'm sorry. I really am. I know how much you cared about him."

I waited for more, but there was none. Maybe Lewis was being sincere. "Thank you," I told him.

"I could come over, if you like," he murmured.

Of course. "Why?"

"To keep you company. Offer you my shoulder to cry on."

I'll bet, I thought. But I said, "I'm fine. I'm going to spend a quiet evening with Rayna."

"But she's gonna head to bed sometime soon, right? In the next hour or two. And after that, you might need someone."

I narrowed my eyes again, wondering why I had even considered giving Lewis the benefit of the doubt. Whenever he called, it was about one thing.

Sex.

I'll be the first to admit that my feelings for Lewis had started out as pure lust when I met him at a South Beach nightclub. I always knew he was a smooth operator, the kind of guy you can't completely trust in terms of a relationship. And that was okay, because I didn't want anything serious with him. He was a guy I enjoyed spending time with because he was a lot of fun. Goofy. Whether pulling off lame Michael Jackson moves on a crowded dance floor or tickling me while we were naked in bed, he never failed to make me laugh.

I loved how I felt when I was out on his arm, the way women stared at me with envy. And I loved the passion we shared in the bedroom. He treated me well, wined and dined me in style. We had an easy rapport and some serious chemistry. And he got along well with Rayna, too, on the occasions when he'd come over and spend time with both of us.

After a while, what had started as lust had turned into love.

"What time should I come over?" Lewis asked, his voice husky.

"I'll be fine, Lewis."

"I'm not sure you should be alone right now. The first night is always the worst after a tragedy like this. Let me come by, hold you in my arms and help you sleep."

"I can't believe you. You are *not* suggesting we hook up tonight."

There was a moment of silence, and I fully expected Lewis to deny my accusation—if only halfheartedly. Instead, he said in a low voice, "I miss you."

"You're unbelievable."

"No, seriously, I do. In fact, I've been thinking a lot about you lately, and how things ended between us. I feel really bad about that."

I rolled my eyes. If I hadn't moved on, Lewis's words might actually have me taking a trip down memory lane. But I still remembered vividly how he'd told me we couldn't be together because of Rayna. Actually, he'd used the lame excuse that Rayna's father, my no-good ex, who only wanted to be a father when the mood struck, might come back into our lives, leaving him out in the cold, heart-broken.

Of course, he'd come up with this lame excuse *after* I'd found a red thong in his pocket.

At the time, I'd been crushed. Now, the absurdity of it all made me want to laugh out loud.

"Lewis, you're a trip."

"Let me come over."

Because I knew him, and knew that he might just decide to drop by in hopes of seducing me, I lied. "I have plans."

"You said you were spending a quiet evening with your daughter," Lewis said, his voice full of doubt.

"Yeah, well…in all the chaos of the day I forgot that my sister said she was going to come over."

"Tell her to come tomorrow."

Something struck me, a thought I hadn't considered before. "It can't wait till tomorrow, because I have to contact the police about Eli. To make inquiries about his body. Nikki said she'd be there for me as I did that."

"Oh." Lewis sounded convinced, though unhappy. "May-be after that?"

I heard a thud, then Rayna's loud cry. "Lewis, I have to go. Rayna just fell."

"Call me later," he said quickly.

I hung up the phone and raced into the living room. My daughter was on her back on the hardwood floor, bawling at the top of her lungs.

"Oh, baby." I lifted her into my arms and gently cooed, offering her comfort.

But as she cried, her raw emotion triggered the overwhelming sadness inside me that needed an outlet for release. It overpowered me, refusing to be contained any longer.

My own tears started to fall, my anguished cries mixing with my daughter's.

chapter five

Thankfully, an hour later, Rayna fell asleep. I'd fed her, bathed her, read her a story, and then she was out like a light. It wasn't like her to fall asleep before eight o'clock—trust me—but it was just what I needed, and I was grateful.

She was so tired, she didn't even ask about "Daddy." I knew the question would come, but hopefully, when it did, I'd be in a better frame of mind to answer it.

The phone hadn't stopped ringing while I'd put together a quick dinner of chicken strips and broccoli, so I'd taken it off the hook. Now, I gave Rayna one last kiss on her forehead, content with the fact that she was sleeping peacefully, and made my way to the kitchen to replace the receiver.

By now, the reporters were certain to have given up in their attempts to reach me, and I needed to use my phone. I would have to call my sister because she had no doubt tried calling me. After that, I would contact the police and find out what a person was supposed to do when her fiancé had been murdered.

But before I did anything, I needed a glass of wine. I poured myself an extra large glass of white zinfandel, then went to the living room and plopped down on the leather sofa.

For several moments I sat there, unmoving. Myriad thoughts ran through my mind like little feet trampling my brain, leaving me with a headache. There was so much I needed to do, but I wasn't ready for any of it. Alaina had asked if I'd told Rayna about heaven. I hadn't, and maybe I should head out tomorrow to buy some books on the matter. Children's books, of course—something that could explain the concept of death to a child.

Or I could simply tell her that Eli was gone on a trip. That was something Rayna would understand. Every day, if she asked, I could tell her that Eli was coming home soon. Surely, one day, she'd just stop asking about him....

I took a sip of my wine and frowned, knowing I couldn't take the chicken's way out of the scenario. However I explained it to Rayna, she needed to know that Eli wasn't coming home. It would be grossly unfair to lead her on, and ultimately make her think Eli had abandoned us. Kids didn't forget things like that, and I'd be guaranteed to foot the therapy bill later if I dared to venture down that road.

My thoughts were disrupted by the shrill ring of the telephone. There was a cordless handset on the coffee table beside the sofa, and I quickly glanced at the caller ID.

It was my sister's home number. I inhaled deeply, then picked up the phone. I knew I'd have to talk to her sooner or later but, Nikki being Nikki, I wasn't relishing the idea.

"Hey, Nikki," I said, offering her the most upbeat greeting I could muster.

"*When* were you going to call me?" she demanded.

I counted to three before answering. "It's been a crazy evening. The media is camped outside my building, my phone has been ringing off the hook."

"I called at least twenty times."

"I was just going to call you."

A beat passed. Then my sister asked, "How are you?"

Wow, genuine concern. "I'm…okay. As okay as I can be, I guess."

"Is Rayna sleeping?"

"Yes. She went down a little while ago."

"Good. So you can talk."

I sipped more wine. "For a bit."

"I've got to tell you, Vanessa," my sister began, "when I saw the news earlier, I nearly crapped my pants."

How did you respond to that? I decided not to.

"It was so disturbing—seeing the cops all over the crime scene, hearing the gruesome details, hearing *your name* in association with that creep… I had to turn the TV off. I didn't want my boys seeing that."

"Right," I said absently.

"Didn't I tell you?" Nikki demanded. "Didn't I tell you that Eli was going to hurt you sooner rather than later?"

"Nikki—"

"Not only did the jerk have a girlfriend on the side, he still had a wife."

I reeled backward, caught off guard. "What?"

"I turned on the TV five minutes ago and there was a

news crew outside Eli's wife's house in Atlanta. They were hoping to get a comment from her or something."

Suddenly, I understood what was going on. And leave it to my sister to find a way to rub salt into my wound without trying to decipher fact from fiction. Nikki had a way of getting under my skin without much effort. She never approved of any guy I dated, nor most of my decisions as a parent. When I got pregnant and found myself alone, she'd chastised me for having dated Byron in the first place, instead of offering me comfort over my predicament.

Nikki married the only man she'd ever slept with, her high school sweetheart, had two children with him, and was a stay-at-home mom. I was single, parenting without any help, and couldn't find a decent guy to save my life.

Compared to her, I was a failure. At least that's the way she made me feel.

"Eli's *ex*-wife," I corrected her.

"Why would they be at her house if she's his ex?" Nikki asked.

"You know the damn media. The juicier they can make this story, the better. Besides, Eli was married while he played for the Braves. I'm not surprised they would want her comment, given what's happened."

"You sure he didn't lie to you about her?"

I felt a surge of anger, but drew in a deep breath to keep it under control. "Of course I'm sure. I did an Internet search when Eli and I got serious. I saw with my own eyes the articles about his marriage breaking up. Apparently it was a bitter split. And that was back in 2002." The various archived article headings in the *Atlanta Journal-Constitution* had all proclaimed the same thing—that Eli Johnson and his wife of six years were headed for divorce court. The headlines were all I could scan without paying a fee to read the full stories, but that had been enough. I wasn't interested in seeing the entire articles and reading about Eli's love affair with another woman, even if it had gone sour.

"Oh." I wasn't sure, but my sister sounded disappointed. "Even if he didn't lie about being married, I knew he was a player as soon as I met him. That's probably why he and his wife got divorced. Former professional athlete. Did you need a bigger clue than that?"

I rolled my eyes.

"Do you *know* how many women guys like that sleep with?"

"Nikki—"

"You remember that one basketball player—the one who bragged about sleeping with more than ten thousand women? Vanessa, you'd better get an AIDS test. Like, yesterday."

"Nikki!"

"I say we go together tomorrow. If you've got AIDS, you need to know."

"Nikki!"

She finally stopped. "What?"

I exhaled sharply. "Why can't you just call and tell me you're sorry that Eli's dead? Sorry that I'm going through this? Why do you have to preach to me like you're my mother? I'm a grown woman."

"A grown woman who keeps making colossal mistakes with men. You worry about penis size and pretty-boy looks. That has gotten you nothing but heartache."

"Ahh, now I get it. Morris has got a small penis. No wonder you're so damn uptight!"

I couldn't help the words that came from my mouth. My sister's phone call was doing more to send me into a deep depression than to help me out of my funk.

"Fine. Lash out at me. I'm not the one who screwed around on you."

"Do you take special pleasure in telling people 'I told you so'? Because my fiancé just died. My *fiancé*. I don't need a lecture from you. I need…" My voice broke, croaking with emotion. I did my best not to cry; she'd probably get some warped sense of satisfaction from it.

I heard her sigh. "You're right. And I'm sorry. I…I was out of line."

"Thank you."

"It's just that I love you so much. And when I see you heading for disaster—"

"Nikki," I said firmly.

"Right. Okay, no more lectures. And I am sorry this happened to you. I might have had my doubts about him, but I really was hoping that Eli was the one."

"So was I."

"What have you told Rayna?"

"Nothing. I don't know what to tell her."

"The good thing is she's young. She'll bounce back from this in no time."

"You think so?" I asked. "Because I'm so worried that she's going to be scarred. One minute, she's got a daddy. The next, he's gone, and she won't understand why."

"She'll be fine," Nikki said. "Not that she won't be upset

at all, or confused, but this won't have a lasting effect on her. She'll grow up and not even remember Eli."

Such a blunt statement, and yet a valid one. "I guess that's a good thing," I said. "Even if it doesn't exactly sound like it."

"I'm not trying to be crass. Just letting you know that she won't be scarred emotionally because of this. And hopefully you'll meet someone great who'll become a fabulous daddy for her."

"I can't even think beyond the moment, much less consider the idea that I might meet someone else."

"I know. I'm just saying—"

"I know what you're saying. You're actually trying to make me feel better." Score one for Nikki.

A moment of silence passed. Then Nikki asked, "You had no clue he was stepping out on you?"

"You think I'd stay with him if I knew he was?" Nikki didn't answer. "Honestly, that was the most shocking news I learned today, more so than finding out he was dead. Eli was always so romantic, so thoughtful, so great with Rayna… It's so hard to believe that any of this has really happened."

"It's quite the salacious story. And that woman—she was quite the looker."

Not what I needed to hear.

"The worst part," I said, "is that we had a fight last night. It was a stupid fight, but he walked out on me. Maybe he met this woman at a bar and this was the first time he cheated. You know, because he was angry, and stupid. Obviously stupid. But I keep thinking, if I hadn't gotten mad at him, maybe none of this would have happened, and he'd be here right now."

Nikki was silent, and I could imagine her biting on her bottom lip to keep from speaking. No matter who I dated, she believed the guy was a no-good loser.

"It's possible," I told her. "Neither of us knows for sure."

"Yeah, I guess," she grudgingly agreed. "But however it happened, it doesn't make this any easier. You're living in a lavish penthouse. How are you gonna keep up the payments?"

"I was worried about that, too, but my boss pointed out that we must have had mortgage insurance when we bought the place. And if not that, then Eli must have had a will. I know you think I'm irresponsible when it comes to those kinds of things, and maybe I am, but wills and insurance aren't things I pay attention to. Anyway," I quickly said, "there'll be a record of them somewhere. I'll call the bank tomorrow and see if I can find some papers here regarding his lawyer."

"That's one less headache."

"Yeah, thank God for insurance."

"If you need to," Nikki continued, "you can come over here for a while. Even if it's just for a change of scenery."

"Thank you," I said, meaning it. The offer surprised me—and touched me. However, in my wildest dreams, I couldn't imagine myself taking my sister up on that offer. I loved her, but I could handle her only in small doses. She had endless advice about my love life that I didn't ask for and never appreciated. Not to mention her thoughts on how I could improve myself as a mother.

In my sister's defense, she had become a surrogate mother to me after our parents had died in a boating accident when I was twelve. Seven years my senior, Nikki had naturally fallen into the role of caregiver, even though we'd moved from Detroit to Miami to live with our aunt Lola.

"Or even bring Rayna over for the weekend," my sister continued. "You know I love having her."

"That might be an idea," I told her, but again had no intention of following through on that. Now more than ever, I wanted Rayna close to me. She was the one person who had the capacity to get me through the coming rough days.

"Oh, hello," I heard Nikki say, and it took me a moment to figure out she wasn't talking to me. "I didn't realize you were going to be coming home this late."

"Nikki?"

"Sorry. Morris just got home."

"I'll let you go then," I told her, more than happy to get her off the line.

"Yeah, I'd better warm his dinner for him. He puts in such long hours, it's the least I can do."

There was a smugness in Nikki's voice as she spoke—or was I just imagining it? Maybe I was, since I was supersensitive to the fact that I'd just lost my future husband and would never be making any meals for him again.

As I hung up, I thought about turning the television to CNN. I wanted to, but the idea of seeing pictures of Eli's lover had me changing my mind. I couldn't handle that. At least not yet. It was hard enough to deal with his death, much less his infidelity.

Still, I couldn't help wondering if what I'd said to Nikki wasn't true—that after our fight, Eli had ended up at a local South Beach hot spot, and then found his way into this woman's bed.

It could have very easily been the first time he had cheated on me.

It would certainly be the last.

chapter six

I decided not to call the police after I spoke to my sister. Emotionally, I was drained, and needed a night's rest before I dealt with that awful task. I was a little surprised that I hadn't heard from them; it would be so much easier if they contacted me, as I didn't have the first clue as to where to start.

I had enough to cope with heading to bed—the bed I had shared with Eli for three months in this apartment. The reality that he wouldn't be joining me was too overwhelming to contemplate. It required me having a second glass of wine before I dared to get under the covers.

The stress of the day had clearly worn me out, because I fell asleep almost immediately. The sound of the ringing phone woke me up. Startled, I first glanced at the bedside clock and saw that it was 12:04. Then I rolled over toward the night table and checked out the illuminated call display.

PRIVATE NAME.

Falling back onto my pillows, I groaned loudly. Damn it! A friggin' reporter! My God, did these people *never* give up?

After I'd hung up with my sister, there had been no calls at all, giving me the false confidence that the media had given up—or at least had gone home for the day.

No such luck, clearly.

A few minutes passed and sleep wouldn't come to me, so I crawled out of bed and went to the window and peered outside. My building had only six floors, and even being on the top one, I had a good view of the street below. To my chagrin, I saw that there were still camera crews and vans parked out front. As if they expected me to leave the building and go out partying in the wake of my fiancé's death.

"Morons," I muttered.

I lay back down, trying once again to sleep, but failing. The bed was too big and Eli's presence sorely missed. Damn those vultures for waking me up. Wasn't there some movie star doing Ecstasy in a local club that they could go and harass?

The minutes ticked by. A quick look at the digital clock told me it was 12:48. Nearly one in the morning, and I was wide awake.

I needed to fall asleep again. Because, come morning, bright and early, Rayna would be up—and I needed to be rested to deal with her.

I forced myself out of bed and went to the kitchen. There, I opened another bottle of white zinfandel. I'd already had two glasses, but if I was ever going to fall asleep again, I needed another one.

Or two.

Or even three.

I opted for one. I might have wanted to drown my sorrows in alcohol, but I had a two-year-old in the next room who needed me sober and alert in the morning.

I curled up on the sofa, the first piece of furniture Eli and I had bought after putting the down payment on this place. The leather was amazingly soft and supple, the nicest I'd ever felt.

I could still smell Eli in the leather, could still remember how we'd enjoyed lying together on this sofa and watching a movie after Rayna went to bed.

It was irrational, but a huge part of me expected him to walk through the front door, a lazy smile on his face. I even kept glancing in that direction.

Waiting.

And waiting.

As I finished off the third glass of wine, it hit me anew that Eli would never walk through that door again.

I'd never share a bottle of wine over dinner with him.

Never watch him tickle Rayna as she climbed on his lap.

Never have a chance to find out what had sent him into another woman's arms.

It was that last thought that was the hardest to deal with.

"It doesn't matter why," I told myself as I went back to the bedroom. "All that matters is that he *did* cheat on you. He doesn't deserve your tears."

But as I climbed back into the big empty bed, I couldn't stop the tears from falling. I buried my face in the pillow and cried like a baby.

When the tears ended, anger took over. I gripped the pillow as if it were Eli's neck and squeezed hard—like I wanted to break it with my bare hands.

My emotions spent and my breathing ragged, I finally sat on the edge of the bed and rested my toes on the cool floor. "Damn you, Eli. Damn you for destroying all our dreams."

This time, when I lay back against the pillows, sleep claimed me quickly.

Something hard landed on my stomach with the force of a cannonball, immediately jarring me awake.

"Eli, what are you *doing?*" I asked, my eyes flying open. But instead of Eli, I saw Rayna.

And in that moment, I remembered.

Rayna's smile was as bright as the morning sun as she beamed at me, pushing any sadness from my heart. "Hi, Mommy."

Easily, I returned her smile. Oh, to have that childlike exuberance at simply greeting another day.

"Hi, baby."

"Go Carwa?" Rayna asked.

I glanced at the digital clock on my bedside table. Seven-fourteen in the morning.

Normally, I'd be up and getting ready for work. But my head throbbed from fatigue and a hangover, and all I wanted to do was close my eyes and sleep for another couple hours.

I pulled Rayna close. "How about lying down with Mommy for a while?"

"It's morning," she replied, as if the idea of sleeping in was a crazy one. Then she wriggled free of my arms and eased her body off the bed.

So much for sleeping in.

Groaning, I forced myself to sit up. Coffee was the first order of business.

I trudged out to the kitchen. Rayna was dragging a chair from the table toward the fridge.

"No, no, no." I hurried to her and lifted her into my arms. "Let me get what you need, okay?"

She pointed to the freezer. "Popsicle."

"Popsicle? Honey, you need breakfast."

"Popsicle," she reiterated.

I didn't bother protesting, and opened the freezer door. In Rayna's mind, freezies and Popsicles were an essential food group.

"You want red?" I asked.

She bobbed her head up and down.

I lowered her to the floor so I could find a pair of scissors, and cut the top edge off of the freezie. When I handed it to her, she grinned widely and wandered into the living room.

I followed her, sat her on the sofa so she wouldn't make a mess, then turned on the television for her. Moments later, I was back in the kitchen pouring coffee grinds into a filter.

As the coffee percolated, I went to the bathroom and took two Advil. My head was throbbing, and I knew I'd need them.

I was back in the kitchen, opening the cupboard to retrieve a mug, when I heard, "Where Daddy?"

Glancing down at Rayna, I lowered the mug onto the granite countertop.

"Oh, sweetheart." I lowered myself to her level and drew her close. "Mommy has to tell you something."

She extended the empty freezie container to me, which I took and placed on the counter. Then I picked Rayna up and carried her to the kitchen table.

"Daddy gone?" she asked.

Sitting on a chair, I cradled Rayna on my lap. I pressed my lips to the top of her head, inhaling her clean scent. She was so innocent, so fragile. And I had to destroy her world.

"Oh, baby." I closed my eyes and sighed before continuing. "Daddy is…"

Dead.

No, not dead. I couldn't say dead. She wouldn't understand what that meant, anyway.

I wracked my brain for something appropriate to say. "Daddy is…gone away. He didn't want to leave, but he had to. And now he's in a place called heaven." I paused. Rayna was listening intently. "The thing about heaven is that when you go there, you can't come back. It's a very beautiful place, with lots of pretty waterfalls and animals. So it's a place where Daddy is very happy. It's just that, since he's there now, he won't be coming back here. When people go to heaven, they stay there forever. Which means we won't be seeing Daddy again." I ran my hands over Rayna's hair. "But we can't be sad, because Daddy is happy there. It's just that we're going to miss him very much."

I steeled myself, waiting for Rayna's tears, but she did something I didn't expect. She wriggled out of my arms, then looked up at me and said, "Circle cereal."

"You're hungry?"

She nodded.

"And you want circle cereal?"

"Circle cereal!" she agreed enthusiastically.

That was her way of describing Cheerios. I stood up. "All right, then. Let's get you some cereal."

She ran to the cupboard ahead of me. My daughter hardly ever walked. If she wasn't running, she was skipping. If she wasn't skipping, she was galloping.

My sweet baby, I thought as I watched her. She'd just lost the father she adored, and she didn't understand.

I guess it was a blessing.

At precisely eight o'clock, the telephone rang. I plucked the receiver off the kitchen wall and put it to my ear. "Hello?"

"Vanessa Cain, this is Dean Musselman with CNN. I was wondering if I could schedule—"

"No comment," I quipped, and hung up.

Dean's call was only the first of many—six more from reporters, and three from acquaintances who'd heard the story and were calling to offer condolences. Soon, the constantly ringing phone had my head pounding. I took the receiver off the hook and went to the bathroom to down another Advil.

Then I got my cell phone from my bedroom, turned it on and dialed Carla's number.

"Carla," I said, relieved when she answered.

"Sweetie," she said warmly. "How are you doing?"

"I've been better," I replied. Then added, "Understatement of the century."

"I'm so sorry."

"It's not your fault," I told her. "Please don't apologize." I finally understood why some people hated pity after they'd suffered a tragedy. It left you feeling even more helpless in the wake of their sadness.

"Will you be home today?" I asked.

"Yeah. Why? You want to do something? Maybe take the girls to the park?"

"Actually, I was hoping that you could watch Rayna, same as always."

"Watch Rayna?" she repeated, sounding surprised.

"Yeah. I'm gonna head to the office."

"You're joking."

"I'm not."

"Your boss expects you to go to the office today?" Carla asked, and I'd never heard her sound more mortified. "You know what, that woman is a total—"

"It's not her," I interjected. "It's me. I want to go to work."

There was a pregnant pause, and I could easily picture Carla's face—her mouth slightly ajar, her eyes narrowed in confusion.

"This was your idea?"

"I can't stay here," I said. "Stay here all day and think about what happened. Plus, have you looked outside your window? With the Jerry Springer media circus downstairs, how long before our building becomes a new South Beach attraction? And how long will it be before the reporters get brave and come knocking on my door? No, I'll be far better off at work, away from all this."

"If you're sure," Carla said, but she didn't sound convinced that I was making the right decision.

I groaned softly. "I have no clue what's right. I've never been in this situation before. I don't know what the protocol is."

"I'm just worried about you, that's all."

"I know. And you're probably wondering how I can even consider going to the office. But if I stay home and see Eli everywhere, what good am I going to be to Rayna? Not to mention the endless phone calls from the reporters, which is only making all of this worse."

"I'm not judging you," Carla said. "Obviously, you have to do what you feel is best. And you know I'll be here as I am every day, more than happy to babysit Rayna."

"Thank you, Carla. You're the best."

"Anytime."

Fifteen minutes later, I dropped Rayna off at Carla's place on the second floor and returned to my apartment to get dressed. My head still throbbed, and when I walked into my bedroom, all I wanted to do was collapse onto the king-size bed and let sleep take me away from my problems. It was tempting, but I feared that if I lay down, I'd spend the day in a catatonic state of depression, and that would get me absolutely nowhere.

So I drank a second cup of coffee, dressed in a smart blazer and skirt, and headed out of my apartment.

I was halfway down the elevator when the realization struck me that I had to drive out of the parking lot, and that the media likely had every conceivable exit or entry point of the building covered. And by now, I was certain they knew what I looked like.

Sunglasses wouldn't cut it.

I made my way back to up to my apartment, where I found a colorful scarf in my closet that I'd purchased at a boutique on Ocean Drive, but had never worn. One of those impulse buys that had made perfect sense at the time, but not the morning after.

Well, it would be put to good use today. The media might

snap off shots of me and get video footage as I drove away, but at least they wouldn't be able to see my face.

"Why does it matter?" I asked myself as I opened the door to my car minutes later. It wasn't like I had anything to hide. These reporters weren't hounding me because they secretly thought I'd murdered Eli. So what if they caught me looking grief-stricken, or less than perfect? Wasn't that par for the course when a person suffered a devastating and public loss such as I had?

As I planted myself behind the wheel of my car and started the engine, it instantly dawned on me the reason I was so mortified at being seen on TV.

Shame.

Sure, Eli's cheating wasn't my fault, but people could be tremendously cruel. They could—and would—form judgments of me without even knowing a single thing about me. They'd say, for example, that I was a pathetically hopeless romantic who should have known better. Or worse, that I was a gold digger for being involved with a man who'd been a well-paid athlete.

I didn't even want to imagine what Eli's ex-wife would say about him if she decided to talk, considering I knew their split had been nasty. If she was still bitter, she'd likely paint an ugly picture of him that would only make me look more desperate for having been with him.

Was it really the public's opinion I was worried about, or my own sister's? Nikki had told me that I was blind where Eli was concerned—in fact, blind where most men were concerned—and that she *knew* my relationship with Eli would fail.

Now it had.

And the last thing I wanted to do was publicize my shame and humiliation to the entire world.

Yes, I sucked at being able to choose the right man. But it wasn't like I was the only woman in the world with that problem.

Slowly, I started to drive out of the indoor parking lot. I didn't realize I was holding my breath until my chest began to hurt. I let the air out of my lungs in a rush, then gulped in more as my car rolled outside.

Every member of the media surrounding the garage entrance came alive. It didn't take more than a second for all of them to rush the car. Clearly, they'd done their homework. Probably had gotten my records from the DMV so they knew what I was driving. They swarmed my car like ants, and my heart lurched with fear. Then adrenaline took over, and I pushed my foot down on the gas. The car surged ahead, and I screamed when a Fox News cameraman had to jump out of the way to avoid being hit.

"Oh my God, oh my God!" My car hit the asphalt of the street, and still people converged on me. My hands shook, but I tried to control the steering wheel as best I could. I didn't let up on the gas, though, determined to get away as fast as possible.

I drove right through the stop sign, nearly colliding with a Mercedes. Screaming, I jammed both feet on the brake. The driver swerved to avoid me, tires squealing in protest as he did. The man hit his horn and gave me the finger out the window.

For a moment, I was so terrified I thought my heart

would implode. And I was suddenly wondering if I was up for the drive into downtown Miami. A quick look in the rearview mirror told me I had no choice, when I saw all the video and still cameras pointed my way, reporters racing down the street after me as if I were a fleeing felon.

Absently, I turned right on the first street I came to, my thoughts on what was happening rather than where I was heading.

"Good Lord, what is going *on?*" I asked aloud. Fine, Eli had been murdered. Yes, he had been murdered in a very lurid and juicy fashion. But why the heck were these reporters so interested in me?

Wasn't the story intriguing enough with Eli's background as a sports star? What did I, the clueless and unfamous fiancée, really have to add to make it more interesting?

chapter seven

As I hurried toward my office building from the parking garage, I realized that my nightmare was only beginning.

Either the camera crews had hightailed it to my Miami office, or secondary crews had been there bright and early, hoping to cover all possible grounds to ensure that they'd get to me.

Damn, I should have stayed at home. Better yet, I should have headed to the airport with Rayna in the middle of the night and gotten on a plane to Timbuktu.

My only hope, of course, was that no one would recognize me. Which was a ludicrous thought if ever there was one. Still, I strode forward purposefully, trying my best to act unfazed. Of course, the colorful scarf on my head was *not* helping me look inconspicuous.

A man holding a microphone with CNN's widely recognized logo was the first to rush toward me as I neared the doors to my office building.

"Vanessa Cain? I'm Dean Musselman from CNN."

I sidestepped him and picked up my pace.

"Ms. Cain, the world wants to hear your story. Tell us how you felt when you heard the gruesome news."

From everywhere, reporters stuck microphones in my face.

"I have nothing to say!" I yelled, then grabbed the heavy door and scurried inside the building.

My sigh of relief died in my throat when I saw the reporter from the *Miami Herald* standing in the lobby. Cynthia Martin had a book in her hand, as if she was simply hanging out reading, but the moment she saw me, she started in my direction.

I broke into a run, quickly flashing my pass to Edgar, the Hispanic security guard, who knew me well. Then I sprinted past him to the bank of elevators.

"Ms. Cain, why won't you talk to me?" Cynthia Martin asked from behind the turnstile. "People want to hear your story. Especially now."

There was a FedEx man standing at the bank of elevators, and at Cynthia's comment, he looked at me quizzically. Thankfully, an elevator opened a moment later and I hurried inside.

The FedEx guy didn't ask the obvious question, but I was certain he knew who I was. I hadn't watched any of the late-night newscasts, but my picture had likely been broadcast alongside Eli's. For all I knew, my face might be on the front page of the *Miami Herald* right now, with a caption I didn't even want to imagine.

Which was the very reason I had avoided turning on my television last night. I didn't want to hear what was being said about Eli, or even me. I needed to deal with my fiancé's death in my own private way, not with the slant of public opinion.

When I stepped off the elevator onto my floor, my shoulders sagged with relief. "Holy crap," I muttered, leaning against the wall to collect myself. "Is it really that slow of a news week?"

If I was lucky, some young starlet would check herself into rehab in the next few hours and save me from this madness.

About a minute later, my breathing had returned to normal, and I was ready to get to work. I walked through the doors to the agency and said hello to Alaina, who returned my greeting with wide-eyed shock.

"Vanessa?"

"Yes, it's me," I chirped. I pulled my scarf off my head so she would be one hundred percent sure.

"But—why are you here?"

"I work here," I snapped. My tone was unnecessarily harsh, but I wasn't upset with her. I was upset with the sudden drama plaguing my life. Eli hadn't been hounded by the press when he was alive. What was with all the hoopla now?

The reception phone rang, preventing Alaina from asking me the next question on her tongue. She answered the phone with her standard greeting, and I took that moment to scoot past her to my office. I saw her hold up a finger in hopes of halting me, but I pretended not to notice.

Seconds later, I was stepping into my office when I suddenly stopped dead in my tracks.

A woman was sitting behind my desk.

"Good morning." The greeting in a British accent threw

me off. The woman had grayish-blond hair and appeared to be in her early fifties. She smiled warmly at me.

I took a quick glance around the room to make sure I was indeed in my office.

"Uh," I began, walking forward cautiously, "who are you?"

"I'm Bonnie Bluegrass, dear."

"Bonnie Bluegrass," I repeated, the name sounding a little too…stagelike. Perhaps I was still at home in bed, dreaming about some British television show.

"Office manager," she added, her tone far too chipper. "May I help you with something?"

At once, I understood what was going on. Someone— likely Debbie or her assistant—had called in a temp to replace me.

"Why did they do this?" I mumbled.

"Pardon me, dear?"

"Sorry—not you. I'm thinking out loud." I moved farther into the room and placed my belongings on the floor beside my desk. "I think there's been a bit of a misunderstanding."

"Oh?"

I nodded, then took off my sunglasses. "Yeah. This is my office."

She looked confused. And then recognition flashed in her eyes. "*Ohhh*. It's you. You're the one in the picture with this darling little girl." She looked momentarily at the framed photo of me and Rayna when Rayna was just nine months old. "But I thought… Aren't you off on bereavement leave?"

"I decided to come in," I replied cheerfully.

Bonnie looked—as I'd heard in the occasional British film—gobsmacked.

"You'll still get paid for your trouble, of course, but we won't be needing you today."

I placed my sunglasses on the edge of my desk, straightened my blazer, then waited for Bonnie to vacate my seat. When she didn't, I asked, "Is there a problem?"

"It's just that the temp agency told me I'd be here for two days. Possibly more."

"Fine." I smiled pleasantly. "Two days' pay. I'll take care of it." As the office manager, I oversaw the company's finances and would authorize the expense.

Slowly, Bonnie rose. "You're sure? You don't need the time off to…"

"To what?"

"Well, to grieve, dear," she replied. Her expression softened, becoming motherly and, oddly, I found myself missing my own mother.

How much different would it be right now if I had my mom around to comfort and coddle me? To hold me against her chest as she'd done when I was a child, and gently stroke my hair? In my mother's arms, I could cry freely, without shame, without fear of being judged. I would have someone to hold me up, keep me from falling apart. I had supportive friends, but their comfort would never equal that of my mother's.

My parents had died when I wasn't yet a teenager, and I'd missed their presence hugely. I'd gone on, as I'd had to do, but I'd never quite been the same. My mother's only sister, Lola, had become a surrogate mother, for which I was grateful, but there was still a big void in my world. A person wants her parents around for the key moments in her life.

Like when I graduated from high school. My aunt had been there, and she'd assured me that my parents would have been very proud that I'd graduated with honors. But by the time I gave birth to Rayna, my aunt, who'd been single until her forties, was living in Hawaii with her new husband. My sister had been at the hospital with me, of course, but I'd still wept uncontrollably when the doctor handed me my little baby, knowing my parents had missed that monumental moment in my life.

Then I'd consoled myself with the thought that they were in heaven, watching and beaming with pride at the sight of their first granddaughter.

I needed to believe that.

"Oh, look at you." Bonnie tsked. "I can see the sadness in your eyes, dear. I do believe you could use a hug. Do you mind if I give you one?"

It was a strange offer, but one that I welcomed.

She opened her arms in invitation, and I walked into her embrace. She gave me a warm, earnest hug, and I closed my eyes, imagining that my mother was channeling her energy through this woman to me.

After a few moments, we pulled apart. I looked at Bonnie and said, "Thank you."

"You're sure you don't want to go home?" she asked, genuine concern for me evident in her eyes. "I came to work. I'm more than happy to stay."

"I'm better off here," I told her. "Thank you so much for coming in, though. And for the hug. It helped. Whenever we need another temp, I'll be sure to call and ask for you."

Bonnie Bluegrass nodded, got her things together and quietly left my office.

If I ever needed a nanny, I'd track the woman down. I had a feeling that Bonnie would be fantastic in that role.

With her gone, I settled in behind my desk. I did a quick scan to see if anything was out of place. I should have known that Debbie would hire a temp in my absence, but I hated anyone but me being at my desk. I was proprietary that way.

But everything was in order. Not even a pen in the wrong spot. And something good had come of me running into Bonnie. She had unexpectedly helped boost my spirits.

I went to the office kitchen to pour myself a third cup of coffee. A few of the office staff passed me, and they all gazed at me in astonishment, as though I had been the one to die yesterday, and they were seeing a ghost.

Trisha gaped at me as I passed Debbie's office, but mumbled a hello. Debbie's office door was closed, which meant she either wasn't in or was on an important call. With Eli getting himself killed, I hadn't even asked her the details about signing Lori Hansen. Lori was a fitness guru turned motivational speaker who had the utmost credibility when it came to inspiring people to lose weight and be their personal best. She had once weighed close to three hundred pounds and now was a lean and muscular one hundred and thirty. People were paying big bucks to hear her words of wisdom.

When I returned to my office, I closed the door because I wanted privacy. Then I sat down at my desk and opened a file on the computer that I hadn't touched the day before. It was a spreadsheet of last month's out-of-pocket expenses for the agency's four agents, which I would verify before cutting checks to reimburse everyone.

My phone rang, and I snatched up the receiver. "Vanessa C—"

"Hello, Ms. Cain. This is Riley Baltimore with the *Sun-Sentinel.* Can you tell me—"

Click. I hung up before he could finish his spiel, then set my phone to go directly to voice mail.

Oh, hell. Remembering something else I hadn't gotten to the day before, I quickly opened another file, a schedule of the events and seminars the clients were either booked for or considering. The University of Houston wanted to book Manisha Talbot for a one-day conference on women in business. It was my job to make sure I confirmed all the details of the event.

I lifted my phone to call the contact at the university, but didn't get to punch in the number because my door burst open.

It was Alaina.

"Alaina—"

"I had to come talk to you," she said. She closed the door behind her. "I have been fielding calls from the media all morning. Girl, it's like you're some megastar."

"You're serious?"

"Oh yeah."

"How many calls?"

"CNN, ABC, CBS, NBC, FOX News—all the major networks. Some station from Atlanta. Not to mention all the local papers. And a reporter from *USA Today.*"

I gaped at Alaina as I settled back in my leather chair. "This is insane."

"Tell me about it. Have you seen the *Miami Herald* yet?"

"No."

"You should. There's a picture of you and Eli at some—"

"Fund-raiser we attended to benefit Jackson Memorial Hospital," I finished for her. Damn that Cynthia Martin.

"I thought you didn't see it."

"I didn't. And I don't want to. But that was the one time Eli and I posed for a picture when we went out publicly as a couple. He was very private when it came to the press."

The pause that followed was ripe with all that was left unsaid. I stared at Alaina, who was pressing her lips together as though making a valiant effort not to speak.

I didn't want to know, but I also didn't want to *not* know. I finally asked, "What is it that you're dying to tell me?"

She approached my desk. "Now, I don't know what this means, and you and I know that the media gets things wrong all the time—"

"Just tell me."

"The paper said there's been a new twist to the story. That you were Eli's mistress because—"

"Mistress?"

Alaina nodded, her expression grave. "Some lawyer in Atlanta said that Eli's *wife* is going to give a statement later today."

"Ex-wife." I laughed without mirth. "What is this bull-shit? My God, what these papers won't do to sell a few copies. Understatement of the century."

Once again, Alaina pressed her lips together.

"What?" I asked, not sure I wanted to know.

"It's just that…well, the paper didn't say ex. What if Eli never got divorced?"

"Of course he was divorced," I replied. "He was *engaged* to me, remember?" I wiggled my finger, flashing the engagement ring I hadn't taken off. "Why the hell would he propose and buy a place with me if he was still married? You said yourself that the media gets information wrong all the time. I already went through this with my sister last night. And I did check that he was really divorced, okay? On the Internet. It happened back in 2002."

Alaina nodded, but didn't seem convinced.

"Eli said it was a really nasty split, and that he didn't want to talk about the details. I respected that."

"The paper also said—"

"Enough!" I pushed my chair back and stood. "Alaina, you know I love you, but I came to work to escape all the craziness."

"I'm sorry. I just thought you'd—"

"Don't think. Please. That's the last thing I need."

"Okay." She nodded. "I didn't mean to make you feel any worse."

"I don't think anything could make me feel any worse. I just want the reporters to go away."

"I take it you don't want me putting any more calls through?"

"Only if it's business. Someone from Hewlett-Packard is supposed to phone me about that color copier, so if he calls, put him through right away. And anyone calling about confirmed bookings or enquiries, naturally. Everyone else, bump to voice mail." This way, I could open my phone line up again and have Alaina screen my calls. I didn't want to have to avoid the phone in my place of work.

"All right," she said.

As soon as she was out the door, I locked it behind her. I had come in to work to avoid the shit I'd have had to deal with if I'd stayed at home. I wanted to lose myself in work, forget all about the real world and my problems for at least a few hours.

I went back to my desk, hoping to do just that.

chapter eight

I stayed locked in my office until after five that evening, having only a granola bar I'd found in my desk for lunch. By the end of the day I was starving, but staying inside had been a smart move, because when I finally ventured downstairs, the camera crews had gone.

I grinned widely. Thank God, they'd finally given up.

There were also no camera crews lining the entrance to my condo. Either the reporters had realized I was never going to speak to them, or the building management had asked them to leave, or a bigger story had broken sometime during the day.

Whatever the reason, I was grateful.

I was in a much better mood than the previous night when I went to Carla's apartment, feeling for the first time since the news of Eli's murder that I was going to get through this all right.

I did have to make sure I called the police—something I had been putting off all day. And I also had to search the condo for the name of Eli's lawyer. There would be a funeral to plan, but I'd watched enough crime shows to know that couldn't happen until the medical examiner released Eli's body. Though the cause of death seemed clear, there was always an autopsy to be absolutely sure.

Calling the police and searching for Eli's lawyer were tasks I could deal with tomorrow, I told myself, the sudden calm after the media storm making me want to put all things negative out of my mind.

As soon as I got to Carla's door and she opened her mouth to speak, I said, "Not one word about Eli, okay? I don't want to think about him right now."

Carla nodded in agreement, then proceeded to tell me what had happened on the day's episode of *The Young and the Restless,* even though I only caught the show once in a while. I didn't mind. Hearing someone else's drama, even fictional, was a welcome change.

She invited me to stay for dinner, but I declined. I wasn't in the mood to be social. I took Rayna up to our place, where I placed a frozen pizza in the oven. The red message light on my phone was blinking, but I didn't check my voice mail. Just as I hadn't checked the messages on my cell phone.

What was the point? There were no doubt endless calls from reporters, and I didn't want to talk to any of them.

Rayna was in the living room watching a Barbie movie, so I opened the fridge in search of wine. A quick glance reminded me that I'd finished off the wine the night before. There were two vodka coolers remaining from an eight-pack Eli and I had bought on the weekend. I took one out and twisted the cap off.

As I brought the bottle to my lips, I hesitated. On the weekend, I'd been completely happy. Now I was in hell. In a matter of days, my life had gone from one extreme to the other.

I sipped the lime-flavored beverage, recalling how Eli and I had sat in bed propped up on pillows, sipping these very same coolers and watching a thriller starring Clive Owen. Eli had had his arms wrapped around me, and I'd been resting my head against his shoulder. As a gruesome battle between the hero and villain ensued, I'd turned my face into his chest. Eli had pulled me closer in a protective gesture. And the next thing I knew, we were in each other's arms, kissing deeply.

Eli was pressing his lips to my stomach when he suddenly said, "Maybe we should try and make a baby."

"What?" I asked, stunned.

"Maybe we should make a baby," he repeated. "I know we're not getting married till late next year, but that doesn't matter, does it?"

I didn't know what to think. The idea was overwhelming.

"What?" Eli asked.

"You know I want to have your baby, but I figured we'd wait until after we get married. I don't know that I want to be dealing with wedding plans while I'm pregnant."

"We'll hire the best wedding planner in the city."

"Then there's my job. And the fact that I haven't even met your family."

"You will. At that huge family reunion in the summer."

"I know. But I'd rather not be…" My voice trailed off. "Even if we are engaged. I just—"

Eli placed a finger on my lips to silence me. "It's okay. You're right."

"It's not that I don't want to," I assured him. "You're so fantastic with Rayna. I want to have lots of babies with you."

"Lots?" He kissed my stomach again.

"Ideally, two. Maybe three."

Eli pressed his lips to the inside of my thigh. "No, no. That won't do. I want at least six."

"Six!" I exclaimed, laughing. "You want to have me barefoot and pregnant for years?"

"I guess I just want you naked and in my bed, getting lots of practice at making babies." He slipped my panties down my legs. "Kind of like this…"

The sweetness of the memory was all the more painful because of the reality that he was gone. I stifled a moan. How could Eli have been talking about making babies with me on Saturday night, then in another woman's bed only days later?

"Mommy. Let's draw pictures!"

I whipped my head around and saw Rayna smiling at me. She was holding a box of crayons and a few sheets of paper.

"Oh, honey. Mommy doesn't feel like drawing any pictures right now."

Rayna's smile faded. "Want to draw pictures."

"I know, but…I have to get supper. Why don't you draw a nice picture while I get the pizza?"

Rayna didn't move, just looked at me with curious eyes. As if she were trying to figure out what was wrong with me.

Of course she was. I might have been trying to put up a brave front for Rayna, but kids were incredibly perceptive. Eli being gone aside, she had to know something serious was going on in my world.

Rayna needed normalcy so *her* world would be secure.

"I'm sorry, honey," I said. I lowered myself onto my knees and gave her small body a hug. "Of course I'll draw pictures with you."

She beamed.

"Let's go to the table." I lifted her and carried her the short distance to the kitchen table, where I placed her in her booster seat. I set the crayons and papers down, then sat in a chair beside her.

Rayna reached for the crayon box, opened it and dumped all the crayons onto the table. She scooped up the red one right away, her latest favorite color.

"What are you going to draw?" I asked her.

"A pony!"

Of course. My little girl was fanatical about ponies and horses. Last month, Eli and I had taken her to a petting zoo, and she had been beyond ecstatic when she got to sit on a real pony.

I passed her a sheet of paper and took one for myself. With a green crayon, I began making blades of grass across the bottom of the page. "You know what I'm drawing?" I asked Rayna.

"Grass!" she said excitedly.

"That's right." I picked up the brown crayon. "And do you know what I'll draw next?"

"A tree!"

"You want to draw your pony on this nice grass?"

Rayna nodded, so I handed her the sheet. I watched her draw a rectangular body and stick legs. Then she met my eyes, seeking my approval.

"That is a beautiful pony, sweetheart."

"You draw now," she told me.

I attempted to draw a pony beside the one Rayna had. Mine didn't look much better than hers, but Rayna was impressed.

I spent the next ten minutes drawing pictures with Rayna while the pizza baked. After we ate our dinner, I snuggled up with her on the sofa to watch the movie *Cars*. Rayna had seen it at least a dozen times, but would never tire of it.

Halfway through the movie, the phone rang. I reached for the cordless handset on the table beside the sofa and saw a number I didn't recognize. It had a 404 area code, and I wondered if perhaps a former teammate of Eli's had gotten my number and was calling me after hearing the awful news of his death.

I pressed the talk button and put the phone to my ear. "Hello?"

"Vanessa Cain?" The contemptuous voice immediately put me on edge.

"This is Vanessa," I answered. "Who's calling?"

"So you're the bitch who was sleeping with my husband."

The words were like a slap in the face, and I actually pulled the phone back from my ear and stared at the handset. "Excuse me?"

"Let's not play games. You know why I'm calling. And you should be ashamed of yourself."

"Excuse me?"

"You know exactly what's going on here. You dirty skank!"

It couldn't be Eli's ex-wife on the other end of my line, could it? Of course not. The two hadn't been together for years. There was no reason for her to be calling me up ranting and raving *now*.

And then it hit me. This woman was some psycho who'd somehow gotten my phone number. Eli used to tell me stories about deranged fans, women who thought they were meant to be his wife. With all the media coverage, some nutcase who'd had a crush on Eli had decided to call me up and give me a piece of her deluded mind.

"I'm hanging up now," I said, though why I bothered to give notice was beyond me.

"Oh, I wouldn't if I were you."

For some reason, I paused. Maybe because I was already angry about Eli's betrayal, the media intrusion in my life and the general stress that went along with losing someone you loved. But I was more than ready to take my frustration out on someone, and this woman had started it.

I got up from the sofa, leaving a comfortable Rayna watching the movie, and hurried to my bedroom.

I closed the door. "Look here, lady—"

"No, *you* look here, bitch."

"Bitch?"

"You may have stolen my husband from me," the woman snapped, "but you will not take my property. That penthouse you're living in, it's mine."

The idea was so preposterous, I laughed. "I suggest you go see your doctor and get some medication, because you have some major screws loose."

"How dare you talk to me that way?"

"You're the one who called me on the attack. And I don't have to deal with your shit, so bye-bye."

"I'm Eli's *wife*," the woman hurriedly said, and again, I didn't hang up.

"That's a lie."

Suddenly, the woman sniffled. "Well, I *was* his wife. Guess I'm his widow now."

This was bullshit. And I'd put up with enough of it. "Look, I don't know who you are, but your number is on my phone, so the moment I hang up, I'm calling the police and having you charged with harassment." Whether or not the police would do that, I didn't know, but I wanted to put some fear in this woman.

"Eli and I were married on July 30, 1994 at the Ebenezer Baptist Church in Atlanta. Check the record books. You'll find the information."

If this was really Eli's ex, then I understood why he hadn't liked talking about how bitter things had gotten between them. The woman was one crazy bitch.

"If you are who you say you are," I began, "then you and I both know that you and Eli were married and divorced. He and I were *engaged*. Already planning our wedding for next year. He couldn't very well do that if he was married to someone else."

"*Ehh.*" The woman made a sound like a buzzer going off. "Wrong answer. We were separated, yes, and even started divorce proceedings, but the divorce was never finalized. I think because of the children—"

"Children?" I exclaimed, my heart slamming against my rib cage. "Now I know you're lying."

"If you want to live in your fantasy world and think that your sleeping with my husband didn't ruin lives—"

"Stop this! Just stop." Why didn't I hang up?

"Do you know where Eli's body is?" she asked.

"I will not divulge that information," I replied, my tone indignant. This imposter didn't need to know it was because I didn't *know* the information. The question nagged me. Why *hadn't* the police called me?

"You don't know where his body is because I asked the medical examiner and the police not to give out any information to anyone but his family. And you are not his family."

"I've heard enough," I said.

I pressed my thumb on the talk button to end the call, then blew out a long, loud breath.

Children? I forced a laugh, but nothing that the woman had said was remotely funny.

And it obviously can't be true, I assured myself.

If Eli had had children, why wouldn't he have told me that? Hell, if he was still married, why would he propose to me? It didn't make any sense at all.

Because it wasn't true.

Eli loved children. He'd proved as much with Rayna. He had accepted her as though she'd been his own, and wanted to officially adopt her after we were married.

A man like that didn't ignore his own biological children, even if he was no longer with the woman who'd borne them.

Frowning, I wandered back out to the living room. The moment Rayna saw me, she stood on the sofa and stretched her hands toward me.

I took her into my arms and sat back down with her on my lap.

Children. Right.

I dropped the cordless handset onto the end table. At least I'd learned one valuable lesson. The next time a crackpot called, I would hang up immediately.

Better yet, I would call BellSouth tomorrow and change my number.

chapter nine

After I put Rayna to bed, I called the police department in hopes of getting some answers about Eli. However, I was transferred from one department to another, to another, and eventually put on hold.

For ten minutes.

I finally hung up and decided I'd call the next day.

I told myself I wasn't avoiding the situation, but I was more upset by that crazy woman's call than I should have been. Part of me wanted to turn on the television and catch the late-night news, get confirmation that Eli had lied to me about only one woman. And yet I couldn't bring myself to watch it.

Something was suddenly bothering me, a snippet of a conversation I'd overheard when I'd been at a Christmas party with Eli at Christian Blake's lavish home in Coconut Grove. I'd made my rounds, saying hello to wives and girlfriends, and was making my way back to Eli. I saw him chatting with his friend Leroy's girlfriend. As I neared them, I heard Eli saying, "It's tough. The way things are, I don't get to see them."

"That's awful," Tina had said. "Those boys must miss you."

I'd stepped up beside her and Eli at that moment, and he had looked down at me in surprise, his eyes wide.

"What are you talking about?" I asked.

Eli quickly put his arm around my waist. "There you are, baby. Tina, will you excuse us for a moment?"

"Of course."

When the tall, thin blonde had walked away, I'd stared up at Eli and asked, "What boys, Eli?"

He hesitated briefly. Then he said, "My nephews."

"Nephews?"

"Yeah. In Atlanta. My former sister-in-law and her two boys used to live with us after she and her husband split. I kind of became like a surrogate father to her kids."

I frowned slightly. "You've never mentioned this before."

Eli shrugged. "It's rough, you know? My wife and I split, and it's like her whole family was cut out of my life. They took her side, stopped talking to me. I don't miss them, but I do miss those boys."

"Oh, sweetheart." I rubbed Eli's arm. "I'm sorry."

"Let's not ruin a perfectly good party by talking about this, okay? I say we find us some mistletoe."

My thoughts returning to the present, I closed my eyes and grimaced. Had Eli so brazenly lied to me? Were his "nephews" really his sons? The story had flowed from his lips so easily, there was no reason for me to believe that he was lying.

But was he? Was I more wrong about Eli than I could ever have imagined?

It was a question I asked myself for the rest of the evening, and as I lay in bed later, I still had no answers. To believe that Eli might have lied about a wife *and* children...that was deception on a scale I couldn't even begin to comprehend.

The more I thought about it, the more I had to wonder if maybe the caller really was Eli's ex-wife. An ex who was pissed that her husband had moved on, and wanted to feed me a line of bull to rattle me.

Unfortunately, I *was* rattled.

Even more so the next morning, when I saw that the camera crews were back. Not as many as the first day, but enough to have my pulse quickening.

I didn't bother to disguise myself as I drove out of the condo's parking lot. Nor did I cover my face as I walked toward my office building. I finally accepted that I wasn't going to be able to avoid the media any longer. It was evident that they were going to hound me until I gave them a statement.

Sure, I could hide out on some remote island until they forgot about me—but that simply wasn't feasible.

And after last night's talk with the woman who was likely Eli's ex-wife, I had a feeling it was important for me to tell the media my side of the story.

"Vanessa Cain—Dean Musselman with CNN." The attractive, dark-haired man hurried toward me before the other reporters did as I neared the building. "I'd love to sit down and have a chat with you about the latest developments in this case."

Latest developments? Oh, Lord, it's true. Eli lied to me about everything!

"Call me in my office in five minutes." I handed him my card, my insides twisting with anxiety. The rest of the reporters swarmed. "Please—no questions now. I'm going to arrange a press conference so we can do this in a civilized manner." The last thing I wanted was to be a public spectacle on the street.

An excited buzz arose from the crowd. I made eye contact with Dean. "I'll expect your call in five minutes. You can relay my message to everyone else."

Dean beamed at me. "Will do."

Three minutes later, I was in my office and calling Debbie's extension.

"Debbie Noble," she said.

"Hi, Debbie. It's Vanessa."

"Vanessa, are you at your desk?"

"Yes."

She sighed. "I can't believe you've been coming into the office."

I ignored the comment and said, "Debbie, I need a favor. I'm sorry to have to ask you this, but CNN is downstairs, as well as other news stations, and the reporters just won't leave me alone. I figure I should give them a statement about this whole Eli fiasco and get it over with."

"Right."

"I suggested they could come up here and that I could hold a press conference. Since the boardroom is empty, I was thinking that'd be the best spot to do this, but if you think it's a bad idea…"

"Are you kidding? I think it's a fabulous idea."

"You do?" I asked skeptically.

"Of course. Just make sure you plug the agency. In fact,

I'll have them set the cameras up where they can see our agency sign in the background."

"Oh." I frowned. "Okay."

I should have known that Debbie would think about the company's bottom line. As long as we potentially got business out of my exposure, it was fine with her.

A minute later, Dean Musselman called and I told him to relay the message that everything was set and that all the news crews could come up.

It took them a while to sign in at security and get visitor badges. As the camera crews set up in the conference room, I kept thinking about Dean's words.

Latest developments.

Did that include a wife Eli hadn't divorced? And perhaps a couple children?

"Stop doing this to yourself," I muttered. Then I glanced at my engagement ring. I tried to smile, remembering when Eli had given it to me. It had been New Year's Eve, and he'd taken me on a dinner cruise around Bayside. When the waiter had arrived with my after-dinner champagne, I'd noticed the ring at the bottom of the glass.

It had been the most romantic moment of my life.

Eli told me how much he loved me, that he couldn't imagine his life without me in it. And Rayna, he'd also assured me. He loved my little girl and wanted to be her father officially. He said that he'd already been looking for condos where we could move in together, that he'd found a spot in South Beach that was available for immediate occupancy.

I said yes to his proposal, and ten days later, we moved into our beautiful penthouse.

"That can't all have been a lie," I said softly. I could accept that he'd run to another woman after our fight. I couldn't accept that he was still married while he'd proposed to me.

I heard a knock, and my eyes flew to the door. Dean Musselman grinned at me.

"We're all set," he announced.

"I'll make my way there in a minute," I told him.

If my sister were here, she'd scowl at me, telling me I ought to keep my private business private. And I wouldn't disagree. I wasn't keen on talking about my relationship with Eli for all of America to hear, but the way I saw it, I didn't have much choice.

I quickly applied a fresh coat of makeup so my face wouldn't look shiny on film. Then I took a deep breath and started for the conference room.

But before I got there, I stopped by the reception desk. "Alaina, how do I look?"

"Fabulous as always."

"Are you sure? What about my clothes?" I was wearing a pale green suit, which I couldn't help thinking might make me look a lot wider on the small screen.

She waved off my concern. "You always look fantastic."

"But you know what they say—the TV adds ten pounds."

Alaina rolled her eyes. "If you're worried about your looks, then what hope is there for the rest of us?"

"My face is okay? Enough makeup?"

"You're gorgeous. Stop worrying. Just go enjoy your moment of fame."

"Fame?" I gaped at my friend. "You can't be serious."

"Girl, it's like a movie premiere up in here. CNN, FOX

News, CBS, NBC, the *Miami Herald,* the *Sun-Sentinel.* I'm just waiting for Will Smith to walk through the door."

"All right. I get the point."

Alaina made her way around the desk and rubbed my arm. "Don't be nervous," she told me. "You're famous!"

"For being with a guy who cheated on me and got himself killed." *And might have been married when he proposed to me.* "Yeah, great legacy."

"All you do is tell them what they want to know. They'll run it on the news, then forget about you."

"I hope so."

Her gaze focused over my shoulder, Alaina bit down on her bottom lip. "*Dios míos,* he is hot."

I turned my head, quickly following Alaina's line of sight. One of the reporters, I think from the local CBS affiliate, was strolling up to the reception desk.

I recognized him as Michael Sanchez, and he was indeed hot.

Michael grinned first at Alaina, who smiled back and blushed. Then he turned to me.

"Everybody's ready if you are."

I nodded slowly. "I'm as ready as I'll ever be. I'll be there in a minute."

As Michael walked away, Alaina mumbled, "I wonder if he's single."

"Wait a minute. What happened to Richie, that guy you went out with on the weekend?"

"We had a great first date," Alaina said. "But he hasn't called me since."

"Really?"

Alaina nodded. "We'll talk about it later, though. You go do your interview."

I had some theories about Alaina's love life—or lack thereof—but I pushed the thoughts out of my mind and headed into the boardroom. Somehow, I kept my nerves in check. Inside, Debbie was talking to the CNN team. The table had been moved and the cameras were facing the wall that boasted the agency's name.

She hadn't been joking.

Someone ushered me to a chair at the far end of the conference table. Someone else primped my hair.

And then it was showtime.

"Vanessa," Dean Musselman began, "tell us about your relationship with Eli Johnson."

For a moment, I didn't say a word, and somewhere in my brain it registered that I must look like a deer caught in headlights. So I forced myself to open my mouth and speak.

The sooner you talk, the sooner you get this over and done with....

"I was Eli's fiancée," I replied. "I met him last September at a charity event, and we got involved romantically after that."

"When did you get engaged?" Michael Sanchez asked.

"New Year's Eve."

"That was a very short courtship," someone commented wryly.

I forced myself not to roll my eyes. No one had the right to judge me. "Yes it was, but—"

"Did you know he was married when you got engaged to him?"

My eyes grew wide in horror. *Oh, God. It's true! Eli was still married when he proposed to me!*

"Vanessa?" someone prompted.

"N-no." I drew in a slow breath, willing myself to calm down. "No, I didn't."

"He never told you he had a wife?" someone else queried, and I could swear I heard skepticism in the woman's tone.

"Absolutely not," I replied. "Are you sure he was still legally married? I'm certain he was divorced. Like I told you, we were engaged. It simply doesn't make sense for him to propose to me if he was still married."

"It appears divorce proceedings were started, but never finalized," Michael Sanchez answered.

Just like his wife had said. *Lord have mercy....*

"Mrs. Johnson says that she and Eli had a change of heart and decided to stay married," someone stated.

"That makes no sense," I retorted. "He was living with *me*. Engaged to *me*."

"According to Mr. Johnson's widow, you knew about her and seduced her husband nonetheless." This comment came from Cynthia Martin, the *Miami Herald* reporter.

"That's a lie!"

"How do you respond to Tassie Johnson's claims that you were a 'home wrecker'?"

I swallowed, feeling as if I were on a witness stand. "I don't know her. I—I never met her. I thought she was ancient history!"

Debbie suddenly appeared beside me. "Ms. Cain has already told you she didn't know Mr. Johnson was married." She spoke as though she was my defense attorney. "Next question, please."

I glanced at her and smiled softly. Then I turned back to the crowd. "All I can tell you is that if Eli has a wife, he lied to both of us."

"How did you feel when you learned he was murdered in the gruesome way he was?" a man with a notepad asked.

"I didn't break out the champagne, if that's what you're asking. Though maybe I should have."

That elicited a few chuckles.

"Do you plan to be in court when Conrad Redgrave goes on trial for Mr. Johnson's murder?"

I pondered the question. Going to the trial of the man who'd murdered his wife and my fiancé was something I hadn't yet considered. But given the lying schmuck Eli had been, what I really wanted to do was put my relationship with him behind me. Forget I'd ever been duped by Eli, and move on.

"I'm not sure," I answered honestly.

"Tassie Johnson claims that you're a gold digger. How do you feel about that?"

"Gold digger?" I scoffed. "That's—"

"Bullshit," Debbie finished for me. "And you can quote me on that one."

My eyes began to water as I surveyed the reporters in the room. Did they actually think I was a gold-digging husband thief?

"I was with Eli because I loved him," I said. "No other reason."

There were more questions, all along the same vein, and after about five more minutes, I felt that we were going in circles. Debbie clearly felt the same way, because she stepped in front of the crowd, held up her hands and said, "I think Ms. Cain has answered enough questions. If you don't mind, I need her back behind her desk."

A few reporters hastily threw out a couple more questions, but Debbie reached for my hand and helped me out of the chair. Then she ushered me out of the room with authority.

Cynthia Martin was the last reporter I passed before I left the room. She held my gaze as though she had another question on the tip of her tongue.

She didn't ask it.

Debbie didn't release my hand until she deposited me in my office. She closed the door behind her, then stared at me with a serious expression.

"What a son of a bitch Eli turned out to be."

"Tell me about it." I grunted in aggravation. "When they first started talking about his wife, I thought they meant *ex*-wife. That they wanted her reaction to his crazy death simply because she'd been married to him."

Debbie shook her head. "Look, I know I'm not a paragon of morality, but at least I wouldn't deceive a guy by pretending I was unattached. And you told me he had no kids, but every article I've read has talked about his two young boys."

A wave of nausea gripped me. "He said…he said he had nephews." I had to stop, take a breath. "Last night, some crackpot woman called me claiming to be Eli's wife. She mentioned their children. I thought she was lying. *Fuck!*"

As I cursed, I pushed the entire contents on my desk onto the floor in one fierce shove. Instantly, my breathing grew ragged, and I stood gripping the edge of my desk like a woman possessed. Debbie looked at me as if she feared I'd start breathing fire.

"All this time, the asshole was married!" My ring finger felt suddenly heavy with the weight of Eli's engagement ring, which I hadn't had the heart to remove even in light of his infidelity. Because on some level, I'd accepted my share of the blame for him ending up in that woman's bed, and ending up dead, telling myself that he had cheated for the first time and paid the ultimate price for his sins.

But now…knowing he'd been married when he'd proposed to me, knowing that his "nephews" were likely his sons… Had he secretly been hoping to get a divorce before I would ever find out?

"And you wonder why I'm having an affair?" Debbie asked, her tone sour. "You can't trust men. They look out for number one, so we need to as well."

Slowly I stood upright, taking a deep breath as I did. "This woman who called, the one who claimed she was Eli's wife, she said she wants *my* condo." As I said the words, my stomach lurched, and I thought I might puke. "She thinks because she was married to Eli, that it's *her* property."

"She sounds like a nasty bitch."

"She can't do that, can she?" My anger was gone, replaced by fear. "Tell me she can't take my home." I needed reassurance.

Debbie shrugged. "I don't know. If she was still legally married to Eli…I don't know."

Not what I wanted to hear. "My name is on the deed as well as Eli's. With Eli dead, the condo should be mine."

"It would seem only fair…but one thing I've learned, the law isn't always fair. Have you checked about mortgage insurance from the bank? Who was the real estate attorney who closed the deal?"

"I don't know." I glanced away, slightly embarrassed. "It's been hard enough coming to terms with Eli's death. And I…I haven't been able to find the mortgage papers."

Debbie gave me a doubtful look. "You? Queen of organizational skills?"

"Okay, so I haven't looked yet," I admitted.

"It's not like you to put things off."

And it wasn't. As the company's office manager, I was highly efficient. There was a file for every piece of paper, and I knew where every piece of paper relating to the office was filed. It was my job to keep the office running smoothly, and I couldn't do that being unorganized.

"I know," I said to Debbie. "It's just that since Eli's murder, my life has been one dark hole. I haven't been able to muster the energy to do anything."

"Oh, hon. I'm so sorry you're going through this. And all these new revelations about Eli…"

"A wife? Children he never told me about? My God, I didn't need this. Wasn't it bad enough with Eli dying?"

Debbie didn't say anything. What could she say?

After a moment, she glanced at her watch. "Shoot. I've got a ten-thirty conference call. I have to get back to my office."

"Of course. You go to work. I've got a lot to do myself."

Debbie's lips lifted in a sympathetic smile before she opened the door and headed out of my office.

Once she was gone, I sank onto my chair. I wondered if my life would get any worse than it was right now.

And I wondered what the hell was wrong with me. Sure,

it wasn't my fault that Eli had lied to me, but I felt like the world's biggest fool for believing without question everything he'd told me.

"I'm sorry. I've rambled on and on about my daughter, her deadbeat father, and the losers in my life." *I gazed out at the view of the illuminated courtyard and enticing pool before looking at Eli again. "Tell me about you. Were you ever married, have any children?"*

Eli sipped his wine before answering. "I was married. Really bad experience that I don't like talking about."

"Oh, I know all about bad experiences."

"It's a beautiful night." Eli gestured to the courtyard. "I'm here with a beautiful woman. I say we talk about beautiful things."

"Like...?"

"Like where's your favorite South Beach spot to get a bite to eat?"

"I'm a huge seafood lover, so I love Blue Door."

"Fantastic spot," Eli agreed.

I frowned. "But I used to go there with my last boyfriend."

"Then how about we make some new memories there? Say, tomorrow night?"

I chuckled softly. "You're smooth."

"No, I just go after what I want."

There were times I'd catch Eli with a faraway look on his face as he regarded Rayna, and once I asked him what was on his mind. He'd told me that he'd always wanted a big family, at least four kids, and hoped that was okay with me.

A painful lump formed in my throat, and I swallowed. I had been an utter fool to believe Eli. But after our romantic relationship and how he'd been a great father to Rayna, how could my heart accept that everything he'd claimed to feel for me was a lie?

I did my best to push that devastating thought to the back of my mind, and instead tried to concentrate on the situation at hand. Yesterday, I thought the media had finally given up on me, but now I could only guess that they'd all rushed to Atlanta the moment Eli's wife had decided to talk. Then they'd come back to Miami to hear from me, the "mistress."

I hated that word, especially since it was in no way accurate when it came to me. Hopefully, now that I'd talked to the media, the newscasts would stop labeling me with that term.

By the end of the night, Americans would learn that I, like Tassie Johnson, had been one of Eli's victims.

chapter ten

At twelve-thirty, I went to a nearby deli for a quick lunch. I wasn't really hungry, but knew I needed to eat something.

Despite what the supposed *Mrs.* Eli Johnson had told me, I'd called the police and medical examiner's office after the media left, figuring they'd tell me what the next step was in this whole mess. Eli had to be buried, and I figured it was up to me to arrange a funeral.

But I got the shock of my life: neither the police nor coroner would divulge any information to me.

"But he was living with me!" I'd protested. "I was his fiancée!"

"We've been in touch with his next of kin," the medical examiner had explained. "Tassie Johnson."

Enraged, I'd hung up.

My turkey sandwich on rye was tasteless, my mind preoccupied with the insanity going on in my life. Could

Tassie—and what kind of name was Tassie, by the way?—
really take my home from me?

Over my dead body, I thought.

When I got back to the office after lunch, Alaina saw me
and her eyes lit up. She had the phone pasted to her ear, and
I assumed she was on a social call.

But instead of her typical non-work-related gossip, I
heard, "Oh, she just came in. Will you hold please?"

I looked at her in confusion. "For me?" I asked.

"Yeah. And it sounds official. Like a cop or something."

Now I frowned. "A cop?" Maybe someone in the department had had a change of heart about not giving me any
information. "Put the call through to my office."

Less than a minute later, I had dumped my purse and
coffee on my desk, picked up my phone and took the call
off hold. "This is Vanessa Cain."

"Ms. Cain. This is Bradley Harris of Harris, Lawton
and Stein."

"Ohhh," I said, immensely relieved. "Thank God. You
must be Eli's lawyer. I was trying to find your information."

"Actually, I'm Mrs. Johnson's attorney."

My body froze, as if the man had snapped his fingers and
I'd instantly turned to stone.

"I understand you've spoken to Mrs. Johnson about your
situation."

It took me at least five seconds to speak. And when I did,
I wasn't too eloquent. "Situation?"

"The Johnsons' marital property that you're currently
residing in."

I wanted to scream. Cuss a blue streak that would make

my mother roll over in her grave. "The only property I'm residing in is the one Eli and I bought together. I didn't know he had a wife."

"Mrs. Johnson has proposed a meeting to talk about this, but says that you denied her request."

"She most certainly did not. Although if she did, I would have told her to go to hell."

There was a pause, then the lawyer said, "I understand this must be a shock to you, as it was to Mrs. Johnson. But the fact remains, you are living in a condo that rightly belongs to her."

"The hell it does!"

The man pressed on. "In the wake of Mr. Johnson's death, and given that Mrs. Johnson and the children are the heirs to his estate…"

Children. I no longer heard what this lawyer was saying. My mind was stuck on the "children" and "heirs to his estate" parts.

Despite knowing that Eli had lied to me, every time I heard the word *children,* my stomach tightened in a sickening way. I would never be able to come to terms with the fact that he'd lied to me about his sons.

"This is all so surreal," I said, not caring that this guy didn't know me from Adam. "I have a daughter, okay? And day after day, I witnessed Eli with her. He happily accepted her as his own. Eli was great with children. You should have seen him cooing over babies at the park or in the mall. How could a man like that neglect to tell a woman that he'd fathered children with someone else?"

"I'm sorry he lied to you, but unfortunately, that doesn't change things legally."

"That's bullshit!" I snapped.

"Ms. Cain, I understand this situation is complicated, but there's no need for hostility. I'm sure we can reach an amicable agreement."

"Are you really a lawyer?"

"Excuse me?"

"Or are you a friend of Tassie Johnson's, playing this sick game with her for the fun of it?" I was grasping at straws, and I knew it.

"I assure you, this is no game."

"This is America. Sh-she can't take my home. She can't!" I slammed down the receiver.

I dropped my head onto my desk and stifled a scream. God, this Tassie character was one evil wench. I would never get to ask Eli what he saw in her, but I could only imagine she'd manipulated him into marrying her.

Manipulated him into marrying her... Slowly, I raised my head. A thought began to grow in my mind, like a seed. Just how manipulative was Tassie Johnson?

Enough to have stolen the divorce papers from city hall? It wasn't impossible, was it? Maybe she had a friend who worked there. Maybe...

Maybe nothing. I frowned. It was a stupid idea. Something like that could happen on *The Young and the Restless,* but not in real life.

But what if... My heart soared with hope. What if Eli had divorced Tassie in another state? Precisely *because* she was such a manipulative character? A state where one person could initiate a divorce without a requirement of residency?

Oh my God. That had to be it.

Eli *had* gotten divorced. Tassie Johnson just didn't know it.

Obviously, the media hadn't checked the divorce records in every state. I would.

I went online and first tried to find information about Eli's marriage. I figured if I was going to do a search for divorce records, I ought to have Tassie's maiden name. I typed in "Eli Johnson Atlanta Braves wedding" and within seconds was at the home page for the *Atlanta Journal-Constitution*. As I knew from doing this before, I couldn't get more information without searching the archives. I used my credit card to pay the $12.95 fee, then began.

My heart faltered when I saw a wedding picture of Eli, much younger, with a gorgeous black woman. As Tassie had said, the date of their wedding was July 30, 1994. It wasn't that I didn't believe her, but seeing the truth in print made it absolutely irrefutable.

Atlanta Braves outfielder Eli Rohan Johnson married Tassie Janelle Brigham in a lavish ceremony yesterday…

I scribbled Tassie's full name on a scrap of paper. Then I quickly typed in Eli's name, with the word *divorce* added to the search.

The same three headlines I'd found when I searched the Web months earlier came up. As I read the articles, I was more convinced than ever that Eli and Tassie *should* have been divorced. There was talk about the two of them heading to divorce court, claiming irreconcilable differences as the reason for their split, but no article that stated their divorce had become final.

That didn't mean it wasn't, of course. Just that, as I'd suspected, Eli hadn't gotten divorced in Atlanta.

I spent another thirty minutes trying to find divorce records, but learning it wasn't that easy. I'd have to pay fees all over the place. I tried in Nevada, assuming it was easier to get a divorce there, but nothing appeared.

Thirty dollars down the drain.

I could keep this up, but not on the agency's time. I had an office to run.

In fact, maybe I could find a private investigator to dig up this information for me.

While I'd been searching the Internet, my phone had rung four more times. I'd let all the calls bounce to voice mail.

Now I checked the messages.

The first one, as I'd suspected, was from the man claiming to be Tassie's lawyer.

"Ms. Cain, this is Bradley Harris calling again. Somehow, we got disconnected. Please phone me at your earliest convenience. I understand your frustration, but there are options available. Mrs. Johnson said she doesn't have to live in the apartment. You could buy out her half, allowing us to resolve this very quickly."

I erased the call before the lawyer recited his number.

By the end of the day, I had a migraine. I left the office promptly at five, two thoughts giving me comfort as I headed home.

One, of course, was the thought of seeing my daughter.

The other was the thought of watching the news.

Thus far, I'd avoided watching any coverage about Eli's death. With this Tassie Johnson character likely giving her warped spin on my character to anyone who would listen, it was highly likely that I'd been portrayed as the Whore of Babylon in the press.

Tonight, however, I would be vindicated. Seeing my side of the story aired wouldn't erase all that had happened, but it would be a small victory—and I desperately needed something to feel good about.

Once Rayna was sleeping, I settled on the sofa with a glass of wine and turned the television to CNN. It took ten minutes to get to the day's headlines, and I inhaled a nervous breath when the newscaster announced, *"Also coming up, the latest in the soap opera surrounding Eli Johnson's murder. Yesterday, we spoke to Eli's widow, Tassie Johnson. Today, we spoke to his mistress."*

"No," I muttered. "Don't call me his mistress! I was his fiancée!"

The first piece of news to run was about a suicide bombing in Iraq that had claimed forty lives. Then I saw Eli's smiling face appear on the corner of the screen.

"Eli Johnson may be dead," the female newscaster said, *"but the fallout from his womanizing continues."*

"Exactly," I agreed, relaxing a bit. With a word like *fallout,* it was clear they were going to get the story right.

Before they got to my clip, they showed a woman on a sofa, tears streaming down her face. They didn't have to identify her as Tassie Johnson for me to know who she was. I recognized her from the wedding picture I'd found online.

Even distraught, she was strikingly beautiful. Beautiful enough to be a model. High cheekbones, full lips covered in clear gloss, and wide, expressive eyes that were swollen from crying. She didn't look as if she'd gained a pound since her wedding in 1994. The marked difference was her hair, which was black and straight and hung to her shoulders. In the wedding photo, she'd had some puffy, curly do beneath the tiara she'd worn atop her head.

There was an elegance about her, even in her grief. She sat poised upon an antique-looking chaise that was deep rose in color. A vivacious painting of sunflowers hung on the wall behind the chaise, reminding me of Van Gogh's work. The color around her clashed with the simple black dress she was wearing to indicate she was in mourning.

"Mrs. Johnson was devastated to learn that her husband had not one, but two mistresses," the newscaster continued.

"I always expected him to come home to me," Tassie said, her voice ripe with emotion. "He said he was taking some time to sort things out."

I didn't want to admit it, but the clip of the distraught Tassie was moving. Though I didn't believe for a minute that she thought Eli was going to reunite with her. He'd been with me for eight months—and I refused to believe he was in touch with her during that time.

In fact, when I met Eli, he'd been living in Miami Lakes. According to him, he'd been there for five years.

Which meant he wasn't in Atlanta during that time.

What did Tassie think Eli had been doing in all the time he'd been apart from her—getting therapy?

"Today, Eli's surviving mistress, Vanessa Cain, finally gave our Dean Musselman a statement."

Next, I came on the screen, looking rather frazzled as I sat at the conference room table. My pale green suit looked like a tasteless choice for a woman who was supposed to be grieving. At least compared to Eli's wife, who'd had the good sense to wear black.

"How did you feel when you learned he was murdered in the gruesome way he was?" came the question.

And my reply: *"I didn't break out the champagne, if that's what you're asking. Though maybe I should have."*

Then Dean Musselman appeared on screen, saying, *"Obviously, she's not a happy woman. But can you blame her?"*

The newscaster went on to a new bit of news, and I shot to my feet, enraged.

"No, no, *no!"* I yelled at the television. "That *can't* be it! It can't be!"

After everything they'd asked me, *that* was the sound bite they'd chosen to show to America? Taken out of context, my words made me sound like a cold, unfeeling bitch.

Where was my side of the story, the statement of the facts that would vindicate me in the court of public opinion?

I turned to FOX News, hoping for a fairer story.

And saw the same sound bite.

At eleven, I watched the local news broadcasts.

"I didn't break out the champagne, if that's what you're asking. Though maybe I should have."

I dug my fingers into my scalp as though I was going to have a nervous breakdown.

Feeling a massive headache coming on, I went to the bathroom and took two Advil, then went to the kitchen and poured myself a second glass of wine.

This is exactly why I hadn't wanted to talk to the media. They had deliberately made me out to be a…a whore.

Really, there wasn't a better word for it. Calling me *mistress* implied I knew about Tassie. People would watch the news and sympathize with Tassie—and hate me.

As I sat on my sofa, desolate, my mind wandered back to my past. How every serious relationship I'd had had ultimately failed.

First Byron, Rayna's father, whom I'd been dating for two years before I got pregnant, became a different person when I told him I was with child. Shock of all shocks, the man who had claimed to love me and wanted to spend the rest of his life with me had flat out asked me to have an abortion. It took me a while to get over the distressing blow, and when I did, I told him there was no way in hell that I would kill our baby.

So he left me. Just like that. He even quit his job as a security guard at my office building, which is where I'd met him. He quit so that he wouldn't have to see me every day when I went to work.

I think Byron's cold rejection of his responsibility as a father, and the way he deserted me when I refused to have an abortion, helped me get over him real fast. There's nothing like an ultimatum to have an abortion that will kill your love for a man.

I didn't let it get me down, however. For one thing, I didn't have time to be sad. I was going to be a mother. I had a life inside me to think about, and I can tell you, the first time I felt my baby flutter around in my belly was the best moment of my life.

Before I was thrown unwillingly into that situation—having a boyfriend who would demand I kill his child—I wouldn't have been able to imagine how I'd deal with something so horrible. And yet, when I was in the middle of that real-life nightmare, somehow I survived. You don't realize how strong you are, or what you're capable of handling, until you're smack in the midst of a trying situation.

After Rayna was born, I went on a few dates here and there, but for the most part was content to concentrate on her and my role as a mother.

And then I met Lewis Carter.

Smooth-talking Lewis, who had a knack for charming the ladies. He was just what I'd needed to make me feel like a woman again, a guy who was fun and sexy. A guy who opened me up to a whole new world beyond the one Byron had been able to show me. His money allowed us to dine and travel in style, and bought me some very nice gifts.

"Oh my God," I exclaimed, an idea coming to me in a flash. "Lewis!"

Lewis could be the answer to my problems!

As an extremely successful real estate developer in South Florida, Lewis was very, very rich. And unlike most of the guys I'd once dated, he was still a friend.

Sure, he was a friend who enjoyed getting some on the side, but I could work around that. The main thing was that Lewis was someone who could help me out of my financial dilemma.

Earlier, I had ignored the lawyer's comment that I could buy out Tassie's share of *my* condo. It was an idea I wasn't willing to even contemplate at the time. Now, I wondered if Tassie would make my life a living hell by trying to force me out of my home if I couldn't pay Eli's share.

I had to be prepared for the worst-case scenario. A scenario Lewis could help me with.

If I called him up and asked for a loan... He would do that, wouldn't he? Considering we'd been romantically involved once, and hadn't ended up on negative terms.

I didn't waste another minute. I reached for the cordless handset on the end table next to the sofa and called Lewis.

When his voice mail picked up, I said, "Hey, Lewis. Vanessa here. How're you doing, babe?" *No, I shouldn't have said "babe." He'll get the wrong idea.* "Listen, I have a favor to ask you. Call me as soon as you get this message?"

As I replaced the receiver, hope surged through my body.

Yeah, Lewis could be the answer to all my problems.

chapter eleven

The next day, I didn't dare leave my house without my sunglasses and a scarf around my head, but as I drove out of the condominium's parking lot, I didn't see a camera crew in sight.

Of course not. Now that the media had publicly humiliated me on the news, what more could they do?

I didn't even want to look at the newspapers, fearing how I'd been portrayed in print.

There were no reporters lurking around my office building when I got downtown either, and I actually felt a little pissed. I wanted to see every last one of those vultures who had "interviewed" me yesterday and give them all a piece of my mind.

No such luck, so I went upstairs to my office, where the first thing I did was check my messages.

"Vanessa, it's Cynthia Martin from the *Miami Herald*. I saw the news coverage of your interview on television last night. All I can say is that if you want a chance to tell your story—*really* tell your side—call me."

Snorting, I deleted Cynthia's message. *Yeah, right.* Like I could trust any reporters after how I'd been vilified.

I spent the next two hours catching up on a ton of work—payroll, work scheduling, ordering office supplies, confirming talent bookings and dealing with various office expenses. It was good to throw myself into my work, but after two hours I found myself thinking about my predicament once again.

It was hard to avoid.

This was Thursday, and Eli had now been dead for three full days. In so many ways, it felt like weeks had passed, not seventy-two hours.

Calling the police yesterday had proved fruitless, and I doubted more calls would garner me any information. I'd been completely shut out, as if I'd never been in Eli's life at all.

As I swiveled in my chair and faced my window, sadness washed over me. Despite learning about his lies and deception, it was hard to deal with Eli being suddenly gone. How bizarre it was to lose someone without the chance to say goodbye.

I turned back to my desk. Eli, at some point, was going to be buried. Likely this weekend, if his body had already been released.

I might have been furious at him for how he'd betrayed me, but he'd been my fiancé, and there was no way I was going to miss his funeral. I had to say goodbye—which was as much about me needing to put closure as anything else.

I called the medical examiner's office and asked about Eli's funeral arrangements.

"The body has been released to the family," the coroner told me.

"All I want to know is where the funeral will be."

"You'll need to contact the family for that information."

The man I was talking to may as well have been a robot. Defeated, I hung up and slumped in my seat. Then I sat up straight, refusing to give in to frustration.

There was a way to get the information I wanted.

There had to be.

I looked up all the prominent churches in Miami on the Internet but, forty minutes and dozens of phone calls later, I'd gotten nowhere.

I left my office and went to see Alaina. My friend had the gift of the gab and could charm almost anyone.

"Hey, Alaina," I said sweetly as I rested my elbows on the reception counter. It was a rare moment not to find her on a call, personal or otherwise.

"What's up, *chica?*"

"I need a favor."

"Uh-oh."

"It's nothing huge. Not really. I just need some info—about where Eli's funeral's gonna be—and I'm hitting brick walls everywhere. I've called all the prominent churches in Miami, and no one has been able to give me any concrete info."

"You said his wife lives in Atlanta, right?"

"Ri…" My voice trailed off. "You don't think—"

"Oh, I think."

Why hadn't I considered the idea that Tassie Johnson might bury Eli in Atlanta? But it made perfect sense. Anything to make my life a little more difficult.

"I hate that woman," I said.

"Could be that with her and the kids in Atlanta, it's the most convenient spot."

The kids. My throat constricted, but I tried to find my voice. "Eli hasn't lived in Atlanta for eons. This is his home."

"Tell that to the wife."

The phone rang, and while Alaina answered it, I bit my lip and I pondered the situation. "There must be a million churches in Atlanta."

"Where did he live there?"

"I don't know. But I know the church where he was married."

"Then call and ask if that's where the funeral will be. If it's not, you can still find out with a quick Google search. I'm sure it will be a prominent church, one that rich athletes attend."

"You are such a pro," I told Alaina.

The phone rang again, and she did her thing. Then she turned to me and said, "Let me know how it goes."

"Actually…I was hoping you wouldn't mind making the calls."

"Me?"

"This has been so exhausting, so frustrating, and no one wants to help. I keep thinking that they know I'm Vanessa Cain, Eli's *mistress.*" I looked pleadingly at Alaina. "Do you mind? Would you, please?"

She held up a finger to quiet me as she took another call. While she spoke, I wrote down on a pad of paper the name of the church where Eli had been married.

When Alaina was finished, I handed her the pad. "This is where he was married," I told her.

"All right. I'll make some calls and see what I can find out."

"Thank you. You're a lifesaver."

"I haven't performed a miracle yet."

"But you will," I said confidently.

I left the matter in her hands.

At precisely 4:45 p.m., Alaina called me. "I got it."

My stomach fluttered. "You do?"

"Yep. Eli's funeral will be held at World Changers Church International in College Park, Georgia."

"College Park? Where's that?"

"A suburb of Atlanta."

"Oh. Okay."

"The funeral is on Saturday at 2:00 p.m.," Alaina added, "followed by his burial at College Park Cemetery immediately afterward."

"I can't believe we're actually talking about Eli's funeral."

"It looks like it's going to be quite the affair. Lots of important people will be attending this one."

I blew out a shaky breath. "Thank you, Alaina. You're terrific."

"Are you planning to go?"

"I…think so. Yeah, yeah I am."

"I don't know, Vanessa. I'm not sure you should."

"Why not?"

"Because with the high-profile guest list—which includes, by the way, Michael Jordan and Eddie Murphy—this is the kind of funeral where they have bouncers and shit. You don't want to go all the way there just to have his crazy wife throw you out."

Alaina had a point. A good one. And yet I didn't want to let Eli's wife take this final moment away from me.

I hadn't even been able to see Eli's body after he'd been murdered. I couldn't let him be buried without saying goodbye.

"What about the visitation?" I asked.

"Friday, 2:00 p.m. and 7:00 p.m., and Saturday at one, right before the funeral. Apparently that's at the church."

"Perfect. I can make it for Saturday."

"Perfect? Vanessa, the viewing's an even worse time to show up. The wife will surely be greeting the mourners."

"But maybe there'll be too many for her to see us all." And this way, I could get up close to the casket, see Eli for myself and know that he was really dead.

I didn't doubt it, of course. But it was still taking time to sink in. The last time I'd seen him, he had stalked out of our apartment. I needed to see the body for my heart to believe the information my brain was telling it.

"What do you say—wanna go with me?"

"Me?" Alaina shrieked.

"If anyone knows how to play like they fit in, that's you, Ally. I need you. Please."

"What about my kids?"

"Your husband gets them on the weekend, doesn't he?" She didn't answer.

"Ally, I totally need you. You know I can't ask my sister. And I'll need my babysitter to watch Rayna. But you—you can do this. With your lead foot, we'll make it to Atlanta in record time."

"Girl…"

"Think of it as an adventure. You might even meet someone nice."

"Oh, I hate that you know how to tempt me."

"Is that a yes? Because if it is, we can leave tomorrow evening, make sure we've got plenty of time to be there for Saturday morning. I'll go online tonight and book a hotel."

I heard Alaina sigh.

"Please, Ally. *Please.*"

"All right," she agreed. "But we'll leave as soon as the funeral is over, right?"

"Of course. Unless you hook up with some rich, available man," I added in a teasing tone.

"That will be the one exception, yes. And anytime I need a favor—"

"I'll be there for you, one hundred percent."

Hanging up, I was grinning. Mrs. Bitch Johnson wasn't going to cut me off like I'd never mattered to Eli.

I was driving home when my cell phone rang. I dug it out of my purse and glanced at the caller ID. Instantly, I recognized Lewis's number.

I pressed Talk and put the phone to my ear. "Hey, Lewis."

"Vanessa," he said, his tone already thick with sexual suggestion. "Getting a little lonely, are you?"

"Huh?" I asked, caught off guard. Not that I should have been. This was Lewis Carter, who always thought with his lower head first. "No. *No.* I didn't call about that kind of favor."

"Oh," he said, now the one sounding surprised. "Then why were you phoning?"

I blew out a frazzled breath. "Lewis…you're my friend, right?"

"You know I'd do anything for you. Just tell me what you need."

"A loan."

"How much? A grand? Two?"

I bit my lip, contemplating how to break the news. The truth was, I didn't know what kind of cash Lewis had, though I was sure it was in the seven-figure range. He bragged often about how much money he made in real estate, and everything he wore had a designer label. Still, the amount of money I needed...

"I have a...situation."

"Go on."

"It's my condo. Eli's wife wants it. I'm not sure she can legally take it from me, but I want to be prepared for the possibility of having to buy her out if it comes to that."

"Whoa, whoa. Hold up a sec. Did you just say Eli's *wife?*"

"Yes," I mumbled in reply. "Haven't you been watching the news?"

"I was in the Cayman Islands for a couple of days. Just got back, heard your message." He paused. "A wife. Damn. And you gave me a hard time because I didn't want to get married."

I ignored the comment. I didn't want to go down that road with Lewis. Clearly, he had a selective memory. Our problem wasn't that he didn't want to get married. It was that he didn't believe in monogamy. When I'd found proof of his infidelity, he had quickly used my daughter as the reason why he was afraid to give me his whole heart.

"Is there any way," I began, "any way at all that you might be able to help me buy this woman out? Maybe cosign a loan for me, and I can get a second job to make the payments. Like I said, it will be a loan. I'm not asking you for a gift."

"Why don't you just sell the place?"

"Because I love it. And real estate prices have gone up even more since Eli and I moved in there. Once I sell it and give that bitch her share, I won't be able to afford a place on South Beach."

"Interesting dilemma. Why don't we meet?"

I hesitated.

"You're asking a lot. At least we can discuss this over dinner."

It was a reasonable request, but I knew Lewis. The last time he wanted to meet as "friends"—after I'd told him about my engagement to Eli—he had started to grope me at the restaurant table. Not only had I been embarrassed because people had seen his actions, but I'd been angry. Lewis and I might have been involved sexually in the past, but he had no right to treat me like his on-demand sex toy.

"A friendly dinner," he stressed.

"You're sure? Because—"

"Would I lie to you?"

"All right," I agreed. After all, I needed him. "When and where?"

"How about the Clevelander?" he suggested. "I can make it in an hour if you can."

Oh, Lord…not the *Clevelander!*

"Vanessa?"

"S-sure." I cleared my throat. "I'll be there."

chapter twelve

I'm a mature adult, I told myself as I strolled toward the Clevelander one hour later. *I can handle this, despite what happened the last time I was here with Lewis.*

In spite of my words, my stomach was twisting. I was no fool. I knew why Lewis had chosen this South Beach hot spot that catered to tourists looking to get laid.

Because the last time we'd met here, while dating, we'd ended up sneaking into the bathroom and having a quickie.

A very hot quickie that still made me blush when I thought about it…

One thing about me and Lewis—the chemistry between us had always sizzled.

Our undeniable mutual attraction was the last thing I wanted to remember, at least not on a nostalgic level. I didn't want to recall how much fun it was to be with him, how sexy he made me feel, how easily we got along. But I did need to keep in mind just how quickly Lewis could ignite my body with one look. That way, I could maintain complete control in the situation.

"Keep it cool, calm and collected," I mumbled, "and you won't give him any ideas."

I wished I didn't have to resort to asking Lewis for a favor, but I was desperate. If he wanted to set up this meeting in a cow field in Wyoming, I would have gone there if that meant obtaining the necessary help to get me out of my predicament.

Lewis was already sitting at an outdoor table when I approached the restaurant. It was an ideal evening to be sitting outside. Warm, not humid, with a gentle breeze that smelled of the ocean. Each table had a decorative umbrella overhead and a lit candle between the place settings. Even with the pulsing salsa music coming from the Clevelander's outdoor club, the mood on this stretch of sidewalk was definitely romantic.

Seeing me, Lewis stood. Then let his eyes roam over me from breast to thigh in a blatantly sexual stare.

"Wow, Vanessa. You look fantastic."

"Thank you," I told him.

I headed to the empty chair, and he quickly pulled it out for me. I eyed him skeptically, wondering if he was being nice simply because he was happy to see me, or for another reason altogether.

I avoided his gaze as he stared at me, instead looking to my right. The beach was dark now, but that didn't stop couples from heading in that direction through the park that bordered the street. It was no mystery what they were going to do once they reached a deserted spot on the sand.

Something Lewis and I had done more than once after a night of partying...

I finally met his eyes.

"So," he began.

"So," I echoed.

"You need some cash."

"Yes." There was no sugarcoating the situation. "Like I said, if you could cosign a loan for me, I'll take on a second job to pay you back. Or..."

Lewis raised an eyebrow. "Or what?"

"Or, I was thinking. You're in real estate. Maybe there's a property you know will turn a quick profit. I can buy it, flip it. Make some quick cash. I'd still need a cosigner for the loan, but at least that way the profit would be fast. Then I could pay this woman off and keep my property."

Lewis was regarding me carefully, his fingers linked beneath his chin. "Interesting."

"I know you're probably wondering why you should give me a chance to make money off of a property that you could easily buy and flip yourself."

"The thought crossed my mind."

"And it's a valid question. And here's a valid answer. Because you're my friend."

Lewis pursed his lips. "And if I help you..."

"You know I wouldn't ask if I weren't desperate. I'm completely, horribly desperate. Understatement of the century."

Lewis suddenly smiled. "You still say that. That 'understatement of the century' phrase."

"Only when it's fitting, and it's definitely fitting right now. Please, Lewis."

"What do I get in return for my...my kindness?"

"A feeling of satisfaction?" I offered, my voice cracking slightly as my stomach sank.

Please be able to do this for me with no strings attached. Please.

"It's a nice idea," Lewis said. "But I'm a businessman."

"Then loan me the money. Let me pay you back with interest."

Lewis flashed a look of doubt at me. "How are you going to do that?"

"My boss is going to make me an agent," I lied with ease. Well, it wasn't entirely a lie. I hoped she would. I hadn't officially broached the subject with Debbie, but becoming an agent was unquestionably one of my goals. "Once I land some clients of my own, I'll make some serious cash."

The waiter appeared and took our drink order. I asked for a sweetened iced tea, and Lewis ordered a Corona.

When the waiter disappeared, Lewis said, "I need to think about this."

I gnawed on my bottom lip. "How long? Not that I want to pressure you, but I'll need to figure out what I'm doing sooner rather than later." And, if possible, I could happily tell Tassie that I'd be buying her out when I saw her at the funeral on the weekend.

Lewis met my gaze with unwavering eyes. "Oh, I'm sure you can help me make my decision faster."

"How?" I asked, though I had a pretty good idea what he meant.

"Come on, Vanessa." He reached across the table and covered my hand with his. "You know I'm crazy about you."

"I do?"

"You should."

"Really? Because the last thing I remember was you telling me you never wanted to marry me."

"I didn't say *never.*"

Rolling my eyes, I pulled my hand away. "Lewis, let's not go there. And to be clear, I'm not holding a grudge against you. We're friends."

"What if I said I was stupid to let you go?"

God help me, this wasn't happening. Not in a real sense, anyway. From Lewis's mouth, those were just words. Words I could never, ever trust.

"Vanessa?" he prompted, reaching for my hand again.

I moved both my hands to my lap so he couldn't touch me. "I don't believe you."

He chuckled. "You don't believe me?"

"Lewis," I said in a low but frank tone. "Do I need to remind you that minutes before you told me you didn't see yourself marrying me, I found that red thong in your jacket pocket?"

"I told you—that was a practical joke."

I shot him a cynical look, then counted to five. There was no point going down this road. Lewis and I were over. *Finito.* Kaput. Even if at one point I'd been crazy about him.

"We're not dating. We don't need to fight about what happened in the past."

"One night," Lewis said.

"Excuse me?"

"One night of passionate, limitless sex. One night, and I'll give you the money you need."

I didn't answer right away. I wanted to say no, but I

couldn't form the word. I immediately contemplated how much it would mean to have the kind of cash I could never raise and likely wouldn't be able to repay even if I took on a second job to do so.

I could keep my condo.

Rayna wouldn't have to endure another change.

Mrs. Bitch Johnson wouldn't be able to come into my life and take what was rightfully mine.

"One night," Lewis said.

"One night?" I repeated.

"Wasn't it fun the way we used to walk along the beach at night, how we'd make out with the sound of the ocean behind us? What was it you said—that you felt we were one with nature?"

I covered my face. "Lewis, please—"

"Don't be embarrassed, baby. I felt the same way."

"Right."

"Look at me."

Grudgingly, I lowered my hand.

"I've had a lot of flings, Vanessa—"

"Really? That's a shock."

"But I always end up calling you. Wanting to see you. You're the one woman I can't seem to forget."

His words gave me pause. A year ago, I would have been elated to hear Lewis say this. Maybe even after he'd broken my heart, but before I'd met Eli. But now, in the wake of Eli's deception and the realization that I clearly sucked at choosing the right man, I didn't dare let myself believe a word Lewis was saying.

"I meant what I said." He spoke softly. "That I realize

how much of a fool I was to let you go. I want another chance with you."

"Lewis—"

"Remember the last time we were here?"

How could I forget? It was the reason I'd practically broken out in a cold sweat when he had suggested meeting here.

Thankfully, the waiter arrived with our drinks, saving me from having to answer Lewis. But before we could order any food, Lewis told him we needed another few minutes.

"What do you think you'll have?" I asked. "I can't stay too long, so I'll go for something light."

"You and me, up against the stage. Surrounded by the crowd, yet it was like we were the only two people on earth."

"Lewis—"

"Remember how you begged me to make love to you? 'Just pull my skirt up and give it to me,'" he said, feigning a female voice.

"Stop."

"I had to convince you it wouldn't hurt to wait the five minutes it would take to make it to the bathroom. You walked right in there, not caring if anyone saw you."

My face flamed. "I was drunk."

"And horny. Remember how we finished up on the beach, with you riding me…."

I cleared my throat. "Lewis."

"Didn't we have the best sex that night?"

I didn't answer. I was too embarrassed.

"One night," Lewis reiterated. "And baby, it'll be the best night of your life."

It hit me then, with total clarity. I couldn't get involved with Lewis. Even one night with him was too steep a price to pay for the money I needed.

I couldn't pimp myself out like a common whore.

And I couldn't allow my heart to take a step backward in time.

Maybe if I didn't have Rayna to think of, I could carelessly have a fling with a guy I knew didn't care about me. But I was past that, past Lewis.

The waiter reappeared and asked if we were ready to order. I pushed my chair back and stood.

"You know what, I'm not really hungry."

"What are you doing?" Lewis asked.

"Leaving."

"You're upset."

"No, I'm not."

"Then don't leave."

I shook my head. "I have to go."

"Vanessa—"

"This was a mistake, me coming here."

The waiter quietly slipped away.

"It wasn't a mistake," Lewis insisted, also getting to his feet.

"We can still be friends," I told him. "Just not friends who…have sex," I finished, changing my mind at the last minute to avoid the cruder description.

Lewis reached for my hand. I won't deny I felt a slight *something*. It was hard to completely erase from my mind the memory of how great he was in bed. How lust had turned into love.

But I was in control of my libido, not the other way around.

As if to prove that point to myself, I kissed Lewis on the cheek. "I'll see you around."

"Vanessa…"

I pulled away from him, thinking that he smelled incredible. And looked incredible.

Lewis stared at me, his gaze unwavering. "Are you going to deny that we were fabulous together?"

That was exactly the problem. Sexually, we had seriously connected. I could never deny that.

It would be all too easy to fall back into bed with Lewis, especially given the fact that I didn't feel the need to honor Eli's memory after his public betrayal. And if I did, I was certain I would be able to protect my heart this time.

But it was how I would feel when the morning came that I wouldn't be able to live with.

"Bye, Lewis." I offered him a small smile, then started off down the street.

He called my name as I walked away, but I didn't look back.

chapter thirteen

Friday evening, Alaina and I drove to Atlanta as planned. When we arrived, she wanted to get dressed up and hit the clubs, but I had a sick, nervous energy I couldn't shake, and didn't want to go out.

We compromised by having a few drinks at the bar in the Marriott Marquis, where we were staying.

I hardly slept. My anxiety level was through the roof, but I'd traveled all the way to Atlanta, and I was going to go through with my plan to attend the visitation.

On Saturday morning, Alaina and I got up around ten and took our time getting ready. I'd brought all black for the occasion, and a large black hat with a veil, hoping that Tassie Johnson wouldn't recognize me if she saw me. Alaina dressed in a body-hugging, above-the-knee black dress that said she was heading to the funeral in hopes of hooking up, rather than to grieve.

"Ready to do this?" she asked when we got to the car in the hotel's underground parking.

I nodded. "But I'm too nervous to drive."

"No problem. I'll get us there."

Alaina got behind the wheel, and I settled in the passenger seat beside her. "You have the MapQuest directions?"

"In my purse." She dug them out and handed them to me.

I navigated the trip, and within twenty-five minutes, we were on Burdett Road. I didn't have to see that large, dome-shaped building to know that that was where Eli's funeral was being held. The sea of people easily gave that away.

"Look at all those people!" Alaina exclaimed.

"Look at the church." It was one of those ultramodern structures. "It's massive."

Personally, I preferred old churches with stained-glass windows. But I supposed for the amount of cars in the parking lot, this place was perfect.

"I had no clue it'd be this busy," I said, noting that my hands were shaking. "And, oh, hell—the media is everywhere."

Alaina glanced at the camera crews that lined the exterior of the church, then at me. "You're nervous."

"Very."

"Having second thoughts?"

"Hell, yeah."

"I know we came all this way, but if you want, we can turn around and leave. Find a great pancake house, stuff our faces…"

"Very tempting right now," I told her, then rubbed my hands together. "But I came here because I needed to, because I wasn't going to let Eli's wife shut me out…and I'm going to do this." My mind made up, I breathed in and out deeply. "Besides, don't you want to meet a man that your ex-husband can't get to?"

"You know I do!"

Alaina and I had joked in the past that the reason the guys she went out with didn't call for a second date was because her ex-husband, a cop, somehow got to them and threatened them to back off.

"Ready, girl?" Alaina asked.

"Uh-huh."

She squeezed my hand in support, then opened her door. I followed suit.

I slipped on my big, dark sunglasses, then positioned my hat on my head. Originally, I'd been worried that I might stand out with such a lavish hat, but it was clear I wouldn't. The women exiting their S-Class Mercedes and 7 Series BMWs were all similarly dressed.

Together, Alaina and I strolled toward the church. When we got near the entrance, Alaina muttered, *"Dios míos."*

My heart slammed against my chest. "What?"

"Him. On the right, getting out of the Beemer. With a body like that, I'll bet he plays for the Falcons."

"I *think* so. He looks familiar but I don't know his name," I supplied.

"I wonder if he's single." Alaina continued to look his way, her lips curled in a lustful smile.

"Can you wait until *after* the viewing to try and hook up?" I whispered.

"Right. Okay."

"And you'd better take the lead, because I'm terrified right now."

"All right. This is how you do it, honey."

Alaina picked up her pace. Her walk could only be described as a confident strut, with a little sexy hip action thrown in. I did my best to follow her, fearing all the while that people were seeing through the protective layers I'd put up.

In reality, they were minding their own business, probably being thoughtful about Eli's untimely and scandalous death.

My hands began to sweat anew when we ascended the steps. At the top, on either side of the front doors, were two men in dark suits and sunglasses. If they weren't bodyguards, they were doing a pretty good job of pretending they were.

I held my breath, expecting the worst, but Alaina linked arms with me, nodded solemnly at the man to the left, and then walked with me into the church.

"Mission accomplished," she whispered.

We simply followed the crowd. Everyone was moving into the sanctuary. Even though I couldn't see it through the throng, it didn't take long to realize that Eli's casket was at the front, and that people were filing past it in a steady stream. Family members were on both sides of the casket, shaking hands with the people who passed by.

The sanctuary was the largest I had ever seen, and filled with hundreds of floral bouquets. Their scent hung in the air, one that would from that point forward remind me of death.

As Alaina and I walked forward, I moved this way and that, angling my head for a view of the casket through the dense crowd. When three men who had the build of professional athletes moved to the left, I finally saw it.

I wasn't close enough to see anything but the glazed cherrywood and a portion of the brown face lying within.

My knees buckled.

Alaina threw an arm around me to help me up.

I recovered, not wanting to draw attention to myself. And even though I'd told myself that I wouldn't cry, I felt the tears building.

"That must be her," Alaina whispered.

"Where?" I asked, the thought of seeing Eli's widow stopping my tears cold.

"There. On the far right of the casket, sitting."

I spotted the woman quickly, and drew in a sharp breath as I did. Even though she was at least thirty feet away from me, it was easy to see she was as stunningly beautiful in person as she had been in her wedding photo. She had fair brown skin, black hair that hung well past her shoulders, and a graceful demeanor even in grief. A man was standing beside her, and she was gripping his hand as she sobbed into a silk handkerchief.

She was, of course, dressed all in black, with a simple strand of pearls around her neck. She wore a hat as well, but a small one that had no veil.

One by one, people filed past the family and the casket.

"How can I do this?" I asked as we got ever closer. "If I go past the casket, I can't avoid speaking to her."

"She won't recognize you," Alaina assured me. "And remember, I'm with you."

Alaina was right. I hadn't come all this way to chicken out at the sight of Eli's estranged wife, who, for all I knew, could have been crying crocodile tears.

Still, my legs were numb as I moved forward, and if not for Alaina, I'm not sure I would have made it.

I shook an older black man's hand, then an older white woman's hand. I had no clue how these people were related to Eli, and I didn't dare ask. All I said was, "I'm sorry for your loss," as I went by them.

When I caught sight of two young boys, maybe nine and ten, sitting on a pew at the front of the church, it was as if someone had hurled a fastball into my gut.

I was seeing miniature versions of Eli.

"We're almost there," Alaina whispered.

At the first good sight of Eli, lying on a bed of white satin, a lump of emotion lodged in my throat.

"He looks good," Alaina commented.

I could only nod. He did look good. But he also didn't look real. Almost like a wax version of himself.

"I can't believe that's Eli," I said softly. "I can't…"

My knees wobbled and my hands trembled. No longer could I hold off the tears. They gushed from my eyes, hot and heavy, accompanied by a loud moan.

I pressed my lips together to stifle my cry. Alaina linked arms with mine and urged me away from the casket. It was then, even in my grief, that I noticed Tassie Johnson glancing curiously my way.

My grief gave way to panic. Her eyes still on me, Tassie slowly rose. I lowered my head so I didn't have to look at her, and took a step backward. I hoped she would ignore me, deal with the next mourner. But she said, "Excuse me?"

I wanted to turn and run. But I couldn't without drawing attention to myself.

Tassie approached. I held a handkerchief over my face, dabbing at my eyes beneath my veil.

Thank God for Alaina. She spoke, saving me from having to. "We are so sorry for your loss, Mrs. Johnson."

"How did you know Eli?" she asked.

"We, uh, we have a flower shop," Alaina answered. "In Buckhead. We used to fill Mr. Johnson's flower deliveries all the time. For you, of course. Some beautiful arrangements."

I raised my head ever so slightly. Saw Tassie eyeing both of us inquisitively. *Oh, damn. She's onto us.*

"Right." Tassie nodded slowly, seeming content with Alaina's answer. "You make such beautiful arrangements. Thank you for coming."

"We wouldn't miss it," Alaina said.

"It's been so hard. Dealing with Eli's death."

"Oh, I know." Alaina tsked. "If it's any consolation," she added in a hushed tone, "I don't believe all those negative things they're saying about him in the media."

I pinched Alaina's hand. Hard.

"Oh, look," she suddenly said, spinning me around. "Isn't that Denrick near the door?"

All I could do was nod in agreement.

"Denrick will be upset if we don't say hi," Alaina quickly said to Tassie. "So good to meet you in person."

Alaina started with me toward the exit. But we didn't get far before we heard, "Wait!"

I cringed, then gripped Alaina's hand, my signal for her to keep moving and not turn.

She halted.

"Ally!" My voice was an urgent whisper.

"We can't just run away," Alaina whispered back.

"Do you have a business card?" Tassie asked, and my heart sank when Alaina turned around.

"No," she said, her voice full of regret. "We didn't even think to bring one."

"Too bad."

Alaina had partly turned when the next question came. "The name of your store?"

Now I knew that Tassie was onto us. If she wasn't, there was no reason for this inquisition. She had mourners to greet, and was spending far too much time with us.

"Ally…"

Alaina raised her hand and waved at someone. "We'll be right over," she called, and my shoulders drooped with relief.

But before we could go anywhere, Tassie was suddenly blocking our path. "Why doesn't your friend say anything?" she asked, her tone dripping with suspicion. "She won't even look at me."

Alaina hesitated for a moment. Then she blurted, "Because she's—well, she's—she's mute."

Oh, shit…

"Mute?" Tassie asked doubtfully.

Screw the sham; I started to hustle across the floor. I saw the interested glances coming my way, but didn't care.

I was almost at the door, almost home free, when my hat was yanked from my head. I was so startled, I screamed as if I'd been struck.

Tassie quickly scooted in front of me. And as her gaze scanned my face, her eyes narrowed.

"Take those sunglasses off," she demanded.

"Vanessa, let's just go."

"Vanessa!" Tassie exclaimed. "I *knew* it!" Now she yanked my sunglasses off my face, but I quickly snatched them from her fingers. The Chanel shades had cost me two hundred and fifty dollars, and I'd be damned if I was leaving without them.

"How dare you?" The woman's voice was low and threatening. "You come here to disrespect the memory of my husband? Haven't you done enough?"

Alaina was tugging on my arm now, but I was the one who wasn't budging.

"What, exactly, have I done?" I asked Tassie. "I had no clue that Eli was still married."

Tassie snorted.

"Despite the lies you want the media to believe, you and I both know that the two of you hadn't been together for a very long time. He wasn't living with you. He was living with me. And he died in another woman's arms."

Tassie's eyes flashed fire. "Did you come here to gloat— you filthy home wrecker?"

"Home wrecker? Lady, you obviously did a great job wrecking your own home, considering Eli didn't ever tell me you existed!" I didn't mean to yell those last words, but this woman was getting on my last nerve.

Tassie threw a hand over her heart and gasped. Then her tears came. "You dare to come to *my* husband's funeral and speak to me this way?"

"I came to say goodbye to Eli. That's all."

"You have no right—"

"He was going to marry me," I stated. "I was a part of his life, whether you want to accept that fact or not."

Tassie sneered at me. An older woman standing near Tassie clutched a Bible to her chest and softly sobbed. Eli's mother?

"I know your type," Tassie said. "You want a man to give you the finer things in life. Well, consider yourself lucky that being with my husband afforded you a very nice lifestyle. But the free ride is over. Anything Eli owned is now rightfully mine."

Panic washed over me. "I have a daughter," I quickly said. "Fine, you don't have to like me, but think of her. She's only two. Please don't take her home from her."

"You mean *my* home." As if on cue, Tassie's expression changed from coldhearted bitch to dejected widow. She dabbed at her eyes. "Please, get out of my sight. I have nothing more to say to my husband's filthy mistress."

The words stung—mainly because everyone in the room probably saw me that way, even though it was completely untrue.

"You and I both know the truth," I said as calmly as I could. Everyone was watching us, but I was beyond caring. "Yet you've made me out to be the Whore of Babylon in the press—"

"Perhaps because you are," Tassie replied equally as calmly, with no hint of grief in her voice, just coldness.

I wanted to belt her. I think I even balled my hand in a fist to do so. But then Alaina pulled hard on my arm, jarring me out of the ugly scenario with Tassie.

"Let's go," she said.

I started for the door with her, but behind us Tassie cried, "Security!"

Damn her. Like we hadn't been on our way out!

Around the corner and into the sanctuary came the two burly men we'd seen outside. "These two women have crashed my dear husband's visitation," Tassie said, her voice cracking. "Get them out of here!"

I turned to shoot Tassie a look of disgust. When I did, she rolled her eyes backward and proceeded to faint.

Nice, I thought, not buying any of it. Then two thick hands locked around my upper arms. My eyes widened in alarm, and instinctively, I started to struggle.

"Don't touch me, you jerk!" Alaina yelled, and I glanced her way in time to see a man wrap his arms around her wriggling form and lift her off her feet.

My beefcake did the same to me.

Just before the guard whisked me out of the sanctuary, I glanced in Tassie's direction. People were fawning all over her, fanning her face, helping her sit up.

She was playing the part of the grieving widow perfectly. But as the woman's eyes locked on mine, her mouth lifted in the slightest of smirks.

The bitch.

And then I was being carried through the parlor and out the front door.

"Watch your hands, you slimeball!" Alaina yelled in disgust.

The beefcake dropped me onto the step's concrete landing as though I were a bag of garbage to be disposed of.

It was then I remembered the news cameras we'd seen earlier. Seeing the commotion, cameramen and photographers frantically rushed closer to get a better shot of us.

"Oh, God," I muttered.

Alaina shoved the guy who'd removed her from the church. "If you ever lay another finger on me…" Her words trailed off. It was an empty threat, and the bodyguard didn't even respond. He just resumed his stance outside the door, looking straight ahead.

None too gracefully, I bounded down the front steps. I darted past the cameras, ignored the questions being shouted from reporters, and sprinted to the car as fast as I could in my Manolos.

I heard the beeping sound that indicated the locks had opened, and I said a silent prayer of thanks that Alaina had made sure to use her keyless remote.

I yanked the passenger door open and jumped inside.

Alaina did the same on the driver's side. Only after she was in and the doors once again locked did I remember my hat.

"Ally—my hat!"

She gaped at me. "You want to go back for it?"

I groaned. Of course I didn't. But it pissed me off that Tassie Johnson had snatched the hat I'd paid eighty bucks for.

Looking at the church as Alaina peeled out of the parking lot, I thought to myself, *You can have the hat, Tassie, but I'll be damned if you take my home.*

chapter fourteen

About two hours into our drive back to Miami, I started laughing. Hysterically.

Alaina looked at me. "What's so funny?"

"Oh my God," I said between chuckles. "Was that crazy or *what?*"

"Girl, you've lost your mind."

"And when Tassie fainted…I mean, come on! Then that gorilla had you, and your feet and hands were flailing…"

"You think this whole thing is funny?"

My laughing tapered off. "Ally, I've got to laugh about it, or I'm gonna—"

I didn't get the last of my words out before I burst into tears. I wasn't even sure why I was crying, because even though the situation had ended badly, I'd accomplished what I had set out to do.

I'd seen Eli, and knew without any smidgen of a doubt that he was dead.

The thought made me cry even harder.

"Oh, sweetie. Don't cry."

"I just… That bitch has the nerve to be acting like a grieving widow, when she knows she and Eli hadn't been together for years. Now she wants to take my very home from me? How can this be right?"

"You want me to pull over?"

"No," I said, wiping at my tears. "I want to get home to Rayna."

"Hon, I've got some savings. Not much, just around five grand, but—"

"Absolutely not. You need that money for you and your kids."

"I'm happy to loan it to you."

"And when would I pay it back?" I shook my head. "I appreciate you caring, Ally. I really do. And I can't thank you enough for going to Atlanta with me. But I need to find a way to have Eli's wife back down once and for all. I'll bet she's got some huge multimillion-dollar house in an exclusive area of Atlanta. Why does she need my condo in South Beach?"

"I hate to even suggest this, but maybe you have to go to Lewis for a loan."

"No," I said without hesitation. "I can't go to Lewis."

"Do you have a choice?"

The question was valid, but I didn't want to hear it. And I didn't want to tell Alaina that I'd already spoken with Lewis, and that if he was going to help me there was a string attached I couldn't deal with.

"Something's seriously wrong with me, isn't there?" I asked.

"Why—because you wanted to see Eli one last time?"

I shook my head. "Because time after time, I end up with guys who break my heart."

"There aren't a lot of decent guys out there," Alaina said. "It's really easy to find the bad ones."

"I didn't even think outside our little circle," I mused. "It was me and Rayna and Eli, and I was fine with that. Never once did I think about the bigger picture. His family, whether they would like me, should I meet them before I said yes to his proposal… It never mattered to me. Like I was dumb enough to believe that the three of us would live in our own world for the rest of our lives."

Alaina gave my hand a quick squeeze. "Don't be so hard on yourself."

"How do you date a guy for two years and not know he'll be the type to abandon his own child?" I asked, speaking now of Byron.

"Sometimes you just can't know a person, no matter how much time you spend with them."

"And Lewis. I should have known better where he was concerned, but I let myself fall in love with him anyway."

"In your defense, Lewis is seriously fine."

"And Eli." I shook my head slowly. "Damn Eli. When I think back now, I can see some of the signs I missed. Issues I never pressed him on. Like why he was so upset when I placed our engagement announcement in the paper. I should have known his answer was bullshit. And like why he didn't want to tell his mother about me. And why he sometimes seemed so sad when he looked at Rayna. Why didn't I press him on all this stuff? Maybe because deep down, I didn't want to know something that would ruin the illusion of perfection. I'm so stupid."

"Aw, sweetie. Don't say that."

"I'm pretty sure I saw his mother at the church. The older lady standing near Tassie…looking at me with such…*disappointment*. What must she think of me?"

"Unfortunately, you can't help what she thinks," Alaina said.

"You think he loved me, don't you?" I asked. Alaina had met Eli. "But if he loved me, why all the lies?"

"I wish I had answers for you. I learned the hard way that men can claim to love you, and still hurt you."

"I know," I said. I paused as I thought. "Leroy was Eli's best friend. He had to have known that Eli was married, that he had kids. Yet never once did he mention it. But he's damn well gonna give me some answers now."

I dug my cell phone out of my purse and called Leroy's number. It rang until his voice mail picked up.

Of course. He was certainly in Atlanta right now, at Eli's funeral.

"Leroy, it's Vanessa," I said matter-of-factly. "We need to talk. About Eli. Call me at home as soon as you get this message."

No sooner had I ended the call than my cell phone rang. I exchanged a quick look with Alaina, both of us wondering the same thing. Was Leroy calling me back already?

I lowered my eyes to the caller ID screen. It was Carla's number. I pressed the talk button and said, "Carla, everything okay?"

"Tell me that wasn't really you I just saw on CNN."

"What?" I shrieked.

"Being dragged out of some church in Atlanta where Eli's funeral is being held."

I closed my eyes and moaned. "Yeah. That was me."

"Vanessa!"

Lord only knew how the media had portrayed what had happened. And hell, I didn't want to imagine the statement Tassie had likely given to the press.

"Is it bad?" I asked weakly.

"Mistress crashes her lover's funeral? Yeah, it's pretty bad."

I groaned long and loud. "I just wanted to see him. I needed to say goodbye."

"That you did."

"Is Rayna okay?"

"Yeah. She didn't see the television."

"Good. I'm on my way home. I'll see you this evening."

"Okay, hon."

I ended the call and turned my ringer off. I knew—just knew—that the next call would be from my sister, and I couldn't deal with that.

I settled back in my seat, wishing this whole situation was a simple nightmare, but very aware that it wasn't.

When we reached Miami, Alaina drove to her house in Kendall, where I'd picked her up. She turned to me and asked, "You want to come in for a drink?"

"Any other time and I wouldn't mind, but it's been a long couple of days. I just want to head home and see my little girl."

Alaina rubbed my arm. "I hear you."

"Sorry you didn't get to meet any hot guys at the funeral."

"No big deal," she told me. "My ex would only squash that, anyway." She smiled, but I knew that was a very real concern. Jorge, though divorced from Alaina, still seemed to believe he should be able to control what she did.

Alaina and I both got out of the car. I gave her a hug, then got behind the wheel and drove off.

Forty minutes later, I was at the door to Carla's apartment. When it swung open, Carla had Rayna in her arms.

A smile as wide as the Atlantic erupted on my daughter's face, and she flung herself forward, reaching for me. I took her in my arms and hugged her long and hard.

I stepped into the apartment, sighing loudly as I did. Carla shook her head. "Girl, you have had quite the day."

"Understatement of the century. At least I didn't see any camera crews downstairs."

"You're our resident media starlet."

I huffed. "Yeah, right."

Rayna kept her little arms securely around my neck as I sank onto Carla's plush sofa. I guessed she was tired. Or maybe she missed me terribly last night and didn't want to let me go. It was a rare occasion when she slept over at Carla's.

"How was Rayna last night?" I asked.

"Oh, a little testy. She took a while to fall asleep."

I kissed her forehead, and she snuggled closer to me. "I'm sorry I had to leave you, baby."

"Don't go."

"It's okay. Mommy's not leaving you again."

I spent the next twenty minutes filling Carla in on all that had transpired, and concluded with my feeling that Tassie

Johnson was going to try to screw me out of my home simply for the joy of it.

"You should have seen the smirk on her face after she pretended to faint," I told Carla. "She's a piece of work."

"You're not going to want to see the CNN clip," Carla warned.

"That bad?"

"Tassie's spin on things is…let's just say, quite different than yours."

"Great." I sighed. "All this grief because of a man. If you ever hear me talk about dating again, shoot me."

An hour and a half later we were back home and Rayna had unexpectedly fallen asleep. I forced myself to turn on the television. I might as well find out now if I'd need to have facial reconstruction to protect my identity from here on in.

I had a glass of wine in hand, however, knowing I might need it.

It took nearly fifteen minutes before CNN got around to the spectacle in Atlanta. And trust me, spectacle was the nicest way to describe it. The newscaster described it as another "bizarre" twist in what was a "verified soap opera."

On the audio, you could clearly hear Alaina threatening the bodyguard who had escorted her out of the church. And you could see me fleeing the church like a convicted felon on the run from the police. Then the camera got a close-up of my face, showing me in a state of total panic.

I downed my glass of wine and poured another. It was becoming a habit, yes, but I had nothing else to take the edge off of what had been a surreal week.

The worst part, by far, was the interview with Tassie, who appeared so distraught by my "crashing" Eli's funeral that one would believe her on the edge of a nervous breakdown.

"I am too much of a lady to repeat all the evil things that immoral woman said to me. She came here to gloat, to make me feel like I had failed as a wife. As if it wasn't bad enough that she tried to steal my husband from me in life, she wanted to mar these final hours that his friends and family could be with him. For that, I will never forgive her. She is a gold digger and a whore. A truly despicable human being."

Then Tassie burst into loud, gasping sobs and needed to be helped to a seat.

I turned the television off and vowed never to watch another newscast for as long as I lived.

I gulped down one more glass of wine, then contemplated looking up cosmetic surgeons in the Yellow Pages. Because after the latest news coverage, it was official.

I wouldn't be able to show my face around town again.

The next morning, Alaina called. She told me she had her boys back and, after yesterday's stressful day, suggested we get together for a play date with the kids at the beach.

"Do you mind if I invite my neighbor Carla?"

"Sure," Alaina agreed.

Three hours later, we were all at Lummus Park Beach. Though the play date was nothing fancy, for the kids it was like we'd taken them to Disney World. We had a picnic on the sand, lots of toys for them to play with, and for the moms we had a couple of coolers, as well.

Rayna got along with Alaina's twins fabulously, as did Amani.

I couldn't say the same for Carla, who seemed to be off in another world.

Carla stood suddenly. "I'm gonna dip my feet in the water."

"We'll watch the kids," I assured her.

When Carla was gone, I turned to Alaina and repeated a question she had ignored when Carla had been beside me. "I'm dying to know," I began. "What happened with Richie? He really didn't call you back?"

Alaina tipped her vodka cooler to her mouth, then shook her head. "Nope."

"I thought you had to be kidding. Surely not another one."

She shrugged nonchalantly.

"That's what—six guys since your divorce became final?"

"Seven, but who's counting?"

This couldn't be coincidence. Either every guy was scared off by the fact that she was a single mother, or something else was going on. In the past we'd joked about her husband possibly following her, and now I had to wonder if that was the reality.

"Did you call Richie?" I asked.

"Oh, I called him. Last night."

"And what did he say?"

"That he liked me a lot, and for that reason didn't want to lead me on, but that he just wasn't *into* me."

"Get out." I couldn't have been more shocked. "The guy who gave you an emerald bracelet on your first date isn't into you?"

"So he says."

A beat passed. Then I said, "We've joked about this before, but do you really think your ex is behind this somehow?"

"Oh, I'm sure he is." Alaina spoke with a conviction she previously hadn't. "This morning, when he dropped off the kids, he asked me if I'd been on any 'hot dates' lately. It's like he knows."

"Oh my God."

"Tell me about it. It just makes sense. I don't know how he does it, but he knows where I've been and who I've been out with, and I wouldn't put it past him to show up at the guy's place in his uniform and *intimidate* him."

"Using the badge to be a jerk. He shouldn't be allowed to get away with this."

"I guess he meant what he always said—if he can't have me, no one can."

"But that doesn't make any sense," I protested. "He's the one who cheated on you!"

"With several women."

"Exactly!"

"I don't know." Alaina shrugged. "Jorge is the typical macho Cuban guy—it's okay for him to stray, but his woman can't look twice at another man."

"That's the problem. You're not his woman anymore."

Alaina took another swig of her cooler, then her gaze moved ahead of her. I followed her line of sight and saw that Carla was heading back toward us.

She was completely wet. "The water's a bit nippy, but it's warm once you go in."

"That's an idea," Alaina said, standing. "I'm gonna take the boys to the water."

When Alaina was gone, I turned to Carla. "Everything okay? You've been a bit quiet. Is it Alaina—you don't like her?"

"Your friend is fine."

"Then what's going on?"

Carla didn't answer right away, and alarm spread through me. "You upset with *me?*"

Rayna suddenly jumped up from her spot on the sand and ran over to me. Smiling, she pressed her head against my stomach.

That smile warmed me right down to my toes. "Hi, baby," I said. I stroked her face. "Having fun?"

She nodded, then stood upright and took my hand. "Come see castle."

The castle she and Amani had been building was only a few feet away, but I let Rayna lead me to the spot. "What a beautiful castle," I said of the pile of wet sand. "Want Mommy to help you make some windows?"

"Yes, yes!" Rayna jumped up and down. When she settled, I poked her distended stomach, and she giggled. Then I pulled her onto my lap. "Let me show you how to make some windows and doors."

By the time I carved one window with my finger, Rayna and Amani were already following my example. I glanced over my shoulder at Carla, who still seemed unhappy.

Leaving the sand castle in the girls' hands, I went back to my chair. "You sure you're not mad at me?" I asked Carla.

"No. Of course not. But I was wondering if you're free tonight?"

"I have no plans."

"Then do you mind watching Amani?"

"I'd be happy to." I paused. "What are you up to?"

"I'm gonna hit the strip with Allette," she said, referring to a friend of hers who lived on the third floor. Like Carla, she was also a military wife. Unlike Carla, Allette had a job. She was a very successful science fiction author. I'd seen the eccentric-looking redhead a few times, but didn't know her.

"Ah, so you're gonna spice up your Sunday night with Allette." I felt a small stab of envy that Carla hadn't thought to invite me, but I knew it would be hard to arrange the babysitting. "Sounds like fun."

"I can't wait. I haven't been out in ages."

She should have been more excited, which led me to wonder if there was something going on that she wasn't sharing. Surely if she was upset with me for some reason, she would tell me.

Two women strolled by me, and I swear, they both pointed and sneered.

"Did you see that?" I asked Carla. "How those women looked at me?"

Carla shook her head, seemingly lost in her own thoughts.

I didn't think I was being paranoid. Those women *had* given me a dirty look. They'd likely seen me on CNN and had the worst possible opinion of me.

We spent another hour at the beach, the kids playing happily in the sand, us women making small talk.

"We should do this again sometime," I said as we all ambled toward the street. "The kids loved it."

I gazed happily at Rayna, Amani, Rob and Eric—all

walking hand in hand. It made me long for that big family Eli had promised me.

"Look at them," I said wistfully. "They're so cute."

No sooner had Alaina agreed with my sentiment than Rayna broke free of the group and took off. She ran faster than one would think possible for two little feet. I saw immediately what had attracted her—a colorful beach ball bouncing around in the middle of the road.

"Rayna, stop!" I screamed, and when she didn't, I gave chase. I reached her just as she was about to run off the sidewalk and into the path of certain death.

Fear that she'd jump in front of the approaching car had me grabbing her by the arm and propelling her backward. But I guess I grabbed her a little too hard, because she screamed and burst into tears.

I scooped her up. "Rayna, you have to listen to Mommy. When Mommy says stop, you stop!" My stern words only made her cry louder, so I took a breath and continued in a softer tone. "You see the cars, honey? If you run in the road, you're going to get hurt. Hurt very badly."

"Daddy," Rayna sobbed, and the simple word made my heart ache. Typical child, having been scolded by one parent, she wanted the other to comfort her.

But of course, her daddy wasn't coming back.

I held Rayna close as she bawled, thinking that had been a close call. And if I'd lost Rayna…well, there was no way I could go on.

"Was that necessary?" I heard a voice ask.

I turned to my left to see a dark-haired man, fortyish, staring at me as though he thought I was Psycho Mom.

"Excuse me?"

"She's only little. She needs comfort, not to be yelled at. And the way you yanked her…"

I couldn't believe this man. Who the hell was he to accuse me of treating my child improperly?

"What would you have preferred I do? Let her run into traffic and get hit by a car?"

Alaina placed her hand on the small of my back. "Let it go."

"There are other ways to control your kids," the man insisted.

I wanted to tell him exactly where he could shove his opinion, but I had Rayna in my arms and didn't want to subject her to further ugliness. Instead I said to him, "Mind your own damn business."

"You're lucky I don't call the police," he said.

And that was when I snapped. I was dealing with so much grief already, I didn't need this.

"You know what—go fuck yourself."

Angrily, I marched off.

Rayna, no longer quiet, seemed curious. She said softly, "Fuck yourself."

My eyes bulged. *Oh, shit.* "Rayna, sweetie. Don't say that."

"Fuck yourself," she repeated, and this time laughed. So did Carla and Alaina.

"Oh my God," I groaned. "I can only imagine what that jerk would say if he could hear Rayna repeating my crass words. Maybe I am a bad mother."

Alaina rubbed my shoulder. "Don't say that! Of course you're not a bad mother."

"Really, though—what did he expect? It's like people

would rather you take the wimpy approach to parenting. Oh, Rayna—watch for the cars," I mimicked in a feeble tone. "Oops, she's dead. Gimme a break."

"He's clueless," Carla said. "It doesn't matter what he said."

"It just makes my blood boil," I fumed. "I am trying so hard to do this all on my own. When Eli came into my life, I thought…" I didn't finish my statement, not wanting to once again think about how all my dreams had so abruptly ended almost one week ago.

"It's not easy," I continued. "But I'm doing the best I can. And it seems that all people want to do is criticize me. Do they say, 'Excuse me, miss, it looks like your hands are full—can I help you carry those groceries to your car?' No. But if you leave your child in the car for one second to return the cart, they look at you like you're neglectful. I'm so sick of all the judgmental people in the world."

When I finished my rant, I was well aware that I'd vented about the laundry list of things that had irked me since I'd become a mother, and not the current situation.

Carla put a hand on my shoulder and made me stop. "This is about Eli's wife, isn't it? What she said about you on television."

Just hearing the words *Eli's wife* made me want to find a toilet and puke. "Maybe it is," I admitted sadly. "She called me a gold digger. Me. She has no clue how I met Eli, how our relationship developed. Eli was the one who pursued me."

"She doesn't matter," Alaina said. "Don't let her worthless opinion get you down."

"Well, she made her worthless opinion very public on national television. Even walking down the street, I've seen people stare at me, give me dirty looks. What makes people feel they have the right to judge me?"

"No one has the right to judge you," Alaina concurred. Then she pulled me into a hug. "Everyone who knows you, loves you."

"Thanks," I said.

"You gonna be okay?"

"Sure. I'm fine."

Alaina nodded. "My car's right over there, so I'm gonna run. See you tomorrow?"

"Bright and early."

"Thanks for agreeing to this play date," she added. "It was fun." She turned to Carla. "It was great to meet you."

"Likewise," Carla said.

We both watched as Alaina took her boys to the car. Once they were settled in, Carla and I continued strolling down the street.

Very obviously, a middle-aged woman looked at me, then glared.

"You saw that?" I asked Carla.

"Yeah, I did."

"People *hate* me. And they don't even know me."

"Why don't you take that reporter up on her offer? You said she left you a message, saying you could give her your exclusive—your side of the story. Maybe she wants to help."

"So in order to salvage my image, I have to get into the media ring and slug it out? I don't want to play that game. Besides, after the way the media crucified me, I'll never trust another reporter."

I started to walk again, and Carla fell into step beside me.

"Maybe I can change my plans tonight. Get Allette to watch both our kids and we can go out."

"It's okay," I said. "You and Allette go out. I'd be no fun tonight."

"No. Don't stay at home and mope. You've had a really awful week, dealt with some really tough stuff. If anyone needs to have some fun, it's you."

"Trust me, I'm not prepared to have any more strangers looking at me with scorn. People who saw the poor, grieving Mrs. Johnson on television and think I'm the biggest bitch on the planet."

"You sure? I think it could be good for you…"

"Yeah. I'm sure. But you go out. I know it's been a while since you've let loose."

Carla grinned. "Thanks."

I squeezed her hand, thankful to have her and Alaina in my life, women I knew would never betray me the way the men in my life had. "Anything for you, Carla. Anything."

chapter fifteen

Hours later, as I sat on the living room floor with Rayna and Amani, playing a board game for kids, the phone rang. I left Rayna and Amani with the game and made my way to the cordless handset. When I saw Leroy's number, I quickly snatched up the receiver.

I pressed the talk button and said, "Leroy."

"Hey, Vanessa."

"Thank you for getting back to me." My tone was clipped. I deliberately avoided a friendly greeting because I was angry with him. Yes, I'd been engaged to Eli, and Eli should have come clean about his wife and kids, but Leroy had to know they existed. And I'm sure he knew Eli had neglected to tell me about them. In fact, I distinctly remembered Leroy mentioning Eli's "nephews" to me after that night at the Christmas party. Eli had likely told him I'd overheard Tina's question, and Leroy had perpetuated the nephew story a week later so I wouldn't have any doubts.

"How're you holding up?" Leroy asked me.

"Oh, I've been a helluva lot better."

"I know the feeling."

"I'm not sure you do," I said. When Leroy didn't speak, I got the feeling that he'd caught my meaning, so I went on. "You were Eli's best friend. You had to know he was still married, that he had kids. How could you not tell me?"

The pause that ensued was long and heavy. "I saw you at the funeral. I was trying to get to you as you were leaving the church, but…"

"But what?"

"You want the truth?"

"That's exactly what I want. No more bullshit."

"I was ashamed to face you. Yeah, I knew Eli was still officially married. I knew he had a couple kids. I'm sure you hate him for lying to you. Maybe you hate me, too."

Did I hate Eli? Was there any point in hating him? "I want to understand," I said. "I thought Eli was my everything, and then I learn our whole relationship was a lie."

"No! That's just it, it wasn't a lie."

I snorted in derision.

"Seriously, Vanessa. Hear me out. Eli loved you. He wanted to marry you."

"Except he already *was* married," I couldn't help interjecting. I didn't want to have this conversation in front of Rayna and Amani, so I slipped out of the living room and went to my bedroom. A *My Little Pony* movie was playing on the television, so if the girls got bored with the game, I hoped the movie would hold their attention until I was finished talking to Leroy. "Not to mention the married woman he was *sleeping* with," I added sourly as I sat on my bed. "You know—the one whose husband killed them?"

"Admittedly, Eli had a roving eye. That always was his thing. He had a weakness for pretty ladies."

That wasn't what I wanted to hear. Ultimately, it wasn't what mattered.

"But he loved you with a passion," Leroy insisted.

"So much so that he lied to me about everything that mattered most!"

"You think it was easy for Eli to keep the truth from you?"

"Obviously."

"It wasn't. Trust me. And since you said you want no more bullshit, I'll tell you something else. It's my fault Eli didn't tell you about his wife and kids."

"What?"

"He wanted to. It was eating him up most of the time. But you have to understand how evil that bitch he was married to is. Sure, he cheated on her, but he also set her up real nicely. And she was nothing but a thorn in his side."

"What's your point? I told Eli all about my crazy exes."

"You remember you and Eli originally wanted to get married this September?"

"Of course. We rescheduled for late next year because we needed time to adequately plan the wedding."

"That's one reason," Leroy said slowly. "The main one, however, is because Tassie was giving him a hard time about the divorce. She knew about you—found out about you after you placed that engagement announcement—and she flipped. She'd been a royal bitch before but, man, she got even worse. Eli and Tassie had been going back and forth over the divorce terms for years, and Tassie always wanted more. At one point, it just became easier for Eli to move on. But he started the proceedings again when he knew he wanted to marry you. Nothing he offered her was good enough. He'd hoped to have it all ironed out by the end of the year so he could go forward with his plans to marry you."

I took a moment to process what Leroy had told me. So Tassie had known about me before Eli's murder. And I knew from my brief experience with her that she was an überbitch. "Okay, let's say I can understand why Eli might have kept the fact that he was still legally married from me. How could he not tell me about his kids? Was he secretly seeing them and keeping that from me? Or did he have nothing to do with them? What on earth could be his motivation for lying to me about his kids when I'm a single mother myself?"

"Tassie poisoned the boys against him."

"That's no excuse—"

"You don't know Tassie. Eli loved his boys. More than anything. For the first few years after they separated, he saw the kids pretty regularly. Then, one day, Eli noticed a change in them on his visits. They'd act up, throw tantrums. The older one straight up told him he didn't want to see him anymore. They wouldn't talk to him on the phone, told the judge in a custody hearing they didn't want to see him. It broke his heart, and there was nothing he could do because of Tassie's brainwashing. But the worst thing was, Tassie said if Eli went ahead and tried to get joint custody of the kids, she'd tell the world he used to molest them."

I gasped sharply. "No!"

"It was a nightmare for Eli. He couldn't see his kids, they seemed to hate him… After a while, it was just too hard for him to talk about them."

Poor Eli. What kind of woman could so viciously use her children to hurt the man she'd once loved? How awful it must have been for him to go through that.

I said softly, "He still could have told me."

"And how would that look to you? The guy you'd fallen in love with had a couple kids he wasn't in touch with? Plus a wife he was technically still married to? Eli didn't think you'd understand."

"He should have trusted me."

"Eli told me what you said the night you two first met— that you didn't understand how any man could walk away from his children."

"This is an entirely different situation," I argued.

"Is it?" Leroy asked. "Maybe you would have thought he could have fought harder. Maybe your own situation with Rayna's father would have made it impossible for you to *not* judge Eli harshly."

Was Leroy right? Would I have understood?

"He wanted to tell you, though," Leroy continued. "I was the one who warned him not to. I told him, 'You really like this girl, you can't tell her any of this. Not till you've worked your shit out.' I told him you'd dump him in a New York minute, even if you understood. A nice girl like you, you wouldn't want to deal with all that drama. Eli finally agreed. As long as the divorce went through before your wedding, there'd be no problem. As for the kids, he figured he'd tell you about them once you were married."

"Gee. Great plan."

"Eli didn't want to lose you."

"Right." I drew in a shaky breath. I'd actually been feeling sorry for Eli while listening to Leroy, but I suddenly remembered the circumstances under which he'd been killed. "All this stuff about his wife, his kids…fine. Let's say I get it. Nothing justifies the fact that he was killed in *another woman's bed*."

"I know, I know. Eli was weak that way. But he'd been faithful to you until that night you had that fight. He used to mess around with Alyssa in the past, and I guess that night he got foolish. He told me she'd been calling him nonstop, telling him how much she missed him."

"She was married!"

"To some rich guy she didn't love. And, man, she was hot."

"Of course, that makes it perfectly all right," I said snidely. I got off my bed and walked out my bedroom door to spy on Rayna and Amani. They were both sitting on the floor watching the movie. I slipped back into the bedroom.

"Hey, I told Eli not to do it. He called me after your fight, fuming, wondering if you'd ever accept him as a father for your child—"

"I already had!"

"Yeah, but he was also feeling guilt over the lack of relationship with his own kids…. He told me that sometimes being around Rayna made him miss them so much more. I guess he wanted an escape from it all, even for one night."

"And he got it." Emotion was threatening to overwhelm me. I needed to end this call. "Look, Leroy, I've got to go."

"I mean it when I say Eli loved you. He really did. You were good for him."

Just not good enough for him to be faithful to me.

"He made a mistake," Leroy said. "Try to forgive him. And I hope you can forgive me."

I hung up just as the tears started to roll down my cheeks. Damn it, I didn't think I was going to cry over Eli again, not with everything I'd learned about him. But talking about him at length, and Leroy's affirmation that he loved me, were too much for me to deal with.

I had answers. Answers I wasn't sure I'd ever understand, even if on some level I could see why Eli had taken the easy way out of a difficult situation. Still, it didn't excuse his behavior, but I could cling to the belief that Eli's feelings for me had been real.

And oddly enough, I also felt a little better about Leroy's assertion that Eli had been faithful to me until the day he'd been killed. In a way it was comforting to know that it *had* been our argument that had sent him into another woman's arms, rather than the fact that he'd been screwing around behind my back for months.

I brushed away my tears, then slowly made my way back into the living room. It was almost eight-thirty. Time to get Rayna and Amani to bed.

By nine-thirty, I was on the phone with Alaina, and I'd filled her in on everything Leroy had told me. My emotions were going up and down, down and up, like they were traveling on a roller-coaster ride. One minute I understood Eli's motivation. The next, I didn't see how he couldn't trust me with what he was going through.

"I want to understand, to forgive him," I said to Alaina.

"Eli was so great with my baby. But I don't care what his wife was threatening to do. Why didn't he think he could tell me about his kids? Didn't he trust me enough?"

"I don't think it's that," Alaina said. "My cousin Pedro did the same thing. He got married when he was young, and when things got ugly between him and his wife, he left her and their young son, married someone else, and hasn't even seen his kid since then. Not because he doesn't love him, but because he can't deal with Elisabeth. He's got two more kids now, loves them to death... He's a great father."

"You're serious?"

"Absolutely. And he really is a great dad."

I digested that information for a moment, tried to come to grips with its seemingly paradoxical nature. "Then this just goes to show that I'll never understand men as long as I live."

"Some women are evil, evil bitches. They'll make men do things they'd never even consider under normal circumstances."

I sipped my iced tea. "He could have told me. He's not the first person in the world to deal with a crazy ex. I would have supported him."

"Maybe it's like Leroy said. He didn't want you getting caught up in all the drama."

"And tell me everything after the wedding when he figured I wouldn't divorce him?"

"You know how men are. They want to fix a problem on their own. I guess he figured after you were married, there wouldn't be an issue with Tassie anymore."

"And I'd just forgive him for not telling me about the kids," I said wryly. "Nice plan."

"Would you have divorced him when he told you about the kids after you were married?" Alaina asked, the hint of a challenge in her voice.

I thought for a long moment. I would have been angry, absolutely. But divorce him? "I guess not," I answered honestly.

"Then it wasn't such a dumb plan, after all."

Alaina had me there. But still. "You think I'm making a big deal out of nothing?"

"I'm not saying that. I'm just… I guess I'm saying that I do believe he really loved you, but that he handled the situation badly. Now, him screwing that other woman, that's a whole other issue. But lying about the kids? Think about it. What if he'd told you that his wife's plan was to scream 'child molester' if he went to court for joint custody? Wouldn't you just maybe wonder if where there's smoke, there might be fire?"

I hadn't even considered that.

"Exactly. So, Eli could have lost you based on this bitch's *allegation*. Girl, I see why he kept all this shit secret."

I couldn't believe it. Alaina was giving Eli her complete support.

But she had a damn good point. I'd dealt with Tassie personally now. I knew how evil she was. But if Eli had given me his side of this twisted story before I'd ever had the misfortune of dealing with the woman…I can't say I wouldn't have erred on the side of caution, for Rayna's sake.

"Well, none of it matters anymore," I said, wandering to my bedroom window. "And given what Leroy told me about Eli's roaming eye, I guess I should be happy we didn't end up getting married."

"You'll find someone else," Alaina assured me. "You know you always do."

My eyes widened at the comment, but I let it slide. I didn't always find someone else. Sure, I had my share of dates, but nothing ever worked out for me. Eli's murder had to be proof of that. I had more man drama than one person should have to experience.

I rested my hip on the window ledge and looked down at the street, at the few people strolling by. "Alaina, thanks for letting me talk your ear off. I appreciate it."

"No problem."

"I'll see you at work tomorrow."

"Sleep well."

"Thanks."

I ended the call and continued to stare out the window. And then my eyes narrowed as they focused on a person below.

Was that Allette?

Sure enough, Allette was strolling hand in hand with her husband toward the building's front doors. The two were nicely dressed, as though they were returning home from dinner.

Carla was nowhere in sight.

I frowned. Carla had claimed that she was meeting Allette at her apartment at eight, and that the two were heading to Mango's to party at least until midnight. Yet Allette was with her husband.

Obviously, she and Carla hadn't met, after all.

So where *was* Carla?

And more importantly, why had she lied to me?

chapter sixteen

The month that followed was far less insane than the week Eli had died. Thankfully. But that's not to say it didn't have any drama—because it did.

First, it was clear with each day that passed that my situation was getting no better. I'd heard from Tassie's lawyer five more times.

Four times, I hadn't returned his calls. Until his last message, three weeks after Eli's death, threatened legal action. I did call him back then, and told him that I was working on a way to pay Tassie off. I also asked about Eli's will, and he confirmed my suspicion that neither Rayna nor I had been left even a penny. I doubt Eli thought he would die when he did, and therefore hadn't seen the need to update his will.

The good news was that I'd spoken with the bank and learned that, yes, with Eli's death, the mortgage would be paid off. That was great news. But the last thing I wanted to do was hand over the condo I considered rightfully mine to someone who had plenty and didn't need it. It'd be one thing if Tassie and her children were destitute, but that simply wasn't the case.

I'd done my own digging, courtesy of a cheap private investigator, and had learned that she lived in a house worth three million dollars—with the mortgage paid off.

My low for the month had come last Friday, after work, when I'd learned—much to my embarrassment—that the ring Eli had given me was very nice, and very fake.

But, the pawnbroker had assured me, likely quite expensive for cubic zirconia.

"Yeah, this is a real nice fake," the overweight, bald man had said. "I'll give you three hundred for it—for the white gold. And that's being generous."

My mouth fell open in unabashed shock. "You're telling me this ring—this stunningly gorgeous ring—is *fake?*"

"It sure is, lady."

I snatched the ring up off the counter and left the shop with my head hanging low, even more depressed about what I was going to do. The idea had come to me that I could pawn my ring and get some sizable cash to help pay off Tassie.

And now…

Eli had screwed me yet gain.

I told myself that he had been duped when he bought the ring. I wouldn't allow myself to believe anything else.

Our relationship was real. I know it was. Even if he lied to me, he would never propose to me with a fake ring—not deliberately.

Ultimately, it didn't matter. The bottom line was that I was far from my goal of being able to pay Tassie off.

When I got home that Friday evening, I tossed the ring into my jewelry box and put Eli out of my mind. Then I picked Rayna up from Carla's, not bothering to tell her what I'd learned about the ring being practically worthless.

After all, a girl had to have a few secrets.

Carla clearly had hers.

I still hadn't asked her about that Sunday, when she'd claimed she was heading out with Allette. And she hadn't said anything.

I had my own issues to deal with.

It was all I could think of this second weekend of May, causing me to sleep fitfully on Saturday night. I really did need a plan to keep my home. I couldn't put off Tassie's lawyer much longer. On Sunday night, I did something I didn't typically like to do: took a sleeping pill to help me get some rest.

At last, I was able to fall into a deep and peaceful sleep—until the sound of my door opening jarred me awake.

My body froze with fear. Then I heard Rayna's happy laugh and her little feet scurrying into the room.

I threw a glance at my bedside clock: 1:24 in the morning. *Oh, God.*

Rayna climbed onto the bed, giggling. "Hi, Mommy."

"Rayna." My voice was a rumbling croak, my head in a drug-induced fog. "Sweetie, it's nighttime."

"Light on," she said.

Not tonight. God, why tonight? "Rayna, it's time to sleep."

"Light on," she repeated.

I didn't move, just closed my eyes and hoped that she would get the hint. Moments later, I must have drifted off, because I was jarred awake when she began to pat my face the way she liked to in the mornings if I was lying in bed and she wanted me up.

"Rayna…" I protested.

"Want chocolate milk."

Groaning, I sat up. I'd taken Rayna to the pool earlier, and she'd fallen asleep around seven—a disaster in the making, I knew. Far too often, if she fell asleep before 9:00 p.m., she woke up at some time in the night, refreshed and ready to play.

I reached for the lamp on my nightstand and turned it on. Rayna wore a smile far too bright for this time of the night.

"I don't know how you do it," I said as I stood.

"Up, up." Rayna stretched her arms to me so that I would lift her.

I did, pain already shooting through my head. Feeling like a zombie, I trudged to the kitchen, where I poured some chocolate milk into a bottle for her. Then I took a yogurt from the fridge and ate that before heading back to the bedroom.

My sister would say that I should put Rayna immediately back to bed when she woke up in the middle of the night, and not bother to get her anything to eat. On one level, I agreed. But I also knew Rayna, and when she was up, she was up. Besides, she'd barely eaten her supper before falling asleep, so it was reasonable for her to be famished.

I put her in her bed and left her drinking her bottle. Then I went back to my room to let sleep claim me once more.

But within minutes, she'd returned.

"Rayna…"

"Want to sleep with you, Mommy."

Damn, I wish I hadn't taken that sleeping pill. Come the morning, when I had to go to work, what kind of shape would I be in?

Once again, I turned on the light, ready to scold my daughter and insist that she stay in her bed. Then I stared at Rayna, into her big, dark eyes—and knew I couldn't say no.

"All right." I helped her up onto the bed beside me. "But it's still dark outside, which means it's time for sleep."

Rayna lay still for about five minutes, giving me hope that she'd make my life easy and fall back asleep. Then she climbed on top of me and started to bounce on my stomach.

Rayna was nowhere near ready to sleep again.

I secured her to my side. "Lie down, Rayna. And close your eyes."

She giggled.

No one takes me seriously, I thought. *That's my problem. Not Byron, not Lewis, and clearly not Eli. No wonder I can't keep a man.*

When Rayna sat up, I gave up the fight. I grabbed the remote control off my night table. Might as well turn on the TV and find some boring infomercial that would put both of us to sleep. It had worked in the past.

I flipped through channel after channel, searching for something that would work.

"My wittle pony," Rayna told me.

"Not right now, sweetie," I said. If I put on a movie she was interested in, she would be wide awake for the next ninety minutes.

I kept channel surfing. But I paused when I got to a station and saw a face that I knew very well.

Chaz Anderson, motivational speaker, was gracing the screen, talking about how to be your personal best.

I watched him. Not just because of what he was saying—which interested me because I was in the business—but because he was so darn beautiful.

Chaz Anderson was as hot as Denzel Washington, with a smile that rivaled Taye Diggs's. Chaz was a man who, in the past few years, had made a huge name for himself. It wasn't hard to see why. Seriously gorgeous looks and charisma that came through the screen. I wouldn't be surprised if the majority of the people making him rich were women.

"If you are serious about changing your life," he was saying, "you need to get real with yourself. You need to understand that what you put out in the universe is what you get back. If you put out negative energy, you'll get negative results."

I listened as Chaz went on, wondering if I unconsciously sent out the message of "desperate for a man" and if that was why the men in my life ended up hurting me.

Chaz was, of course, plugging his book and series of tapes in this infomercial. The book, *Unlocking the Door to Your Emotional and Financial Wealth,* was on sale for $29.99. The series of tapes were $59.99. But if I called in the next thirty minutes and bought the entire package, I would save thirty percent.

I worked in the business because I thought it was a fun industry, but a lot of the self-help/motivational/life coach stuff was pretty much the same. At least the core message was: believe in yourself and you can achieve anything you want.

Debbie had capitalized on that theme with the name of the agency.

From a business perspective, I could see the appeal of

being on the selling end. There was huge money to be made. People were looking for guidance, and were happy to pay a pretty penny for it. They were willing to be publicly humiliated on national talk shows to figure out how to lose weight, control their finances or to build their self-esteem.

From a personal perspective, I pretty much thought that a person was able to pull herself up by her bootstraps if she put her heart into it—without having to spend thousands to achieve that goal.

Absently, I snaked an arm around Rayna's waist. When she didn't react, I glanced down at her and saw that she was asleep.

Even though she'd woken me up, I smiled as I gazed at her. She looked like a little angel.

My little angel. No matter how trying it could sometimes be to parent alone, I would always be thankful for my precious gift from God.

I gave Rayna's cheek a soft kiss, then switched the television off.

As I snuggled my head against my pillow, my mind drifted back to that infomercial. Was I wrong to think that a person could pull herself up by her bootstraps on her own? Maybe it was harder than I thought.

Heck, perhaps *I* could benefit from some of the professional services my agency offered. Because from Byron to Lewis to Eli, I had clearly been doing something wrong.

The next morning, my brain still in a fog from fatigue, I turned on the *Today Show* as I got ready for work.

And saw Chaz Anderson's face.

"Exactly," Chaz was saying with a smile. He was sitting

back on the armchair, one foot resting easily on the opposite knee. Everything about him said he was comfortable—and confident—in his own skin.

You had to be confident to build an empire out of teaching people how to achieve their personal best.

"This weekend," host Ann Curry began, "you'll be in the Bahamas. Tell us about that."

"Absolutely. I'll be at the Atlantis Resort in the Bahamas, Paradise Island, where I'm hosting a four-day seminar on self-empowerment. It's the first of three I plan to hold there. The second will be in September, and the one following that in January."

"When people will be happy for an escape from winter," Ann pointed out.

"That's right."

"So your book, *Unlocking the Door to Your Emotional and Financial Wealth*." Ann held up a copy. "Tell the viewers at home what it's about."

"In this book, I lay out the three basic principles for success."

"Three?"

"Yes. I believe that there are only three. Spiritual, mental and physical. I go into more detail, of course, but if you can conquer those three areas, you've got it made."

"It doesn't sound very complicated."

"It doesn't have to be, but the reality is that for most of us, we don't always find a way to make these areas mesh." He linked his fingers. "And that's the key. If one area is out of sync, it puts everything off balance."

Chaz demonstrated with his hands, by holding one higher than the other to give the viewer a visual hook.

"It sounds fascinating," Ann said.

There was more chat about the upcoming seminars in the Bahamas, and then Ann started talking to him about his background.

"Now, is it true that you were homeless for a year?"

"Eleven months," Chaz said, almost proudly.

"Wow."

"I'd had my own business, then lost everything in the dot-com bust. I was married at the time, and down but not out. Only things got worse."

"Oh, no."

Chaz nodded. "Oh, yes. I had another idea—"

"You're not short of ideas, are you?"

"No." Chaz chuckled warmly. "But this idea my wife and business partner stole out from under me."

"You're kidding."

"No. Not only did I lose my marriage, I lost my home, and that's when I ended up homeless."

"Incredible," Ann said thoughtfully. "What did you do?"

"I lived with my brother for a year while I tried to rebuild, and spent much of the time being depressed. Then I realized that I had two choices—to spend the rest of my days moping over what I'd lost, or to pull myself up by the bootstraps and start anew."

"And that's when you took five thousand and turned it into a million dollars."

"That's right. I sold my car, got the five thousand cash and invested it in an idea I had."

He went on to talk about an invention, something to do with online security that I didn't understand, but the gist of it was that he'd been able to sell his idea to Microsoft and he'd earned a million dollars for it.

"After that, I realized I had a story to tell. That if a guy like me could go from being homeless to becoming a millionaire, I needed to share my experience with the world. The best way to do that was to write a book. Easy, right? Wrong. I couldn't get an agent to touch me, or a publisher, so I decided to self-publish my book, and that's when things took off. I did it on my own, and I've had lots of offers from agents since. But I feel like no one gave me a chance before. I got to where I am today on my own, and I'm happy to keep doing that."

"So you don't work with an agent?"

"No."

"Not even for your speaking engagements?"

"I arrange everything on my own."

As I sipped my coffee, I had an epiphany. I suddenly understood why I'd seen Chaz both last night and this morning. It wasn't coincidence.

Fate was at work.

He didn't work with an agency.

He was going to be in the Bahamas this weekend.

If I brought a high-profile client to the agency, I'd get a $25,000 bonus.

Twenty-five grand would be a good start in helping me resolve my issue with Tassie Johnson. And in the best-case scenario, enough to make her go away.

And if I brought Chaz to the agency, I would be one step closer to my dream of becoming an agent myself.

The answer to all my problems was instantly clear.

I had to go to the Bahamas and meet Chaz Anderson.

chapter seventeen

I went straight to Debbie's office as soon as I got to work. I told her about the interview I'd seen with Chaz, how he didn't work with an agent, but that I was determined to change that.

"It's fate," I said to Debbie. "For me to see him on television at two in the morning, then again on the *Today Show*—it was a huge sign."

Debbie eased her chair back and rested her designer-clad feet on the edge of her desk. "Let me get this straight. You want to go to the Bahamas to try and get Chaz Anderson to come to this agency."

"Right."

She laughed. "Nice thought, but I assure you it will be a waste of time."

"I don't think so."

"I read an article about him once. He boasted about how he'd been responsible for every bit of his own success, and saw no reason to have an agent."

"That doesn't mean he can't change his mind."

"And I suppose in another hundred million years or so, pigs might have wings."

"Nothing is impossible. Every day we work with clients who preach that mantra."

"I know. I'm just saying it's a stretch. A long one."

"But when will we ever have a better opportunity? I know where he'll be. I can register for the conference, pull out all the stops to meet him and talk to him. It's worth a shot, and I'm hoping you'll agree to give me Thursday and Friday off. Well, likely Wednesday as well, since I'll have to travel that day."

"You mean *this* week? As in two days from now?"

"He'll be in the Bahamas this weekend."

"This is the week I head to New York," Debbie said, lowering her feet from the desk. "I like for you to be here when I'm not."

"I know, but…someone else will be able to take the helm. Maybe that temp you brought in last week—Bonnie Bluegrass. She seemed very efficient." Not that I really knew, since I'd sent her home.

I took a seat opposite Debbie's desk, sighing. "Debbie, I know it's a big risk, but nothing ventured, nothing gained. I've got Eli's wife breathing down my neck, trying to take my home from me. I have to do something. If I can convince Chaz to sign with our agency, I'll get that signing bonus— and, Debbie, to say that I need it is the understatement of the century. I just feel like this is my one chance to make something really big happen. That if I can meet Chaz face-to-face, make an impression on him…"

Debbie's eyes slowly lit up. "Ahhh…I see where you're

going with this. Yes, yes. He's an attractive black man, you're an attractive black woman. You meet him, let nature take its course…"

"Well." I cleared my throat. "That's not exactly what I was saying."

"But it's a strategy. A damn good one." Debbie nodded enthusiastically. "And you just finished telling me that you need the signing bonus."

"I do. You know I do."

"And I want Chaz Anderson at this agency. Damn, I wish I didn't have those meetings in New York with Lori Hansen. I'd head to the Bahamas myself."

Debbie looked thoughtful for a moment, as if she was considering if she could reschedule her trip.

That was exactly what I *didn't* want. If she snagged Chaz, she wouldn't have to pay me the bonus.

"You *have* to meet with Lori," I said. "You just signed her. How would it look if you canceled your plans with her already? She might not be too happy with you."

"You're right," Debbie said after a moment. "No, I have to go to New York. Which means you need to go to Paradise Island."

"You'll let me go?" I asked excitedly.

"Yes."

"On official business?" I asked next, then held my breath.

"Of course on official business. Go ahead and book the flight and hotel from the agency account. But when you get to the Bahamas, you have to pull out *all* the stops to land Chaz as a client." She raised an eyebrow and looked me dead in the eye. "Whatever it takes."

I nodded. I was fairly certain that Debbie was suggesting I seduce him.

"Chaz is worth God only knows how many millions. He's doing very well, but we can take him to the next level. Tell him that we have contacts all over the world, that we can turn his millions into billions." She rolled her chair closer to her desk. "I can give you a list of key points to cover."

"All right," I agreed, but the truth was, I knew this agency inside and out. I might not be an agent, but as the office manager I was privy to how the business was run.

And I was ready for my chance to shine.

Back in my office, I called Carla and asked if she'd be able to watch Rayna for me for the entire four days that I would be away. I should have asked her before getting Debbie excited about the idea, but if Carla wasn't available, I'd beg my sister to care for my daughter.

Thankfully, Carla was available. It was going to cost me two hundred dollars extra in babysitting fees, a steal, quite frankly.

Not that I could afford the extra cash, but I'd make that money back a hundred times over once I got Chaz to sign with my agency.

Child care arranged, I called the travel agency we dealt with and booked my flight and secured a hotel room.

Only then did my stomach tighten with anxiety.

This was really happening.

I was a step closer to my dream.

Murphy's Law sucks big-time.

Of course, when I *needed* to hit the road so I'd get to the airport on time, Rayna decided to have a total meltdown.

She'd been sulking the entire morning Wednesday, while I prepared for my trip, as though she suspected what was coming in just a couple hours. Normally the only cereal she wanted was Cheerios, but not that morning. She flicked the spoon out of the bowl and splashed milk in my face and on the black Gucci dress I'd picked up on sale.

"Damn it!" I yelled, and Rayna had started to cry. She didn't stop crying even as I got her toast, nor while I got myself redressed.

And when I took her to Carla's place, she clung to me as if I were leaving her with the exorcist.

"Rayna," I cooed. "It's okay."

"Mommy! *Mommeee!*"

She must have realized that this wasn't a normal day. First, I didn't take her to Carla's place as early as I usually did, since my flight was leaving in the early afternoon and there was no point in me heading to work. Adults rarely give kids credit for being as smart as they are, and I firmly believe that Rayna knew I was leaving without her when she saw me packing my suitcase.

"You're going to stay with Carla, sweetie," I said. "The way you always do."

"Hey, Rayna," Carla said softly. "Come to Auntie Carla."

"Noooo!"

"I'd better just take her," Carla said, then tried to pry Rayna's fingers from my neck. This caused Rayna to scream at the top of her lungs.

What am I doing? I asked myself. *Heading to the Bahamas on a lark when I should be here with my baby.*

But she was the reason I was heading to the Bahamas.

Why I had to take this leap of faith and see if a miracle happened.

When I thought I was going to marry Eli, I'd considered giving up my dream of becoming an agent to become a full-time mother. In fact, Eli and I had talked about that. He asked me how I felt about being a stay-at-home mom, especially once I had another child. He had the money to support a family, and claimed he would have more once his music career got off the ground. I figured we'd wait and see how that all panned out, but now it was clear.

What had been a nice idea would never become reality.

"Oh, baby." I held Rayna close and gave her a big kiss. Her crying calmed to a whimper. Then I mumbled, "Maybe I shouldn't be doing this."

"Don't be silly," Carla said. "Rayna's going to be okay."

"But this isn't like her. She loves staying at your place." I felt her forehead. "She's a bit warm."

"I'm sure she's fine. But I can take her temperature as you head downstairs, and you call me when you get to the car. If she's got a fever, you can decide what to do—but I wouldn't cancel your trip for that."

"Sweetie, Carla's going to take good care of you." Rayna's fingers gripped my shirt, and her crying grew louder. "Mommy's going to see you soon, okay? I love you."

As I extricated her from my body, my heart broke at Rayna's shrill cry. Every maternal instinct inside me told me I should stay until my baby was okay.

Which meant I would miss my flight.

Rayna's misery couldn't have been more profound.

"God, I hate this," I said.

"Just go," Carla told me. "She'll be fine once you're gone."

Would she? I couldn't remember the last time she'd acted like this.

But I said, "You're right. I'm sure you're right. I just hate seeing her like this."

"I'll take her temperature. Call me in five minutes. We'll go from there."

I took two steps back, away from Rayna's reaching fingers, and felt like the worst mom in the world. "I'm sorry," I exclaimed. "Mommy loves you."

Then I turned and ran out the door, and Carla quickly closed it behind me. Rayna's cries only grew louder.

I ran down the hallway to the elevator, trying to block out the sound of my daughter's angst-filled screams.

If only Eli hadn't gotten himself killed. I could leave on a business trip without this wretched guilt. Rayna would be with the man she considered her father, and she wouldn't miss her mother as much.

Then again, if Eli hadn't gotten himself killed, I wouldn't need to be heading to the Bahamas on a long shot in hopes of finding a way to keep my home.

Back upstairs in my condo, I got my suitcase and carry-on bag ready, then called Carla before leaving my apartment.

"Does Rayna have a fever?" I asked without preamble.

"Rayna's fine."

As if to emphasize that point, I heard her laughter in the background—the same child whose cries had indicated she was being tortured the moment I left.

"Not even a little one?"

"She and Amani are playing with their ponies, and Rayna is having a grand old time."

"Okay," I said. "Okay, good. Remember, if you need to, you can call my sister for some relief. If anything crazy happens."

"We'll be fine."

With that, I put any concerns out of my mind and went downstairs to my car.

As I drove out of the parking lot, I said aloud, "Chaz Anderson, here I come."

chapter eighteen

I left my home for the Miami International Airport at ten o'clock, and by one-fifteen I was getting off the plane in Nassau.

One step closer, I thought, smiling.

But my smile soon wavered. I remembered all too well that Eli had once promised to take me to the Bahamas, how he'd said that we would stay on a private island and that he would treat me like royalty.

At the time, it had sounded like the ultimate fantasy. Now, I had to wonder if it was a fantasy Eli had enjoyed in the past.

With his wife.

Just remembering that vile woman had my stomach turning. I drew in a deep, warm breath and held it until my unease passed.

You didn't come here to think about Eli, I told myself. *You came here for your future.*

That thought in mind, I went to baggage claim to retrieve

the large suitcase I'd traveled with for my four-day trip. That had my clothes.

The carry-on had my shoes.

Hey—a woman can never have too many pairs of shoes on a trip.

I waited at the conveyor belt, and as I did, I overheard Chaz's name. Clearly, the people beside me were here for the series of seminars, too.

"And he's *so* cute," one of the two forty-something women commented.

"I wonder if he's single."

"We'll try to locate him at the bar, get him drunk and find out."

Both women laughed.

The women's luggage came, and they went. Other people's luggage came. But mine was nowhere in sight.

I waited.

And waited.

And didn't see the bright red suitcase holding my clothes.

Another thirty minutes, and after everyone I'd recognized on my flight was gone, I was fairly certain that my suitcase wasn't arriving.

Great. I had a carry-on full of shoes, and no clothes to wear.

Cursing my crappy luck, I made my way to the American Airlines counter, waited twenty minutes in line, then went through the process of filing my missing luggage report. I had to look at pictures of various suitcase styles and pick the one that best matched my own.

"Look," I said wearily when all that was done, "what's the

bottom line here? Did my suitcase somehow not make it on the flight, or is it lost somewhere on another plane?"

What I really wanted to ask was how on earth an airline could lose a piece of luggage on a direct flight.

"We'll investigate this promptly," the attendant told me. "And we'll get it to you as soon as it arrives."

"Will I have it by this evening?" I asked.

The woman smiled brightly. "There are six more flights scheduled to arrive from Miami today, which means it's likely your luggage will arrive by tonight."

"So my suitcase was left in Miami," I said, drawing the obvious conclusion.

"I can't be certain of that, ma'am. But we'll investigate this promptly."

"And what if my suitcase doesn't come in? I have no toiletries."

"I'll be happy to give you a toiletry kit." The woman produced one from behind the counter.

"Thank you," I mumbled.

My shoes and toiletries in hand, I headed outside to get a taxi.

I hoped this negative start wasn't a bad omen for the rest of my trip.

The Atlantis Resort was absolutely stunning, making me think I'd truly arrived in paradise. There were actually several hotel towers on the property, but the main building was by far the most magnificent. The focal point of the resort, the Royal Towers, actually looked like five buildings fused together. They ascended in height from the left and right sides to the middle. A suspended archway connected the two tallest ones. It was an opulent, peach-colored complex.

The resort grounds spanned acres and were also spectacular, with dazzling waterfalls, lush greenery, lagoons filled with marine life, and even a dolphin cove.

It was a place I'd love to bring Rayna one day.

I'd decided to splurge and stay in the Royal Towers, by far the most luxurious and upscale part of the hotel, from what the travel agent had told me. I justified the expense by telling myself this was where Chaz would be staying, unless he'd opted for one of the private residences. I doubted that, although that could have been wishful thinking.

My room was bright and pleasant, accented in blues, greens and peaches—tropical colors. I had a king-size bed, a desk, a twenty-seven-inch plasma television. But I was most impressed with the outstanding view I had of the property from the floor-to-ceiling windows.

I ordered room service, not in the mood to go downstairs to eat. Not only did I not want to dine alone, I wanted time to simply chill. So I sat and ate my burger while taking in the view of the grounds and the ocean from my tenth-floor balcony. With the chaos since Eli's death, it was nice to sit down and relax like this.

Soon, I would head down to the lobby and find out where I needed to register for the conference. But before dealing with conference business, I decided to go downstairs in search of clothes.

My fear that I'd possibly have to wear the same outfit the next day was assuaged when I saw the many shops in the hotel atrium. Shops like Gucci, Versace, Cartier and Ferragamo—all the high-end designers.

Though I was tempted to go straight to Gucci or Ferragamo, I refrained. With Tassie wanting to take my home, I could no longer afford the occasional impulse designer buy. So I strolled the shops until I found a small store that sold swimwear, clothes and shoes.

Exactly what I needed. I could buy a clean outfit and some underwear.

Fifteen minutes later, I had my arms full with lots of cute dresses, skirts and shirts—far more than I would ever need for the next four days.

But combined, they didn't total even one dress from Gucci.

"May I help you?" an attractive young woman asked me, with the hint of an island accent.

"Uh, no," I replied. "I'm still looking."

"I can take some of those clothes to a fitting room for you."

"Oh, sure. That'd be great."

The woman awkwardly shifted the mound of clothes from my arms to hers. I smiled sheepishly, knowing she had to be wondering if I was staying on the island for the next three months.

The clerk walked off with my clothes, and I wandered over to the shoes. I couldn't help it, they were so pretty.

Don't, I told myself. I didn't need shoes. I had a carry-on full of shoes.

But still, there was a pair of gorgeous black strappy stilettos with jewels on the top that were calling my name.

"Just walk away," I said aloud.

"Ma'am?" the clerk said, and I whirled around to face her. "The clothes are in dressing room number four."

Saved by the clerk. "Thank you," I told her, then headed that way.

I bought two casual skirts, two casual shirts, a red bikini, a black sarong and a long black sundress that had a belt around the waist and spaghetti straps.

More than I needed, but I'd at least be able to go to the pool or beach later and look good when I went to register for the conference.

With my new purchases in hand, I was perusing one of the hotel's gift shops in search of decent toiletries and makeup when I became aware of someone familiar—and then I stopped breathing.

Chaz Anderson was in the store, one aisle over from me.

And at a time when I was hot, sweaty and looked like a contestant from *The Amazing Race.*

I turned away, hoping he wouldn't catch a glimpse of me. I wanted to meet Chaz, yes, but not in my present unflattering condition.

He rounded the corner. I dropped to my haunches and picked up the first package I could.

Tampons.

Oh, jeez. Smooth, Vanessa. Real smooth.

I replaced the package of tampons and, with my head down, breezed around the corner.

I dropped the toothpaste and facial cleanser I'd picked up earlier onto a table near the front, then all but ran out of the store. I glanced backward, wondering if Chaz had been watching me, wondering if I was a crackhead. I saw him casually perusing the magazine rack.

Well, that had been close.

I don't know why I was so damn bent out of shape over him possibly seeing me, but I didn't want his first impression of me to be anything less than my best.

Standing outside the store, I stared through the glass, allowing myself a good, long, luscious look at Chaz Anderson. The man was seriously fine. He had to be about six foot three, and looked even better in person than he did on television.

He lifted his head and glanced my way. I quickly turned and started to walk.

All the way to my room, my heart was beating fast, with a mixture of fear and excitement.

Somehow—after I was dressed in clean clothes—I needed to find a way to introduce myself to Chaz.

I had to find a way to make my plan work.

That opportunity came sooner than I expected, later that evening when I decided to venture to the Lagoon Bar and Grill for a bite. And it proved to me that fate was at play.

It was a bit of a trek to get there from the Royal Towers, the highlight of which was the walk through an underwater glass tunnel filled with colorful fish. I loved Miami because it was subtropical, and the palm trees, floral shrubs and brightly colored buildings made the city look so pretty. But the Bahamas was even more beautiful. The water was a magnificent shade of turquoise along the shore, then morphed into a darker blue as the water got deeper. The sand was very fine and almost white. It was the most gorgeous stretch of beach I had ever seen.

The Lagoon Bar and Grill was a circular building surrounded mostly by water—lagoons that had been designed as part of the hotel's stunning grounds. The waters were filled with various marine life, like sharks and stingrays. There was even a lagoon-style pool. On the patches of land between the lagoons, there were lush green shrubs and countless·palm trees.

Paradise Island was the perfect name for this place. The resort was nothing short of spectacular, celebrating both nature and architecture. From the restaurant, I could see the Royal Towers. The long, arched section that connected the two tallest buildings was actually a suite, the Bridge Suite, the concierge had told me. He'd also said that it went for close to thirty grand a night.

"Table for one?" the hostess asked me.

"Yes, please."

The petite and cheerful-looking young woman led me through the restaurant. When she stopped at a table and my gaze went to the left, I froze.

"Is this okay?" she asked, picking up on my shock.

"Um, yes." I quickly pulled out a chair. "It's perfect."

The hostess placed a menu on the table. "Enjoy your meal."

As she walked away, my heart beat out of control. The concierge had suggested this open-air, casual restaurant, and now I was pleased for more than one reason.

The hostess had seated me at a table behind Chaz Anderson!

He was there with a man, his brother by the looks of it, likely around five years older than him.

Chaz's back was to me as I sat, and yet I was as nervous as if he was staring across the table at me. My mind scrambled for a way to introduce myself.

"The timing couldn't be worse," I heard one of them say. I thought it was Chaz, but I couldn't be certain.

"I hear ya," the other replied. "What did the doctor say?"

"Food poisoning. Likely from the shrimp she had for dinner last night." He gave a loud sigh. "I don't know what to do. I've got you to help, yeah, but I need Claire to make this weekend go smoothly. She oversees everything. Without her…"

My, oh, my, I thought. It distinctly sounded as though Chaz had lost a member of his team to a bout of food poisoning.

"No chance she'll be better by tomorrow?"

"She has been violently ill all day, with no signs of her condition letting up."

There was a pause. "We'll get it done, bro. You just tell me what you need done."

This is fate. It has to be. Chaz has lost a member of his team, and here I am, someone who works in the business, sitting at the table right beside him.

Excitement washed over me like the waves crashing at the Bahamian shoreline. This was my foot in the door.

I was pushing my chair back when the waiter arrived. "Leaving so soon?" he asked.

"No," I told him.

"Then can I get you a drink?"

"I'd love one," I responded, "but I haven't had a chance to look at the drink menu. Can you just give me a minute? I need to make a call."

"Certainly."

My purse in hand, I stepped away from the table to phone Carla. It was a long-distance call, and I had no clue how much it would cost, but I couldn't stop myself. I had to share this fabulous news with her. With *someone*.

I moved to an open area overlooking the water and punched in her number.

"Carla, it's me," I said when she picked up.

"Vanessa?"

"Yes."

"Aren't you in the Bahamas?"

"Yes, but I just had to call with some fabulous news. That motivational speaker I came to see—Chaz—I just overheard him talking to someone. His brother, I think, but that doesn't matter. Apparently his assistant became violently ill. Some sort of food poisoning."

"Uh-huh…"

"Well, you know how much I wanted to be able to meet him and convince him to sign with my agency. His assistant getting sick—that gives me a great excuse to approach him. Let him know I'm in the business and that I can work for him if he needs me to."

"Where are you?"

"In a restaurant," I replied. "And Chaz is at the table behind mine. How incredible is that? If I hadn't been put at that exact table, I never would have—"

"That's great," Carla said, cutting me off. She sounded less than enthused—or perhaps distracted. "Are you going to talk to him now?"

"Yes, but…" I trailed off. "You okay, Carla?"

"Yeah, sure."

"And Rayna's fine?"

"Rayna's terrific. She's taking a nap right now."

My lips curled in a soft smile as I thought of Rayna. I missed her. I hated having to be away from her at all, but if I accomplished my goal on this trip, then it would be well worth it.

"You sound sort of down," I said. "Or is it just that since you're not in the business, my news isn't exciting to you?"

"I'm fine," she said, and I didn't need to strap her to a lie detector to know that she wasn't being honest.

"Hey," I began softly. "You're my friend. If something's wrong, you can tell—"

"I met someone," she blurted.

Her words caught me completely off guard, so much so that I didn't get her meaning at first. Then I did, and I asked, *"What?"*

"I met someone," she repeated. "He's cute, and he's nice—"

"Wait a second," I said. "Are you…having an affair?"

"I'm thinking about it," she quickly replied.

I couldn't have been more stunned if she announced she'd been abducted by aliens. "Carla, why? You love Paul."

"Yeah, but he's not here. And any day now he could be killed and make me a widow."

She wasn't making any sense. "What's really going on here?"

"I'm lonely, Vanessa. I knew Paul was in the military when I married him, but I'm here alone all the time, and he's missing all these wonderful moments with Amani. And then there are the times when I just need a break

from Amani, no matter how much I love her. Time to be
by myself. To be able to go out and get a pedicure. Hell,
to have Paul around to get up in the night when Amani's
got a cold…"

"He's fighting for our country, not off on vacation."

"I know, I know. I get that. But you don't know what it's
like, Vanessa. I hate having to stay home all the time. I can't
go out to dinner with him, have nice adult time with someone my age. Except you, of course. But you have your job…
I swear, my daily thrill is watching the *Y and R*."

"When I get back, we'll plan a spa day," I told her. Carla
was clearly having some sort of breakdown. The timing
couldn't have been worse. Here I was, wanting to share my
good news…and I got her shocking news instead.

"We'll find someone to watch the kids for us," I added. "And
we'll make a day of it. A full day. That'll be fun, won't it?"

"And I miss having sex."

"That I can't help you with."

"Sometimes at night, I get so horny…"

This was too much information, and I tuned Carla out.
Tuned her out and stared back toward Chaz's table. He and the
man I believed to be his brother were finishing their desserts.

"…you just want a real man beside you, ya know?"

"Right," I agreed absently. Then, "No! I mean, yes I
know you miss Paul, but you're *married*. Till death do you
part—remember that vow? You don't get to go out and find
some other man just because you're lonely."

"I've been thinking about this for a while now."

Oh, hell. Chaz's waitress had arrived with his bill. "Carla, I hate to cut you off, but the guy I told you about is

leaving the restaurant. And I have to talk to him before he disappears."

"Oh. Of course."

"But please don't do anything impulsive."

"I'll try not to."

"Do more than try. You love your husband! Don't you dare jeopardize what you have with him just because you're horny. I'll never forgive you, you hear me? Look, Carla, I really have to run. I'll call you later."

I flipped my cell phone shut and started back toward my table. I didn't get three steps before being blocked by someone in my path.

I went to sidestep the man, but he matched my move.

"Excuse me," I said, looking down him. He was at least five inches shorter than I was.

The man, who appeared to be in his mid-fifties, grinned up at me. "Wow. You're a beautiful woman."

"Thank you," I told him, then started to move. But the next thing I knew, I felt his hand on my arm.

I whirled around and gazed down at him.

"What's your name?" he asked me.

Oh, God, I thought. *Tell me this man isn't flirting with me....*

I always have a problem with being impolite. So I found myself saying, "Vanessa. But I'm in a—"

"That's a nice name. My name is Billy. Now tell me, why is a pretty woman like you here alone?"

I threw a glance in Chaz's direction, and noticed that the waitress was handing him back his credit card.

"Billy," I began, pulling my arm free of his grip. "This isn't a good time."

"When would be a good time? I'd love to buy you a drink."

I stared at him in disbelief. Did this fifty-something, short, balding man really believe he had a chance with me? Or did he think he had nothing to lose, so why not go for it? It wasn't the first time a guy who was clearly not my type had hit on me, and I could never understand the nerve.

His boldness, however, didn't matter. Because as I once again looked in Chaz's direction, I saw him putting his wallet back into his jacket. Then he started to move.

"I'm sorry, Billy, but I really have to go." I shrugged helplessly and started off.

"Bitch," he muttered behind my back.

I stopped cold in my tracks, anger quickly consuming me. I hadn't been rude to this guy, and he had the nerve to call me a bitch?

And so I snapped. With the dirty looks people had given me after seeing me on TV, with Tassie making my life far more difficult, I simply didn't feel like taking any more shit from anyone.

I spun around to face him. "Let's make one thing perfectly clear, *Billy*. The only way I'd go out with you is if I were dead. You're not even close to being my type, you…you jerk."

The stunned look on his face was priceless. But the next moment, I remembered Chaz. I turned and saw him starting to rise from his table. I trotted across the restaurant before my perfect opportunity to approach him wouldn't be lost.

Right before Chaz got to the exit, I was at his heels. I whipped in front of him and his guest, and his eyes widened in surprise.

"Excuse me," I said, hoping he wouldn't think I was some crazy person. "Sorry to interrupt you like this, but I wanted to introduce myself."

"Okay," Chaz said warily, as if trying to decide if I was sane or not.

I extended my hand. "My name is Vanessa. Vanessa Cain."

He reached forward tentatively, and when his palm touched mine, I swear I felt an electric shock. I'd always thought Chaz was great-looking on television, but in person, he was even more attractive.

"Hello, Vanessa," he said, his voice smooth, his lips curled in what I considered a flirtatious smile. Obviously, he'd decided I was harmless.

In fact, he must have thought I was on a very different mission than I was, because he held my hand for a couple beats longer than I expected, leading me to wonder if he thought I was some groupie who wanted to get into his bed. Taking my hand back, I reached inside my purse for my business card holder.

"Not that I was eavesdropping, but I couldn't help over-hearing your conversation," I told him. Grasping the metal case in my purse, I lifted it out and extracted a card. "That your assistant took ill."

Chaz didn't respond as he glanced at my card. "You're in the business."

"Yes," I said. "An agent." A little white lie, but he didn't need to know the truth. My business card had my name and the agency information on it, and not my title, so he would never question what I told him.

He extended the card back to me. Gone was his smile and

friendly demeanor. "And I'll bet you're here to try to convince me to sign with your agency. No, thank you."

I didn't take the card. "I can help you," I told him. "You need someone. Why not let that someone be me? I was here for the conference anyway, and I have extensive experience in the business. I'll have no problem getting done what you need doing."

Chaz looked at the man who was with him and said, "Sean, why don't you go on without me?"

"You're sure?" Sean asked. He gave me the once-over, as if he thought I was threatening or something.

"Yes, I'm sure. I can deal with Ms. Cain."

Deal with me? I didn't like his words. So as soon as Sean was out of earshot, I quickly started talking again.

"I'd be lying if I said that I didn't want to woo you over to my agency, but you'd be remiss in refusing my help for that reason alone. I'm a good, hard worker. I live and breathe this business every day. And I'd even be willing to help you for free."

I regretted the last words as soon as I said them, because I didn't want him having the impression that if I did help him, there would be strings attached.

"Let me think about it," he said.

"Your seminar is starting tomorrow."

"Give me a way to reach you. When I make my decision, I'll let you know."

"All right," I conceded, knowing I couldn't twist his arm. "I can write it on the card."

"Right." Chaz returned the card to me.

I fumbled around in my purse for a pen, but like an idiot,

couldn't find one when I needed it. "I know I've got a pen in here somewhere…"

"Allow me." He produced one from the breast pocket of his jacket, something I was surprised he was wearing in this weather. I guess he always wanted to look professional and successful.

"This is my room number," I told him. "I assume you're staying at the hotel."

"I am."

I passed the card back to him. "I hope to hear from you. It would be my pleasure to help. I'm a big fan."

Glancing at the card again, he nodded. Then he met my gaze. I smiled, hoping a little flirtation from me this time would help sway his decision in my favor.

"Thank you, Ms. Cain."

"Vanessa," I told him.

He gave me a polite nod, then turned and sauntered out of the restaurant. After a few seconds, he looked over his shoulder at me.

I waved.

He smiled.

Then he rounded the corner and was gone.

Excitement bubbling inside me, I returned to my table. I ordered a lobster salad, but I was no longer hungry.

Should I call Debbie, let her know I'd been able to establish contact with Chaz?

Not yet, I decided. I wouldn't call her until Chaz gave me an answer as to whether or not he'd use me.

"He *will* use me," I told myself. Power of positive thinking and all that.

Hopeful, I stared out at the tranquil view of the water, far more blue than I'd ever seen in South Florida.

No doubt about it, this place was beautiful.

I was determined that coming here was going to be a new beginning for me.

chapter nineteen

To my disappointment, when I returned to my room, I discovered that my suitcase had not yet arrived. I immediately went to the phone and called American Airlines.

"Hi, this is Vanessa Cain calling. I flew to the Bahamas earlier today. Unfortunately, my luggage didn't arrive with me, and it's now nearly 9:00 p.m. and I'm wondering if I can expect it tonight."

"What is the claim number?"

I gave the woman the information and waited while she searched the computer. "I'm showing that the luggage still hasn't been found."

"What do you mean, it hasn't been found?"

"It's not in the system."

My stomach dropped. "Do you realize I'm on vacation without so much as my makeup bag? No, not vacation," I corrected. "A business trip. I need to look professional."

"I'm sorry, ma'am."

"How, exactly, does a bag get lost, anyway?"

"We're looking into the matter and as soon as we find your luggage, it will be delivered to you."

"Great." I hung up. *Thanks for nothing.*

What was I going to do now? I'd foolishly worn the nicer dress to dinner—the black one—which I counted as a smart move, since I'd run into Chaz. But that meant that for the first day of the conference, I needed something else to wear—especially if Chaz called and said he needed my help.

I decided to wait until the morning. Hopefully, I'd get my suitcase bright and early. If I didn't, I'd deal with the situation then.

Next, I called my home number and checked my messages. As soon as the first message started to play, my stomach sank.

"Ms. Cain, this is Bradley Harris, Tassie Johnson's lawyer. The message you left said you were working on some arrangement, but I haven't heard from you since. I'm afraid my client isn't happy about your attempts to dodge a very serious legal situation. We have agreed to give you thirty days to come up with a solution, after which we will be forced to take action."

Snorting, I hung up. "I'm afraid I'm not too happy about your client trying to screw me out of my home," I retorted mockingly.

Honestly, was Tassie really so hard up in her three-million-dollar mansion?

Of course not. She just wanted to push the knife even farther into my back, make me suffer because Eli had chosen me over her.

Well, that wasn't entirely accurate. Eli had chosen cheating over being monogamous. Tassie should be pissed with him, not me.

Thirty days. I didn't doubt for a minute that the lawyer was serious—that Tassie was serious.

Which meant I had to put my time here to the best use possible.

"Please, Chaz," I whispered as I lay in bed that night. "Please give me a chance."

My future depended on it.

Shortly after seven the next morning, my phone rang. I rolled over in bed and snatched up the receiver before it rang a second time. "Hello?"

"Vanessa?"

"Yes?" I answered, my voice hoarse and unsexy.

"This is Chaz Anderson."

"Oh, hello." I sat up. "Morning."

"Still want to come to work for me?"

"Yes. Yes, I'm definitely still interested."

"Sorry to call this early, but my assistant is in even worse shape than yesterday, so I could really use your help today."

"I am more than happy to help."

"Can you meet me in the Atlantis Grand Ballroom in the conference center? In an hour? We can go over the details then."

"Absolutely. No problem." But I was thinking, *an hour?* To my knowledge, my suitcase still hadn't arrived, and an hour wouldn't give me near enough time to go downstairs and find something decent to wear, if the shops were even open at this hour.

"Vanessa, I appreciate this. You're a lifesaver."

"Looking forward to it," I told Chaz.

As soon as I hung up, I swung my legs off the bed and went into panic mode. There was no way on earth I could wear the dress I'd worn last night, no matter how smashing I had looked in it.

I dialed zero and got the front desk. "Hi. This is Vanessa Cain. I'm wondering if there's been a delivery for me from American Airlines. You might not have wanted to call because it was too early."

I heard fingers clicking on a keyboard. Then, "No, Mrs. Cain. I don't see anything."

"*Ms.,*" I corrected. Why did everyone assume a woman couldn't be single? Sometimes I felt as if I had a scarlet *S* on my forehead.

Once, I'd sat through a time-share presentation in Orlando, and had even succumbed to the pressure to buy one (I canceled the purchase four days later). When the man filled out my application, he wrote across the top in big, red letters, "A SINGLE WOMAN."

I kid you not.

I was only twenty-eight, still in great physical shape and taking care of myself. Why did people have to make you feel insufficient because you didn't have a husband?

It wasn't a subject I had time to think about. I bolted to the shower.

Chaz Anderson wanted me to work for him! This was the first crucial step in securing him as a client. I would do a fabulous job, impress him with my organizational and people skills.

He would be hiring me as an agent in no time.

I dressed in the pale pink shirt that hugged my breasts, plus the white skirt and a pair of sandals. This was far more suitable for a day of shopping in town than as Chaz's right-hand person. But there was nothing I could do about it at this point.

I made sure my face and hair looked good, then went downstairs to the conference center. My stomach started to rumble as I made my way into the ballroom, a reminder that I was hungry—and nervous as hell.

Chaz was standing at the front of the room with the man I'd seen him with the day before. Both of them were wearing suits, and the sight of Chaz in his loose blazer and white shirt unbuttoned at the collar—well, all I can say is that it shot a delicious jolt through me that early in the morning, waking me up as surely as a cup of java.

When he saw me approaching, he grinned widely.

"Vanessa. I'm so glad you could make it." He pumped my hand firmly.

"Like I said, I'm happy to help out."

Chaz's gaze roamed over me from head to toe. Self-conscious, I raised a hand to my hair. "About my attire, I'm really sorry I don't have any of my proper business suits. My suitcase hasn't arrived—"

Chaz waved off my concern. "Don't worry about it. You look great."

My gaze wandered to the other man, who was organizing what appeared to be stacks of handouts.

"I didn't officially introduce you to Sean last night," Chaz said. "Vanessa, this is my brother, Sean. Sean, Vanessa."

I shook his hand.

"So you do have some help," I said.

"Sean takes care of the handouts and audience questions. Things like that. I'll need you to help me organize the whole production, for lack of a better word. Talk with the hotel staff about what I might need. Like an overhead projector. It hasn't arrived yet. And at the end of every session, I always sell my tapes and books. If you can man that for me—with help from the hotel staff if necessary—that'd be fantastic."

I nodded.

Chaz took me gently by the elbow and led me out of earshot of Sean. "Now, we didn't discuss your fee. How's twenty-five hundred for the next three days?"

"Twenty-five hundred?"

"Okay, I can do three. That's a thousand dollars a day."

A thousand dollars a day!

I nodded. "That's fine."

"You're sure?"

"Yes. Absolutely."

Chaz's smile was wide and warm. "Great. If you want me to draw up a contract—"

"That's not necessary."

"But it's the smart thing to do," he stated. "Give me a few minutes."

As Chaz walked over to his laptop, I nearly had heart failure. *Three thousand dollars!* Good Lord in heaven. This was unbelievable—far more than I expected.

With three grand, I could easily pay Carla the extra money it was costing me for Rayna's care, and also save a little toward the get-Mrs.-Bitch-Johnson-off-my-back fund.

It was an amount that was hard to really fathom.

Then I thought about the fee I'd paid for this conference—eight hundred dollars—and realized that if even fifty people had registered, it would be an incredibly profitable weekend for Chaz.

He approached me a couple minutes later with a sheet of paper. "Here you go."

I glanced at it. And gulped. "This says four thousand dollars."

Chaz nodded. "I figured it was only fair to return your registration fee. I made it an even four grand, and I'll pay you on the last day."

I nodded jerkily. Things had gotten even better.

I went over some of the logistics with Chaz. In the next twenty minutes, the hotel staff would be setting up pastries and coffee outside the conference room. It was a very large space, with a huge stage area, and that was where Chaz would be at all times. Between me and Sean, we would monitor those entering the room, making sure that they were wearing badges.

Chaz gave me a clipboard with a checklist, and I made my way to the lobby outside the conference room to take care of the first order of business.

The smell of fresh coffee wafted toward me, reminding me I'd started the day without a cup. There were platters and platters of Danishes and fresh fruit, bagels and jams. My mouth began to water, and my stomach grumbled.

"Feel free to eat something."

I jumped and spun around to see Chaz standing behind me.

"I'm sorry," he said. "I didn't mean to frighten you. It's just that, in about half an hour, things are going to get really hectic, and you won't have time to eat. I know I got you out of bed this morning."

I nodded. "Sure."

Not wanting to appear gluttonous, I chose a bagel and some fresh pineapple. I put the bagel into the toaster and then poured myself a cup of coffee.

Chaz still stood there, and I was a bit unnerved.

"Can I help you with something else?" I asked.

"Sorry," he said. "I get a bit frazzled before one of my seminars starts. I wouldn't mind a cup of coffee."

I poured him a cup and passed it to him. "How many people are you expecting for your conference?"

"Two hundred," Chaz replied.

Two hundred! Two hundred people, at eight hundred dollars a pop. I quickly did the math and was left a little breathless.

Sure, he'd obviously had to pay a good sum to the hotel for the continental breakfasts and the lunches scheduled over the next few days, but still. The amount of money Chaz stood to make this weekend alone would go a long way in buying out Eli's wife.

I was impressed. And I could see why Chaz worked alone. He'd built a following on his own, and was able to keep one hundred percent of the profit. Still, I had to find a way to convince him that having an agency work for him would increase his numbers. Our clients often did seminars for crowds of one thousand and higher.

"Vanessa."

The way Chaz said my name made butterflies go crazy in my stomach. My gaze rose to his. "Yes?"

"Do you mind checking with the hotel liaison to make

sure that the lunch is scheduled for twelve-thirty, and that everything's on point? His name is Calvin Cassidy."

"I sure will."

I noticed that the registration desk was manned by local hotel staff. I made a note to ask Chaz if he always hired locally, as opposed to traveling with a bigger team.

By the time the first person came down to the buffet spread, Chaz was somewhere backstage. I guessed he didn't want to be seen. Strobe lights danced over the stage's dark surface, giving people the impression that something amazing was about to happen.

And it did. The morning session was electrifying. Watching Chaz, I realized he was in his element before an audience. He spoke candidly about his own personal experiences, how he'd had success, only to lose everything, and how he'd rebuilt his life from nothing. I saw dozens of moist eyes in the room as he spoke.

After those very moving first two hours, Chaz opened up the floor for people to ask questions, or give their own testimonials about overcoming hardships in their own lives, which was followed by half an hour of selling and signing books and tapes.

Of course, even as the autographing finished, people still lingered to talk to him. The same thing happened after the afternoon session, and because there wasn't an official dinner scheduled, an even larger group hung around. After twenty minutes of Chaz graciously giving his time and answering questions, Sean and I had to herd people out of the room, assuring them that they'd have time to talk with him the next day.

When the last person left, finally giving him a break, I saw the relief that passed over Chaz's face. I quietly approached him. "Wow. That was one incredible day. People were moved to tears, you were so inspiring."

"Thank you," he said, his modesty obvious.

"You look exhausted."

"I always am. The lead-up to the first day, with all the preparations—it's draining. And then I'm worried that something will go wrong."

"Everything went well. You don't need to worry about that." I paused. "Are you up for dinner? Away from the hotel? I asked the concierge about places we could go, and he recommended Columbus Tavern at the Paradise Harbour Club and Marina."

"You are a mind reader."

I smiled. "Excellent. We can meet at the concierge desk in half an hour, if that works for you."

"You're on."

He went back in to talk to Sean, and I sprinted out of the conference center. I jogged all the way to the front desk and was out of breath when I got there.

My plan was to inquire about my luggage, but I drew up short when a little girl in a pink bathing suit, around Rayna's age, saw me and gazed up at me with curiosity.

She appeared to be Hispanic, with her short dark hair in two pigtails. She was holding the hand of a woman who was talking to another woman. There was a mix of excitement and exasperation in the young girl's eyes, and I knew exactly what she was thinking.

Get me to the pool already!

An intense feeling of longing gripped me as I stared at this little girl. So intense I had to swallow.

It's amazing how sometimes what you want most in the world is a break from your child, a moment to rest and not have to be Mommy. And yet, when you get that, you will inevitably see other children and then desperately miss your own.

I smiled at the little girl, and she rewarded me with a radiant one in return. Holding on to that small reminder of everything that was right in my world, I continued on to the front desk.

I went up to an available staff member and told her my name and room number. "Can you tell me if my luggage has arrived?"

The hotel clerk checked her files, then smiled. "Yes, Mrs. Cain. I see here that a suitcase arrived at three-forty this afternoon and was delivered to your room."

"Thank God."

"Is there anything else I can help you with?"

"No," I told her, and was about to turn when I said, "Actually, yes. There is something else you can help me with."

"Certainly."

"Please change my name in the computer so it says *Ms.,* not *Mrs.*"

"*Oh.*" She nodded slowly, a look of understanding in her eyes. "Everyone refers to you as Mrs., as though being single is some sort of crime."

"Exactly."

She nodded. "Consider it done."

That resolved, I went upstairs to change for my dinner engagement with Chaz.

chapter twenty

Half an hour later, I was dressed to impress, in a casual yet sexy red dress and low-heeled gold sandals. Chaz opted for a more casual look than the business suit he'd sported earlier, instead wearing a polo shirt and khaki pants.

The Columbus Tavern looked like a floating house, as it had been built on a platform that was surrounded by water on three sides. Two pelicans and one seagull stood on wooden poles sticking out of the water, either waiting to catch food or taking a break from the hunt.

A variety of yachts, catamarans and powerboats were moored at the marina, and glancing out the restaurant's windows gave you the impression that you were on a houseboat.

The interior was what you'd expect on an island—not stuffy and pretentious, but cheerful and laid-back, right down to the white plastic chairs.

The hostess greeted us with a warm smile. "Welcome to Columbus Tavern. You've caught the last fifteen minutes of happy hour. Feel free to help yourself to the complimentary conch fritters at the bar."

"Nice," I said. "Thank you."

She led us to a quiet table in a corner of the restaurant, where we had an unobstructed view of the ocean. In fact, all the square tables lined the windows, so that patrons would be able to gaze out at the water.

The hostess gave us our menus, and we settled in our seats.

I glanced at the bar area, where lots of happy people were munching on appetizers and drinking beer. "The place is busy. Thankfully, most of the guests are at the bar."

Chaz nodded as he surveyed the surroundings. "I like this place."

I looked across the table at him, trying to make sure he really was pleased. For all I knew, with his millions in the bank, he might not like eating in any restaurant that wasn't a five-star establishment.

"Yes," I murmured. "The decor isn't necessarily fine-dining, but I've been told the food is top-notch."

"This is exactly the kind of place I enjoy," Chaz said. "The kind of place that has heart. And it's exactly what I needed," he added. "You were very smart to book something away from the hotel."

"I figured you'd appreciate that." I lifted my menu briefly, then without looking at it, placed it back on the table. "Chaz, I just want to say something. Thank you again for giving me the opportunity to work for you. No strings attached," I added.

"Stop." He held up a hand. "I'm the one who should be thanking you. I worked you hard, had you running around like a crazy person, and you did a fabulous job today."

"Oh, I often run around like a crazy person," I told him, laughing. Which was true. My job as an office manager required it.

"You certainly were a great help. And the timing of our meeting couldn't have been better."

"It's like it was fate," I commented.

Our eyes met right then, and held—and something hot and intimate passed between us. It was as though my comment about fate had us both suddenly thinking about far more than work.

Feeling uncomfortable, I looked away, breaking the moment. Outside, seagulls flew around the restaurant, clearly hoping to spot a morsel of food. It didn't matter where in the world you were, if something edible was near, so were the seagulls.

"I do have an idea," I said, getting back on the business track. "Something that could help maximize your audience."

"Oh?"

"Yes. Sort of like a reward program. Or referral program, whatever you want to call it. If some of the convention goers tell someone else about your seminars and get them to register for your next convention, they'll get a discount on their next seminar package. If they get two friends to go, they get an even bigger discount. And if they get three people to go, then their fee is waived."

I paused, trying to read Chaz's reaction to my suggestion. I couldn't. "You don't like the idea," I stated.

"It's brilliant," Chaz said. "In fact, I'm surprised I didn't think of it before."

Pride swelled inside me. "And I had another idea."

"Go on."

The waitress arrived at that moment, making me have to hold my thought. She looked from Chaz to me, then asked if we wanted to order something to drink.

Chaz quickly scanned the wine menu. "How does a bottle of pinot grigio sound to you?"

"Fine," I replied.

"But?" Chaz asked. "I sense a bit of hesitation."

"Nothing, really. I guess I'm just a cheap date. My favorite wine is white zinfandel."

"Then that's what we'll have," Chaz said.

"No. Please, order something decent."

"A bottle of white zinfandel," Chaz told the waitress.

"Certainly," she said, then sauntered off.

"You didn't have to do that," I told him.

"I wanted to."

It was hard to argue a point like that.

Chaz looked at me and said, "You were saying?"

"Right. My other idea. Are you at all flexible in terms of where you hold tomorrow's session?"

"What do you mean?"

"Well, I was thinking it might be nice to change the venue to outside. Here we are in the Bahamas, on Paradise Island, and people are cooped up for the entire day. I checked with Calvin after lunch, and he said there are outside venues where you could hold your seminar. I thought it might be a nice idea. Change it around a bit, let people enjoy the tropical background."

Chaz nodded, his expression thoughtful. "I suppose it could work."

"And if you're concerned about having a staging area, Calvin said the hotel could build one for you. There might be an issue if you wanted to use the overhead projector, but I noticed that even today, everything on the projector you already had written in your handout."

Chaz paused. Then he said, "Let me think about it."

"Okay. Even if you don't do it for tomorrow, perhaps Saturday could be an option. Or, if you think the idea is crazy, we don't have to do it at all."

"The idea's not crazy. Nothing you've suggested has been crazy."

"Thank you."

"But, schematically, I'm going over things in my head… It might work. It might not."

"I think today was a huge success. Everyone seemed really excited. You're a phenomenal speaker. And I'm not just saying that to butter you up," I quickly pointed out. "Though you know I want you to sign with my agency. But it's true. You're a natural."

"You know what would be nice?" Chaz suddenly asked.

"What?"

"If we didn't talk about business."

"Oh, I'm sorry. You think I'm giving you a total hard sell, don't you?" I covered my face, embarrassed. "I really am sorry."

"Don't apologize." He dismissed my concern with a wave of his hand. "Your ideas are great. And I don't think you're giving me a hard sell. I valued everything you did today. You picked up the ball and ran with it as if you'd been a member of my team for years. I guess I'm just saying your work for the day is done, and mine, too, so let's enjoy each other's company."

With his words, a frisson of heat shot through me. For the second time since we'd arrived at the restaurant, I wondered if he might actually be a little interested. I had hoped earlier, during the seminars, to see a spark when he glanced my way—anything, really—but he'd been all business. Had I read him wrong?

"What do you want to talk about?" I asked.

"You," he replied, so frankly that my heart raced with anticipation. I *had* read him wrong.

"Me?" I chuckled nervously.

"Yeah."

"I don't know what to say."

"Oh, I don't believe that. You're very fascinating."

Fascinating? I almost repeated the word aloud. Did he really believe that, or—my stomach sank—was this his way of trying to flatter me so that I'd end up in his bed later?

"You're much too kind," I told him matter-of-factly, my hope that he was genuinely interested having deflated like a balloon. "I'm not fascinating at all."

"I beg to differ," he said. "A beautiful woman like you…you must have done some modeling, or perhaps acting." His eyes narrowed. "I don't know why, but you look really familiar to me."

"Nope. Never a model or an actress."

He pressed his lips together thoughtfully. "I could swear I've seen you before."

As he continued to study me, I decided to fess up. "You did see me before. In the hotel gift shop yesterday afternoon." And I'd thought that I had made a clean getaway.

"No, not that." Now he frowned, like he was racking his brain to figure out where he'd seen me before.

"I guess I have one of those faces. People always tell me I remind them of someone else."

"A face like yours a man doesn't easily forget."

I let this compliment go over my head, determined not to be susceptible to Chaz's charm. I was actually a bit disappointed in him for being so…

So male.

Disappointed in myself, really, for having been flattered in the first place.

It was just that he was such a charismatic creature, so deliciously good-looking… I'd always found him attractive on television, and in real life, I couldn't help but be drawn to him.

But Chaz was a man. And I had to keep in mind that men—men like Lewis and Eli—always reacted to attractive women. I could be any other pretty face and Chaz would be reciting the same lines, much like he said the same things in each of his seminars.

Not that I should be concerned about any guy showing interest in me after what had happened with Eli, and merely a month after his funeral. It was time to refocus my energy on work.

"I've got it," he said, and I raised my gaze to his. His eyes were wide, and he was grinning. "Now I know who you are."

"Enlighten me." I tried to keep my lack of enthusiasm out of my tone.

"The one who was on the news a while back. Dating that former baseball player who was murdered."

I couldn't help it—I groaned. "Oh. *That.* Not exactly my shining television debut."

"Why do you say that?"

"Other than the fact that the media made me out to be the biggest gold digger on the planet?"

"I didn't think that when I saw you."

"Then you thankfully missed most of the CNN coverage."

"I do recall seeing some interview with the guy's wife—"

"And to set the record straight immediately, I did *not* know that Eli was married. He and his wife had been separated for years—something he'd neglected to tell me when he proposed to me."

The waitress arrived with the bottle of wine, opened it and poured a glass for each of us.

"Are you ready to order?" she asked.

"Actually—" I lifted the menu "—I haven't even looked yet. What do you suggest?"

"The lobster flambé is very popular."

"Sounds delicious," I said. "I'll try it."

"I'll have it, too," Chaz said. Then he glanced at me. "Do you feel like splitting the crab cakes as an appetizer?"

"That'll be great," I told him. "But maybe we can share an order of the shrimp spring rolls, as well." I was famished from all the running around I'd done earlier, especially since I'd only had an apple at lunch.

"Works for me," Chaz said.

The waitress took our menus from the table, then smiled pleasantly before walking off, something I noticed that people in the Bahamas did a lot. Maybe there was something to be said for living in a place called Paradise Island.

When the waitress was gone, Chaz looked at me and said, "Just so you know, I'm not judging you."

At first, I didn't know what he was talking about. Then I got his meaning. He was continuing the conversation that had been interrupted when the waitress appeared.

I eyed him skeptically. "You're not?"

"Absolutely not. I know a thing or two about being with deceptive women."

"Really?"

"Yes. You sound surprised."

"I am. Someone in your position…" I hesitated a moment. "I can see being burned once, but wom*en?* That's a little surprising." The words were quite hypocritical coming from my mouth, considering my own past. But as far as I was concerned, men didn't have nearly as much trouble finding a decent woman as the other way around.

"Why—because you think money can buy love?"

"No. I just…" I didn't finish my statement, realizing that whatever I said would be based on my own sexist perception. I'd been screwed over enough times to be biased when it came to thinking men even had the capability of being hurt.

Not a sentiment I wanted to share with my new boss.

Instead, I said, "I saw you on the *Today Show* only a few days ago. You mentioned something about having been married and how your wife hurt you."

"Mistake number one," Chaz said.

"That bad?"

"Worse." He said it without emotion, which told me that he wasn't bitter.

I heard what he'd said to Ann Curry, but asked nonetheless. "What happened?"

"She'd been my college sweetheart," he told me. "I thought she'd be there for me through thick and thin. You know—the kind of woman who was with you at the beginning so you can trust her with your success?"

I nodded.

"Instead, she changed when my dot-com company went bust. Refusing to give in to failure, I quickly thought of another money-making opportunity. But Jill took the first opportunity to screw me over. Stole a business idea right out from under me, and I had no clue it was happening."

"What was the idea?"

"I was working with a friend of mine, a nutritionist, on a diet supplement that would help people lose weight. I know, it sounds too good to be true, but it wasn't. The idea had come to me after years of training and eating a certain way, and I asked this friend of mine, who was working for a company that made vitamin supplements, what he thought of the idea. He liked it, got to work on it. Jill was excited, too."

"Oh, no…"

Chaz nodded. "Uh-huh. All the while, my wife was sleeping with this guy who I thought was a friend, and they went on to sell my idea to his company for five million dollars."

"Oh my God."

Chaz took a sip of his wine. "I ask myself, how could I have protected myself? Should I have seen it coming?"

"And?"

"And I think that if I were to do things over again, it would play out the same way. Jill was my wife—how could

I not share my idea with her? Anything I'd gained would have been for both of us, our future. I thought she felt the same way."

"Incredible." I shook my head in disbelief. "She was your college sweetheart?"

"Yep."

"So what'd you do about the idea your wife and friend stole?" I asked, intrigued about Chaz's life. "They sold it for millions, yet you were still married to her, so whatever she earned you were entitled to half of, and vice versa." I couldn't help thinking of Eli's wife, and how she was trying to take half of the condo that she didn't even need.

"I let it go," he told me.

"You what?"

"The court battle would have been long and ugly, and I just wasn't up for it."

"Five million dollars," I said, my tone suggesting he was out of his mind.

"Everything I'd worked for," he added. "But I knew even then that money can't buy you love, and it certainly can't buy you happiness."

"Amen to that," I exclaimed, suddenly wondering if I was wrong about Chaz. Maybe he wasn't the average guy who would sleep with a woman and discard her without a second thought.

Certainly a guy who let his wife have everything—when she'd stolen from him—couldn't be that shallow.

"You're definitely living well now," I commented. "Which, as they say, is the best revenge."

"I prefer to think of it as karma. I had an idea that was

wrongfully stolen from me, and the universe provided another outlet for me to be successful."

"You're amazing," I said.

"Why?"

"Because you seem to harbor no bitterness or resentment at all where your wife is concerned. And after what she did, you're entitled."

"I'm not perfect," Chaz said. "I don't trust people as much as I once did. If I catch a person in a lie, I'm far more likely to end the relationship than work on it. The one thing that matters most to me in a relationship is honesty."

"After what your wife and friend did to you, it's no wonder."

"And you wouldn't have wanted to see me after this all happened. For a few months, I was consumed with anger. But I woke up one day and realized that the anger was eating at my soul. Taking away my creative energy, my happiness. The day I let it all go, I started to find joy in living again. My brain started working productively. I began studying security issues on the Internet, loopholes I could find. Long story short, I sold my idea to Microsoft for a million dollars. That wouldn't have happened if I was still hanging on to my anger."

I stared at Chaz in amazement. I'd been impressed with him when I'd heard him speak on television, and earlier in the day, but I didn't know how much of his spiel, for lack of a better word, was contrived to put millions in his pockets. But now, talking to him one-on-one like this, I was hearing firsthand how he had motivated himself onto a path of success, after having lost everything.

He had a powerful story to tell, and was a living example of his own prophecy.

"What about you?" he asked.

"Me?" I chuckled without mirth. "After that story, anything I say will sound excruciatingly shallow."

"No it won't."

"Yes." I nodded. "My ex was murdered by a jealous husband after being caught in bed with the man's wife. Then I found out he was also married. And had kids he never told me about. I've been angry with Eli for deceiving me, for getting murdered, for sending my life into turmoil. I've dated my share of losers. Never have I walked away with the grace that you have."

"Forgiveness isn't about the other person. It's about you—helping you heal so you can move on."

"Like I said, you are an amazing person."

The waitress arrived with our crab cakes and shrimp spring rolls, and we indulged. The subject changed from exes to how delicious the appetizers were, and then to the festive atmosphere when the reggae music coming from the speakers grew louder.

"Would you like to dance?" Chaz asked after our plates were cleared.

"I would love to."

The man was a gentleman. First, he helped ease my chair back, then he took my hand and led me to a tiny dance floor at the far end of the restaurant.

He pulled me close, but not close enough for me to feel that he was getting out of line. We danced to the slow reggae beat in comfortable silence, and when the second slow song started, I was the one to lean into him.

His body was warm, his chest strong, and I thought that

I could easily stay like that for the rest of the evening and not get bored.

"Vanessa," Chaz said softly.

I shifted my head from his shoulder to look at him. "Yes?"

"You're an incredibly beautiful woman."

My heart slammed against my rib cage, then excitement shot through my veins. A huge part of me told me I should be wary of his words, that I would be a fool to trust another man, but another part...

Another part of me still believed in love.

I *needed* to believe in love. I didn't want to think that I would spend the rest of my days alone. My aunt Lola had finally found the man of her dreams at the age of forty-four, and had been happily married for two years. That was exactly the kind of story that gave me the hope I needed to keep believing I'd have my own happy ending.

My heart told me that Chaz seemed too much a gentleman, too much of a good person, to talk this way to just any woman he happened to be with. Which meant he was saying this because he felt there was something special between us.

I was blushing when I said, "Thank you. You're incredible yourself. Both inside and out."

He pulled me a little closer, held my body a little tighter. And I swear, it felt like heaven.

I can't tell you why, but my attraction for Chaz was instant and powerful, something that surprised me immensely. Not lustful, the way it had been with Lewis. And I wasn't in need of a distraction, as I had been when I let Eli sweep me off my feet. I was at a point in my life where all I really wanted to do was concentrate on my career.

And yet there was something about Chaz that was drawing me to him. He had a genuine quality that I hadn't noticed in any other man I'd been with, and as we danced, I allowed myself to think that this connection we felt could be the start of something wonderful.

When the third song began, it was an upbeat reggae tune. I thought Chaz might want to get off the dance floor, but instead, he kicked things up a notch, releasing me and moving his feet faster to the beat.

"So the man can dance, too," I commented, my own hips moving faster to keep up.

He grinned.

It was a grin that could charm a woman's panties off—seriously. Chaz looked good enough to eat, but surprisingly, didn't act as if he knew it. He was as down to earth as they came, something I wouldn't have believed if I hadn't seen it for myself.

I was the one to notice the waitress approaching with our main course, and we headed back to the table. The lobster was the best I'd ever had. We topped off the evening with a flaming coffee, which was prepared right at our table.

When our bellies were full, Chaz leaned across the table and asked, "Feel like heading back to the hotel?"

I was disappointed, only because the evening had been going so well and I didn't want it to end. But I said, "Sure. After all, we've got to get ready for tomorrow."

"Actually, I was thinking we could hit the casino."

My lips spread in a wide grin. "A man after my own heart."

"What's your game?"

"I like blackjack," I told him. "Even if the house always takes my money. Mostly I play the slots."

"Up for some blackjack with me?"

I wasn't keen on losing any of the cash I was going to earn this weekend, but I was nowhere near ready to say good-night to Chaz.

So I looked at him and said, "Let's go win millions."

chapter twenty-one

For the first hour I watched Chaz win five hundred, then lose eight. When he dropped another two hundred in two quick hands, he got up from his chair and said, "I should probably quit before I lose my shirt. You want to try?"

"I don't know," I told him. "Looks like the house is cleaning up."

"Come on," he urged.

"Oh, all right. But I'd rather go to another table. This one isn't lucky at all."

"Pick your spot."

We wandered around until I found a table where the minimum bet was five dollars, something I was much more comfortable with than the fifty-dollar table Chaz had been at.

"You like this one?" he asked.

"I think so."

"If you feel it, own it."

"Okay," I said, more confidently. "This is the table I want."

"All right."

There were only three other people there, and I approached and took a seat. The dealer, a young man, grinned at me.

"You might not be smiling in half an hour," I warned him. "Because I'm here to win."

Before I could withdraw my wallet from my purse, Chaz was handing the dealer a hundred-dollar bill.

"Chaz."

"It's on me," he said.

"But—"

"But if you do insanely well, then I can recoup some of my losses. Deal?"

I had a feeling he would have it no other way. "All right. Deal."

The dealer gave me the equivalent of one hundred dollars in chips, and since I was playing with Chaz's money, I decided to bet twenty.

And won the first hand.

Squealing with delight, I turned to Chaz and gave him a high five.

"That's the way to do it," he said.

Three more hands, and I was up one hundred and forty dollars—and ready to move on to a table with a higher limit.

"Time to win your money back," I told Chaz.

"If you believe it, you'll achieve it."

I was determined to put his theory to the test, so went

right on by the fifty-dollar tables to the ones that required a minimum hundred-dollar bet.

I put two hundred down.

And won.

Now, I screamed. Four hundred dollars, just like that!

"You're on a roll," Chaz said, laughing.

And I certainly was. I took a hit, but immediately won three times in a row, betting one hundred dollars each time. Some excitement was generating around me, partly because a number of conference goers were nearby and wanted to see how Chaz and I were faring.

When I was up six hundred dollars, I looked at Chaz. He read my thoughts.

"You want to bet it all, don't you?"

"It's your money."

"Do what your heart tells you."

"I feel it," I said. "And I want to win back what you lost."

"Then do it."

I pushed the entire mound of chips to the middle.

The first card that came up for me was an ace. My heart started to pound from both excitement and fear.

When the dealer came back to me with my card, it was a ten.

I screamed as if I'd won a million dollars in the lottery.

Cheers erupted all around us. The dealer, an older man, winked at me as he passed me my stack of chips.

I looked at Chaz and said, "I'm out. I won back your money. That's what you call a successful night."

"You sure?"

"I told myself if I won, that'd be the last round."

"Gotta follow your instincts," he agreed.

We went to the cashier's booth to trade in my chips. I handed the bills to Chaz, but he waved his hand and shook his head.

"Chaz…"

"No, you won that."

"With your money."

"Keep it."

"You're being far too kind. I can't. You said I could win your money back for you, remember?"

I extended the bills, and Chaz obviously saw the resolve in my eyes because he said, "All right. We did have a deal. But I only lost a thousand. So you can keep the profit." He handed me two hundred dollars. "A deal's a deal."

I accepted the bills, knowing now that he would have it no other way.

"Thank you for a wonderful evening," he told me.

"Thank *you,*" I said.

And I thought, *I could get used to this.*

The next morning, I noticed an envelope slipped under my door when I was en route to the bathroom. I scooped it up, wondering what message I had from the hotel, and absently thinking that they had very nice stationery.

My fingers made quick work of opening the seal. Inside, I saw a flash of gold and the edge of a card.

Odd.

I withdrew the card and read the words *THANK YOU* embossed in gold, and then it hit me that this card wasn't from the hotel.

It was from Chaz.

A laugh bubbled in my throat. I opened the card and read the words he had written.

Vanessa—I can't thank you enough for all your help yesterday, and for giving me a most enjoyable evening. I look forward to what today will bring.

I closed the card, held it against my chest and released a happy sigh. It was the nicest thank-you card I had ever received, and had me once again thinking about fate.

Was this really happening? Was Chaz really interested in *me?*

Despite all odds, it appeared to be the case. I felt like I was living out a real-life romantic movie, and that I was at the part where I knew I'd finally found love and would live happily ever after.

All the heartbreak with Eli had to have happened to get me to this part of my story.

It was fate.

I was tempted to run to the phone and call Carla, or Alaina, to let them know how well my trip was going. In fact, it was going better than I'd ever expected.

But those phone calls would have to wait. First, I needed to shower and get ready.

I wanted to look my absolute best today.

After my shower, I applied a slightly darker shade of lipstick than I normally wore in the day, and a shiny coat of gloss, making my lips look luscious.

I decided not to wear the typical business suit. Nothing I'd brought seemed quite right. After getting to know Chaz much better the previous night, I wanted to play up my feminine, sexy side. Wear the kind of outfit that would have him following my movements wherever I went in the room.

I could hear my sister now, telling me that I was once again letting myself care too quickly, but I couldn't help myself. My brain could scream, "Slow down!" but once my heart was hooked... Well, my heart had a mind of its own.

And right now, it was feeling very much like it wanted Chaz.

He was the real deal, a good man. With the heartache he'd suffered, and how he'd handled it, it was clear that he was inherently decent and trustworthy. Our paths were crossing for a reason—how could I ignore that?

I tried on a burgundy sundress I loved, one that flowed around my knees, but then frowned. A little too casual. Great for the last morning brunch on the last day of the conference, but I had to remember that Chaz was paying me to oversee things, and I needed to make a respectable impression not just on him, but on the conference goers.

I glanced at the clock. The time was ticking away quickly. I had another fifteen minutes, max, before I needed to be downstairs.

I rummaged through the drawers where I'd placed my blouses, and came up with a body-hugging red top with a V-neck.

I held it up and glanced in the mirror. *Perfect*.

I'd brought a loose-fitting black blazer that I loved, and it would look perfect over this blouse, along with a straight black skirt that hung just below my knees. It was the perfect blend of business and femininity.

After a light spritz of a vanilla-scented body mist—a scent men always noticed when I wore it—I went downstairs eight minutes before I'd planned to be there.

When I got to the conference area, I saw Chaz immediately. His back was to me, and he was near the table where the hotel staff were setting up the buffet.

I drew in a deep breath and approached.

Then stopped cold when he moved to the left, and I noticed that two thirtysomething women were standing with him, their eyes as wide as their smiles.

My disappointment was so profound, it felt as if someone had thrust a hand into my body and squeezed my stomach, hard.

Chaz laughed, a warm sound that carried across the room.

He turned suddenly, almost as though he'd sensed me. His laughter died as his eyes locked on mine.

When his lips curved at the sight of me, I released a breath I didn't know I'd been holding. And in that moment, I realized how much I had come to care for Chaz in such a short time.

I had been deathly afraid that his face would drop, surprise in his eyes when he saw me—proof that I'd caught him flirting with these women, as he had with me the day before.

Instead, I saw a man who was genuinely happy to see me—and my spirits soared.

"Vanessa," he said, and started toward me.

I pasted on a smile and walked forward once more.

Ever the gentleman, he quickly turned back to the women and excused himself, then proceeded toward me.

His eyes swept over me slowly, taking in everything I wanted to flaunt. "Morning, beautiful."

"Good morning. Did you sleep well?"

"Not too badly. But a certain someone had me waking up early and unable to get back to sleep."

I didn't catch his meaning at first, until his eyes narrowed playfully on me.

"Oh. You mean me?"

He nodded.

I swallowed, unsure what to say. "Hopefully not in a bad way," I murmured.

"Definitely not in a bad way." Briefly, he glanced over his shoulder at the women, who were now filling plates with pastries. "I just had an interesting conversation with two of the conference participants."

"Mm-hmm?" I tried not to let any emotion into my voice, because I could only imagine how interesting those women wanted to seem to Chaz.

"They asked if we were going to be spending any time outside for any of the sessions."

"Oh…"

"Seems they think the Caribbean background is too beautiful to ignore."

"Is that so?"

Chaz nodded. "So I was thinking—"

"I'll talk to Calvin about it immediately. I don't know about today, though."

"Tomorrow's fine. It'll give us time to prepare, and let everyone know about the change of venue."

"I'll confirm with Calvin if Ripples is still available."

"Thank you."

"I'll take care of it now."

I had a walkie-talkie, but went to a nearby house phone and dialed Calvin's extension. A short while later, I was able to announce to Chaz that the change was a go.

"Amazing," he said. "You've been such a great help."

"I'll make the announcement at lunch."

I turned to walk away, but Chaz placed his hand on my shoulder. I slowly faced him. "You wanted something else?"

"Yes. What are you doing tomorrow night?"

"Uh…nothing."

"Good. Because with the extra time we have after tomorrow's sessions, I was hoping you might be free to spend it with me. Unless you're taking one of the excursions?"

My stomach fluttered. Yesterday's and today's sessions were full days, but tomorrow's would end at noon, allowing people to participate in one of three prearranged trips: a tour of Nassau, which included dinner at a local hot spot, a cruise of the various nearby islands, or a marine adventure. All the trips cost extra, and I had opted not to book one.

Now I was very glad I hadn't.

"Sure," I said to Chaz. "What would you like to do? Go over strategy—"

He shook his head, dismissing that idea. "No strategy. Something fun."

"I'm game," I told him, amazed that my voice sounded level and cool considering I wanted to jump up and down like an excited child.

"Excellent. I'll give you all the details tomorrow. As for tonight, how about dinner?" he suggested. "We both need to eat. It'll be my treat."

"It was your treat last night."

"And it'll be my treat again."

I bit my lip so I wouldn't smile. I almost wanted to pinch myself, things were going so well with Chaz.

"All right, then," I said. "That'll give us time to go over some details about tomorrow's schedule."

"That, yes. But mostly I want to enjoy your company."

Despite myself, I started to beam. God, I was so pathetic. You'd think I'd gone to the Bahamas to attend a Women Desperate for Men convention.

Chaz's lips quirked in a charming smile, which put me at ease. Did he really like me, or was he just interested in passing the time while we were both here for the weekend?

There was only one way to find out.

"I'd be honored to accompany you for dinner tonight," I told him.

"Great. We can meet at the concierge desk at six this evening if that's all right with you."

I nodded in agreement. "Perfect."

"Oh—and I forgot to say, about tomorrow. Make sure you bring your bathing suit."

My mouth fell open. "Excuse me?"

"Don't sound so alarmed. I'm sure you look like dynamite in a two-piece."

Now my face flushed. Hopefully, Chaz didn't notice.

"I'm taking you somewhere very special," he stated. "I'm sure you'll like it."

I'm sure you'll like it.

Chaz's words kept replaying in my head as I made my way

up to my room at the end of the day, my heart beating fast from excitement.

Mention the words *bathing suit* and I break out in a cold sweat....

The real issue was that I liked Chaz. A lot. His image on television and in pictures was enough to have me drooling, so being here and actually spending time with him was sending my libido into overdrive.

But the fact that he was sexy was the last thing drawing me to him. Well, almost the last thing. I loved that he was genuinely nice. He was a great guy, with a fantastic career—and he was taking *me* someplace special for the evening.

Upstairs in my hotel room, the first thing I did was call Debbie. With my trip going so well, I figured it was time I gave her an update. She might not be in the office, since it was after five, but at least I could leave a voice mail message.

I dialed her direct extension. The phone rang three times, and I thought it was going to voice mail when someone finally picked up.

For the first several seconds, no one said a word. But someone was there. I could hear the phone moving as if it had fallen to the floor or was brushing across the desk.

"Hello?" I said. "Hell*o?*"

"Ohh... H–hello?" Debbie sounded breathless, as if she'd done a hundred–meter sprint to get to her phone.

"Debbie?" I asked cautiously.

"Oh...Vanessa..." She giggled. "Hi."

I frowned. Five-thirty in the afternoon, and Debbie didn't sound at all like her normal professional self.

Then I remembered that she had been in New York on

business. Maybe she'd just arrived back at the office, and was a bit off-kilter from the flight.

Though why she would bother heading to the office on a Friday afternoon…

I asked, "Are you drunk?"

"Me…? No, not drunk."

"Then why do you sound…?"

"Ohh…" came a reply.

Another giggle cut me off, followed by a moan.

"Debbie, what are you doing?"

"I'm not alone," she said hurriedly. "I've got to—" Once again I heard a loud—and clearly sexual—moan.

Oh my Lord. "Jason!" I said accusingly. "Didn't you just get back into town?"

"Yes…" I wasn't sure if Debbie was replying to me, or responding to something Jason was doing with his tongue ring.

"What has gotten into you?" I asked.

"I don't think you want to know the answer to that… Ooh, ooh. Gotta go."

The line went dead.

I replaced the receiver, groaning in disgust. Had Debbie lost her mind? Receiving sexual favors from Jason when at least some of her colleagues were sure to be in the offices around her? Answering the phone while doing something X-rated? Sure, no one could fire her, but still.

And her poor husband. I felt really awful for Ben. I loved my friend, but he deserved better.

Frowning, I made my way to the floor-to-ceiling windows in my room and looked outside. It was another spectacular day, the sky a clear blue, the ocean calm. People were strolling the grounds and splashing around in the pools. I was in paradise, and yet I was suddenly feeling down.

Hearing Debbie in the midst of an adulterous rendezvous had unexpectedly dampened my spirits.

Debbie was cheating on her husband, Carla was contemplating an affair. Lewis had cheated on me, and so had Eli. Chaz's wife had cheated on him. Some people believed that being monogamous until death was an unrealistic expectation. Were those people right? *Was* it impossible to stay faithful to one person, no matter how much you loved them? Were we all supposed to stay faithful only as long as we felt like it and throw morality out the window?

No, I said to myself. I couldn't believe that. I absolutely believed in fidelity, and there had to be at least a few men on the planet who felt the same way.

Men like Chaz…

Clinging to that thought, I got ready for my date. I went through every single item of clothing I'd brought for this four-day trip, and *nothing* was suitable for a date with Chaz Anderson. Not a single thing.

So I did the only thing I could under the circumstances. I headed downstairs to the Gucci boutique, where I spent a fortune on a sexy little number that *was* flattering.

Two sexy little numbers, really. One for our dinner date this evening, and one for the surprise date the next night.

I know, I know—it didn't make sense. Not given my financial predicament. But I reasoned that I hadn't expected to get paid for helping Chaz, so that money was an unexpected bonus.

Plus, any cash I spent on clothes to impress him was an

investment. Because when he agreed to hire me as his agent, it would be well worth it.

And if he fell for me…well, that would be the best bonus of all.

chapter twenty-two

Chaz took me to a local Nassau eatery for our dinner on Friday night, and it was clear to me from our heated looks and body chemistry that our relationship was deepening. But never in my wildest dreams could I have anticipated his surprise for me on Saturday.

His Thursday seminars had dealt with the mental aspect of success. On Friday, he'd dealt with the emotional aspect. All of Saturday morning, he'd focused on the spiritual component.

I can tell you right now, I became a believer.

Not in God—I've always believed in God. But on Saturday I came to believe in Chaz and the fact that something real was brewing between us.

After spending an hour with the dolphins at the hotel's Dolphin Cay, Chaz took me to the marina, where we boarded a catamaran-style, motorized yacht. I had to pick my jaw up off the floor when I saw the impressive boat. I didn't imagine I'd get close enough to touch a vessel like this, much less board one.

The captain took us far out in the ocean, where Chaz and I spent an hour swimming in the warm, clear water. From this distance, the Atlantis Royal Towers looked like a toy figurine. I was a little nervous about swimming in the ocean, but the salt water really did help keep a person up, and the water was calm. A passing shower had us heading back on board, where a light lunch of fresh fruit and deli sandwiches was waiting for us. The crew kept the Bahama Mamas coming.

I thought that was the end of it, but Chaz told me there was more to the surprise.

"What more could there possibly be?" I asked.

"You'll see."

Now, as the motor yacht, a Queensland 60, skipped over the gentle waves with ease, I pinched myself to make sure I wasn't dreaming.

I definitely wasn't. I was very much awake, and very much alive.

My hair blew around my face as we gazed out at the water from the top deck.

"Look!" Chaz suddenly said, his eyes lighting up with excitement.

I whirled around to peer in the direction he was pointing. "What?" But I saw them immediately—sleek creatures jumping out of the water.

"Oh my goodness!" I giggled. "Dolphins!"

Chaz slipped his arms around my waist, and together we watched the school of dolphins as they played.

When they disappeared, I turned in Chaz's arms. "This

is absolutely incredible. Every minute of this experience with you…it's more than I could ever have dreamed of."

"It's only going to get better," he assured me.

I felt like a child going to Disney World, eagerly anticipating every experience to come.

Chaz left me for a moment to talk to the captain. After a few minutes, he returned to me.

"We're almost there," he announced.

We were standing at the stern, facing the back of the boat. I turned to look where we were going, but didn't see anything ahead of us but water. "Where?"

"I've kept the secret long enough. I'm taking you to a private island." Chaz's smile was bright and sincere.

"A private island!" I couldn't help exclaiming.

"There are plenty around here. I figured it'd be a nice treat to get off and enjoy one."

The ride on the yacht had been exciting enough, but a private island? Talk about the icing on the proverbial cake.

"Want to go downstairs?" Chaz asked.

"You mean…inside?" He had already shown me the striking interior: ultra-sleek cream-colored sofas set off by warm, polished mahogany. Every part of the vessel screamed of luxury, and I was surprised at how much the ambience was that of a posh hotel, rather than a boat. Then again, I'd never been on anything except casino and dinner cruises that sailed the waters of South Florida, which didn't even begin to compare to this.

"No, not inside," Chaz answered. "To the front."

I felt a modicum of relief. With the captain steering the boat, there was nothing to stop me and Chaz from going to the exquisite salon and screwing like rabbits. And while that thought was extremely appealing, I didn't want to give in to temptation.

Because I didn't want any part of this incredible time with Chaz to be simply about sex. My emotions were already invested in this man.

He reached for my hand. "Come on."

Anxiety caused my stomach to flutter. "The boat's moving kind of fast right now. I don't want to fall."

"You won't."

Chaz spoke with an easy confidence, the kind that made me trust him without doubt. He led me down the stairs and cautiously walked with me along the right side of the boat to the front, where we sat side by side on the raised deck.

"I see it!" I exclaimed, noting the shoreline in the distance. "What a lovely place. It's so small!"

The island couldn't have been more than a mile wide, and with the mass of brush, palms and pine trees just beyond the beach, it didn't look as if anyone had ever set foot on it.

Several beats passed, then Chaz said, "Can I ask you something about Eli?"

Eli…what a way to mar an otherwise perfect moment. I drew in a deep breath, then let it out slowly. "I don't particularly care to talk about him. I'd rather forget about that period in my life."

"Understandable," Chaz said. "But you became something of a star, being on the news. When my brother realized who you were, he was a little excited."

A hollow laugh bubbled out of my throat. "Come on."

"I'm serious. And I called my mother, told her I'd met you, and she remembered you from TV, as well. She wants your autograph."

I shot Chaz a doubtful look, but he nodded. I almost blurted that his family must not get out much, but I refrained. These days, I was hard on myself for ever having dated Eli. Looking back on our relationship, I saw all the pieces that didn't fit. Little inconsistencies here and there, but enough that I should have known he was keeping something from me.

"Hey." Chaz placed his finger beneath my chin and angled my head upward. "I didn't mean to make you sad."

"I'm not sad," I told him. I gestured to the ocean. "How can I be sad in surroundings like this?"

But I wasn't being honest. The lawyer's call and the threat that I would lose my home hung over my head like a dark cloud. The only ray of sunshine right now was Chaz.

He smiled then, a look that was totally arresting. What was it about his smile that made me melt every time?

"I guess," he began slowly, "what I really want to know is if you have any residual feelings for him."

"For Eli? The guy screwed me over—understatement of the century. No, I absolutely do not have any residual feelings for him."

"Good. Very good."

And then, without warning, Chaz kissed me. Finally. And I swear, it was like an electric charge passed through both of our bodies when our lips met. Not just a passionate charge, but something else. It was a feeling I hadn't quite experienced before, not even with Lewis, a man I'd been fiercely attracted to.

As we pulled apart, as Chaz gave me that sweet and sexy smile again, I knew why.

He *liked* me. This wasn't about just getting into my pants. I would bet my life on it.

What was happening between us was as sudden as it was powerful.

If this was an act, then Chaz had gone into the wrong career. He could be making millions in the movie business if this was all a game to him.

"Wow," I said softly.

"Wow is right."

The yacht slowed dramatically, and both Chaz and I looked over the bow. We'd been lost in each other and hadn't even noticed we were fast approaching the beach.

I got to my feet and squealed. Yes, me. Squealed as if I'd never been on a date before.

And it was almost true. I'd never been on a date like this one.

On the beach, about fifty feet away from where the men were now securing the boat, was a table covered in a white cloth, with two place settings and a candle. Obviously, we hadn't stumbled upon this island by accident. This was the kind of scene I'd read about in the romance novels I loved.

"You didn't," I said.

"You like?" Chaz asked.

"*Like?* Chaz—this is utterly amazing. When did you have the time?"

Out of nowhere, a man appeared pushing a cart across the

sand. It couldn't have been easy, but he looked cheerful, as though he routinely did this sort of thing.

And maybe he did. For the rich and famous.

People like Chaz.

Chaz got off the boat, stepping into the water. Then he helped me off. I clutched my sandals in my hand, knowing I'd need them when I got to the hot sand. I'd bought that sexy new Gucci dress just for this date, but when Chaz had told me that we'd be heading to the Dolphin Cay, I hadn't ended up putting it on. I'd spent the entire date in a bathing suit and a wrap.

I'll just have to save the dress for next time, I thought. *When I see Chaz in Miami.*

He took my hand and we walked together. My eyes devoured the scene in front of me, wanting to forever etch every detail in my brain. The romantically set table. The pristine white sand. The lush background of palm trees and thick vegetation. The smiling waiter in a crisp white suit. Even the birds soaring overhead. I wanted to remember it all.

By the time we got to the table, the waiter was pouring wine.

"White zinfandel," Chaz explained. "Since that's your favorite."

"You remembered."

"You only told me the day before yesterday."

It wasn't so much that he remembered. It was that he cared. I recalled the first time I'd gone out with Lewis and ordered white zinfandel. He'd laughed, saying that it wasn't sophisticated and proceeded to order an extraordinarily dry German wine that I hated.

Chaz and I sat, sipped wine, and then the waiter proceeded to tell us the soup choices. Yes, *choices.* When I would have been happy with anything served in this idyllic setting.

"I'll have the ginger carrot," I told him. Chaz asked for the same.

"There's only one main course," he explained, "then a couple desserts."

"Chaz, you couldn't improve upon this evening if you tried."

"No? Well, how about this?"

As if on cue, I heard music playing, and quickly whipped my head around. About ten feet away was a saxophonist, also decked out in a white tuxedo. My mouth fell open in complete shock.

"Chaz—"

"Did the evening just get better?"

"How did you plan all this?" I asked him.

"I made a few phone calls. And voilà."

My stomach suddenly lurched, making my excitement fade and skepticism take over. I remembered how Eli had promised to take me to the Bahamas and wine, dine and romance me. It was a vacation I couldn't wait for, and yet everything with Eli had ended in the worst way possible.

Was I a confessed hopeless romantic, being conned once again? Should I really accept this situation for what it seemed to be—or assume there was a dark, ulterior motive behind Chaz's actions?

After all, this was a bit over the top. If he was interested and wanted to impress me, he didn't have to go to such dramatic lengths.

Then again, what if this was proof of just how much he cared for me? Was it *impossible* that he could be one of the few truly romantic men on the planet?

"A toast," Chaz said. "To getting to know each other better," he said simply.

Just like that, I put my concerns aside. I decided that tonight was a night for hopeless romantics.

Both Chaz and me.

"Let's dance."

Chaz didn't wait for me to answer, just pushed his chair back, got to his feet and extended his hand to me. I took it and let him lead me a few feet away from the table, where he drew me into his arms.

We danced. With the romantic island setting, with the saxophonist playing a love ballad, we danced as though we were a couple here on our honeymoon, rather than two people who had met only a few days before.

"I'm already feeling a bit sad about tomorrow," Chaz said, his warm breath fanning my cheek.

"Why?"

"Because the seminar ends then. And it's back to the real world."

Back to the real world… Words I didn't even want to contemplate—except for my daughter. I missed her fiercely.

But there was no reason what I was experiencing with Chaz had to end here.

"There's something I've been meaning to discuss with you," I said tentatively.

Chaz pulled his head back to look at me. "What's that?"

"Maybe this all doesn't have to end…our getting to know each other, working together…"

"Go on."

I cleared my throat, stalling for time as I gathered my courage. "Well, you know that I work for an agency. I told you that when we first met."

"Right."

"And I know you don't work with an agent—and that you said you never want to."

"Right again."

"But I was thinking…maybe you might consider changing your mind?"

"Go on."

"I like you, Chaz. Even without this incredible setting, I still like you. And if you reject my offer, I'll still like you. I just want you to know that what's happening between us is sincere on my part, even if we never do business together."

"Okay."

"How long did it take you to organize this four-day conference? How much of *your* precious time did you spend dealing with the little details?"

"A lot."

"I think it's been a success. No doubt about that. But it could have been better attended," I added, hoping he wouldn't recoil at my frankness.

He didn't. In fact, he pulled me closer.

"There's no reason you couldn't have had four hundred people here instead of two hundred," I continued.

"And the punch line is?"

"Let someone else deal with the mundane details. Let

someone with experience reach the widest audience possible, get you even more speaking engagements and seminars. In the end, even with the commission you'll pay an agent, it will lead to more money in your pocket."

Chaz didn't say anything, just continued to hold me. With each passing second, I feared the worst. I just knew that he was going to say no.

Instead, as I glanced up at his face, he seemed to be seriously contemplating my offer.

"You would be my agent?" he asked.

"Yes," I said without hesitation, though I'd still have to hammer that out with Debbie. I would tell her that it was a deal breaker. Either I was Chaz's agent or he walked.

"And just so you know, people come to us. People in search of motivational speakers. I firmly believe that if you sign with my agency, a whole new world of opportunity will open to you."

"It's tempting."

"But?" I asked.

A few beats passed. "But you know what's even more tempting?"

"What?"

"You."

"Chaz—"

He silenced me with a kiss. A kiss that was as tender as it was passionate. When we pulled apart, I was breathless.

For a moment, I forgot there were people around us, that's how into Chaz I was. Until the waiter cleared his throat, breaking the spell between us.

"I do not mean to disturb you," he said in his light Bahamian accent. "But the dinner will soon get cold."

"Right," Chaz agreed. He turned to me. "We should eat."

"Absolutely."

The saxophonist continued to play all through dinner, which was a Bahamian favorite—deep-fried conch. I'd never tried it before, but the firm meat was textured and flavorful. For dessert, we enjoyed crème brûleé and chocolate mousse.

After taking a walk along the shore of the small island, we went back to the beach, where we watched the sun begin to set while we drank more wine.

The sky was a mix of brilliant oranges and maroon when Chaz stood. "I hate to do this, but we should get going before it's completely dark. It'll take about an hour to get back."

"Of course." I sounded a little too chipper, courtesy of all the wine and Bahama Mamas I'd consumed.

"And then, I have to prepare for tomorrow. It'll only be a half day, but I need to be awake and alert for the brunch."

"Right."

Chaz offered me his hand and helped me to my feet. I was more drunk than I'd thought, easily losing my footing and stumbling into him. He braced both hands on my shoulders to steady me.

"You all right?" he asked.

"I'm fine." My words slurred. I turned to the saxophonist. "Thank you, Mr. Saxophone Player. You were really awesome."

To my own ears, I sounded over the top. But I couldn't

stop myself. I turned to the boat's three crewmen. "And you guys—you know how to sail a boat!"

Chaz secured his arm around my waist and walked with me through the shallow water to the catamaran's steps.

"Oh, God. I'm being loud and obnoxious, aren't I?"

"No."

"Of course I am. Two glasses of wine, I'm good. Three and I become an idiot. Not to mention those yummy cocktails earlier."

"You're beautiful," Chaz told me. "Adorable, really."

"You're not lying?"

"I would never lie to you."

Despite the drunken cloud in my brain, I knew I could believe his words. At least, he sounded one hundred percent genuine.

I had no clue what might come out of my mouth next, so I pressed my lips tightly together so that I wouldn't speak.

Chaz helped me onto the boat, where I none too gracefully stumbled onto a seat. Then he climbed aboard and sat beside me, wrapping an arm around me.

I rested my head against his shoulder, reveling in the comfort of being so close to him. The next thing I knew, we were back at Nassau Harbour, ready to disembark.

I was instantly awake, and wiped at my mouth in case I'd been drooling. To my mortification, I saw a wet spot on the shoulder of Chaz's shirt.

"We're here, Sleeping Beauty."

"I was out like a light," I commented.

I gathered my belongings, and we got off the boat. And then I started to wonder what was going to happen next.

I'd spent the most romantic afternoon and evening of my life with this man. While we'd refrained from having sex in one of the boat's cabins, I was certain he was going to ask me back to his room, the typical denouement to such an evening.

Just as certain as I was of that, I also had doubts. That nagging thought that this was too good to be true popped back into my head. What had been the most incredible day ever for me could be par for the course for Chaz. He could easily set up such elaborate displays at all his conferences, and bed eager and gullible women. He no doubt had the resources to make that happen.

But when we got to the bank of elevators leading upstairs, he turned to me and said, "Thank you for a very lovely day."

"Thank *me?* No, thank you."

He took a deep breath before continuing. "I hope you won't be disappointed if I don't invite you up to my room."

"Oh?" I gaped at him.

"I like you, Vanessa. Really like you. And I don't want to give you the wrong impression by spending the night with you. But make no mistake, there's nothing I want more than that right now."

I couldn't have been more shocked—nor more pleased. My feelings must have clearly shown on my face, because Chaz said, "You look stunned."

"You continue to amaze me," I told him. "I like you, too. So much that I don't want this to be just about sex."

He looped his arms around my waist and planted his lips on my forehead in a soft kiss. "Know that every minute tonight, I'll be thinking of you."

My entire body grew hot. I suddenly felt the urge to lock my lips to his and beg him to make love to me. But I didn't.

I said, "I'll be thinking of you, as well."

"I hope to be able to spend time with you after the brunch tomorrow."

"Yes, definitely." I didn't want to ruin things by telling him that our time together would be limited, because I had a six o'clock flight to Miami.

He gave me a soft kiss on the lips. "See you tomorrow."

chapter twenty-three

If I'd been smoking joints all afternoon, I couldn't have been more high. I went into my room, kicked my sandals off and collapsed onto my bed with a sigh of utter pleasure.

I think I'm in love.

Suddenly, what I'd felt for Eli had seemed like a grade school crush at best. The emotions I was feeling for Chaz were in a whole other league.

When the phone rang, I rolled over on the bed and snatched it up before it could ring a second time. If it was Chaz calling to invite me to his room, I was going to throw caution to the wind and say yes.

"Hello," I answered, my voice deep and provocative.

I wasn't sure, but I thought I heard some sort of croak. No, a gasp.

"Chaz?" I asked, alarm spreading through me.

"Vanessa?"

I narrowed my eyes. Was that— "Nikki?"

I heard more gasping, followed by sniveling.

Now I sat up. The grief in my sister's voice was obvious, which, I reasoned, could mean only one thing.

"Oh, God, Nikki. What happened to Rayna?"

"Rayna's okay," she croaked, and then burst into tears.

I held the receiver and listened to her bawl. This wasn't like my sister. She was grace under fire, calm even in the midst of chaos. She was supermom, superwife, my elder and my superior.

"Nikki?" Had my sister come down with terminal cancer?

She sobbed and sobbed, making me regret the fact that we weren't close. Not that I didn't want to be. It was that she'd always treated me like I was the family's greatest disappointment.

"If you're dying," I said cautiously, "please tell me. I'll check out of the hotel and head home right now."

"I'm not dying," she said, her voice suddenly loud. "It's Morris!"

My heart slammed against my chest. "*Morris* is dying?"

"No!" she snapped, and I was taken aback by her tone. "He's having an affair!"

It took a full five seconds for her words to register, and when they did, I actually laughed. "Come on, Nikki. Morris? You know the man adores you."

"He is," she insisted. "He's screwing some filthy slut."

Now I rolled my eyes. The Morris I'd known for eight years was too boring and predictable to be screwing a filthy slut.

And hell, why was it that when I was in the Bahamas, hoping to enjoy my time on this beautiful island, my friends and family saw fit to drag me into their crises?

"What happened?" I asked. "You two had a fight?" More likely, Morris had stood up to her. "It's completely normal to have a spat every now and then, even every day. That does not mean Morris is—"

"He said I'm controlling."

All right, so it was just as I thought. Morris had grown some balls and my sister couldn't deal with his "rebellious behavior."

Unfortunately, I couldn't disagree with the fact that she was controlling, but I didn't think she would appreciate me saying so.

Instead, I said, "Words spoken in anger. That doesn't mean anything."

"Then how about chlamydia?" she asked in an angry whisper.

The words sent a chill down my spine. Surely, I must have misunderstood. Or she had misunderstood. Something was seriously off here.

"Chla-*what?*"

"Chlamydia!"

Oh, Lord… I cleared my throat, wondering if my sister had lost her mind or if the unspeakable was true. "Why would you think you have chlamydia?"

"Other than the green discharge coming out of me?" she asked, and the image was so crass, I almost vomited the fried conch. "Because I saw my doctor today, and I've been calling you ever since."

"You have chlamydia?" I asked in a whisper, as though the people in the next room could possibly hear me.

"Yes."

"Oh my God."

"I'm moving out."

"Where to?"

"To your place," she answered, and if possible, I felt even sicker than when she'd dropped her bombshell.

"M–my place?" I stuttered.

"You can't turn your back on me at a time like this!" she cried.

"I'm not! I would never do that. But *my place?* There's not enough room for you, me and the kids."

"You expect me to stay here? With *Morris?*"

My mind scrambled for an answer. If my sister did indeed have chlamydia, then I could see her point.

But still.

"What about kicking Morris out? That's what wives do. Especially wives with kids. You make sure *he* leaves. He's the one who cheated. He should be the one to have to find a new place to live."

"And what if he goes to her?"

"After she gave him chlamydia?"

Nikki burst into tears.

"Oh, Nikki. I'm so sorry." I thought about everything my sister had said to me in the past about the men I'd dated, how she was certain they would hurt me in one way or another. And when Eli had been murdered, she had practically gloated when she'd said she'd been right about him.

This was my perfect chance for some payback. I could easily rub salt in Nikki's wound, point out that while she'd spent so much time being hard on me, she clearly hadn't been paying much attention to her own marriage. And after she'd told *me* to get tested for HIV, she was the one who'd ended up with a sexually transmitted disease.

Of course, I didn't say anything like that. In fact, my heart broke for Nikki. I didn't know how to comfort her in the face of her grief.

"I'm so sorry," I told my sister again. "I'd be less surprised if you told me that Morris was gay."

"He's out late again tonight. I haven't even gotten to talk to him about the 'present' he gave me."

"He doesn't know?"

"If he doesn't, he's a moron. I hope his dick falls off."

"Incredible."

"You know, I think you're right. Why should *I* be the one to leave this house, the house *I've* made a home? I'm going to pull a *Waiting to Exhale* on his ass."

"Nikki…?"

"Oh yeah, that's exactly what I'm gonna do." She sounded like she was on the move. "He's got a lot of expensive clothes in his closet. Enough to make quite the bonfire on the front lawn."

"Maybe that's—"

"Thanks for listening, sis. Gotta run."

And with that, Nikki hung up.

Oh, damn.

I debated calling her back, but then decided against it. If Morris had cheated on her, he deserved what he got. And quite frankly, I wished I'd learned of Eli's betrayal while he was still alive, so I could have lashed out and done something that would have hurt him—like burning all his baseball memorabilia. If my sister needed to do this to get over Morris's brutal betrayal, who was I to tell her not to?

Her call did put a damper on my mood, however, making me doubt the existence of true love and romance. It was the same way I'd felt after my call to Debbie. I was back to wondering if fidelity was a nice idea, but only a fairy tale.

Of all the men in the world, Morris was the one I never thought would cheat. But if *he* could cheat…

"That doesn't mean Chaz would," I said aloud. I refused to believe that our time together hadn't meant anything.

Unfortunately, experience had taught me that both men and women sometimes betrayed each other. But there were still decent people who believed in honoring their word. Honoring their love.

People like my parents. My aunt Lola and her husband, Vince.

And wasn't Chaz honoring me? If I were in his bed right now, maybe I could discount the evening as one huge, overly dramatic, excessively romantic effort to get me naked.

But Chaz didn't want me to doubt his sincerity, and for that reason had *not* wanted to sleep with me.

If that didn't count for something, then nothing did.

The next morning, brunch was the first order of the day, so I wasn't required to be there the moment it started. The plan was to meet Chaz at the brunch, have a relaxing meal, then get on with business.

The event was at an outdoor venue called Shark Bites. Amid palm trees and blue skies, the place was picturesque. It was packed when I arrived. The hotel staff seamlessly made the rounds, pouring coffee and clearing plates. The buffet options stretched a span of at least twenty-five feet.

I searched the area until I saw Chaz—at a table in the middle of the room.

My stomach sank. He was surrounded by women.

I quickly turned my gaze away and shuffled across the floor to the buffet. My heart was thundering in my chest, my hands shaking slightly.

Chaz can enjoy the brunch with some of the conference attendees, I told myself. *Don't get bent out of shape over this.*

Still, my heart wouldn't calm down. I was back to thinking that I was probably a fool to believe in love. I went through the buffet line, piling food on my plate without paying much attention. It was only when I was at the end of the line and someone commented, "You must be hungry," that I looked down at my plate. Toast sat atop scrambled eggs, which were on top of thick oatmeal. Bacon and ham and hash browns somewhere in the mix, as well.

I must have looked as though I hadn't eaten in a year.

Smiling sheepishly, I set down my plate at the edge of the buffet table.

I stole a quick glance at Chaz. He and the women—three of them—were all smiling, then laughing.

My stomach clenched.

Why was I letting this get to me? So what if Chaz was having brunch with three women who looked like they were hanging on his every word? He hadn't taken *them* to private islands for a once-in-a-lifetime dinner.

Obviously, he had to be nice. His goal was to sell his books and tapes and videos. He wouldn't accomplish that goal by being inaccessible to people who'd paid a pretty penny to be here.

Still, I couldn't help feeling glum as I glanced around the restaurant, looking for a spot to sit. I couldn't help wondering if I was lying to myself. If I was desperate to believe in a happily ever after I would never find.

My eyes once again wandered to Chaz. This time, he saw me. His face lit up like a neon sign.

Quickly, he got to his feet and beckoned me to his table. I shrugged, letting him know I didn't think that was a good idea. But inwardly, I was beaming.

Stop being so damn insecure. Fate is at play, remember?

I got a new plate and went through the buffet again, but this time I paid attention to the selections and took some eggs, some bacon and whole wheat toast.

I turned—and nearly lost my plate as I almost collided with Chaz.

"Morning," he said.

"Hey," I responded, trying to sound cool.

"Why don't you join me?"

"The table's full."

"We can make room."

"You're about to do your talk soon. I think it's better that I find a seat right up front."

"Nonsense. I want you near me now."

"All right, then." He'd twisted my arm enough, and I wanted nothing more than to spend every possible moment close to Chaz.

The hostile, possessive looks from the woman at Chaz's table were obvious—even if they were disguised with smiles.

Regardless, brunch was uneventful. When Chaz gave his final speech, people stood up and cheered. The man oozed charisma, and at the end of his talk, people who hadn't yet bought books or CDs lined up to do so. Again, some asked him to pose for pictures, and Chaz graciously obliged.

It was an hour after his speech had finished that the last of the patrons gave me cash for the entire series of his books. I counted out the change, gave it to the man, then closed the till.

Chaz slipped his arms around my waist from behind, surprising me. "I thought that would never end," he murmured.

"What are you talking about?" Warmth spread through my body at being this close to Chaz. "You love every minute of this stuff."

"I love it," he said, and turned me in his arms, "but I'm dying to spend more time with you."

Brazenly, he kissed me. After a couple seconds, I pulled away and glanced around nervously.

"What's the matter?" he asked me.

"Are you sure you want people seeing us like this?"

His arms tightened, giving me my answer.

And, Lord, did I feel good.

"I was thinking," Chaz began, "that we can do something fun today. Oh, wait a minute," he suddenly said. "I'm forgetting something."

"What?" I asked.

"To pay you."

"Right," I said slowly. I'd forgotten, too. Being in Chaz's arms made me forget lots of things.

He walked to the till and opened it. He spent some time

counting silently, then said, "Four thousand." He put it all in an envelope and handed it to me.

As crazy as this might sound, I wasn't as excited about the cash as I thought I'd be. I guess it was because this meant goodbye, and there were no guarantees that I'd see Chaz again.

"Hey," he said softly, and placed his finger beneath my chin to lift it up. He smiled softly as he stared into my eyes. "What's the matter?"

"I hate that I have to leave," I told him.

"I'm not through with you yet," he stated. "I'd love to go parasailing today, if you're game. Or do something you'd like to do."

"It sounds wonderful," I admitted. "But I...I don't have much time."

His eyebrows shot up.

"My flight is at six. Which means I should be leaving here in the next few hours to get to the airport."

Chaz's disappointment was palpable. "Is there any way you can change the flight time? Perhaps stay another couple days?"

"I would love nothing more—"

"But you've got to head back to the office," he finished for me.

"That, yes. But there's something else." I suddenly felt nervous as I looked at him. "Maybe we ought to sit down."

Chaz eyed me curiously, but didn't say anything. Instead, he led me to a table a few feet away, where we sat.

"You're not married," he said, chuckling uneasily. "I know that, because your fiancé was recently killed. Right?"

"Married?" My eyes bulged. "No! Chaz, there's no way I would be married and getting close to you the way that I have."

His relief was evident in how his grip on my hand loosened. "Big relief," he said. "It's happened to me before."

"You're kidding."

"No."

"And here I thought only men were capable of that kind of deception." I grinned to soften the blow to his gender. "*Some* men."

"I've had my share of bad experiences. When a woman sees dollar signs, sometimes there's nothing she won't do."

It sounded as if Chaz and I could sit and swap bad experiences for hours, but we were getting offtrack. I had to let him know about Rayna.

"I can't stay," I began, "because I have to get home to my daughter."

I watched as my words settled over Chaz, and was prepared for the look that would come next: disappointment. Instead, his eyes lit up, a reaction I hadn't expected. "You have a daughter?"

"Yes."

"And here you had me worrying that there was another man in the picture. How old is she?"

"Rayna is two."

"Two. Such a wonderful age."

His comment made me realize that he might have children himself. "You have kids?" I asked.

He shook his head. "No. But I was dating a woman once. A single mother."

My spirits lifted incredibly. "You were?"

"Yeah." He shook his head ruefully, which was like a pinprick on my enthusiasm.

"Obviously, it didn't work out…"

"And not for the reason you might think. The child's father was still involved, more than I thought. More than this woman had told me. He was apparently still in love with her, and once he knew she was involved with me, he protested our getting together, to the point where she ended things."

"Oh."

"It's made me a bit wary," Chaz admitted. There was a pregnant pause as he studied me. "What's the situation with Rayna's father?"

"He's, uh…" Oh, God. What should I say? I couldn't let Byron rob me of what I'd found with Chaz. "Well, he's dead."

"Dead?" Chaz asked.

Now that the lie was out, I had to keep going. "You know—the story you saw on the news."

Chaz's eyes widened. "Oh! That guy. Of course."

I didn't quite meet Chaz's eyes as I nodded.

"You have a picture of your daughter?"

"Of course." I pulled my wallet out of my purse and produced the latest photos of Rayna.

Chaz took them. "Wow. Look at that smile. She looks like you."

"Thank you."

"She's beautiful."

"I like to think so, but hey, I'm not biased or anything."

"You're lucky," he said softly. "Family. That's what it's all about."

As I stared at Chaz, my feelings for him grew. He was a very sentimental human being. I wasn't used to that in a man. I was used to men having soft sides on occasion, but the guys I'd been drawn to had all been strong types who didn't necessarily show their emotions.

Chaz was quite different.

He handed the photos to me and said, "Nothing on the news mentioned Eli had a little girl."

Oh, shit. Did he suspect I was lying?

"I—I asked the media to please respect my daughter's privacy," I lied. "Considering the circumstances."

"Gotcha. Well, at least I know you're not trying to blow me off by leaving."

"Absolutely not! And like I mentioned yesterday, I hope this won't be the end of our association. I'd love very much for you to come to Miami and meet with me, my agency, and continue the discussion we began."

Chaz's eyes locked on mine. I held my breath. I waited for him to shoot the idea down, because I wanted to prepare myself for the worst. But the way he was looking at me…

"Absolutely."

"I really believe that you're going to see the value of working with an—"

He placed his finger over my mouth to silence me. "How much time do you have?"

"A couple hours."

"Then what do you say we head to the pool? Because I'd love to see you in that sexy bathing suit again before you leave."

My lips spread in a slow smile. "That sounds like an offer I can't refuse."

chapter twenty-four

I'd just retrieved my suitcase from baggage claim at the Miami airport when my cell phone rang. Seeing my sister's number, I quickly answered the call.

"Nikki, what's happening?"

"It's not Nikki," said a timid voice. "This is Morris."

"Oh. Morris. Hi." I headed outside.

"Look, I know you know."

"Good, then that means I don't have to pussyfoot around the issue. How could you do this to my sister?"

"I made a mistake," Morris said softly.

"A mistake? You gave my sister an STD." The bulging eyes of the woman next to me at the curb made me realize I'd spoken too loudly. I crossed the street at a brisk pace toward the airport parking. "That is not a mistake. That's…that's evil."

"It's not like I did it on purpose."

"Your penis just fell into another woman's vagina, did it?"

"That's not what I mean. And that's not why I'm calling." I didn't speak, so he continued. "Your sister's been arrested."

I stopped suddenly, shrieking, "What?"

"She went crazy. Lost her mind. Threw all my clothes on the front lawn and started a bonfire. The police arrested her for misdemeanor arson."

"Jesus." Drama, drama, drama. When would my life be free of it? I'd simply wanted to return home, rush to Rayna and squeeze her to make up for the past four days.

I started walking again and asked, "She's in jail right now?"

"Yeah, until the morning at least."

"For a misdemeanor? That's excessive."

"There's more."

I wondered if I'd die of a heart attack before I got to see my daughter again. "Tell me."

"I called the police because she was out of control. They only wanted to talk to her, reason with her. But she freaked out, and when one of them stepped toward her, she punched him in the face. She's been charged with assault."

I cussed a stream of expletives.

"I know," Morris said. "I thought you'd want to see her or something."

An image of me heading to the county jail with a file in a cake filled my mind. How was it that in the four days I'd been gone, all hell had broken loose?

Now at my car, I opened the trunk. "You're going to fix this, right? Get a lawyer, do what you have to do. Right?"

"Of course. Your sister can be impossible at times, but I still love her."

"Funny way of showing it."

"It was the first time, I swear. And the last. You need to make her understand that."

"I'm not the one who slept with another woman." This time, a man in his forties at the car beside mine glanced my way. Then winked.

I quickly put my luggage in the trunk, then got behind the wheel. I turned on the car and cranked the air-conditioning to high.

"I can't imagine what you think of me," Morris was saying.

"Not very much, I'll admit. These days, I'm all out of patience for cheating men."

I ended the call, dropped the phone onto the passenger seat, then gripped the steering wheel.

My sister. Arrested.

What else could go wrong?

I called the police and confirmed that, yes, my sister had been arrested. Yes, the charge was serious. Assaulting an officer was a charge that had jail time attached to it.

I'd wanted my sister to be able to get a bit of revenge, but I hadn't expected it would go this far. If only I'd known, I would have called her back and talked her out of it.

An hour later, just after 8:00 p.m., I was back home, and I pushed my sister's plight out of my mind. The only thing I was concerned about was seeing Rayna.

First, I brought my luggage to my condo. Then I hurried downstairs to Carla's.

I was beaming when she opened her door. "Hey, Carla." I gave her a quick hug. "Where's my baby?"

"Sleeping," she replied.

"What?"

"She fell asleep about ten minutes ago. I told her you were coming home, and she was excited about seeing you. But she tired herself out at the pool earlier."

"Oh," I said, disappointed as I stepped into Carla's apartment. "That's too bad."

"You hungry?" Carla asked. "I made spaghetti."

"Sure. I'll have a plate." I hadn't eaten since the brunch, and was starving. "Beats the pretzels they serve you on the plane."

As Carla got me a plate of food, I noted that she seemed a bit down. My poor friend...she was missing her husband terribly. I couldn't do anything about that, but I could help take her mind off things for a bit. I made a mental note to plan a spa day as soon as possible.

I ate the spaghetti in record time. Then Carla and I settled on the living room sofa with a glass of wine each.

"How did the trip go?" she asked me.

So I told her how I'd met Chaz, gotten the opportunity to work for him, and how I hoped he'd give my agency a chance. Then I told her how he'd romanced me like no man ever had, and I couldn't stop gushing about how wonderful my time with him had been.

"Everything was so amazing," I said, knowing I was wearing a megawatt smile that couldn't be extinguished even if my lips were stapled shut. "Honestly, I've never met anyone like him."

"You said that about Eli," Carla pointed out.

She looked as glum as I'd ever seen her, but I ignored her lack of enthusiasm. "I know what I said about Eli, but this is a whole other league. What I feel for Chaz is...mature. I mean, we had the chance to jump into bed together, but we both made an adult decision not to act on our feelings, and to invest in something more."

"Should I go buy that gun now?" Carla asked.

"Excuse me?" I asked, frowning.

"You remember. You told me that if you ever fell for another man, I should shoot you."

"Oh. That. Well, I didn't mean if I fell for a guy like Chaz."

Carla rolled her eyes.

"You know, Carla, you could try to be a little bit happier for me. After everything I've been through."

"I'm sorry. It's just hard to hear about your revolving sex door when I haven't had sex in five months."

I gaped at my friend. "Revolving sex door?"

Carla slapped a hand to her forehead. "I don't know why I said that."

"Yes, you do. You think that I sleep with man after man?"

Carla met my gaze but didn't say a word.

"No, tell me," I insisted.

"All right. Since you asked. First, there was Lewis—and you thought you were going to marry him. Then Eli, who you got engaged to. Now this successful motivational speaker. All within less than a year. Not to mention the few guys you dated in between Lewis and Eli. It doesn't sound like you're hurting in the love department."

"Lewis couldn't be faithful if he was given all the money in the world," I retorted. "Eli was married, and now his wife wants my condo. Plus, he was killed screwing his lover, and people look at *me* like I was some gold-digging slut. Most of the residents in this building who used to at least greet me with a smile now turn their noses up when they see me. You want to switch roles with me—give me your happily married status and take all my drama?"

"I'm not happily married," Carla said.

"Your husband's gone. You miss him. That's to be expected."

"I cheated on him," Carla blurted, and didn't meet my eyes.

My mouth fell open. Was the whole world going to hell in a handbasket? First Debbie, then Eli, Morris and now Carla? The state of love in the world was at a dismal low.

When I'd arrived at Carla's condo, I was disappointed to learn that Rayna was sleeping. Now, I was glad she was— or Carla and I wouldn't be having this conversation.

"Carla." I shook my head sadly as I stared at my friend. "I told you not to do anything crazy."

"I didn't have sex," she clarified.

I blew out a relieved breath. "Thank God."

"But—we came close to it."

"What does that mean?"

"We kissed. A lot. He started to get naked."

"Carla!" I exclaimed. "Please don't tell me you subscribe to the Bill Clinton definition of sex."

"No! Definitely not. It didn't get that far. I thought I wanted to. He seemed so nice, and sexy, and into me, but as soon as he took his shirt off, I thought, *What am I doing?* And then I kind of freaked out. I told him he had to leave right away, that I never wanted to see him again. He looked at me like I was crazy, then ran out the door."

"Good. Let him think you're crazy. That's fine."

Carla nodded, her eyes downcast. "The thing is, now I

feel like the biggest whore on the planet. Like some ungrateful bitch. My husband is in Iraq, and I almost cheated on him."

"Almost," I stressed. I squeezed her hand in support. "That's the important part. You came to your senses and realized you could never betray Paul."

"I still feel bad."

"Feeling bad is okay. Feeling bad will keep you from doing anything like this again. And by the way, when did you get the time to do this? You've been home with Amani, and watching Rayna."

Carla glanced at me briefly, then looked away. "Please don't be mad."

"You didn't do anything insane like leave the kids unattended, did you?"

"No. Nothing like that. But once they were sleeping, he…he came here."

"I can't believe you brought this guy to your home," I said. "But," I quickly added in a more cheerful tone, "that's not the issue here. The point is you sent him away before you crossed the line."

She nodded.

"Who is he? Forget it, I don't want to know."

Carla drew in a shuddery breath. "Do you think I should tell Paul?"

"Tell your husband?" I was shocked she was even considering it. "Absolutely not."

"You don't think I owe it to him to be honest about this? Especially since I realized I couldn't go through with it?"

I thought about Debbie, who had been forever scarred

by Ben's admission that he'd been tempted to cheat. Nothing good had come of that. Even years later, Debbie didn't trust him, and now she was jeopardizing her relationship and family because *she* didn't want to get hurt first.

I shook my head. "Never tell him, Carla. *Never.* I know you won't do this again. You know you won't do this again. But Paul…he may not be so understanding. This will only hurt him. No, don't tell him. A little omission is not a big deal."

As I said the words, I was thinking about my own situation. How I'd told Chaz what amounted to a little white lie when I'd said that Rayna's father was dead.

Technically, it wasn't true—but if you thought about it, Byron was *practically* dead. He wasn't in Rayna's life in any consistent fashion. He didn't send support payments, and in no way was he a real father to her. Eli, she missed. Byron could die tomorrow and it wouldn't cause a blip on Rayna's radar.

Still, I felt a little guilt at the lie I'd told Chaz. I liked him—a lot—and I didn't enjoy lying to people I cared for.

I heard a door open, then the sound of little feet running across the floor. My heart soared, and I shot to my feet just as Rayna rounded the corner to the living room.

"Mommy!" she squealed.

"Rayna!"

As she charged toward me, I dropped to my knees and spread my arms wide. She leaped at me and wrapped her arms tightly around my neck. My eyes misted as I felt her body against mine. Reuniting with my daughter always made me emotional, as if I'd found a piece of my heart that had been missing.

"Mommy! Mommy, Mommy, Mommy!"

"Sweetie, I missed you so much." I held her tight and inhaled her fresh scent. Then I planted lots of kisses on her cheek and neck that made her start to laugh.

Clutching Rayna, I stood. She couldn't stop smiling, and neither could I.

Carla regarded us fondly. "She must have heard your voice."

"Go home," Rayna said.

"Yes, sweetie. We're going to our place." I faced Carla. "I guess I should head upstairs. It's getting late, and I have to be up early for work." It dawned on me that I hadn't told Carla about my sister, but I could do that tomorrow. "I'll see you in the morning."

"You want me to get Rayna's things?" Carla asked.

"No rush. I can do that tomorrow. I don't feel like doing laundry tonight."

Carla nodded, then walked with us to the door.

As I stepped into the hallway, she asked me in a low tone, "You really think I shouldn't say anything to Paul?"

"Never," I replied without hesitation. "You tell Paul, and all you're going to do is risk ruining everything you've worked so hard for."

As I spoke the words, I was well aware that my advice was as much for myself as it was for Carla.

chapter twenty-five

The next morning, I was preoccupied with my sister's plight. The news that she had been arrested had put a damper on my excitement over how well my trip had gone.

But I was determined to head into the office before dealing with Nikki's crisis. I wanted to give Debbie all the details of the weekend so she knew I hadn't hung around the bar drinking coladas the entire time.

Then I would call that snake of a brother-in-law and find out if he'd hired a lawyer yet.

But for now, I allowed myself to remember Chaz and the time we'd spent together, and how my life was finally taking a turn for the better. Walking toward the security desk, I had a bounce in my step. Even Edgar, the guard at the entrance, noticed my mood.

"Looks like someone had a great weekend."

"I did, Edgar." I couldn't help grinning. "I was in the Bahamas for work."

"Work, right. That smile on your face—looks like more pleasure than work."

"Work doesn't have to be boring and tedious."

"Tell that to my boss. Bahamas." He shook his head. "Some people have all the luck."

I wiggled my fingers at him as I started for the elevators. "Have a good day."

"Hey," Edgar suddenly said, and I turned to face him. "Byron said he's been trying to reach you."

"Byron?" My eyes nearly popped out of their sockets. *Byron McLean?*

"Yeah, I know." Edgar half nodded, half shrugged. "I was a little surprised when he asked me how you were doing. I know you two don't get along so well."

"Understatement of the century."

"I guess he misses you."

I didn't even know how to respond to that. Edgar's announcement was beyond startling, and a little disconcerting. "Are you talking about the Bryon I think you're talking about? The one who used to work in this building as a security guard, then quit to avoid having to see me when he decided he didn't want to support his own child?"

"He said he's trying to work on his issues," Edgar said. "He wanted me to tell you that."

Good God almighty. I started backing away from the security desk. "This is too freaky. I'll see you later."

I turned and all but ran to the elevator. What was going on? Both in their early thirties, Edgar and Byron had been casual friends when they'd worked together at this building, and used to go to the same gym. But I had no clue they were still close enough that Byron would talk to Edgar about me.

I hoped Byron had been drunk when he'd spoken with Edgar, because the last thing I wanted was for him to show up in Rayna's life right now. In the past, he'd appear out of nowhere for a day or two, then disappear for months. Rayna was getting older and understood more. I wanted to protect her from the emotional roller coaster she would ride should Byron keep popping in and out of her life whenever it suited him.

I'd gotten along fine without Byron since the beginning. If all he could be was a once-in-a-blue-moon father, then I'd rather he stay away forever.

You have Chaz to concentrate on, I told myself as I stepped onto the elevator. *Forget Byron and his games. If things go well with Chaz, he'll be your future—and Rayna's father.*

By the time I reached my floor, I convinced myself that Byron *had* to have been drunk, and that he didn't really care to see me or Rayna. Why would he want to reach me now, when the last eight months had passed without a word from him?

As I stepped off the elevator, I was determined to have only positive thoughts floating through my mind. I remembered the precious moments I'd spent in the Bahamas with Chaz. Being on the yacht with him, seeing the dolphins jumping in the water, him kissing me for the first time…

A rush of pleasure ran through my body.

Alaina had the phone pressed to her ear, but when she saw me she said into the receiver, "Arlene, I'll call you later." Then she turned to me. "Girl, if that look on your face is any indication, you had one hell of a trip. Tell me all the details."

Her excitement about my trip boosted my spirits even more, given Carla's lack of enthusiasm about Chaz, my sister's current drama and the disturbing news that Byron had been trying to reach me.

"I'll tell you everything. But not here. You've got to come to my office."

Alaina was out of her chair in a flash. "Ooh, girl—do you have some juicy news?" she asked as she fell into step beside me. "You hooked up with someone?"

"Keep your voice down."

"Right." She cleared her throat and spoke loudly. "The conference went well, then?"

At my office, I opened the door and we slipped inside. Alaina closed the door behind her and said without pre-amble, "Okay, tell me *everything*. What does he do, how was he in bed, and how many inches?"

"Calm down, girl."

"Okay, okay. It's just that you know I live vicariously through you, since I'm not getting any. And it's exciting to hear about all your conquests."

All my conquests? The comment made me remember Carla's words the previous evening, about the revolving door on my sex life.

"Do you really think I have a lot of conquests?" I asked.

"Well, sure. When one relationship ends for you, it doesn't take much time before you're with someone else."

"That's not true." Was it?

"When you broke up with that firefighter—what was his name?"

"Ian." Alaina was referring to the man I'd dated before I'd met Lewis. "But that wasn't serious."

"Ian, that's right," Alaina went on, ignoring my comment. "How long did it take before you and the next guy got together?"

My back stiffened. "If you're referring to Winston, we only went out a couple times. Dinner and a movie. I'm glad I didn't sleep with him, because after two dates, I was certain he was bisexual."

"Welcome to South Beach. Home of some of the world's hottest men who'll bang Brenda on Friday, and Bob on Saturday…."

"He was hot," I said wistfully. Then shuddered.

"And before Eli?" Alaina pressed. "You weren't single two months after Lewis."

"I was single for five months after Lewis!" I retorted.

"No. There was that guy. The taxi driver who wrote poetry."

"Oh." I frowned. "Right. Pierre, the psycho." I'd dated him a few times before I realized the guy had some major issues. I'd been with Alaina the night I'd met him. We'd hit some clubs in North Miami Beach, and when I was in a cab on the way back home the driver had started reciting poetry to me.

All right, I admit—I was foolishly impressed. But no man had ever done that for me before.

"Getting back to you," Alaina said. "You don't think you date a lot of guys?"

"I guess I never thought about it. Since all the men I've

been with have been complete scumbags. And I didn't date for over a year after Rayna was born," I said proudly. Suddenly, I felt my reputation was at stake.

"I'm not judging you," Alaina told me. "I look up to you." She paused. "So…did you hook up with someone, or what?"

"No," I said, and Alaina frowned. "But—"

"Ooh, I love it when there's a but. Hopefully a nicely shaped, firm one."

I shot her a look, and she pressed her lips tightly together. Then I spoke. "You know I went to the Bahamas to try and convince Chaz Anderson that he needed to work with an agency."

"Right."

"I think he's really interested. He's planning a trip here to discuss things."

Again, Alaina's expression was one of disappointment. "That's it?"

"I swear, Alaina—it's like you *want* me to be a slut."

"What's wrong with being a slut?" she asked, and giggled. "No, something else happened. You still have that look on your face. The look you had right after you met Eli."

"Oh, you're right," I admitted, as if she'd forced some secret out of me. "There is more."

"I knew it!"

"No, we didn't sleep together. But, girl, we had the most romantic date I've *ever* had in my life. He's coming to Miami not just for the agency, but for me! We clicked—totally— and I can't believe it, because this guy is superhot and could have anyone, but he's interested in me!"

"Wow."

I spent the next ten minutes filling Alaina in on every detail of the trip to the private island.

"And you didn't have sex?"

"No. And that's the most amazing part. He said he wanted me to know that he was interested in *me,* and that by sleeping with me it would make what we'd shared seem fake. Like it had been a grand setup to get me into bed."

"I had no clue guys like that existed. You sure he's not gay?"

"*Totally* sure."

"Girl, I don't know how you get all these guys."

"You go on lots of dates," I said.

"Yeah, but it's been forever since I've had sex."

"And we both know why. Somehow, your ex is getting to the guys you date." And a threat from Jorge Rivera, one of Miami-Dade's finest, carried a lot of weight. Men weren't too interested in getting a 9 mm slug in the head.

"I don't know how he always finds out who I'm dating. If I have lunch with a guy today, by tomorrow the guy's telling me he doesn't want to see me again."

"Jorge's stalking you," I said, half joking. But seriously, I had to wonder. I also had to wonder why he would even do that. Jorge was the one who'd left her.

"I wonder if he's stalking the other ten women he's screwing?" Alaina asked sourly. After being married for five years, she'd learned her husband's ugly secret: he had slept with no less than ten women since they'd gotten married. It had been a devastating blow for Alaina, whose twin boys had been four years old when they'd split up.

"Wait a minute," I said slowly, an idea hitting me. "You can help me."

Alaina narrowed her eyes. "Sounds like you've already made a major impression on this guy. Why would you need my help?"

"My sister," I said.

"Huh?"

I gave Alaina the condensed version of what had happened with Nikki the day before.

"And you think I can help you *how?*"

"Jorge," I answered. "If you call and ask him to look up my sister's case, maybe he can pull a few strings."

"Oh my God. You did *not* just ask me to call the ex I hate—"

"It's not like you don't talk to him."

"Only because I have to when he comes to pick up the kids."

I walked toward Alaina, my hands joined together in a prayer-like pose. "You can be nice for one phone call, can't you? Long enough to convince him to help my sister out."

"When it comes to Jorge—"

"Please," I begged. "My pair of Jimmy Choo slingbacks you've always wanted—they're yours."

"Really?"

I'd said it, but now I regretted it. However, I couldn't withdraw my offer. Closing my eyes, I said, "Yes."

"In that case…"

There was a pounding on my door, then it opened. Debbie, scowling, appeared.

"Have you seen— There you are. Alaina, what do you think you're doing? You work at the reception desk. Front of the agency, big desk with a phone that's been ringing off the hook?"

"I'm sorry," she said, and scurried past Debbie.

As soon as Alaina was gone, Debbie turned her gaze on me. I expected her to be a bit pissed, but instead her eyes lit up.

"Don't keep me in suspense. How'd it go?"

So I told her my good news. Buttered her up so she'd be likely to say yes to part two of my plan. Because I didn't just *want* to become an agent. I *needed* to become one.

Around eleven, Morris called. He told me that my sister was scheduled for a bail hearing in the afternoon, and wanted to know if I could come to court to support her.

I'd go to court, all right—but prayed I could keep my wits about me so that I didn't end up in jail along with Nikki.

I hung up with Morris and was about to call the reception desk when my phone rang. I picked up on the first ring.

"You owe me," Alaina said. "Big-time."

"Jorge's gonna pull a few strings?"

"One of Jorge's friends was the arresting officer. He already talked to the guy, told him to give her a break."

"And you think he will?"

"I can't make any guarantees."

"Thank you, thank you." It was the best I could ask for. I would keep my fingers crossed and hope that all went well at the bail hearing. "Look, I've got to run. My brother-in-law called and Nikki wants me at the courthouse for support."

"You're gonna owe me more than that pair of Jimmy Choo shoes. Jorge wants the kids for a full week to take them to Disney World—without me."

"Think of the bright side. While he's gone, you can go on all kinds of dates without the men ending up in the Atlantic."

I called Morris to tell him the news, then got my stuff and headed out of the office.

The Miami-Dade County Courthouse wasn't too far from my office in downtown Miami, and without much traffic, I got there in ten minutes.

An hour and a half later, it was over. My sister got a very stern warning from the judge, my brother-in-law got evil looks from everyone in the courtroom, and then Nikki was released.

It took another half an hour for us to get her stuff and have her officially released from custody, and Nikki tolerated Morris for all that time. But the moment she inhaled her first breath of fresh air, she turned to him with a look more venomous than I thought her capable of (which is saying a lot).

"Get lost," she told him.

Even I felt a little sorry for Morris—a little. "Come on, Nikki. He did everything he could to fix the situation."

She ignored me. "Let me make this perfectly clear, Morris. If you don't get out of my face by the time I finish saying this, I'll end up charged with murder this time—and I won't regret a minute of the time I do."

"Nikki," I said.

"I'm sorry," Morris exclaimed. "How many ways can I say it?"

Nikki shoved him, and it was a good thing he wasn't closer to the edge of the steps, or when he stumbled backward, he would have gone down the flight of stairs and likely cracked his skull open.

Which, judging by the look of disappointment on my sister's face, was exactly what she'd wanted.

"Nikki, stop!" I urged.

"Fine." Morris threw up his hands. "You want us to be over, then we're over."

"And don't you dare go back to the house, Morris. Or you'll be the next one going to jail."

Nikki spoke loud enough for the entire world to hear, and I buried my face in my hands. When I looked up again, Morris was running to his car, which was parked on the street.

"Did you have to do that?" I asked my sister.

"After what he did to me?"

"I know. It's just that…maybe if you weren't so…harsh, he wouldn't have—"

"Don't you dare blame me for his infidelity!"

I bit my tongue. But I was suddenly feeling a lot less judgmental toward Morris, knowing that my sister wasn't the easiest person on the planet to live with. Maybe he wasn't a scumbag, but a guy who'd needed an escape from an overbearing wife. I'm not saying that justifies an affair, but perhaps it's immature to look at everything in black and white. Maybe there are shades of gray when it comes to these matters.

I asked, "Where are the kids?"

"At Morris's mother's house. Oh, God. We have to go there. I don't want Morris pulling anything crazy."

"Like taking off with the kids? Are you serious? Morris has had his one act of rebellion. Quite frankly, I don't think he's capable of another."

"And I didn't think my own husband would give me chlamydia!"

"I get the point," I mumbled, but I thought, *drama queen.* There was no way Morris was going to abduct their children. If you asked me, he seemed genuinely sorry for what he'd done. And I was pretty sure that after contracting an STD, he'd learned his lesson.

"We need to make it to Miramar before he does," Nikki urged. "I think I should drive."

"I can get us there."

"Morris is cheap—he'll take the interstate, so we can get there faster if we take the turnpike."

My sister was in one of those moods—the kind where if she didn't get her way, she'd turn into a complete bitch. So I didn't argue.

When we got to Morris's mother's house, we learned that he was on his way there. Nikki whisked the children into my car as if a hit man were on her tail.

Mrs. Godwin watched and said very little. Her face was drawn, her lips tight, and I could only imagine what she thought of Nikki's dramatics.

I shrugged as I looked at the woman, letting her know I was just along for the ride.

Back in the car, Nikki hit the gas and backed out of the driveway.

To pull my thoughts from the current situation, I kept checking my cell phone messages, hoping that I'd somehow missed a call from Chaz.

I hadn't.

chapter twenty-six

I'd been hoping to head straight home after dropping off Nikki, but that was not to be. She insisted I stay for dinner—dinner *I* cooked because she was too *stressed* to do so. Then I comforted her while she cried and bitched about Morris.

By the end of my three-hour visit, I was feeling a lot more sympathy for my brother-in-law. Actually, I wondered why he hadn't cheated before now.

Maybe he had, but I did believe he was being truthful when he'd said this was the first time.

Of course, when I told my sister that, she erupted in a fit of tears. "You might be used to guys screwing around on you, but I'm not. And this hurts! I thought Morris was my soul mate."

I urged my sister to pull herself together, because her histrionics were going to upset her kids.

At the mention of her kids, she'd looked panicked. "Oh, God. I have to call a locksmith. And a real estate agent."

"You don't have to do any of that tonight."

She didn't let me leave until I'd called and set up an appointment with Sheila LaRoche, one of Kendall's top real estate agents, for the next day.

By the time I got home, it felt like I'd been up for seventy-two hours straight. Rayna was asleep, so I carried her from Carla's place to mine and put her in bed.

She didn't stir.

Once again, I checked my cell. No calls. No messages.

I checked my home phone. No messages from Chaz.

I drowned my disappointment in a glass of wine.

By the next morning, I was in a funk. And not so much because I was depressed over Chaz—which I admittedly was—but because if I didn't hear from him, I could kiss becoming an agent goodbye.

And if I had to kiss becoming an agent goodbye, it meant I would have no way in hell to even begin to buy out Tassie Johnson and keep my apartment.

I couldn't pull myself out of my bad mood even when I got to work.

"Here," I said to Alaina, handing her the box that contained my Jimmy Choo slingbacks.

"Don't look so depressed. It's only a pair of shoes, not your firstborn."

I mustered the best smile I could and went to my office.

I was in the middle of a spreadsheet with appointments and bookings when my phone rang. I snatched up the receiver and placed it at my ear. "Vanessa Cain."

"Now why does a beautiful lady like you sound so sad?"

Instantly, I sat up straighter. My spirits lifted and my heart started to race. "Chaz?"

"Yes, it's me."

I closed my eyes and mouthed the word, *Yes!*

Then I tried to play cool, calm and collected. "How are you?"

"I'm good. Very good."

"How was your flight back home?"

"Interesting."

"Meaning?"

"A flight attendant was flirting with me the entire first leg of my flight."

Okay… "And you're telling me this why?"

"To see if you'll get jealous," he said softly, his voice teasing.

"It worked," I told him.

"Good," he said. "Though you have nothing to worry about. That woman's got nothing on you."

Talk about a pick-me-up. Just hearing Chaz's voice had me grinning from ear to ear.

"So, what are your plans for the day?" Chaz asked.

"Oh, work. Going over schedules for some clients. Lots of fun stuff."

"Are you the kind of woman who stays in her office and eats a granola bar for lunch?"

"No, not me. I try to go out with a couple friends, make lunch an event. Or with clients," I quickly added, remembering I'd told Chaz that I was an agent, not an office manager.

"How about meeting me for lunch?" he asked.

I laughed. "Sure. I'll get right on that, have my private plane ready to fly to Chicago in the hour."

"I meant we could have lunch in Miami."

My heartbeat stumbled. "Are you…are you here?"

"I told you I'd come to see you."

"I know, but…where are you?"

"A hotel downtown. Close to a really nice-looking area called Bayside."

Somehow, I kept my squeal of delight inside. But I did excitedly say, "You're close to my office!"

"So can we meet? Or are you taking out another client?"

"For you, I'll clear my schedule."

"Excellent. Now, I don't know what's good from what's not."

"I'll make the reservations. Can you meet me at the front of Bayside Marketplace at twelve-fifteen?"

"I sure can."

"See you then."

The fact that Chaz was in Miami could mean only one thing. He was seriously considering signing with our agency, and if that was going to happen, it meant I had to speak to Debbie first.

The thought was a little overwhelming. I knew Debbie well, and although she was a friend, she liked to be the one to call the shots. If she approached me with the idea of me becoming an agent, fine. But I had no clue how she would deal with me being the one to broach the subject.

Half an hour later, I was outside the door to her office. I rapped softly on the heavy oak.

"Come in," she called.

I opened the door and entered. She smiled when she saw

me. "Vanessa. Did you finish confirming the travel arrangements for Lori Hansen's trip to Dallas?"

"I did, yes."

"And you reached Michael Hoffman at his country home?"

"Yes. Taken care of."

"Good." When I didn't leave, she asked, "Was there something else?"

"Yes." I inhaled a breath for courage. "I was wondering if I could talk to you about something."

"If you tell me that you're quitting—"

"No, definitely not quitting." I sat on one of the two chairs opposite her desk. "Hopefully moving up, actually."

Debbie eyed me with confusion. "I don't understand."

"Well, I've told you in the past that I'm interested in becoming an agent."

"Yes, I know. But—"

"And that's what you say every time I mention the subject. 'I know, *but.*' 'Yes, *but.*' Like you don't think I'm serious."

"Vanessa, you are the best office manager I've ever had."

"And I enjoy the work. It's just…I'm ready to grow. I told you when you hired me that I was interested in opportunities for growth."

Debbie frowned. "I don't know, Vanessa. There are four agents in this office, and no one's going to give up any of their clients."

"That's not what I'm asking. Because I'm on the verge of bringing a client to this firm, one who is high profile, his star rising…and I want to be the one to manage his career."

Debbie's eyes lit up. "Chaz Anderson? He said yes?"

"He flew to Miami this morning to meet with me. I'm taking him out to lunch."

"Why didn't you say so?"

"Because I want to make sure that if he's interested, he gets to be *my* client. I don't want to wait anymore."

Debbie considered my offer. She'd make money off Chaz whether he was her client or not, since she owned the agency, and a percentage of the fees went to her.

"He likes me," I told her. "He's connected with me. And I pretty much told him I'd be the one working with him."

"Sneaky, sneaky." Debbie tsked. "I love it." Slowly, she nodded. "All right. You land Chaz Anderson, and you can be his agent. That's the deal."

"Really?"

"I want Chaz with this agency. Go get him, girl."

"And I still get the finder's fee?"

"Of course."

Smiling like a fool, I jumped to my feet. "Debbie, thank you."

"No, thank *you*. You worked some real magic in the Bahamas. I've heard Chaz speak, and he's very anti-agent. So, if you have him singing a different tune…"

"I don't know for sure, but the fact that he's here makes me hopeful," I told Debbie.

And I was also hopeful for another reason.

That Chaz was here in Miami as much for pleasure as he was for business.

Before I left the office for lunch, I stopped at Alaina's desk. "Alaina, where are my shoes?"

Her eyebrows went on high alert. "Excuse me?"

"Okay, *your* shoes. I need to borrow them. Chaz Anderson is in town!"

"I already put them on."

"Then take them off and let me borrow them. I'll return them after lunch."

Alaina groaned. "This is so unfair." Grudgingly, she slipped out of the spectacular satin slingbacks. I kicked my low-heeled sandals off and put the Jimmy Choos on.

Oh yeah, I thought. *These shoes will seal the deal.*

"I'd better get them back!" Alaina called as I sailed out of the office.

I waved without looking around.

I considered my reflection in the elevator's dark mirror. While it was too dark to fully see myself, it was obvious I needed to freshen my makeup. I dug my hand into my purse and came out with my lipstick, applied a fresh coat, then fluffed my hair.

Stepping outside into the hot sun, I realized that I should have called for a taxi upstairs. What was the point in applying fresh makeup if I was only going to melt before I got to Bayside? The weather had gotten increasingly hot, but it wasn't summer yet, when there'd be daily afternoon showers to cool the city off.

Thankfully, I hailed a taxi without much effort. Three minutes later, I was exiting the cab in front of Bayside Marketplace.

I saw Chaz immediately, and he saw me. His smile was bright and instantaneous.

I couldn't help running toward him. He moved forward

to meet me, and I threw myself into his arms. He kissed me on the mouth, making me realize how much I'd missed him since I'd left the Bahamas.

"I can't believe you're here," I said.

"I wanted to see you again as quickly as possible."

My heart fluttered. Honestly, I've never felt more excited in all my life. Or more lucky. For some reason, I'd been given a second chance at love, and I wasn't going to blow it.

By the end of the lunch, I was certain that Chaz was going to sign with our agency. I was also certain that he and I were well on our way to happily ever after.

"I have to head back to Chicago this evening," he said.

"You do?"

"Uh-huh. I flew in for the day." He paused. "To see you."

The only time I'd been happier than this moment was when I'd given birth to Rayna. "I can't believe you did that," I said softly.

"Are you free this weekend?" he asked.

"I can be."

"Good. Because I'd like to fly back down and spend some time with you. You and Rayna."

"You'd fly down here again?" I asked. "So soon?"

"I have a private plane," he explained. "May as well put it to good use."

"Well, in that case." Suddenly, I frowned. "Hey…you have a flight attendant on your private plane?"

"Of course. She used to be a stripper, so she's great at entertainment."

My eyes widened.

Chaz laughed. "I'm kidding, of course."

"*Ohh.*"

"I took a commercial flight to the Bahamas," Chaz explained. "Hence the flight attendant. But when I travel within the States, I use my plane."

"I could be your flight attendant," I offered. "My years as a topless waitress have taught me a lot about entertaining, as well."

Now Chaz raised an eyebrow, and I was the one to laugh.

"Very funny," he said.

"You're not the only one with a sense of humor."

I loved that we could laugh like this. I loved that everything was going so well.

I reached across the table and squeezed his hands. "Oh, Chaz. I can't wait to spend more time with you."

I was on a natural high for the rest of the day. Debbie was elated that I was one step away from signing Chaz, and Alaina was elated that I was one step away from getting laid.

I was so happy that after filling Carla in on the day's events, I even called my sister to share the news with her.

But before I could tell her my wonderful news, she told me hers.

"Hey, Vanessa. I'm so glad you called."

"Why? What's up?"

"Sheila LaRoche has been great. She thinks I'll have an offer on the house by the end of the week."

For a moment, I said nothing. Then I voiced my concern. "Nikki, don't you think you're moving too fast?"

"Hell, no. If Sheila brings someone in who makes an offer, I'm going to take it."

"*You're* going to take it?"

"You'd better believe it."

"What about Morris?" I asked.

"What about him?" Nikki countered.

"Don't you think he should have a say when it comes to accepting any offers?"

"Are you forgetting what he did to me? He's lucky he'll get anything out of the house when it sells. And he can forget about getting custody of the kids. I've already talked to a divorce lawyer who says I have a very strong case for full custody."

"Whoa, Nikki," I said. "I know you're mad at Morris—and you have a right to be—but selling the house by the end of the week? You're making a really important decision really quickly. I think you should hold off selling the house until you know for certain that you're not going to work out your differences."

"Whose side are you on?" Nikki demanded.

"I'm on the side of your family. You and Morris have been married for eight years. You have two adorable boys. Maybe you won't work things out, I don't know. I'm just saying that you should pause, take a breath, think things through."

"I *have* thought things through. I'm moving on, Vanessa. Maybe you would have forgiven Eli just to have a man in your life, but I'm not that desperate."

My sister's comment was so harsh and insensitive, it made me see red. "You know something, Nikki—I'm sick of you lashing out at me all the time. Sick of you judging me. You're always on my case about the guys I date. Never once have you been supportive. You act like you're Miss Perfect, like you know everything. Funny how you didn't know you were pushing your husband away."

"Van—"

"The wonder isn't that Morris cheated on you," I said, barreling on. "The wonder is it took him so long! You treat him like a child, beat him down whenever you can. I may not have a man in my life, but at least I can't say that I was afraid to love. I'll never regret that."

And then I hung up.

For a few minutes, I felt awful. Then Rayna, who'd been playing with her dolls on the floor, climbed onto the sofa and onto my lap. She gave me a kiss on the cheek, as though she knew that was just what I needed.

I forced myself to think about *my* future, not my sister's. My future in the love department was looking very bright.

And by the end of this weekend, it could only be brighter.

chapter twenty-seven

On Thursday evening, I went grocery shopping in preparation for Chaz's arrival. Nikki hadn't called me back all week, and I felt awful about our fight, but I wasn't about to phone her.

I concentrated solely on the good things in my life—Rayna, and the upcoming weekend with Chaz.

For the most part, people didn't snicker or sneer when they saw me anymore, the CNN footage of me all but forgotten. But there were some occasions when I could tell people recognized me.

Today was one of them.

"That's her," I heard one of two women whisper as I made my way down the bread aisle. I'd noticed them staring at me two aisles over, when I'd been buying spices.

I gritted my teeth, but kept strolling down the aisle at Publix. I wasn't about to get into a confrontation with Rayna in tow.

I was glad to be rid of the two when I rounded the corner,

but a few minutes later, I saw them approaching from the opposite end of the snack food aisle.

I'd have to be blind not to notice that they kept staring at me, but whenever I glanced their way, they turned their heads.

Now I was getting angry, but I was determined to ignore them. I was sick of people looking at me, thinking that they knew me because they'd seen me on CNN. Judging what kind of mother I was because I'd had the bad fortune to be with a guy who had lied to me.

One of the young women started to laugh as I neared them, and that was what pushed me over the edge. Forgetting my resolve to avoid a confrontation with Rayna around, I left the cart behind me and stomped toward the two women.

A person can only take so much.

"You might think I haven't seen you staring at me and snickering," I said to them, "but I have. And I'm not going to be treated with disrespect by anyone anymore. My God, I'm here with my daughter. If you don't like the sight of me, stop following me around!"

Both women's eyes widened in horror as they looked at me. Good. They needed to be shamed.

Satisfied, I whirled around on my heel. And then one said, "We only wanted your autograph."

I stopped dead in my tracks, and slowly faced the two young women again. "What did you say?"

The dark-haired one extended a piece of paper and a pen. "We saw you on TV and wanted your autograph. But we were a little afraid to approach you."

Now I was the one who felt shame. "Oh." I swallowed. "I thought… Some people haven't been very nice to me since seeing me on the news. I'm sorry."

"Why wouldn't they be nice to you?" the dark-haired woman asked. "It's so obvious the guy you were with was a total creep."

"Exactly," I agreed, instantly warming to these beautiful young women. "My fiancé lied to me. Like that hasn't happened before."

The brunette was still extending the pen and paper, which I now accepted. "Who shall I make this out to?"

"Shelly and Marnie," they said in unison, then giggled.

No sooner had I signed the piece of paper than I heard a crash. I spun around to see a jar of salsa broken on the floor. Rayna started to cry.

"Oh, shit!" I charged toward her. Remembering the women, I turned to them and said, "It was great to meet you."

They smiled and waved as if they thought I was a movie star.

How stupid had I been? To leave Rayna and go tell people off? Maybe the stress of the past months was causing me to have an emotional breakdown.

"Oh, baby." I unbuckled my daughter from the cart and pulled her into my arms. I couldn't be mad at her. I was the one who'd left her too close to the shelf.

As I continued to comfort Rayna, a smile spread on my face. Marnie and Shelly's comments had proved that not everyone had judged me harshly after seeing me on the news.

I took that as a positive sign that everything negative in my life was finally in my past, and that I had nothing but good things to look forward to.

★ ★ ★

Chaz's plane arrived at the Opa-locka Executive Airport at five-thirty Friday evening. It took him another hour to get to Lummus Park Beach, where I told him I'd be with Rayna.

I was more nervous than I thought I'd be as I anticipated his arrival, more so than when I'd hoped that he might show some interest in me.

Because now I knew that he liked me, but that was only the first step. If he didn't like Rayna… A man who couldn't accept my daughter would never be right for me.

Seeing a black town car pull up to the curb, I held my breath. A few moments later, the back door opened and Chaz emerged. As always, when he saw me, he smiled.

I waved.

Rayna was sitting at my feet, coloring the concrete with pink chalk. Chaz didn't see her until he passed the stone wall that led into the park area. His gaze instantly dropped to my daughter, his grin growing wider.

"Rayna," Chaz said in a singsong voice, going directly for her. He dropped onto his haunches, and to my utter surprise, Rayna threw her little arms around his neck.

Chaz chuckled. "Wow. If that isn't a wonderful greeting, I don't know what is."

The sight of them together warmed my heart.

"Vanessa, she is adorable. Absolutely precious."

"I like to think so."

Chaz scooped Rayna into his arms and lifted her as he stood. "I brought you something," he told her, and that's when I noticed that along with the small suitcase I'd seen his driver take from the car, he also had a small gift bag.

"For me?" Rayna asked in a tone that was both excited and awestruck.

"Yes." Chaz offered her the bag.

Rayna giggled as she reached in and ripped out the tissue paper. And when her fingers closed around a small box containing a toy pony, she squealed and kicked her feet with pure joy.

"You like ponies, do you?" Chaz asked.

Rayna's head bobbed up and down. "Open it."

"Chaz, how thoughtful of you," I said.

"Mommy, here." Rayna extended the pony to me, and I set about opening the package.

"Look," Rayna said to Chaz. She pointed toward her artwork on the ground.

"You made that picture?" Chaz asked.

Rayna nodded.

"Wow. That's beautiful," he cooed. "You think you and I can make a picture together?"

Excited, Rayna tried to ease herself from Chaz's arms. He released her, and she took his hand and walked with him over to her box of chalk.

Chaz bent down, accepted the piece of green chalk Rayna handed to him, then started to color.

As I watched them, I was sure.

Chaz was the Mr. Right I'd been waiting for all my life.

After spending a couple hours at the beach with Rayna, I brought her to Carla's, who had agreed to watch her for the evening. Chaz and I went back to my place, where we both changed for dinner.

I took him to a trendy South Beach restaurant called the Forge, where I insisted on paying for the meal.

Afterward, we went back to Ocean Drive, where we strolled along the beach hand in hand.

"It's beautiful here," Chaz commented. "A great place to live."

"I know," I said. "You've got the excitement of the clubs, the lure of the beach, the beautiful architecture. I love it."

We walked a bit more, the waves lapping at our bare feet.

The beat of Latin music mixed with hip-hop filled the air, coming from the number of clubs on the famous South Beach strip, reminding me that I'd promised Chaz a night of dancing. "Whenever you're ready to hit the clubs, just say so."

"Sure." But he didn't seem the least bit interested in dancing. Instead, he was entirely content to stroll with me along the water's edge.

"Can I say something?" I asked him after five more minutes had passed.

He stopped. "Of course."

"And you're going to think this is corny—but don't laugh."

"I promise not to laugh."

"I feel like we're living in the pages of a romance novel." I paused, waiting for him to laugh hysterically, but as promised, he didn't. "The romantic dinner in the Bahamas, how everything has been going so amazingly well between us in Miami…"

He ran his finger along my cheek. "I know exactly what you mean."

And then my heart started to pound. Everything about this moment was perfect. From the sound of the waves gently lapping at our feet, to the full moon hanging above our heads, to the electric energy I could feel passing between my body and Chaz's.

His finger moved from my cheek to my chin, tilting it upward as he lowered his face.

And then his lips were on mine.

I sighed like a woman who had tasted a sip of water after a trek in the desert.

"Oh, Chaz." I looped my arms around his neck. "Oh…"

The kiss was gentle at first, his full, sensual lips playing over mine. Then it grew more urgent, with his tongue entering my mouth and flicking over mine. The passion inside me came alive with the strength of a tsunami. I was hot and breathless and wanted to make love to Chaz more than I'd wanted anything in my life.

He tore his lips away and framed my face in his hands. I could see in his eyes the same desire that was roaring through my body.

His eyes roamed over my face, and I thought he wanted to say something. Instead, he kissed me again—a kiss that literally made my knees buckle.

Chaz pulled me close as he deepened the kiss, molded his palms to my back. His mouth moved from my lips to my jawline, then lower, to my neck, and I purred from the pleasure.

Nothing had felt this good. This real.

"I want to make love to you so badly," Chaz said. "I can't wait anymore."

I thought about dropping onto the sand and surrendering completely to him, and I just might have done that if it weren't for the two men I spotted casually walking toward us. Chaz saw them, too, and instead of kissing me senseless, he just held me close.

When the men were out of earshot, he pressed his lips to my cheek. Then he whispered in my ear, "I'd like to go somewhere where no one can interrupt us." He nibbled on my earlobe. "Not for several hours."

My body thrummed at the thought of him making love to me all night long.

"My daughter's with the babysitter. I can call and make sure she's okay there for the night."

I took my cell phone out of my purse and called Carla.

"Hello?" Carla said.

"Is Rayna sleeping?" I asked without preamble.

"She just went down. She and Amani were watching a movie in the bedroom, but now they're both out cold."

"Great," I said, relieved. "Do you mind if she stays for the night? Considering it's late, anyway. Obviously, I'll pay you extra."

"Ahh…so things are going that well?"

"Yes," I said simply, not wanting Chaz to pick up anything from my tone.

"You go get freaky with Mr. Chaz Anderson. Rayna will be fine here."

I ignored the comment and said, "I'll probably come by around eleven in the morning."

"That's fine. Have fun!"

I quickly hung up the phone, hoping Chaz hadn't been able to hear any of Carla's words. Then I turned to him and said, "We have the night. Want to head to Mango's for a drink before we go back to my place?"

Chaz shook his head. "I say we go get *freaky.*"

My eyes widened in shock. Then embarrassment washed over me. "Oh my God." My eyes fluttered shut. "You heard that?"

Chaz chuckled softly as he wrapped his arms around me. "No need to be embarrassed."

I groaned.

He whispered hotly in my ear, "I say we don't disappoint your friend."

And when he kissed me again, I knew that we wouldn't.

Back in my apartment, Chaz and I quickly resumed where we'd left off at the beach, only our kisses were immediately hotter.

"Where's the bedroom?" he asked. We both knew what we wanted. There was no point beating around the bush.

"On the left at the end of the hallway," I replied between moans as he kissed my neck.

Holding each other, we moved in that direction. But when we got to the door, about to cross the threshold, I stopped.

"What?" Chaz asked, his breathing ragged.

"Nothing."

But that was a lie. I knew exactly what was bothering me. I felt a little weird. The only man I'd slept with in this apartment was Eli.

"Tell me what's wrong," Chaz urged.

I pressed my cheek against his chest. "This is the place I shared with Eli. He's the only man who slept with me in that bed."

Chaz didn't say anything, just pulled me a little closer.

Then he lowered his mouth and kissed the side of my neck, and suddenly I wasn't thinking about Eli anymore. I was thinking only about being right here, right now, with Chaz.

My mouth sought and found his. As we kissed, he groaned, a low and guttural sound that pushed the last thought of Eli from my mind.

I reached for the hem of Chaz's shirt, freeing it from his pants. He ran his hands over my butt, pulling me closer. My belly pressed against the very firm evidence of his desire for me.

I stepped away from him, moving backward to the bed. As I did, I began to unbutton my blouse. Chaz pulled his shirt over his head.

"You are absolutely perfect," I told him as my eyes greedily scanned his body. "Everything about you."

Before I could finish undoing my buttons, Chaz was in front of me again, placing his hands on mine. He finished the last two, then slipped my cotton blouse over my arms.

His eyes moved over my nearly naked chest. "Oh, baby."

I eased down on the bed, and Chaz lay on top of me. Our mouths met as he tangled his fingers in my hair.

"I've been waiting to do this since you left me in the Bahamas," he muttered.

"Me, too," I told him.

He kissed me again, his tongue plunging into my mouth the way I imagined his penis might plunge into me.

He moved his mouth lower, between my breasts. My body began to throb with delicious anticipation.

And when he pushed my bra down and closed his mouth over one nipple, I moaned shamelessly.

"You like that?" he asked.

"Are you kidding? Nothing gets me hotter. Well, except perhaps one thing…"

"I wonder what that might be?" he asked, chuckling softly.

I didn't get to answer, because he moved his mouth to my other breast, eliciting another long moan from me. He licked, he gently nipped, he suckled so tenderly I thought I would reach orgasm without him touching any other part of me.

As I was panting from pleasure, Chaz kissed a path from my breasts to my navel, then lower, where his mouth moved over my center the way it had over my nipples.

He drove me wild with lust, forcing my body to explode with release.

As I lay beside him, my breathing coming hard and fast, Chaz asked, "You all right?"

"Are you kidding? I'm incredible." I gently stroked his face, then moved to position my body on top of his. "I've never felt this incredible."

"Music to my ears."

I planted a soft kiss on Chaz's lips, then kissed a path from his mouth to his ear. I whispered, "Make love to me, baby. All night long."

"Sweetheart, your wish is my command."

chapter twenty-eight

The next morning, I was on cloud nine. Having spent most of the night making hot love with Chaz, my body was satisfied, and so was my heart.

As promised, I picked Rayna up at eleven, but Carla didn't get to grill me as to the night's events, since Chaz was with me. But she gave me a knowing look, followed by a wink. She seemed to have come around regarding the idea of me dating again, and I was happy for that.

Chaz, Rayna and I went to Perkins for breakfast, and I couldn't help thinking of us as a family. Rayna really took to Chaz, wanting to be in his arms as we walked into the restaurant, then wanting to be in his lap when the hostess sat us at a table.

Seriously, I don't remember ever being happier.

The waitress arrived holding a coffeepot, and offered us some of the delicious smelling brew.

"Oh, yeah," Chaz said, holding up the cup that was

already on the table. "And keep it coming." He winked at me as he said the words, and I blushed. The waitress wouldn't understand our private joke—that we needed all the coffee we could get if we were going to be able to stay awake today.

"I'll give you a few more minutes to look at the menu," she said.

When she was gone, Chaz took a swig of coffee before fixing his gaze on me. "I was thinking that, on Monday, I could go with you to the office. Meet the rest of the team."

Excitement spread through every part of my body. "Are you serious?"

Up to now, I hadn't pushed Chaz about signing with my agency because I was more interested in what was happening between us than winning him as a client. Don't get me wrong, I still wanted that more than ever, but never in my wildest dreams did I expect someone like Chaz to come into my life. A relationship with him was the icing on the cake, so to speak.

"Yeah," he replied. "Obviously, our relationship has… blossomed."

Has it ever…

"I want to be with you. That's always been my first priority. And now that we're on that path, I see no reason for us not to work together."

"Chaz!" I squealed, reaching across the table to take his free hand. "This is so exciting!"

"I'm excited, too."

Rayna got caught up in our excitement, laughing as well.

"And not just because of business," I added, "though my boss will be elated. But because of what's happening between us. It's more than I could have ever hoped for."

Chaz linked fingers with mine, and for several moments we simply stared at each other.

I felt like this was a dream. Here I was with Chaz, a man I was crazy about. And not only was he crazy about me, but he loved my daughter.

It was the most a woman could hope for.

Rayna stretched her little body across the table, reaching for a saltshaker, and in doing so, she knocked over Chaz's cup of coffee. The black liquid splashed onto him.

I jumped forward. "Rayna!"

I expected Chaz to be annoyed, the way Eli had when Rayna had spilled her milk on his lap. But instead, Chaz looked at my daughter with concern. "You okay, sweetheart?"

I realized that he was checking to see if any of the hot coffee had spilled on her.

Rayna nodded, then curled her face into his neck.

"It's okay," he cooed. "I'm not mad at you."

I almost started to cry. Eli had exploded when Rayna had spilled her milk. But Chaz took it in stride.

Like a parent.

I started to wipe up the table with the serviettes we had. "Are you okay? Did it burn you?" I asked him.

"I'm fine."

"But your clothes—"

"Can be washed. No big deal."

Oh, but it was a big deal. Bigger than Chaz would ever know. For me, this proved that Chaz wasn't just husband material.

He was father material.

★ ★ ★

Chaz stayed at a hotel Saturday and Sunday night, arguing that he didn't want to confuse my daughter. As far as I was concerned, Rayna adored him, and I was happy for him to stay with us, but I did understand his point. And more than anything, I appreciated that he'd put Rayna first in making his decision.

The weekend passed all too quickly, but I didn't mind. Because Chaz was coming to the office on Monday, the next crucial step in getting him to become my client.

"Someone looks *very* happy," Alaina said when I entered the office. "And I wonder if this could be the reason why."

Alaina produced a copy of the *Miami Herald*. There was a picture of me and Chaz on the front page of the entertainment section.

My eyes bulging, I snatched the paper from Alaina's hands. "What? When did someone take our picture?"

"You two look quite close," she sang.

Beneath the color photo of me and Chaz was the caption, "Vanessa Cain gets cozy with motivational speaker Chaz Anderson."

My eyes scanned the article.

It seems that South Beach resident Vanessa Cain has gotten over the heartache of recent months, appearing out on the town with successful motivational speaker Chaz Anderson. One wouldn't know that just six weeks ago she was grieving the loss of her boyfriend, famed Atlanta Braves outfielder, Eli Johnson. Johnson was brutally murdered on April 3 by jealous husband Conrad Redgrave, when he caught Johnson in bed with his wife.

The article went on to mention that Chaz and I had been out at the Forge, and even gave a detailed account of what we ate. It ended with the speculation that I'd found love with Chaz, "another successful man."

The byline read, "Cynthia Martin."

"My God," I said, shaking my head. "This woman is still following me around? Of course she neglects to mention that I work for an agency that represents motivational speakers."

"You're a star, girl. I told you you were a celebrity."

I shrugged, deciding not to let the article rattle me. If Ms. Martin wanted to follow me around, so be it. I wasn't about to let anything sour my excitement at the fact that Chaz and I had made love, and that I was one step away from landing him as a client. He was due to come into the office this afternoon and meet everyone, after we first had lunch at Bayside.

"So," Alaina said, wiggling her eyebrows. "Just how well did things go?"

"Very," I admitted. Then, smiling slyly, I started off toward my office.

"Hey!" Alaina quickly jumped out of her seat and followed me. "Girl, you'd better spill the beans."

"Okay, okay." I closed the door to my office and got right to the point. "Chaz and I made love!"

"Oh my God, *chica!*" Alaina grabbed my hands and squeezed hard. "How was it? No, don't answer that. It's obvious by the look on your face!"

"Alaina, everything was amazing." Resting my butt against the edge of my desk, I sighed dreamily. "Not just the sex—which was out of this world—but how Chaz connected with my daughter. This is it, Ally. I've finally met The One."

"Oh, girl. I'm so happy for you!" Alaina stepped toward me and drew me into an embrace. We pulled apart a moment later, giggling like schoolgirls.

"He's coming into the office today. To meet the team."

Alaina's eyes widened. "Get out!"

I nodded. "Mm-hmm. This afternoon. I'm taking him to lunch at Los Ranchos, then bringing him to the office."

"You go, girl!"

"And to think that when Eli died, I thought I'd never be happy again."

"You deserve to be happy." Alaina rubbed my arm affectionately. "You've dealt with more drama than any one person should."

I made my way around my desk, where I turned on my computer. "How was your weekend?" I asked.

"I had a big fight with Jorge. He called me a slut when he picked up the kids."

"Oh my God. That man has some serious issues."

"Tell me about it. But I had some good news this morning, which is making me forget all about my crazy ex."

"Oh?" I asked, intrigued by a look I recognized on Alaina's face. A look that said she was interested in someone.

Alaina grinned from ear to ear. "Some *real* good news."

"Don't keep me in suspense."

Alaina's eyes lit up. "Guess who called me? This morning, not ten minutes before you showed up."

I leaned back in my chair. "I have no clue. Tell me."

"That reporter!"

I narrowed my eyes as I stared at her. "What reporter?"

She looked at me with disbelief. "Mike Sanchez? The one who works for CBS? He interviewed you that day you had the big press conference at the office."

I eased my body forward. "Oh. *Ohhh*. Mike Sanchez. The hottie you were drooling over. He called?"

"Uh-huh. And we're going out tomorrow night."

"Alaina, that's great!"

"My first real date in ages and, girl, I'm so psyched! Mike Sanchez—he's famous!"

"Obviously you made an impression on him, for him to be calling you weeks after he met you."

"Yeah," Alaina agreed. "Maybe he was in a relationship or something and just broke up. Whatever, I don't care. I hope I have as much luck with him as you've had with Chaz. Maybe we'll both end up married to celebrities!"

"Maybe."

"Look, I'd better head back to the reception desk. I don't want Debbie freaking out."

"I'll talk to you later," I told Alaina.

Laughing, she hurried out of my office.

When she was gone, I checked my voice mail messages. There was one from my sister, which surprised me.

She had called to remind me about my nephew Stephen's birthday party this weekend, and also to tell me that the previous Friday, a couple had made an offer on the house she couldn't refuse.

Replacing the receiver, I debated phoning her, then decided against it. Nikki had called my office phone because she hadn't been ready to talk to me.

She might think that I owed her an apology, and maybe I did. But I wasn't ready to give her one. I would call her later in the week, and hopefully we'd iron things out.

She was my sister, after all. I couldn't walk away from her forever.

At twelve-fifteen, I exited the elevator on the lobby level of my office building. Seeing me, Edgar whistled.

"Wow, baby. You look amazing."

I did a little twirl, showing off my sexy red dress with a fitted top and flared skirt. "Thank you."

"Going on a hot date or something?"

"I'm meeting a client at Los Ranchos." But I burst into a grin that said I was a big liar.

"*Client.*" Edgar drummed his fingers on his desk. "Hmm."

"Well, maybe he *is* a bit more than a client," I admitted.

"That motivational speaker from Chicago?" Edgar asked. "The one you were pictured with in the paper?"

"Actually, yes."

Edgar raised an eyebrow. "Is it serious?"

"I think it is, yeah."

"Ah, poor Byron." A smile played on Edgar's lips as he shook his head. "Guess he'll never have another chance with you."

"Like that was even a remote possibility." I rolled my eyes. "Edgar, I'd love to stay and chat, but—"

"You go have fun."

Less than ten minutes later, I strolled into the restaurant. Chaz was waiting at the hostess's stand, and when he saw me, he immediately wrapped me in his arms.

"I hope you weren't waiting long," I said as we pulled apart.

The hostess arrived back at the stand. "I see your guest has arrived." She smiled pleasantly. "Ready to be seated?"

Chaz took my hand as she led us to a corner table that had a view of the water. I loved how romantic he was with me, how he openly hugged me, kissed me, held my hand. It made me feel special.

The hostess left us with menus and promised that our server would be along shortly.

She had barely walked away when my cell phone rang.

"Sorry," I said to Chaz.

"Don't be silly. Take the call."

I flipped open my phone and pressed it to my ear. "Vanessa Cain."

"Vanessa, hello. This is Bradley Harris."

My stomach took a serious nosedive. "Oh. Um, hello."

"I've been waiting to hear from you."

"In my last message, I told you a month, didn't I? How did you get this number?"

I noted that Chaz was looking at me with concern.

"Ms. Cain, we really do need to come to some sort of arrangement regarding the condo. Have you secured the money to buy my client out?"

Damn, I wished I hadn't answered the phone. "Not yet. Can we talk about this later?"

"I'd be happy to set up an appointment right now."

I glanced at Chaz, who still regarded me curiously, then looked away. "I'm at lunch with a client right now, Mr. Bradley."

"Why don't I call you this afternoon," he suggested.

"Fine," I said testily. "Call me later if this can't wait."

Then I snapped my cell phone shut. But in case Mr. Harris wanted to call me again, I decided to turn my phone off.

Chaz reached across the table and covered my left hand with his right one. "Something wrong?" he asked.

I groaned, but didn't answer.

Chaz squeezed my hand gently. "Vanessa…what is it?"

"I… Nothing."

"Hey. Whatever's going on with you, know that you can share it with me."

Sighing softly, I met Chaz's eyes. I saw both care and worry in their depths.

So I told him. Told him how because Eli had still been officially married to Tassie when we'd bought the condo, his wife had a legal claim to half my property. That if I wanted to keep my home, I had to come up with a sizable amount of cash to buy her out.

"What about Eli's will?" Chaz asked. "Didn't he leave you part of his estate?"

I shook my head. "Nothing. And it gets even worse. I thought I could at least get some cash for the engagement ring he gave me, but a pawnbroker told me it was a fake."

Chaz's eyebrows shot up in alarm. "Did you sell it to him?"

"No. He only wanted to give me three hundred dollars."

"Smart move."

I frowned slightly. "Why do you say that?"

"How do you know the pawnbroker wasn't lying to you? I read a story once, about some of these pawnshops taking expensive items and claiming they were basically worthless. Just because this guy said the ring was a fake doesn't mean it was."

"You could be right," I said slowly. "I—I just believed him."

"Take it to a jeweler. Have them appraise it for you."

Once again, I had hope because of Chaz. "Thank you for telling me that. I didn't even consider…" My voice trailed off.

The waitress finally arrived. I ordered a strawberry daiquiri, while Chaz ordered a Corona.

When she was gone, he said to me, "Now, as for your condo—how much do you need to buy Eli's wife out?"

"A lot. At least a couple hundred—" I stopped abruptly, my eyes widening as I looked at Chaz. "If you're suggesting… No, absolutely not. I can't take money from you."

Reaching across the table, he covered my hands with his again. "Vanessa, I love you."

He stared at me, and his eyes said that he was absolutely serious. "Chaz…"

"I love you," he repeated. "I want us to be a team—in every sense of the word. I know we're not quite ready to take that next step. I'll need time to get to know Rayna… But in the meantime, you want to keep your apartment, and Eli's wife sounds like a piece of work. So if I can give you the cash you need to make the problem go away, I'll consider it an investment in our future."

I was so stunned, all I could do was stare at him.

"Why are you looking at me like that? You didn't think I'd help?"

"You said you love me," I commented, my voice a whisper.

"Of course I do. Can't you tell?"

I couldn't believe it. My every dream was coming true.

Chaz loved me, he was willing to give me the money necessary to buy out Tassie Johnson.

He loved me.

"Vanessa…"

I leaped out of my seat and onto his lap. And despite the numerous people around us, I planted my lips on Chaz's face and shamelessly smothered it with kisses.

"I love you, too," I told him.

"And you're not shy about showing it," he teased.

"Not one bit."

Only then did I glance around sheepishly, looking to see how people were reacting. There were smiles, mostly. People happy for our happiness.

But then my gaze wandered toward the restaurant's door, and what I saw there made me freeze.

chapter twenty-nine

Sheer panic had me paralyzed. I wanted to move, get off Chaz's lap and sprint to the bathroom. Or better yet, jump out the nearest window. But I couldn't move a muscle.

"Oh, God," I muttered. "Oh God, no."

"Vanessa?" Chaz asked.

I tried to swallow, but my throat was suddenly parched.

"Vanessa?"

Somehow, I found the strength to move off his lap and back to my own seat. It was pointless, but I blocked my face with my right hand.

"What's going on?" Chaz asked me.

"That's exactly what I want to know," another voice boomed.

I slinked down in my chair, praying that this wasn't really happening.

Byron.

Chaz's attention quickly turned to the man at our table. "Excuse me?"

"Vanessa," Byron said in a hard, angry tone. "So this is the guy? This *metrosexual*-looking brother is your new flavor of the month?"

Now Chaz stood. I slipped lower.

"Who the hell are you?" Chaz demanded.

For a moment, both men stared each other down. Then, Byron asked, "Vanessa, you want to tell him, or shall I?"

I wanted to call, "Anyone here got a gun?" Instead, I glanced at the man who was about to shatter my every hope and dream. My eyes implored him to lie.

Angry eyes turned to Chaz. "I'm Byron McLean. Rayna's father."

Someone shoot me now....

"Rayna's *what?*"

"You heard me," Byron retorted. Then he turned to me. "I heard that you were running around town with some new guy, then I saw that photo in the paper this morning. You gonna get engaged to this guy, too, maybe take my daughter to Chicago?"

Edgar. Damn him! The idiot must have called Byron and told him about my lunch date.

"I'm starting to get concerned about all these men you're bringing into my daughter's life," Byron said.

I couldn't look at Chaz, but I felt his gaze burning my skin nonetheless. Byron's, too.

It was a wonder I didn't spontaneously combust.

"Vanessa?" Gone was Chaz's anger, replaced by confusion. I think I would have preferred unadulterated wrath compared to his soft, questioning tone. "You told me Rayna's father was dead."

"Dead?" Byron laughed out loud. "I'm very much alive, my friend. Very much alive."

Ignoring Byron, Chaz sat back down. "You lied to me?"

I sighed long and loud. "I—I…"

"After everything we've talked about, how the one thing I told you I couldn't stand was to be lied to?"

"I'm sorry," I said lamely.

Chaz's eyes widened. "You're sorry?"

"It wasn't totally a lie," I quickly said. "He's dead to Rayna in every way that matters. And ask him when he last sent a support payment. Try never. Last year, he sent her a present for her birthday. One present—that's all he's given her. And ask him what he told me to do when I announced I was pregnant." My gaze landed on Bryon for a moment, and it was full of contempt. "He wanted me to get an *abortion*— that's how much he loves his daughter. I don't know what this grandstanding is all about, but Byron's not a part of my life. Or Rayna's." I stopped my long-winded spiel and sucked in air. I searched Chaz's face for a reaction, some sign that he understood what I was saying and that he would forgive me.

Instead, he slowly shook his head and looked at me with grave disappointment.

The waitress arrived with our drinks, but seeing the brewing drama, she quickly turned on her heel.

"I thought you were different," Chaz said.

"I am different! You love me, remember? You just told me so. Don't let the lies he's spewing ruin what we've found."

"What did you say?" Byron interjected.

My neck nearly broke as my head whipped in his direction. "You should disappear like you did when I told you I was pregnant! The only reason you suddenly give a damn about Rayna is because someone else wants to make me happy!"

"I love my daughter."

I snorted in derision. "Like hell you do."

Byron's mouth opened, but as he regarded me carefully, he decided not to respond. He took a couple steps backward.

"Fine. I'll leave. But if you think you're going to take my daughter out of Miami-Dade County, you've got another think coming."

Then he left.

I turned back to Chaz. "I'm sorry," I said. "I know I shouldn't have lied. But after what you told me about that single mother you dated, I didn't... I couldn't... I was falling for you. Falling hard, Chaz. And you have to believe, Byron hasn't cared about Rayna from the moment he knew I was pregnant. He hasn't been in her life." My voice cracked. "Please stop looking at me like that."

"You lied to me." For Chaz, it was as simple as that.

The air rushed out of my lungs. "Please try to understand."

"Oh, I understand all right." He pushed his chair back and stood. I watched as he took his wallet out of his jacket pocket and threw some money onto the table.

I shot to my feet. "Chaz, please don't leave. Don't let that loser ruin everything. Come back to the office with me. Meet everyone, just like you planned. Talk to Debbie, get to know everyone at the agency..."

"I can't believe you. You're still trying to give me a sales pitch?"

I reached for his arm, but he stepped back, out of my reach. "You think this is a sales pitch?"

"Maybe everything was. Our *connecting* in the Bahamas. Maybe you've been playing me all along."

I closed the distance between us, gripping his upper arm. "I introduced you to my daughter. Do you think I'd introduce you to the one person who means the most to me as part of a sales pitch? That I'd use my own child that way?" I was silent until he met my eyes. I wanted him to be able to read how sincere I was.

"I don't know." He sighed. "People are staring."

I released him and took a step backward. "Please come to the office with me. Let's talk about this there."

Slowly, Chaz shook his head. "Honesty, Vanessa. It was the one thing I told you mattered most to me."

"I know, but—"

"And your baby's father obviously wants to be part of her life. Probably even wants you back."

"That is such a lie! And trust me, it will *never* happen."

"I'm not going to get caught in the middle of something like this again. I can't."

"Chaz."

He started to walk away.

"Chaz," I repeated, louder this time. But he didn't stop. He didn't even glance over his shoulder at me.

I wanted to run after him, tell him how sorry I was, and that I'd do whatever necessary to make it up to him. But I was well aware that curious eyes all around the restaurant were trained on me.

I also had the feeling that I could run after Chaz, drop to

my knees and cling to his thigh in a dramatic display of grov-
eling, and he wouldn't be moved.

Right now, he was utterly disappointed in me.

So I sank back onto my chair and buried my face in my
hands. I'd lost another man, and this time it was all my fault.

chapter thirty

If it weren't for Rayna, when I got home from work I would have crawled into bed and stayed there forever. As it was, the next morning I slept late, having no desire to get up and face a world without Chaz.

But as if my two-year-old knew exactly what I needed, she came into my bedroom and woke me with her rendition of "Twinkle Twinkle Little Star," forcing a smile from me when I didn't think there was even the hint of one inside me.

"Oh, Rayna." I stroked her face. "What would I do without you?"

Though I didn't want to, I went to work. Everyone offered me their sympathy. They were sorry my relationship had fallen apart, sorry I wasn't going to bring Chaz to the firm, after all.

I was sorry my life seemed so pathetically hopeless.

Somehow, I got through Tuesday without falling apart.

On Wednesday, when I entered the agency, my heart

filled with hope. There was a vase with three dozen red roses on the reception desk.

In my haste to get to the desk, I twisted my ankle. Badly. But I didn't care about the pain.

"Flowers," I said breathlessly, smiling as I met Alaina's eyes. "God, they're so beautiful."

My fingers frantically searched for the card.

"Um…Vanessa…"

My eyes scanned the card. And when I finished reading it, I nearly burst into tears.

"I'm sorry," Alaina said.

"No. Don't be sorry. Michael Sanchez sent you the most stunning roses I've ever seen."

I hustled away from the desk, tears streaming down my face.

"It went real well," Alaina said around a mouthful of garlic bread.

We were at Bayside for lunch, at Lombardi's Ristorante. No way in hell would I return to Los Ranchos.

"Michael's divorced, too," she related, "but doesn't have any kids. The marriage only lasted four months before he learned his wife was sleeping with someone else."

"Another guy who was screwed over by a woman," I said, thinking of Chaz. "Who knew there was more than one of them?"

"Oh—and he *did* recently break up with someone, and get this—because he couldn't stop thinking about me. Isn't that great?"

"Yeah, great," I agreed, though I couldn't muster any enthusiasm.

"Oh, sweetie. I shouldn't be going on about Michael when you're so bummed about Chaz."

And just like that, emotion clogged my throat. In fact, it was suddenly hard to breathe.

"I'm sure you'll hear from him," she said, trying to make me feel better.

I had to take a moment before answering her, a moment to pull myself together so that I didn't end up a weeping mess right in the middle of this restaurant as we waited for our pizza.

"I want to believe that," I said. With my straw, I stirred the red slush at the bottom of my glass. I'd already finished one strawberry daiquiri and was ready for another.

"It's only been a couple days," Alaina pointed out.

"You didn't see the look on his face. His total disappointment in me. And you know what? I can't blame him. I was so mad at Eli for keeping crucial information about his family from me, and what did I do with Chaz? The exact same thing. I lied to him because it was easier to let him believe Rayna's father was dead than deal with the consequences of telling him the truth. I'm no better than Eli."

Alaina's cell phone sang some Latin tune, and she glanced at the phone's display. "Ooh, that's Mike."

I expected her to flip her phone open and answer the call. But she let it ring until it stopped.

"Why didn't you answer it?" I asked.

"I can talk to Mike later. Right now, you need me."

"Ally…"

She reached across the table and covered both my hands. "You are a dynamic, beautiful, compassionate, talented person. If Chaz can't see that—"

"But I lied to him. He has every right to be mad at me."

"Mad, yes. To drop you completely? Uh-uh. You didn't lie to him about having HIV or something *really* serious. You told him Rayna's father was dead. And you know what? He might as well be dead for how often he's been in his daughter's life."

"I know, but—"

"No buts. You should call Chaz. Explain the situation."

"I tried."

"And he didn't listen?"

"No. I hung up."

Alaina tsked. "Vanessa."

"I know, but I was scared. I heard his voice and just panicked. I couldn't live with myself if he told me to never call him again."

"Do you believe he really loved you?"

I thought back to my time in the Bahamas with him, how he'd given me the most romantic date I'd likely ever experience. And then I remembered when we had been strolling along the beach, looked into each other's eyes, and both knew at that moment that we were ready to make love. When I'd taken him upstairs, sex with Chaz had been a soulful experience unlike with any other man.

"Yes, I think he did."

"Then you have to fight for what you want. I don't believe he stopped loving you in just two days."

I nodded, but my heart wasn't in it.

"Since when are you a quitter?" Alaina asked. "You're the toughest *chica* I know. You dragged me to Atlanta with you, determined to say goodbye to Eli even if his wife would make a scene. You weren't scared then."

"I was terrified."

"But you didn't let your fear get to you. That's what you have to do now. Call Chaz in spite of your fear. In fact…give me your phone."

Anxiety gripped my stomach and squeezed hard. "What?"

"Give me your phone. I want to call Chaz."

"No!"

"Do you want me to look his number up at the office and call him when you're not around?"

I groaned. "Girl, you don't play fair."

"Give me your phone. Or give me his number and I'll call from my cell."

For a moment, I debated what to do. I wasn't ready to talk to Chaz.

"Tick tock, tick tock. The choice is yours."

"Fine." I pulled my cell phone out of my purse and flipped it open. Then I promptly closed it.

"Vanessa…"

"You should call from your phone. He'll recognize my number."

"Hit me with the number."

I recited it to her and Alaina punched in the digits. Then my stomach went berserk as she held her phone to her ear.

"It's ringing," she said.

I reached for the phone and she passed it to me.

My hands were sweating, and it had nothing to do with the humid day.

"Hi."

"Hi," I said, and watched Alaina's eyes light up.

"You've reached Chaz Anderson…"

I pulled the phone away from my ear and frowned. "It's his voice mail."

"Leave a message."

I shook my head and closed Alaina's cell phone. "I don't know what to say."

Alaina opened her palm, and I passed her the phone. She immediately pressed some buttons and put the phone to her own ear.

Panic washed over me in waves. "Ally, what are you doing?"

"What you were too afraid to do."

"No—Ally—"

She ignored me.

"Okay! I'll leave a message! Give me the phone."

She didn't, and after a few seconds, said, "Hi, Chaz. This is Alaina Rivera, the receptionist at Vanessa's agency. I'm calling on behalf of Vanessa."

"Ally, *please*…"

"I just wanted you to know that she's hurting like hell. She feels really bad about what happened—but you have to understand the story about her ex. He's the world's biggest deadbeat dad."

I cringed.

"She loves you, Chaz," Alaina declared. "Please call her."

Then she hung up, and I wanted to die. I dropped my head onto the table and moaned.

"Someone had to do it."

"Yeah, but now Chaz is going to think that I was too chicken to call him myself."

Alaina shrugged nonchalantly. "He's going to think

you're so distraught over the breakup that your friend had to intervene."

"I don't know, Ally."

Once again, Alaina placed her hands on mine. "Vanessa, it'll work out. If it's meant to be, it will be."

But the rest of the day passed, and there was no word from Chaz. He didn't call on Thursday, either, and by the end of the day, I was an emotional basket case. I don't know how I held myself together.

Hope, I guess. I didn't want to believe that after what Chaz and I had shared he could write me off forever.

I told myself that he needed time. Time to digest everything that had happened, and to come around to forgiving me.

I had to cling to that, or I would fall apart.

Still, as I left the office that Thursday evening, I was torn. Part of me wanted to drive to the airport and take a flight to Chicago. I'd find Chaz if it took a full week. The other part knew not only that I couldn't, but wondered if I should forget about Chaz altogether. It wasn't like I didn't have enough to deal with being a single mother. No matter how much I loved him, Rayna came first. I had to stay in control so I'd be the best mom to my little girl.

Still, all Thursday evening, every time the phone rang, I leaped for it, hoping Chaz would be on the other line.

He never was.

Around seven, I left my cell phone in my apartment and took Rayna to the video store. I picked up a new *My Little Pony* movie. Back at home, I curled up on my bed with Rayna and a bowl of popcorn, and spent the rest of the evening deriving pleasure from watching my daughter's little face light up as she enjoyed the tale about a princess pony ina fairy-tale land.

We watched the movie twice, then Rayna fell asleep with her head resting on my belly.

chapter thirty-one

Bright and early Friday morning, my office phone rang. I snatched it up on the first ring. "Vanessa Cain."

"Hello, Vanessa," a cheerful female voice trilled.

I narrowed my eyes. "Who is this?"

"This is Lisa Dunn returning your call."

Lisa Dunn? Why didn't that name ring a bell? "I'm sorry. I'm drawing a blank."

"I got your message yesterday about you wanting to list your property. I'd love to come and take a look at it and tell you what I think it can sell for."

My mouth fell open. "Excuse me?"

"Lisa Dunn from Carlson Realty Group," the woman said, sounding a little surprised that I didn't remember her. "The way you described your penthouse suite, I'm certain I can sell it quickly."

"I'm sorry, Lisa. It seems there's some kind of mistake."

"You don't live at Cosmopolitan Towers?"

"I do. But I'm not interested in…" My voice trailed off as I realized what was going on. *Tassie.*

"So you're not interested in selling?" Lisa asked.

"I wasn't the one who called you, but I know who did. And I'm sorry she bothered you, but I have no intention of selling my condo."

"If you change your mind—"

"I won't."

Angry, I replaced the receiver. I wanted to search for Bradley Harris's number and tell him that he'd better warn his client to stop harassing me.

I didn't. This was a childish prank on Tassie's part, and I wouldn't give her the satisfaction of letting her know how much she was pissing me off.

Just before noon, Andrea, one of the agency's agents, peeked her head into my office. She grinned warmly at me and said, "Hey, you."

"Hi." I tried to sound pleasant.

"Thanks for straightening out the scheduling mess with my client. That was almost a huge nightmare."

"No problem," I told her. "That's why I'm here."

"All the same, I'd like to invite you for lunch if you're free. As a way of thanking you properly."

I glanced at my clock. Ten minutes to twelve, and I hadn't even thought of eating until Andrea had shown up.

"Sure," I told her. Heck, I'd just resolved a major crisis for her. I was entitled to a celebratory lunch.

And it would help take my mind off Chaz, if only for an hour.

As I rode downstairs in an elevator with Andrea, I thought

about the fact that it seemed I was able to resolve other people's crises—like my sister's, and Carla's, and now this near disaster because of a scheduling mishap. And yet I was completely unable to rescue myself.

Andrea offered me a small smile as we got off the elevator. I returned it, but I couldn't help thinking that it was weird for Andrea and I to be heading out to lunch. She was a bit aloof at the office, not the type to hang out and chat at the watercooler. In fact, she spent a lot of time behind closed doors in her office. At first, I thought she was a snob, but then decided she was the shy type—an odd thing, given her job.

I didn't mean to be rude, but I found I kept tuning Andrea out as we walked. She was talking about her ex-husband, sharing more with me than she ever had. I wanted to give her my undivided attention, but my thoughts were on Chaz and how I could fix what had gone so seriously wrong.

Alaina had jokingly suggested that I bump Byron off so he wasn't in the picture anymore. "Then he'll really be dead," she had said. I wouldn't do it, of course, but I can't deny the idea held more appeal as each day passed.

"Vanessa!"

Andrea's hand closed around my arm, and she yanked me backward. A car sped by, and I instantly realized that I'd almost walked right in its path.

"My God, Vanessa. Are you sure you're okay?"

I exhaled loudly. "I'm… I've had better days."

"You're really upset about Chaz, aren't you?"

"Yeah," I admitted. "I was so close, and I blew my chance to get him to sign with our agency." I decided not to share that my heart was crushed, as well.

The light turned to green, and Andrea and I started across the street. "For what it's worth, these things happen. Debbie was disappointed, but she knows the deal."

"I know. It's just that I…I really wanted this."

We fell into silence as we made our way to Lombardi's. I perused the menu, hardly seeing a thing. When Andrea suggested we split a pepperoni pizza, I agreed.

"Isn't this a great place?" she asked. "I love sitting here, looking out at the water."

"It is beautiful," I agreed. "Romantic," I added wistfully.

Andrea leaned forward. "Can I ask you something? And you can tell me if I'm crossing the line."

I raised an eyebrow at that, but said, "Go ahead."

"You and Chaz were an item, weren't you?"

How had she known? Had I done that terrible a job of keeping my affection for him secret? Or had Alaina not been able to keep her big mouth shut?

I decided not to lie. "I cared for him, yes."

Andrea shook her head ruefully. "You've had a bad time in the past few months. One dating disaster after another."

"Tell me about it."

"I know how you feel. I was married to my college sweetheart, thought that was it. My happily ever after. Only his version of 'happily ever after' was until he got bored with me and wanted new pussy."

I reeled backward, then quickly tried to disguise my shock at Andrea's choice of words. Alaina could say that to me, and it wouldn't faze me one bit. But from Andrea, who hardly spoke to me if it wasn't about business, that was shocking.

"I hear you there," I said. "I know all about the cheating man."

"I get so sick of them, you know?"

"Oh, I know. If I knew what was good for me, I'd swear off men forever."

"Exactly! So you feel the same way I do."

"It's like you can't live with them, can't live without them."

"That's what I used to think," Andrea said. "But now I realize I *can* live without them. Any woman can."

I wondered where she was going with this. "It's not like I'm going to wither away and die. It hurts, yes. But if it's over with Chaz, it's over."

"That's not what I meant," Andrea said.

"Then what?"

"Vanessa." She paused. Exhaled slowly. "I'm feeling like we're pretty much on the same page here, so I'm just going to say this. I like you."

"I like you, too." And then my stomach dropped. She didn't mean—

"You do?" She laughed, relieved. "I didn't know how you would react, but—"

"Wait a minute." Unconsciously, I eased my chair back a bit. "What exactly are you saying?"

"I think you're an amazing woman. Certainly one who deserves someone who will treat you right. With love and respect." She reached across the table and rested a finger on my hand. "Someone like me."

I pulled my hand back as if I'd been scalded. Then I said in a confused whisper, "Andrea, what are you talking about?"

"Before you say no, think about the men you've dated. Think about how they've hurt you. They're all the same, every last one of them. You can count on them to break your heart every time. But I...I would never do that."

I glanced around nervously, wondering if people thought we were a couple. Why I cared what strangers thought, I didn't know, but I did.

"Andrea," I whispered. "I'm straight. You are, too."

"Being straight is a choice."

"I *like* being straight," I said quickly—and perhaps a little harshly. "Look, Andrea. It's not that I'm not flattered—I am. It's that I'm straight. Ever since my first crush on Lloyd Summers in kindergarten, I knew I was hooked on boys." I couldn't believe I was having this conversation.

Andrea looked... I couldn't quite put my finger on it. Upset? No, that was too strong a word.

Disappointed.

Yes, she was disappointed.

And embarrassed.

"I get it, though," I said, hoping to spare her feelings. "I understand why a woman might want to write off men altogether."

"I just wanted to put it out there." Her voice wavered. "In case."

I nodded. Andrea looked away.

The waiter arrived with our pizza.

To say this moment was awkward was the understatement of the century.

The waiter was almost out of earshot when Andrea called him, and he turned. She beckoned him over.

"Actually, I'm not very hungry anymore. Do you mind putting half of this in a doggy bag for me?"

"Certainly."

"Oh, you're leaving?" I asked, feigning disappointment.

"I think it's best. I—I feel really stupid. I'm so sorry."

"Don't apologize." I waved off her concern. But I was relieved that this awkward "date" would soon be over.

"I'd appreciate it if you didn't mention this to anyone," Andrea murmured. "If you could forget it ever happened." She chuckled nervously.

"Two coworkers out for lunch. Nothing strange about that." To my own ears, I sounded high-strung. Uneasy.

Hell yeah, I was uneasy.

I had to go back to the office and work with her. And I would never be able to look at her the same way again.

When the waiter returned with her packaged food, Andrea couldn't get away fast enough. I smiled politely and waved— then covered my face with my hands as soon as she was gone.

This warranted a glass of wine.

I ate all three slices of my pizza, then ordered chocolate mousse after that. I wasn't really hungry, but I was in no rush to get back to the agency.

"She asked you out?" Alaina all but shrieked later that afternoon in my office.

"Shh! Keep your voice down," I whispered. "I told you she didn't want me telling anyone."

"That's just freaky."

"I don't know if she was really serious. She was married. I know she's not gay."

"She wouldn't be the first one. I had a friend who, after her husband cheated on her over and over again, did the same thing. Lasted a couple years. But now she's straight again. Oh, *chica*—you look so sad."

"I keep hoping I'll hear from Chaz, but it seems now that I never will."

"I'm really sorry."

I shrugged nonchalantly, as if what I was feeling inside my body was anything remotely indifferent. "The one thing Andrea had right—if I don't hear from Chaz, I'm swearing off men." When Alaina's eyes bulged, I quickly continued. "No, I'm not saying *that*. I'm just saying I'm going to concentrate on me and my daughter. And try to find a new place to live," I added sadly. "Obviously, I won't be able to pay off Tassie. Which really hurts. I'll be fine, though. I will."

"I'm sorry you're going through all this drama."

"Hey—what doesn't kill you makes you stronger," I said as cheerfully as I could. I wished I could believe my own words.

"I'd better go back to work. I don't want Debbie firing me."

"Just remember, don't tell anyone what I told you. I had to tell someone, but I don't want Andrea feeling uncomfortable."

Alaina gave me two thumbs up before she headed out the door.

When Debbie entered my office shortly after 2:00 p.m. and closed the door, I didn't expect her to say, "Andrea asked you out!"

"Oh, God." I groaned. I could throttle Alaina. "Who told you?"

"I heard it from Will."

"From Will!" Shit, that meant the whole office probably knew.

"I had no clue she was a dyke."

"Please keep your voice down. She didn't want anyone
knowing." She was going to hate me if this got back to her.
"And for what it's worth, I don't think she's really gay. She's
just…sick of men."

"I know the feeling." Debbie's face twisted in a scowl.

"You?" I laughed without mirth. "What are you talking
about? You're sleeping with that hot stud, you've got a
doting husband at home…"

"Then ask me why I'm on my way to see a marriage
counselor."

"What?" I exclaimed. "You, seeing a marriage counselor?"

"Shh," she said. Then she rolled her eyes. "Ben figured
out that something was going on. He said if I didn't agree
to counseling, he'd leave me—and take the kids."

"Wow." I sat back in my chair. I was surprised he hadn't
left her the moment he'd learned of the affair, the way a
typical man would. "How'd he find out?"

"I…I came home without any panties last week. The one
time I leave my panties with Jason, my husband has to decide
to get frisky when I walk through the door. I tried to turn
him off, but he had a hard-on and a mission. When he found
me without my thong on, he remembered me having worn
one in the morning. He wanted to know what happened to
it."

"And what did you say?"

"I said they ripped when I was in the bathroom."

"And he figured it out."

"No, not right away, actually. He seemed suspicious, but he let the matter go."

I narrowed my eyes as I looked at my boss. "So, why the counseling?"

Now Debbie plopped down onto the chair opposite my desk. "Because last Friday, Jason got the bright idea to follow me home."

"What?"

"Oh, yeah. It was ugly."

"Why didn't you tell me?" I asked. Normally, Debbie wouldn't keep something like this from me for an entire week.

"Look, I only have a few minutes. If I miss this two forty-five appointment, Ben will kill me."

In my wildest dreams, I could never imagine that happening. "Give me the bottom line, then. Jason followed you home…"

"Then he showed up at my door. Ben answered, and Jason asked for me. Before I could get there, Jason tells Ben that we're in love and that Ben needs to let me go."

I threw a hand over my mouth to stifle my gasp. *"No."*

"At that point, I couldn't deny anything. I fessed up, told Jason to leave or I'd call the cops, then had to deal with Ben."

"He must have been *pissed*."

Debbie shrugged. "Actually, he was more sad than anything. But he did lay a guilt trip on me…. He's home with the kids, he takes care of the house, makes the meals, does the cooking. Jeez, he was whining like a bitch."

I had to admit, Ben sounded like a stereotypical house-wife. Debbie had always been the one with the balls in the marriage, a role she enjoyed.

"I finally had to agree to a romantic weekend in Key West on top of the counseling to get him off my back."

"When are you going?" I asked.

"This weekend."

"Wow." I paused for a beat. "I'm guessing you told Jason you can't see him anymore."

Debbie gave me a look that said I was out of my mind.

"After that?"

She glanced at her watch and rose.

"Don't you dare. What happened to Jason?"

"I told him if he pulled any shit like that again I'd have him fired."

"You're still seeing him?" I asked incredulously.

"Tongue ring, baby. Remember the tongue ring."

All I could do was gape as Debbie made her way out of my office. The woman was a trip and a half.

As soon as she was gone, depression swallowed me whole. Talking about her love life—sordid or not—had me remembering the spectacular time I'd spent with Chaz. I simply didn't want to accept that we'd never make love again.

If there was one smidgen of hope, I'd cling to it.

If not, then how could I go on?

chapter thirty-two

Friday night, I took Rayna to the Aventura Mall, where we shopped for a present for Stephen, my oldest nephew, who was turning seven. Then on Saturday, Rayna and I made our way to Kendall for the party.

I hadn't spoken to Nikki since she'd left me a message last week, but I'd called and gotten her voice mail so she knew I'd be at the party. I wondered how she was doing, and if she'd accepted the offer for the house. I knew what it was like to start over again after losing your lover and partner, and it wasn't a pleasant experience.

Maybe we'd cheer each other up.

I was on Kendall Drive, nearing 147th Avenue where I would turn left, when I noticed a police cruiser trailing me. I don't know why, but I got a bad feeling.

As I maneuvered my car into the left lane, so did the cop. And when I got into the turning lane and the cop followed me again, I knew for sure he was going to pull me over.

Even though I'd been driving the speed limit and hadn't
done anything wrong that I could think of, my stomach
clenched. I hated that I was nervous, since I didn't have any
reason to be, but I supposed it was a natural reaction anytime
a person was stopped by a police officer.

When I finished turning, the cruiser's lights began to
flash. I made my way to the far right and came to a stop.
He pulled up behind me, and I pressed the button to lower
my window. Then I turned and put a smile on my face,
hoping the officer would see I wasn't threatening.

But when I saw who it was, my smile instantly disappeared.

Jorge Rivera.

Alaina's ex-husband.

He smiled at me, a creepy kind of smile that made a chill
run down my spine.

But I said cheerfully, "Hey."

"Vanessa, right?"

He had to know who I was. "Yes. I work with your
wife. Ex-wife."

"License, ownership and insurance, please."

Jorge stared from me to Rayna in the backseat. I didn't
like the way he looked at either of us. Rayna was absorbed
in a *My Little Pony* video, and thankfully wasn't paying any
attention to him.

"License, ownership and insurance," he repeated.

I frowned slightly, though I reached for my purse next to
me. "Can I ask what I was doing?"

"I spotted you swerving a ways back. Have you been
drinking?"

"No! Of course not! Actually, I was putting on some lipstick. But I don't believe I was swerving."

Jorge leaned forward, almost pushing his head through my open window. "Lucky for you, I don't smell alcohol."

As I handed him the required information, I couldn't help thinking, *Man, he's being a prick.* But I said, "Here you are."

Jorge left me waiting in my car while he went back to the cruiser, presumably to run my info. Or perhaps to make me sweat. That was the vibe I got, but the question was why.

He came back to the car and slowly handed me my information. I gazed at him, waiting.

He didn't say anything. Just stared at me, and stared inside my car at Rayna again, with a look that had my hair rising on my nape.

Did he think I had a stash of marijuana in my vehicle? With my daughter inside? What was up with him?

"So," he began, drumming his fingers against the window frame. "You took Alaina up to Atlanta."

"Last month, right." So that's what this was about. He was pissed.

"Next time you want to plan a little trip like that—don't."

My eyebrows flew up. I bit my tongue, but if Jorge felt he could threaten me and I'd cower because he was a cop, he had another think coming.

"I did you a favor by helping out your sister. You can return the favor by not involving my wife in your…crazy antics."

How did a person respond to that? I didn't.

"You have a nice day now," he concluded, and stood tall.

"Thanks. Good to see you again," I muttered sourly as he started to walk away.

What an asshole! I had no clue what the guy's problem was. I was hoping he'd drive off so that he wouldn't be able to follow me, but he waited, so I ultimately merged into traffic.

He followed behind me, and now I started to get angry. The jerk was definitely trying to intimidate me.

But when we hit 104th Street, he turned left, and I breathed a sigh of relief.

Then I called Alaina.

"Hey, Vanessa."

"Girl, I just had a run-in with your ex."

"What?"

"Oh, yeah. He pulled me over." I filled her in on the bizarre and threatening nature of the ordeal.

"Vanessa, I'm so sorry. For some reason, he can't get over the trip to Atlanta, and that was what—six weeks ago? I thought he'd finally put it behind him, but when he called last night to say he had to work an extra shift today and couldn't take the kids, he started on about it again, asking me who I'd met, how many numbers I'd gotten. The guy is insane."

"Don't be sorry. The only reason I called is because he scared me. I'm really worried about you."

"Jorge's just…weird. Jealous by nature. I think he gets a secret thrill out of acting possessive or something."

"You sure he doesn't want you back?"

"He's living with someone!"

I made a face. "So he's just an asshole. Like most cops." I snorted. "Most men."

"Someone's calling on my other line. Hold on."

Several seconds later, Alaina came back on the line. "Vanessa, that's *him*."

"Jorge?"

"Uh-huh."

"What's he saying?"

"Oh, he's sounding really sweet. He apologized that he couldn't take the twins today, and says he wants to say hi to them."

"Don't mention I'm on the other line."

"I won't. But look, I'll call you tomorrow, okay? After my date with Mike."

"You're seeing him again?"

"Yep! A second date! Jorge's picking up the boys tonight, so I'll be free all day Sunday."

"I hope you get laid," I said, and laughed.

"I'd better get back to Jorge."

"Of course. Talk to you later."

I ended the call and tossed my phone onto the passenger seat. I glanced at Rayna, who'd fallen asleep. Within minutes, I was pulling up to my sister's house.

Even though Rayna had been fast asleep moments ago, she came instantly awake. "Party," she said.

"Yes, we're at the party." It doesn't matter how young kids are, they understand the concept of party. "And it might be the last one at your auntie's house," I added, more for myself than for Rayna. I didn't see a For Sale sign on the lawn, which meant Nikki had accepted the offer.

The front of the house was decorated with blue and white balloons, plus a wooden dinosaur sign that proclaimed Stephen was seven.

I unbuckled Rayna from her car seat, balanced her on my hip, then got the gift bag out of the car. She bounced her little hands up and down with excitement as we neared the house. It made me think I ought to visit my sister more often.

I might end up seeing a whole lot more of her if we have to move in together....

Not a thought that warmed the soul. I loved my sister, but living with her was a whole other matter.

Not being one to just open a door and head inside, I rang the doorbell. Then Rayna had to ring it, too—once, twice, three times before I was able to pull her small hand away.

The door swung open, and my sister smiled brightly at me, as though our last conversation hadn't ended bitterly at all. "Vanessa! And Rayna." She gave Rayna a kiss first, then hugged and kissed me. I took that to mean we would put our fight behind us without any further discussion of the topic.

Rayna squirmed, wanting to get down. I lowered her to the floor and she took off in search of other children.

Nikki looked fabulous. She was wearing a white mini-dress that showed off her well-toned legs and firm butt. Her hair and makeup were done to perfection. She looked like she was ready to head out for dinner at the marina, rather than stay home hosting a child's birthday party.

"You look great," I said. "How're you holding up?"

"Doing well," she responded.

I nodded and stepped into the house. I wanted to ask her about the house sale, how that had all gone down, but this wasn't the time, as the family room was full of parents.

I greeted the women and few men in the room, then went off in search of my nephews. There were more men outside, drinking beer and grilling hamburgers. The kids were running around, laughing and screaming. Rayna was already among them.

I easily saw Stephen. He was dressed up like his favorite superhero, Spider-Man. I made my way over to him and gave him a big hug and kiss, then did the same with my younger nephew, Clark.

Only as I headed back toward the patio door did I realize that Morris was standing over the grill.

He saw me and smiled, then waved. For a moment I stood there in shock, then finally gave a short wave in greeting.

I hurried back inside in search of my sister. She was in the kitchen now, taking a platter of vegetables out of the fridge. I sidled up next to her and whispered, "Morris is here?"

"Yep," she replied. Then, like the consummate hostess, she strolled past me with a smile on her face, toward the family room.

Clearly, I wasn't going to get answers now, so I poured myself a glass of punch and got a plate of munchies, then went to the family room myself. I watched Nikki offer the platter to everyone, wishing I had her ability to mask my emotions. Morris obviously had to be here because Stephen was his son—and I was glad to see she hadn't shut him out of this important day. But if I were my sister, knowing that my cheating husband was outside, and that because of him, this was the last party I would likely host in this house, I'm not sure I could smile and hand out food without bursting into tears.

Score one for Nikki, though. She was a better person than I.

Well, at least in this regard.

In the family room, the women were talking about dieting. I listened, and added a couple of comments here and there. Then Morris came in and announced that the burgers were ready. People got up en masse.

I lingered, waiting for my sister. It was a protective thing, because Morris was still in the room, and I wanted to be there for Nikki in case things got ugly.

And I knew my instincts were right when I saw Morris approach Nikki. I'm not sure what I expected to happen, but I slowly stood, ready to lunge between the two of them if necessary.

And I almost did, when Morris got too close to Nikki for my liking. I expected my sister to turn and grow alarmed at the sight of him, but instead she smiled.

What the hell?

Then things got more bizarre. Morris slipped his arms around her waist from behind. She leaned her head back so that it rested on his shoulder. Morris turned his head so that his lips brushed her temple.

My mouth fell open in shock.

Nikki's gaze landed on me, and seeing my expression, she giggled. "I swear, you should see the look on your face."

I still didn't get it. "What on earth is going on here?" I demanded.

"Morris and I made up."

I stared at my sister as if she had morphed into a Stepford Wife in front of my eyes. "What?"

Morris released her, and Nikki made her way to me. She spoke in a hushed tone. "We worked out our differences."

"Six days ago, you had an offer on the house—an offer you didn't even plan to consult Morris on. Now, you're suddenly back together?"

"Ironically, it was selling the house that made me realize everything I was going to lose."

"So all the drama—the house-hunting, the divorce lawyer, getting full custody—that was all…all bullshit?"

"Wow. I thought you'd be happy that we worked out our problems. You were the one who said I shouldn't rush things."

I didn't answer. Why *wasn't* I happy?

Because I felt duped. I'd run all over South Florida with my sister, and now I wondered if this was all part of some big dramatic act. I wondered if she knew from the beginning that she had no intention of selling the house. That her plan had been to make her husband sweat, then take him back.

Morris approached, and he was the one who spoke this time. "I love your sister with all my heart. What happened…it was a foolish mistake. I learned my lesson the hard way."

"But it's made us stronger," Nikki said. "I realize that I have some issues I need to work on, and so does Morris…"

And so you're back to being the Cleavers, I thought.

"I'm happy for you," I said, but my words were forced, and I wondered what my problem was. Whether it was Nikki's plan all along to forgive Morris or not, the bottom line was that they'd resolved their differences. Wasn't that what mattered most? And like my sister had said, I was the one who'd told her not to rush things. Yes, Morris had screwed up, but I believed that he deserved to be forgiven.

"I'm just surprised," I continued. "Nikki, you didn't give me any warning. The last I knew, you two were selling the house, and you were looking at apartments…" My voice trailed off. None of this mattered now. "But, thankfully, you're not going down that unpleasant path. And the children won't have to deal with the fallout."

Clark ran into the family room, looking none too pleased. "Mommy, Stephen isn't sharing the Game Boy!"

My sister sighed. "I told you both that the Game Boy was off-limits during the party." Then she took Clark's hand and walked out of the room with him.

Typical mom drama in suburbia.

"I'd better get back to the grill," Morris said.

"Sure," I said, as if I had to give him permission to leave.

As soon as he was gone, I realized what really bothered me about him and my sister getting back together, other than the surprise factor.

It was that my sister was getting her life back in order. She was going to be happy with her man again, while I was still alone.

chapter thirty-three

The next day, Lewis called no less than four times. Each time, I let my voice mail pick up. I could only imagine what he wanted, and I wasn't the least bit interested in talking to him.

When my phone rang just before three-thirty, I assumed it was him again. But a quick glance at the caller ID told me the call was coming from Debbie's cell.

I quickly snatched up the receiver. What was she doing calling me on a Sunday afternoon, especially since she was supposed to be out of town?

"Aren't you in Key West with Ben?" I asked without preamble.

"I'm about half an hour out of the city."

"The trip must have gone well if you're calling before you've even gotten home."

Debbie sighed, and for the first time, I picked up something in her tone—something I didn't like. "Debbie…"

"Sweetie, there's something you need to know."

"What?" I asked warily.

"It's Alaina."

My heart rate accelerated. "What happened?"

"I don't know all the details, but it looks like her ex beat her up—"

"What?" I shrieked.

"Yeah. He was pretty rough with her. She's at Baptist Hospital."

"Oh my God. I have to see her. I'm leaving right now."

"I'll meet you there."

When I got to Alaina's hospital room, the sight of her robbed me of breath. In fact, I didn't recognize her. The only way I knew for sure that it was Alaina was because her older sister, Arlene, was by her bedside.

I approached cautiously. A gasp rose in my throat as I neared Alaina's side. Her face was bluish and purple and she had a bandage over one eye. Stitches stretched across one corner of her forehead.

"Alaina." My voice was a strangled cry.

She was awake, though, because when she heard me, her one eye opened, then her bruised lips lifted in the slightest of smiles.

"Hi," she said, her voice weak and hoarse.

Tears were streaming down my face. "My God." I reached for her hand and gently squeezed it. I turned to Arlene. "What happened?"

"The asshole was following her. Even though he had the kids with him, he was following her. He saw Alaina meet that new guy she's seeing, Mike Sanchez. And he flipped out. Jorge got in the guy's face, called Alaina a whore… Then he started pounding on her, kicked her in the stomach. In the face."

My own stomach lurched with the horrific description of what Jorge had done. "And what was Mike doing when Jorge was beating the crap out of Alaina?" I asked, a bit ticked. "Standing around like an idiot?"

Arlene shook her head. "Jorge took him out first. Hit him with a Tazer gun."

"No!"

"Oh, yeah. Then he beat the crap out of my sister." Arlene's voice broke. "A few passersby jumped on him, got him under control. If no one had helped…"

I didn't even want to think of what could have happened if no one had thought to help—which might have been a distinct possibility if Jorge had been wearing his uniform.

I gently rubbed Alaina's hand. "I can't believe he did this to you."

"He's…crazy…"

"Understatement of the century," I muttered.

After Jorge's irrational harassing of the men Alaina dated, the way he totally wanted to control her even though they were no longer together, I should have seen this coming.

I had feared it, but didn't really think he'd cross the line, especially since he was a cop. I figured he knew the ramifications of criminal behavior, how much he had to lose.

"Tell me Jorge is in the county jail."

"He was arrested," Alaina answered slowly.

"Good. I hope he rots in jail. And that he's gang-raped by a bunch of bikers."

"Don't cry," Alaina said. "I'm fine."

I brushed at a tear. "You're far from fine. I can hardly believe I'm looking at my friend."

"I hope they don't protect him behind bars," Arlene said. "He needs to be with the general population—the rapists, murderers. Let justice prevail."

"Exactly," I agreed, but I could only imagine that Jorge was in a separate holding cell even now, and would be until he pleaded guilty or went to trial.

I pushed the thought from my mind, because if I thought about all that might come and how mentally trying it would be for my friend, it would be too overwhelming.

"I'll be fine," Alaina said hoarsely. "Now that he's in jail…"

That was the ray of sunshine on this very dark day. Now that Jorge had beaten his wife to a pulp, he would surely face jail time, and once he was behind bars, he could no longer hurt her.

"What did the doctors say?" I asked Arlene. "Anything broken?"

She shook her head. "No, thank God. But she has a couple bruised ribs, and the kick to the head gave her a mild concussion."

Anger grew inside of me, to the point where I knew if Jorge were in the room at this moment, I could have killed him.

"I swear, Ally, if I'd seen him doing that to you, I would have jumped on him and squeezed the life out of him with my bare hands."

"You'd have had to get in line," Arlene said sourly.

Again, Alaina's swollen lips moved in what looked like a smile.

The sound of footsteps made me turn toward the door. Debbie breezed into the room.

She cursed a stream of unladylike profanity when she reached the bed and saw Alaina. "Jesus have mercy. Someone tell me where Jorge is. Tell me where he is and I'll go slit his throat."

I turned to Debbie, and we embraced for a moment before she greeted Arlene, then went to Alaina's side.

"With you two here, I'll head downstairs for a bite to eat," Arlene said.

"Please, go," I told her. "Take a break."

When Arlene was out of the room, Debbie turned to me and said, "I never liked Jorge. Every time I saw him, something about the bastard rubbed me the wrong way."

"He straight up creeped me out." I told Debbie about how he'd pulled me over the day before, under the guise of a traffic stop, but had ultimately issued a threat.

Hindsight being twenty-twenty, I wish I'd told Alaina to go to the police department and report her husband's actions. But never in my wildest dreams would I have imagined he'd do this.

"Anything I can do for you?" Debbie asked Alaina.

"No. Just talk."

"Have you seen your kids?" I asked.

"No. Don't want them to…see me like this… Hey, Vanessa. Heard from Chaz?"

"No." My stomach tightened. "But that's not important right now."

"You'll be all right," she said slowly. "When a door closes…"

"How can you say that when you're lying in this bed?" I asked, once again wiping at a tear.

"Because now…I'm free."

Suddenly, Alaina moaned in pain, and both Debbie and I leaned in close. "What, sweetie?" Debbie asked.

I gently brushed Alaina's forehead. "You need a nurse?"

"No," she said after a moment. "I'm…okay."

"You're gonna get through this, hon," I said. "We'll be here for you every step of the way."

Alaina's eye moved from Debbie to me, and her mouth twitched in another attempt at a smile. "I know. That's why I love you guys."

After I left the hospital, I felt emotionally spent. Seeing my friend like that had been the hardest thing I'd had to deal with since Eli's death, and it put a lot into perspective for me.

I loved Chaz—and I didn't imagine I'd stop grieving for him anytime soon—but I would go on. I would go on the way I had after Eli's death.

I'd been hard on myself, thinking myself a failure in the love department and in life, but I hadn't done that bad a job, after all. I had a child who was well adjusted and extremely happy. We both had our health, something I should remember never to take for granted.

Even if I lost my apartment to Eli's bitch of a wife, Rayna and I would be okay.

And maybe there was even a plus side to the idea of losing the apartment—something I hadn't considered before. It would give me the chance to make a clean start in a place that held no memories of me and Eli.

It was a start I'd hoped to make with Chaz, but I had to accept the fact that it might never happen. And if it didn't, I'd be all right.

To be happy, I didn't need a man.

I was almost at the end of the causeway to South Beach when my cell phone rang. I scooped it up and flipped it open without checking the caller ID.

"Hello?"

"Baby."

I paused. That was Lewis's voice.

"It's Lewis," he exclaimed. "Don't tell me you've forgotten me already."

"I know who it is," I said. "What I'm wondering is what you want."

"You haven't returned any of my calls."

"I know."

"Ouch. That's cold."

"What do you want, Lewis?"

"To see you."

I rolled my eyes.

"Don't say no."

"What's the point? Every so often you phone me up, want a booty call… I know you don't believe me, but I'm over that."

"That's not why I'm calling."

I was in no mood to play this game with Lewis right now. "Can we talk later? I've had a really stressful evening. A friend of mine is in the hospital."

"Oh, man. I'm sorry to hear that."

"Thanks. It's pretty awful." Then I heard a horn blaring and abruptly hit the brake. I was so out of it, I'd started to drive through the red light on Alton Road.

"Damn it, damn it, damn it!"

"What's going on?" Lewis asked, alarmed. "Talk to me."

"I nearly had a friggin' collision. I shouldn't be driving."

"Where are you?"

"Just getting onto South Beach."

"Why don't you meet me at 510 Ocean?"

"Sunday evening? It's probably packed."

"Packed or not, you know I can get us in there."

It was true. Lewis had connections that could get him to the front of the line at any club, or into any restaurant, even when there weren't reservations available.

"I can be there in two minutes, Vanessa." When I didn't answer, he went on. "After everything we've been through, do you not consider me a friend?"

"Yes," I admitted. One thing about Lewis, even if I didn't think he was marriage material, I liked him. He could make me laugh.

Which was exactly what I needed right now.

"All right," I told him. "I'll meet you. But as a friend, you hear me?"

"I hear you."

"Good."

When the hostess took me to the table where Lewis was waiting, I rolled my eyes the moment I saw him.

He stood up to greet me. "Hey, baby."

Frowning, I sat. "Lewis, what's with the roses?"

"Beautiful roses for a beautiful woman," he replied simply.

"Let me say this once, clearly, so there's no misunderstanding. I am not going to sleep with you, so you're wasting your time trying to seduce me."

"That's not why I'm here."

My eyes narrowed. "Lewis. Come on."

"Look at the bouquet." He extended it toward me.

"It's lovely. Thank you. I'm still not going to sleep with you."

"Look at the bouquet."

"What?" I asked testily. "Red roses." I shrugged. "I already said it's lovely."

"Look. At. The bouquet."

I had no clue what Lewis was getting at, but I examined the bouquet further. And then I noticed something.

The edge of something dark, buried within the floral arrangement. I reached for it. When my fingers brushed it, I knew immediately that it was a jewelry box.

My heart went into overdrive. "Lewis…"

"I told you that I'm not interested in you for a booty call."

I pulled out the navy box, so dark it was almost black. "What is this?"

"Open it."

I was afraid to. If there was a ring inside, I didn't know what I was going to do.

I turned the box over in my hand. It seemed to weigh a hundred pounds.

"Open it," Lewis urged.

"Okay," I said. Then, knowing there was no point in delaying the inevitable, I opened the box.

Inside was the biggest cushion cut diamond I had ever seen. So big I gasped. A large HW in silver-gold was inscribed on the top interior of the ring box.

Around us, there was spontaneous applause.

"You like?"

I swallowed. "Lewis. I don't understand."

"Marry me, baby."

"*Marry* you?"

"I'm ready now. It took me long enough, but I am."

I glanced around nervously. People were grinning at us like love-starved fools. If only they knew that my relationship with Lewis wasn't even remotely a relationship, that he'd blindsided me with this absurd proposal.

"I...I—"

"Say yes!" someone yelled.

And then Lewis did the unthinkable. He dropped down onto one knee.

OhGodhelpme....

"How romantic is that?" I heard a woman say. And I wanted to scream, *No, you've got it all wrong!*

But I looked at the ring, really studied it. Holy shit, that could pay off Tassie. If not on its own, then surely with Eli's ring—if Chaz's suspicion that the pawnbroker was trying to scam me was right.

The waitress arrived at the table, and when she saw the ring box, she let out a loud gasp and her knees buckled—as though she were the one who'd been proposed to.

"Oh my God," she said. "That is the biggest rock I have *ever* seen! You said yes, right? 'Cuz, honey, if you don't want it, I'll take it."

"Well…"

"Of course you said yes!" The woman went on before I could officially answer her question. "This is so exciting!"

I tried to smile.

"Put it on," the waitress instructed, not at all caring that she could be intruding on our "romantic" moment.

Lewis looked at me expectantly—as did all the people in the immediate vicinity. What could I do but offer him my hand?

"Ohhh…" The waitress's eyes actually filled with tears. Then she started clapping, and everyone around us did, as well.

Talk about no pressure…

As if to seal the deal, Lewis moved toward me and kissed me on the lips. A deep, wet kiss that had me gasping for air when it was done.

I settled back in my seat, grinning nervously.

Lewis was all smiles when he returned to his seat opposite me, as if he were the happiest man in the world.

Honestly, it felt like I was in the twilight zone. Not only did he want to marry me, he now thought *I* wanted to marry *him*.

I wanted to point out that I hadn't really said yes, that I would have to *consider* his offer, but this wasn't the time. When we were alone, I'd set the record straight.

Then I remembered Alaina's words only a short while earlier, that when a door closes, a window opens. Was Lewis that window?

My gaze went to the ring, which was quite heavy on my finger. Stunning clarity, gorgeous cushion cut in the center, with two triangle-shaped diamonds at the sides…

The Harry Winston box alone told me it had to have cost a very pretty penny.

"It's five carats," Lewis said proudly.

Enough to pay off Tassie…

"It's the most beautiful ring I've ever seen," I said breathlessly.

"I promise you, we're going to be very happy together."

"Will you, um, excuse me for a minute?" I asked, already pushing my chair back.

I all but fled from the table, with the people I passed staring at me as if I were a movie star. I grinned sheepishly until I got to the bathroom, where I promptly locked myself in a stall and took out my cell phone.

I dialed Carla's number.

"Hey, Vanessa," she said when she answered. "How's your friend?"

"She's in rough shape, but she'll be okay." I blew out a deep breath. "Carla, something major just happened, and I'm freaking out here. I don't know if I should say yes, if I should think about it, because my heart is still with Chaz—"

"Hey, slow down. What are you talking about?"

"Lewis."

"Lewis?" Carla couldn't have sounded more shocked.

"He just *proposed,* Carla. *Proposed.*"

"Lewis Carter—the guy who couldn't commit?"

"He gave me a five-carat diamond! I—I—I can't even believe it."

"You want to marry him?"

"No! I want Chaz, but… But Chaz doesn't want me, and Lewis can give me the money to buy Tassie out, too. And…you should see this ring. It's incredible."

"You can't say yes," Carla told me.

"Can I afford to say no?" When she didn't respond, I went on. "And it's not like I didn't love him once. Maybe I can again…"

Someone entered the bathroom.

"Vanessa, I don't know."

"I've got to go."

"Huh?"

I flipped my cell phone shut.

But I didn't leave the stall. I stood inside with my eyes pressed shut, a million thoughts running through my mind.

After the other woman left the bathroom, I finally ventured back out onto the restaurant floor. And for the rest of the time we stayed there, I played the part of the newly engaged woman.

Lewis didn't even want to go back to my apartment with me, something that made me wonder if he'd truly done a one-eighty.

By the time I went upstairs, I'd made my decision. I immediately called Tassie's lawyer. It was a Sunday, but I wanted him to get my message first thing Monday morning.

"Mr. Harris, this is Vanessa Cain. I wanted to talk about the situation with Tassie Johnson. Can you let her know that I will be making arrangements to buy her out immediately? We can talk about it when you call me back, but everything's set." I recited my work number, even though I knew that Bradley Harris had it.

Then, with a smile warming my heart, I hung up.

The next morning, the lawyer called me at work.

"Ms. Cain?"

"Mr. Harris. Hello."

"I've spoken with my client."

"Great."

"However, she asked me to tell you that she is rejecting your offer to buy her out."

"What?" Confused, I frowned. "How can she reject my offer? Those were *her* terms. If I bought her out, I could keep the condo."

"I know, but she's had a change of heart. She feels, having had time to think, that she would like to relocate to South Beach."

"In my apartment," I supplied sourly.

"Your shared property."

"So in other words, Tassie Johnson's only interest is in screwing me over."

"She will happily buy out your share of the property."

"Oh, really? Now she wants to buy *me* out?" I gritted my teeth. "So this has been a game all along?"

"My client is prepared to pay above market value," the lawyer told me, and I detected a note of optimism in his voice.

"Am I supposed to get excited about that?" I asked. "You know what? Do me a favor. Tell your client to stick it where the sun don't shine. Oh—and tell her I want my hat back. She'll know what I'm talking about."

And then I hung up.

If Tassie Johnson wanted a fight, it was *on*.

It was while I was staring out my office window that I thought of something. Rather, made sense of something.

The day Alaina and I had gone to Atlanta, we'd seen

Tassie near Eli's casket at the funeral home. I remembered that I'd seen a man beside her, offering comfort.

An attractive man.

Tassie had tried to smear me in the media, making me out to be a manipulative slut while she'd been the doting wife, but it was unlikely that she had been sitting around waiting for Eli's return for seven years. She was an extremely attractive woman, one who could have her pick of men.

She could have cheated on Eli, for all I knew. What if she had some skeletons in her closet that she didn't want exposed?

There was one way to find out.

I searched for the *Miami Herald* reporter's card and dialed her number.

"Cynthia Martin," she said when she answered her line.

"Cynthia, this is Vanessa Cain."

"Oh. Hello, Vanessa."

"You once were interested in helping me tell my side of the story. Does that offer still stand?"

"Certainly."

"Good. Because I need something." As far as I was concerned, Cynthia owed me, especially after the article she'd written about me and Chaz. If not for that, Byron likely wouldn't have confronted me that day at the restaurant.

When, five minutes later, I replaced my receiver, I was grinning from ear to ear.

I was sure that if anyone could help me find the dirt on Tassie Johnson to bring her down, it was Cynthia.

It was high time I played dirty.

A riveting novel by acclaimed author

DIANE CHAMBERLAIN

Twenty-eight years ago a North Carolina
governor's young, pregnant wife was
kidnapped. Now her remains have
been found and a man has been
charged with her murder. Only one
person—CeeCee Wilkes—can refute
the charges against him. But CeeCee
disappeared years ago....

Eve Elliot is a successful therapist
to troubled students, a loving wife,
a mother deeply invested in her
family. But her happiness is
built on a lie. Now, forced
to confront her past, she
must decide whether to
reveal to her family that
she is not who she seems,
or allow a man to take the
blame for a crime she
knows he did not commit.

the SECRET LIFE of CeeCee Wilkes

"Diane Chamberlain is
a marvelously gifted author!
Every book she writes is a real gem!"
—*Literary Times*

Available wherever trade paperback books are sold!

MIRA®

MDC2531TR

The marvelous sequel to
the evocative *Silent in the Grave*

DEANNA RAYBOURN

Fresh from a six-month sojourn in Italy, Lady Julia
returns home to Sussex to find her father's estate
crowded with family and friends—but dark deeds
are afoot at the deconsecrated abbey, and a
murderer roams the ancient cloisters.

When one of the guests is found brutally murdered
in the chapel and a member of Lady Julia's own family
confesses to the crime, Lady Julia resumes her unlikely
and deliciously intriguing partnership with
Nicholas Brisbane, setting out to unravel a tangle
of deceit before the killer can strike again….

SILENT *in the*
SANCTUARY

"Fans of British historical thrillers will welcome
Raybourn's perfectly executed debut."
—*Publishers Weekly* on *Silent in the Grave*

Available wherever trade paperback books are sold!

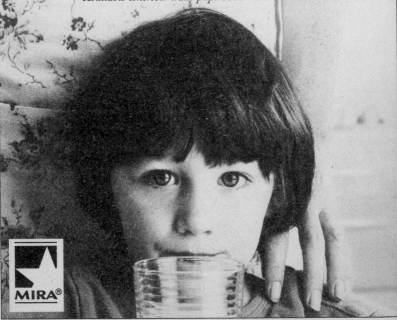